DAN O'SHEA

GREED

EXHIBIT A
An Angry Robot imprint
and a member of Osprey Group

Lace Market House,
54-56 High Pavement,
Nottingham
NG1 1HW
UK

Exhibit A / Osprey Publishing
PO Box 3985
New York
NY 10185-3985
USA

www.exhibitabooks.com
A is for African Diamonds!

An Exhibit A paperback original 2014

Cover design by Argh! Oxford
Set in Meridien and Franklin Gothic by EpubServices

Distributed in the United States by Random House, Inc., New York

ISBN: 978 1 90922 316 5
Ebook ISBN: 978 1 90922 317 2

Printed in the United States of America

9 8 7 6 5 4 3 2 1

To my kids, Danny, Nick and Shannon.
Everybody's got to have a reason. You're pretty good reasons.

PRAISE FOR DAN O'SHEA

"To classify *Penance* as a mere police procedural would be to do it a serious injustice. Because when you crack the cover of this novel, you'll discover there's a whole lot more there, lurking just below the surface. Buy yourself a copy of *Penance*, and prepare to dive in."
Katrina Niidas Holm, Criminal Element

"*Penance* is a rich, gritty, terrific novel. O'Shea can throw a punch and turn a phrase with the very best of them. Even better, he knows the human heart inside out."
Lou Berney, author of Gutshot Straight *and* Whiplash River

"*Penance* is a rare novel, at once staggering in scope and achingly human. A brutal, white-knuckled tale of betrayal and redemption in which the sins of the fathers are laid upon their children tenfold, O'Shea's astonishing debut delivers pulse-pounding thrills and the beating heart to match. Fans of Le Carré and Lehane had best take note."
Chris F Holm, author of Dead Harvest *and* The Wrong Goodbye

"A non-stop adrenaline rush, beginning, middle and end; half Stephen Hunter, half American Tabloid, Daniel O'Shea's *Penance* is a bonafide blockbuster."
Owen Laukkanen, author of The Professionals

"*Penance* has one foot in Bourne and the other in *The Untouchables*, but tells a very human story of loss and atonement. A great thriller that ranges from the streets of Seventies Chicago to the highest levels of modern power, with tight dialogue and righteous violence. One for fans of crime, espionage and mayhem."
Jay Stringer, author of Old Gold

CHAPTER 1

Darfur, 2008

Nick Hardin never thought his first Hollywood party would be in a big-ass tent on the Chad-Sudan border, but there he was, nursing a gin and tonic, hoping he'd set things up far enough west that he was out of RPG range in case some Janjaweed punk got a bug up his ass. Fucking Mooney and his do-gooder shit.

Hardin had run into Jerry Mooney in Khartoum almost a year back. Darfur was heating up as the PR play of choice for socially conscious Hollywood types looking to bump up their Q scores. Hardin had been heading out on his usual fixer gig for one of the networks. Same gig he'd been running since he got out of the Foreign Legion back in 2000 – logistics on a file footage job. Camera guy, sound guy, some former BBC face with the right kind of public school accent and safari-guide outfit. Get ten or fifteen minutes in the can from the hellhole of the week so *Nightline* would have something for a slow news day. Run the film, then cut back to the studio where the talking heads and maybe someone from Médicins Sans Frontières or some Foggy Bottom undersecretary could cluck their tongues between beer commercials. A little of the self-flagellation that a goodly portion of the folks who actually watch *Nightline* like to engage in before bed – helps them sleep better. Hardin's job? Line up some transport and some security that, when you'd bought them for a couple days, stayed bought. Point the talent at the right locations, pay off the right warlords, make sure the face gets his interview without getting his throat cut and the crew gets out without having to buy back their equipment at ten bucks on the dollar.

The face in this case being Nigel Fox. Hardin liked Nigel, and Nigel liked gin. That was why he was spending his twilight years stringing the massacre circuit when he had used to cover No. 10 Downing Street for BBC One. Hardin had done Somalia with Nigel; had done Liberia back in the Taylor days; Kinshasa; Rwanda. It was the beginnings of a beautiful friendship.

Hardin waited at the Khartoum airport by the Twin Otter he'd chartered as Nigel walked across the tarmac with his crew: a couple of stoner Italian adrenaline junkies. And with Jerry Mooney.

Hardin had heard of Mooney, of course. Hollywood's most eligible bachelor. Square-jawed leading man in a dozen chart-topping flicks. Probably more than a dozen – Hardin figured a few had come out that hadn't made it to the flea-bag cinema down the street from his place in Accra back in Ghana.

"Nick Hardin," said Nigel, "meet Jerry Mooney."

"Jerry," said Hardin, shaking hands. He turned to Nigel. "We still shooting news or are we making a movie?"

"Little of both, old boy," Nigel said. "Ran into Jerry here at the Hilton night before last. Splendid chap. Shared a bottle of Boodles and let me have more than half. Anyway, he's headed down to Darfur for a look-see, some video-blog thing for his website. Marvelously technical – beyond me, of course. But his fixer bolted on him, left the poor man stranded. All for one and one for all, of course, so I told him he could pack along with us."

"Nice of you to spend my nickel, Nigel," said Hardin.

"Hey, Nick," said Mooney. "Look, I know I'm imposing, and I know you've got to make a living. The guy I was supposed to meet up with, he'd said $500 a day, American, plus expenses. Nigel tells me we're back tomorrow night, so that's two days. Suppose we say $2500. Is that fair?"

Usury is what it was, but Mooney had thrown out the number. Mooney was starting to smell like the gravy train. With a capital G and a capital train.

"Yeah, OK," said Hardin.

Mooney smiled. Big, dimpled movie-star smile. "All right. Off to the heart of darkness."

Hardin caught the little smirk from Nigel. They always do that, the first timers. Drop the Conrad on you. But the darkness wasn't concentrated in a heart anywhere. It had metastasized into millions of tumors. Some, like Darfur, were a thousand miles wide. But most of them were about the size of a qat-chewing thirteen year-old with an AK-47.

Nigel waved the Italians back to the truck. "You've forgot the bloody gin."

So Mooney had got the Darfur bug bad. Started harping on Congressmen, hanging out with Martin Sheen, the whole nine yards. Mooney's buddies then started turning up, and Hardin ended up with damn near a full-time gig as the Darfur Tour Guide to the Stars. And the stars pay way better than the networks. Then Mooney got his big idea. Dollars for Darfur– a Live Aid type deal, but right here on site. Mooney signed up half a dozen big-name bands, got a mess of Hollywood types to commit. Huge buzz in the media.

Hardin had to admit it made sense from Mooney's perspective. For once, the press would have more cameras looking at Darfur than it had looking up Lindsay Lohan's skirt. But from Hardin's perspective, it was a nightmare – staging a rock concert on the Darfur border was like building a golf course in Antarctica.

Hardin paid the bribes, pulled the strings, got the generators and tents and food and booze shipped in. And he did the other stuff that he couldn't tell Mooney about – like talking to his contact at the Chinese embassy in Khartoum, explaining how, while this liberal love-fest was likely to piss off the masters in Beijing no end, it was still in the PRC's best interest to lean on the Sudanese and make sure they keep the Janjaweed on their leash for a few weeks. Suddenly, you got almost as many publicists in Darfur as you got starving people, and they're making sure every A-list name in town for the show has a camera on them every second. Janjaweed goes on a rampage within a light-year of the place, the PRC's going to have to deal with gang-rapes and mass murder live and covered from more camera angles than the Super Bowl.

And Hardin was twenty-four hours from pulling it off. The night before the big show, Hardin was standing in the corner of the party tent, sipping a gin and tonic with actual ice in it, and watching all the size-one blondes strut around. Drink tasted good, which it should, because when you built in the logistics, it probably cost more per ounce than cocaine. The tent was full of movie stars, rocks stars, a couple of the right kind of politicians, a handful of network news guys – and not the second-string talent that usually got shunted off to Africa either. Couple of print guys, but only the big-time names with hot blogs and book deals. Rest of the print media was outside with the refugees and the aid workers.

Now Shamus Fenn was working on fucking up Hardin's payday. Fenn had the Hollywood radical gene bad, always ready to play footsie with anybody who wanted to badmouth the US. But he also had an alpha male problem – had to know more and be a badder ass than anyone else around. When he got off the chopper that morning with what's-her-face, some actress Hardin still couldn't quite place, Fenn was in full macho mode. Chopper had spooked a mole viper out of its hole, the snake scurrying off for cover. The actress evidently had a snake problem, because she screamed, so Fenn had to get all manly, make a move to grab the snake.

"I'd leave that alone," said Hardin. "Poisonous."

"That little worm?" said Fenn. Mole vipers don't look like much, short little black things, harmless if you don't fuck with them. Fenn started walking after the snake. When his shadow fell over it, the snake stopped crawling and coiled up. Last thing Hardin needed was Fenn getting himself bit on his watch. So Hardin shot the snake.

"What the fuck you do that for? Just wanted to get a look at it," Fenn said, puffing up.

"They coil like that, they're going to strike I doubt if we have any antivenom here. You might have survived the chopper ride out, but you definitely would have missed the party."

The actress was apparently over her snake phobia now that it was dead, and also clearly didn't want her screaming fit to be the last image in the minds of the press guys who'd gotten off the chopper with them.

"Shamus, we've come to save Africa, not to help destroy it," she said, stomping off. A minute ago, Fenn had been halfway into her pants. Now she was marching over to Mooney.

Fenn walked over to Hardin. Hardin was five foot nine, 175 pounds. Fenn had four inches and 20pounds on him. Fenn got in real close. "I don't know who you are, cowboy, but I don't like you already."

Mooney broke things up. "Shamus, this is Nick Hardin. You haven't been out here before or you'd know him. He was just looking out for you."

"I've looked out for myself in worse places than this. Not afraid of some pissant snake," said Fenn.

"Of course not. Come on, let's get you settled in, get you up to speed on the program." Mooney got an arm around Fenn's shoulders, turned him away from Hardin, walked him off.

Within two hours, the story of Shamus Fenn's arrival in Darfur was up on one of the press blogs, complete with video, and nobody was missing a chance to put the needle in with Fenn. And now Fenn was stalking Hardin around the party. Fenn was liquored up, had been hitting it hard for a couple of hours. Every time he saw Hardin, he'd start angling toward him, but Hardin would move off, and somebody would grab Fenn and start chatting him up.

Then Hardin lost his concentration. The actress from the snake scene came over – having been at the booze herself some – wanting to apologize for the whole thing, hitting on Hardin pretty hard; making it clear that, if he wanted to stop by her trailer after the party, she'd be waiting. And Hardin was definitely thinking about it. You get up in your forties, you don't have a lot of hard-body twentysomethings throwing themselves at you. And getting laid was one of the downsides to an Africa career nowadays. Condoms or not, with the AIDS rates, you had to think real hard before you dipped your wick anywhere. So this chick was stroking his arm, leaning forward so that her loose and not-very-buttoned blouse kept falling open, and Hardin had his mind on something other than Fenn long enough for Fenn to get right up next to him.

"You a star-fucker, Hardin? That your deal?"

Hardin turned, and Fenn was right behind him, face red, smelling of Bombay and testosterone.

"I was just thanking Mr Hardin for saving your life earlier, Shamus," said the girl, putting some real bite into it, and all of a sudden Hardin got it. Some kind of history between these two, and she'd come over here to tee Hardin up, get Fenn over, make some scene, get some more face time on YouTube. Hardin thinking how his pecker could still get him in trouble.

Which was when Fenn threw the right. Shitty right. Movie right. Big, long, telegraphed punch Hardin could have slipped twice. But Hardin stood in, just turning with it at the last minute, let it glance off his head, made a show of going down.

"Whoa, nice shot," Hardin said from his knees, showing his ass, still looking for an out. "Look, I guess I had that coming, OK? Just let me get out of here."

But when Fenn went to put a boot in while Hardin was getting up, Hardin lost it. He grabbed the leg, flipped Fenn over onto the bar table, and gave him a good right to the nose. Just one, but the right kind: straight, short, starting from the legs, hips turning with it. Fenn's nose got way broken, and pieces of the highball glass he landed on ended up stuck in his back.

"Oh, Shamus!" The blonde, all concern now, leaning over the semiconscious actor.

"Better get him to the doc," said Hardin, trying to pull her aside so he could get a look.

She reared up and slapped him hard across the face. "Get your hands off of me. You thug. This whole continent is full of thugs." She stomped off, exactly the same carriage as earlier, after the snake. Her exit stomp, Hardin figured. Must have that one down.

That derailed the gravy train, right there. Mooney kept him on through the concert, and he was cool about it after. "Everyone knows Fenn's an ass, especially when he drinks," said Mooney. "But the Darfur story is bigger than us, said Mooney. "Can't afford to let it be about some movie star brawl," said Mooney. "Need to let you go to get you and Fenn off the front page, make this about the people again," said Mooney. "You'll always be a hero of mine," said Mooney. "Here's another ten grand."

Hardin knew there was more to it. The whole Hollywood PR machine was cranked up around Dollars for Darfur. It was their chance to prove what a big heart the industry had, take everyone's mind off the brainless crap they put out – the no-panty starlets and the revolving doors at the rehab clinics. And now, instead of Darfur leading the news, they had video of a drunk actor acting like, well, a drunk actor.

That was five years ago now.

Hardin had tried to get back into the network gigs, but suddenly no one returned his calls. After a couple months, he ran into a producer he went back with a ways, and the guy told him he'd been blackballed. Word had gone out from the agents and PR flacks – any news team working with Hardin gets zero play with their people. And the same media conglomerates who owned the movie studios owned the news networks. The movie studios made way more money.

So five years of scrambling, taking riskier gigs for less money, working with some of the European outlets, Al Jazeera, even. Burning through his savings.

And maybe a few other things... not-quite-legal things. Hardin hadn't always been a glorified gofer. He'd spent eight years in the Marines, Scout/Sniper back in Gulf War I. When a beef back home meant he needed a get-out-of-jail-free card, he spent half a decade in the French Foreign Legion, 1st Co, 2nd Para regiment, the baddest asses in a bad-ass crowd, pretty much his whole time in the Legion spent in Africa. It was no continent for pussies. Not just journalists who needed a little security.

Then Hardin heard some interesting noises about a new twist in the old West African blood-diamond business. That had cooled off after Charles Taylor and his RUF animals finally got run to ground, but there'd always been a Lebanese connection to the diamond trade in West Africa. Now Hardin was hearing that Hezbollah had muscled in on that, and then Bin Laden and the boys had muscled in on Hezbollah, and now Al Qaeda was using diamonds as a way to move capital *sub rosa* since the US was putting the freeze on any above-ground cash flow. Not to mention, if you got Hezbollah in the mix, then you got Tehran holding their leash.

Story felt a little canned, though; had a little Mossad scent around the edges, Hardin getting the feeling maybe the Israelis were trying to play him, get some storyline they liked to come out through Al Jazeera so it would fly on the Arab street, give them some way to muddy up Iran a little in case this was the week they decided to bomb something. So Hardin did a little recon. Far as he could tell, the story checked out.

A couple things, though. First thing was this. Even if he got Al Jazeera to bite, this was going to come to maybe ten grand on his end – ten grand after probably a month with a higher-than-usual chance of getting his ass shot.

Second thing? These blood diamond guys, sometimes their security wasn't what it ought to be.

Hardin figured he'd had a good run in Africa. But he was pushing fifty, and after almost twenty years schlepping around the Sahel, fifty was pushing back. It was time for an exit strategy. A few million dollars in untraceable stones looked like a good one.

That was how Hardin ended up on an Air France flight, headed to Chicago, with eighteen ounces of uncut stones hidden in his bag.

Problem was that was about fifteen ounces too much of a good thing.

A couple ounces were what he had planned on. Al Qaeda moved the stones when they had to finance an operation – usually two or three ounces, $10 to $20 million retail value, out of which they'd get maybe half. So Hardin figured he'd bounce a shipment, get a couple ounces of stones, come out with a million or two on his end, still be pretty much under the radar. From what he'd heard, it wouldn't be the first time they'd had a shipment go missing.

Now he was halfway across the Atlantic with a pound and a half of hot rocks – ten times the size of a usual shipment. Eighteen ounces would cut out to better than $150 million retail. That raised a few questions. Like how was he going to move that kind of weight? And what was Al Qaeda up to that took that kind of financing?

Most importantly, how was he going to get back under the radar now?

Time to talk to Stein.

CHAPTER 2

Chicago, 2013

Detective John Lynch climbed out of the unmarked Crown Vic in the parking lot outside the United Center and hunched his shoulders, pushing the collar of his overcoat up around his ears. United Center... almost had that down now. Lynch could go a month sometimes without calling it the Stadium.

Temperature was near zero and heading down, wind coming out of the northwest like sandpaper. Beginning of March. Even in Chicago, they should be past this shit by now. But the storm had blown in overnight, dumped better than a foot of snow, cold front behind that. Lynch looked across Madison at the chimneys on top of the three flats. The wind flattened the heat from the furnace stacks sideways against the sky in ribbons of vapor and mirage. Powder blew across the snowpack around the edges of the parking lot in braided ropes, the half moon and stars showing in a night sky frozen so clear and hard that you'd swear it would shatter like a plate if you fired a round into it.

Been pretty warm the last week so the shelters had emptied out, a lot of the emergency options closed down for the spring. The uniforms would find the bodies in the morning – the homeless along Lower Wacker – curled up in the basement delivery doorways of the office towers;

more of them frozen into fetus shapes under cardboard and old blankets beneath the underpasses out on the west side, the south side; probably a family somewhere, all of them dressed in everything they owned, choked out from carbon monoxide, huddled on the floor next to a smoldering charcoal grill in some shit-ass tenement where the heat was out because some slumlord hadn't made repairs or paid his gas bill.

The uniforms would call out the wagons, haul all the bodies in so the ME could thaw them out, try to make sure that each death was really an act of God and not the result of some nefarious human agency. Then everybody'd go home and have a drink or six try to figure out why God had to act like that.

"Pretty sky," Bernstein said. "Only time it looks like this."

"Yeah, when standing outside to look at it will kill you," said Lynch. "Let's go see our stiff."

"That Stein?" asked Lynch.

"Hard to tell, just looking at his ass," said the uniform. "Girl outside found the body, says it's him – right size, right suit – nobody seen him leave, it's his box, so I'm thinking yes."

Stein's body was wedged between the toilet and the wall in the bathroom of the luxury box at the United Center, on his knees, face on the floor, ass in the air. Aside from a little mess next to the three holes at the base of his skull, no blood at all.

"Two thousand dollar suit, luxury box, and you still end up kissing the floor next to the john while you take three in the back of the head," said Lynch.

"Are all thy conquests shrunk to this little measure?" said Shlomo Bernstein, Lynch's partner.

"What's that shit?" asked the uniform.

"Shakespeare probably," said Lynch. "He does that."

From the floor of the stadium, the expansive post-game echoey sounds rattled around – the crew breaking down chairs and tables, starting to pull up the floor so they could set up the rink for the Hawks game the next night.

"Got a timeline?" Lynch asked.

"Girl said she'd been in with five to go in the game," said the uniform. "Stein's last guest had just left, so she wanted to see did Stein need anything. Stein said he was good. After the game, she came back in, didn't see him, which she says was weird, cause he's a pretty gregarious guy – saying hello to everybody coming and going. Anyway, she started cleaning up, bathroom door was open, she looked in, saw the stiff, ran out, called security, they called us. We got the call at 9.53. Five to go in the game is like 9.30 – got a twenty-minute window there."

"OK, thanks. We got everybody rounded up that had access up here?"

"Everybody that wasn't gone already, yeah. Got them in the next couple suites up the hall."

"OK, let 'em know we'll get to them when we can. Thanks."

The uniform left the suite.

"So what can you tell me about this Stein, Slo-mo?"

Shlomo Bernstein was an anomaly. North shore, Jewish, big family money, but he always wanted to be a cop. When he tried to go to the academy right after finishing a double major in Economics and Philosophy at Brown, his parents made him a deal – get the MBA just in case you change your mind and want to take over Daddy's brokerage business someday. So Bernstein blew through Wharton in two years, top of his class, and then became a cop, made detective in record time. Smart as hell, but a physical anomaly, too – five foot seven, maybe 140 pounds. Good looking guy, though, like some junior-sized male model. Sharp dresser.

"Abraham Stein. Huge in commodities – one of the lords of the universe down at the Board of Trade. And one of the real big shots in the Jewish community here – Jewish United Fund chair, Spertus Institute named a building after him. Word is he's tight with Tel Aviv. His father was Palmach. Family goes way back in the diamond business – that's where he started."

"What's this Palmach?"

"The elite of the Haganah, which was a sort of unofficial Jewish army in Palestine under British rule. These were the guys who won the War of Independence back in 1948."

Bernstein handed Lynch his iPhone, Wikipedia article on the Palmach up on the screen.

Lynch scanned it, handed it back. "Jesus, Slo-mo, you sleep with that fucking thing?"

"If you want to stick with your talk-only dinosaur, that's your problem. You want to be one of the cool kids, get yourself an iPhone."

Lynch just shook his head. "OK, you and your electronic friend might as well get back to the station, start digging at the business and Jewish stuff. This had to come out of somewhere."

Ashley Urra was in her early twenties with the kind of face that Lynch bet meant she never had to buy her own drinks. Blonde, a short cut with bangs Lynch was seeing a lot of these days. Shiny white teeth. Thin, decent figure, not real tall. Perky. Lynch bet she got called perky, and she probably liked it.

"You were working Mr Stein's box tonight?"

"I was Abe's regular hostess. It was a great assignment. He was very generous, and he wasn't one of these guys who gets off on pushing the help around. He didn't hit on me either."

"Bet you get a lot of that."

She just smiled.

"Nice spread," Lynch said. Table at the back of the box had a chafing dish full of ribs, some kind of pasta, salad, bar set up on the other side of the room. "All this, he's up here alone?"

She was looking across the suite to the bathroom, where the evidence techs and McCord, the ME guy, were working on the body. "What?" she said.

"Lots of food. Seems like too much for him to be up here alone."

"Oh. Abe did a lot of business during the games. People would come and go. He always over-ordered. He'd let us have what was left, after the games. The staff loved him."

"I bet. Security pretty good up here? I mean you can't just walk in, right?"

The girl was looking over at the body again. The interview would go quicker if Lynch did it in one of the other suites, but most people didn't see a lot of dead bodies and it kept them off balance, kept them from working on their answers too hard. If it didn't, then that told him something, too. So Lynch liked to do interviews with a stiff around.

"I'm sorry, what?" she said.

"Security," Lynch repeated.

"Oh, yeah. This level has its own elevators and ramps – you have to have a special ticket just to get up here."

"You need to show any ID?"

"Not if you have a ticket. I mean unless you need to pick it up at Will Call or something."

"Did Mr Stein leave any Will Calls tonight?"

"I don't know. They'd know downstairs, I guess."

Lynch waved a uniform over, sent him down to check; also told him to run down any records on Stein's box, his contract, that sort of thing. The girl was looking at the body again. Lynch waited until she turned back.

"Sorry," she said.

"It's OK. That's not normal for most people. What can you tell me about tonight? Who'd he have up here?"

"People from his firm mostly, I think. Mendy Axelman – he worked with Mr Stein, he's here all the time. He was here early with a lot of younger guys. I think they were traders who work with Abe and Mendy. I recognized a couple of them. They bring them up to the box as a reward or something. Bulls went up by like twenty-five points midway through the last period, and they all took off. The younger guys were all heading for a party somewhere – one of them slipped me his card on the way out, told me I should stop by after the game, that it was going to go late."

"You got the card?"

She handed it to Lynch. Mike Schwartz, Stein & Co. Business contact info on the front, address for a townhouse in Streeterville handwritten on the back along with another phone number – probably the guy's cell. Lynch called another uniform over, told him to get a unit over to that address, make sure everybody stayed put until he could get there. Turned back to the girl.

"Were you going to go?"

"What?"

"To the party. Nice neighborhood."

A weak smile; she shrugged. "Yeah, probably. I mean, not now."

Lynch nodded, straightened his leg, his right knee barking at him some the way it did when it got cold like this. Green Bay had taken him in the third round back in 1985: strong safety out of Boston College. Blew out his knee in his second preseason game, and they couldn't do shit with knees back then like they could now. Came back from rehab half a step slower. Wasn't a half-step he had to give.

"Anybody else?" Lynch asked.

"One other guy came right toward the end of the game. He was different."

"Different how?"

She made a thinking face. "I dunno. Rougher I guess? He was real tan, which you don't see that much around here this time of year. This wasn't a just-back-from-vacation tan, more like, you know, weathered? And he wasn't in the usual clothes. It was mostly suits with Mr Stein. This guy was dressed casual, but not like Banana Republic, you know? You see these guys sometimes in the cargo pants and safari shirts, and it's like Halloween – like they're in a costume? This guy was like whoever it is they're trying to dress up to be."

"You said tan, so a white guy. He tall, short?"

"Not real tall, maybe five foot nine. Not big. Pretty broad shoulders I guess, but lean. I mean you look at some guys and you can just tell. This guy, he was in shape. He just looked hard. Gray hair – not like old-man gray, but like Anderson Cooper gray? Hair was pretty short, not a fancy cut."

"You hear a name?"

"No, which is a little strange. Mr Stein is always introducing everybody. You know, like 'Ashley, this is my friend so-and-so. We go way back. Take good care of him.' I'd seen this guy go in, so I stopped to see if they need anything, and Mr Stein was just 'Thanks, Ashley; we're good for now.'"

"Like he wanted some privacy, maybe?" Lynch asked.

She nodded, like she hadn't thought of that. "Yeah, exactly like that." A look on her face like there was more.

"Something else?" Lynch asked.

"Just this other guy? I could swear I've seen him before. At the same time, I'm positive I've never met him. That make any sense?"

"Seen him here, you mean?"

"That's the weird part. I'm real good with faces, and I know I've never met him. But his face keeps nagging at me."

"OK. Something comes to you, let me know. He was the last guest?"

She nodded. "That's when I went back in to check with Mr Stein, see if he would need anything else. He said he was fine. That was the last time I talked with him."

"He seem OK then, distracted or anything?"

"Seemed the same as usual."

"And you never heard anything – shouting, gunshots, anything unusual?"

"No."

"See anybody up here who didn't belong?"

"You get a blowout like that, toward the end of the game, you got people leaving, trying to beat the traffic. You got the food service guys and janitorial service guys trying to get a jump on breaking things down – there were a lot of people around. Nobody stuck out."

"The mystery guest, you see him after he left the box?"

"I saw him get on the elevator. I didn't see him after that."

"OK, Ashley. Thanks. If I need anything else, I'll be in touch."

Eight blocks west of the United Center, Membe Saturday shivered in the night air, trying to understand why the stars had moved. It had been only eight days since he'd arrived at the shelter run by the nuns he had met in Sierra Leone. His wife and sons had been killed by Taylor's men during the war, and he had been forced to work at the mines near Kenema – until a stone went missing, and the

guards lined up Saturday and the five other men who
had been working near him, and cut off their right hands
with an ax. Since then, he had begged and stolen and
wasted away. Finally, he had gone to the hospital the
nuns ran, thinking he could die there – everyone died
there. But one of the sisters told him they would take
him to a new life in America.

Saturday was beginning to think it had been a bad idea.
It was too cold here, colder than Saturday had ever been.
And the stars were not where they belonged. Saturday
had never listened as a boy when his father would try
to tell him what the stars meant, but now he wished he
had. Saturday had a bad feeling all the time, and he was
sure that these misplaced stars held a message for him.

Then he looked up past the iron fence that ran across
the front of the property by the cement path in front
of the street, and he saw a man he remembered from
Kenema. He knew what the message from the stars was,
and that he had learned it too late.

Six months earlier, he had been begging in the streets
when this man walked into the house of the courier
who worked for the Arabs who sold the diamonds. He
had marched the courier and his wife and his two small
children – a boy, maybe four, and a girl who could not
yet walk – out into the street. The man made them all
kneel there, except for the girl, who started to crawl
away. The man shot the girl first, and then the boy, and
then the woman. All in the head. And then he shot the
man. First in both knees, then in both arms, and then in
the stomach. He left the man to die slowly in the street
with his dead family around him.

Now, the same man was standing on the cement path in
front of the house in this strange city under these strange
stars, and Saturday knew the man must have come for

him. He could not think why, but why else would this man from Africa be here, with Saturday? The man had not yet seen Saturday in the darkness, but Saturday said, "Wetin mek? Wetin mek?" *Why? Why?* in Krio. He did not even know he had said it until he heard his own voice on the air. And then the man turned and pulled a pistol from inside his coat, and he shot Saturday.

Lynch was halfway through the people the uniforms had penned up in the next couple of suites. The rich and powerful and their friends, most of them not taking kindly to being detained. Nothing useful from any of them, most of them so self-absorbed that they probably never noticed anything that wasn't going in or out of their own pockets.

McCord stepped out of the bathroom while the uniform went to fetch the next asshole. "You want the quick and dirty?"

"Sure," said Lynch. "What've you got?"

"Three entrance wounds, small caliber, probably a .22. No exit wounds, so the slugs bounced around inside the skull like lotto balls, figured to puree the brain pretty good. Mob likes to do that, but it's been on every *CSI* episode since the dawn of time, so it's not like it's a secret. No sign the body's been moved. Perp made the victim kneel by the toilet and put his head down on the floor, then popped him. Evidence points to pretty much a contact wound, but we got less singeing in the hair than usual, which means something trapped some of the gas, so you're probably looking at a suppressor. We'll see what's left of the slugs when we get him in to the shop, but they'll be a mess."

"Suppressors usually don't work that good," said Lynch. "Not to where you wouldn't hear something in the next box."

McCord shrugged. "With a .22, you can silence it up pretty good, especially if you load shorts. For this kind of work, you'd want shorts. Just enough to punch through the skull, not enough to punch back out again. Game going on, you'd have a fair amount of background noise here. I could see it."

"Three shots? That over the top at all?"

Another shrug from McCord. "With a .22, you can put a lot of holes in somebody and leave 'em breathing. Better safe than sorry, I guess. What's a .22 short cost you? A dime, maybe? Not like a little insurance is gonna break the bank."

"So a pro. You got anything else?"

"Got a shitload of prints in there," said McCord. "Some from the victim; mess of others. Got at least ten different sets in the can so far, who knows how many out here in the suite. It'll take a while to sort that out. Have to get prints from whatever guests we can track down, from the staff. Gonna be a hairball."

"Plus, if we got a pro who can get in and out of here without being seen, has a .22 with a suppressor that actually works, then he's probably not leaving prints anyway."

"Probably not," said McCord. "But we'll run it out. One other thing that's a little weird. Stein's got some kind of dirt rubbed into the right leg of his pants. His suit costs more than my car, so you gotta figure he keeps it clean. Dirt looks fresh. We'll see what that's about, just in case. Listen, I'm gonna have to let the techs wrap up here. Somebody popped some guy a couple of blocks west up Madison. Drive-by or something. I'm not gonna get any sleep tonight. You either, from the looks of it."

"Job security, McCord."

"Damn straight," said McCord. "World ain't ever gonna run out of evil."

CHAPTER 3

Two days earlier, Dr Mark Heinz rode his horse on his New Mexico ranch, guiding it into the narrow arroyo that led from the higher country down toward the stables next to his home. He had purchased the land five years ago, built his dream house. Every morning, he rode the palomino for an hour, enjoying the early morning, the solitude, the views.

Time to think. He had always been a man of thought.

Today, he thought about whether his conscience should bother him. Well, not his conscience, he supposed. He'd realized long ago that he didn't have one of those. Not didn't *have*, really. Didn't *need*. He was a creature of pure intellect and understood that one shouldn't base ethical reasoning on feelings. One considered the facts of each situation, the causes and effects of each potential course of action, and one acted accordingly. Right or wrong should be the product of thought, not emotion. On the current matter, his thoughts were this:

Yes, the devices he had sold could, and in all likelihood would, result in great harm. And yes, selling those devices, even for the considerable sum he had received, would, by most standard definitions, be considered evil.

But he had invested the early part of his career in defining exactly this evil. In warning against its dangers. And he had been ignored.

And yes, those to whom he had sold the devices were agents of an anachronistic pox on the peace and order of the human society. They had repeatedly demonstrated their implacable intent to impose their horrid, backward barbarism on the rest of the world, to plunge mankind back into superstitious medieval suffering. And how had the world responded to this virulent threat? How had his own country responded? With half measures and the weak will of a society that elevated tolerance and political correctness to the level of policy.

So Heinz had acted for them. With his devices, these barbarians could finally commit an act of such magnitude and horror that the civilized world would have no choice but to respond decisively, in similar magnitude, as it should have long ago. The morally insane leaders who thought it God's will that they infect the world with their inane philosophies would die, and those few adherents who remained would be so devastated that they would hide and quake in fear for generations.

In the end, Heinz's act, one that those with no moral courage would consider evil, would preserve a millennium of human progress at the cost of a fraction of the number of human lives that its enemies would take in any event. By that calculus, by virtue of reason, he was not evil. He was a hero, if an anonymous one. And a rich one. Now a very rich one. That he would also profit from saving mankind, no thinking man would call that fault.

The horse shied, startled by something. Heinz sensed motion to his left, turned and saw just a blur of movement, the sense of a man, before he felt the blow to his forehead. Then he was on his back, on the ground. He had no memory of falling, and he was in no real pain, but he felt blood pouring from just under his hairline, down his face, down the sides of his head.

He heard footsteps and looked up.

It was the man who had paid him for the devices the day before. Heinz tried to rise, to turn, but his limbs were sluggish. Was the man after the money? He must know he would never get the money back with Heinz dead, not without the account numbers and the access codes. To ensure the secrecy of his mission? Surely this man and his masters must understand that Heinz could never reveal his actions. He would be jailed as a traitor, enshrined in the pantheon of evil with the likes of Hitler, Stalin and Pol Pot. Heinz was suddenly furious. To kill him? To still his facile mind? This act served no purposed, followed no logic.

But then he realized the flaw in his own argument. He was dealing with ignorant men who were driven not by reason but by fear. As they lived in fear of their own god, they also ruled by fear, acted from fear and sought to kill anything that made them afraid. Now they were afraid of him.

The man grabbed Heinz by the left shoulder and rolled him onto his stomach, and then pulled his head up by the collar of his jacket. Looking down, Heinz could see a large rock, perhaps a foot wide, with a sharp ridge running along its length. Heinz tried to resist, but could only weakly flail his arms. The man dragged Heinz forward positioned his head over the rock and drove it down onto the sharp, jagged edge.

Heinz didn't think anything after that.

CHAPTER 4

Shamus Fenn sat in his suite at the Peninsula Hotel off Michigan Avenue and slammed another scotch. Just not working anymore; might as well be water. It had started out as a good night. He was in Chicago shooting the next film, Lakers in town; producers got him a courtside seat, so that was cool. And then he'd seen that fucker Hardin.

Goddamn Africa thing a few years back, Mooney and his charity shindig. Last place on earth Fenn had ever planned to go, fucking Darfur. But his publicist had kept riding his ass telling him this thing was sponging up all the press. Fenn was in the running for a couple big roles just then; last thing he needed was to be on the dark side of the moon all of a sudden, so he called Mooney up, said sure, he'd love to help out.

Then he ran into that fucker Hardin.

Leno and Letterman made him their steady punch for weeks after Darfur. The parts he was up for? Nothing. Then the producers on his next picture dropped him, everybody making all the right conciliatory noises, but Fenn knew what it smelled like when they started pushing you downhill. The part went to that Leo Harris punk, kid ten years younger than Fenn. Fucking Harris got an Oscar. Fenn's goddamn Oscar.

Had to go under the knife for the nose twice, and it still wasn't right. His agent kept telling him go with it, said it

gave him some character. What the fuck did he know?
When Fenn went to Darfur, he was *People*'s reigning
Sexiest Man Alive, then his agent starts telling him to go
with the Owen Wilson look?

Some scripts that used to come to him first didn't come
to him at all. Finally, a director who'd had a couple of
arty films tank on him called Fenn in for a meeting. Guy
needed another blockbuster so the studios would keep
bankrolling his vanity projects. Fenn had played the lead
in the guy's two big paydays, so the man was reaching out.
But the producers had written this anger management
shit into Fenn's contract – Fenn had to go see this shrink,
had to get him to sign off that Fenn wasn't going to bust
anybody up.

Fenn figured he was an actor, right? He couldn't
convince some shrink he had his mind right, then he
might as well hang it up. But at their first meeting, quack
actually said one thing that made sense. Said that what
you were angry at wasn't why you were angry. Said you
needed to reach down, find that main hurt and deal with
it.

Just like that, Fenn saw a way out. Sat down that
night, worked up a whole backstory – how some trusted
family friend had abused him as a kid. Ran through the
scenes in his head, even had a guy in mind, guy his dad
used to know. Did his homework, and the guy had been
dead better than a decade, no family left to dispute the
story. And the guy'd gotten in some tax evasion trouble
in the early Eighties, so nobody had him up for sainthood
or anything. Once Fenn was sure he had it down, he
dropped it in the session. Some of his best work – crying
and furious all at once. Screaming at one point, tossing
a chair. Curled up in a ball on the floor blubbering like a
baby later. The shrink ate it up. Signed off, but not before

priming his own pump, telling Fenn that they should continue therapy, that identifying the cause was just the start. Fenn figured what the fuck; it gets him back to work. So if he's got to drop a few bills a month in this shrink's lap, so be it.

Then Fenn's agent cranked up the PR machine; started leaking the abuse shit to the right contacts, until finally they got the big cover story in the Enquirer – "The Dark Secret Behind Shamus Fenn's Fury". So the agent sets up a press conference, Fenn playing the reluctant hero – talking about how he had always been a private man, preferred to keep his business to himself, but then saying, maybe some other kid out there will know he can stand up, maybe some kid won't let this eat him out from the inside the way it had with Fenn. Then they went on the charm offensive, even did the obligatory weepy gig with Oprah.

Fenn was back on top now. Nothing America liked better than a sinner come to his understanding, especially if you could throw in a little prurient sex in the backstory. Looked like he was finally going to get his Oscar, too. Oprah wasn't daily anymore, but he had a sit-down with her a couple days back, her pre-Oscar special for that O network of hers. That interview was airing tomorrow. Meant he'd had to slip into his victim persona again, do the child abuse dance one more time. Old hat by now, had that down, even thought he sort of had a handle on the anger management thing.

Then he saw that fucker Hardin heading for the entrance to the luxury boxes. The one thing that had kept Fenn sleeping nights since the Darfur fiasco was knowing he'd fixed Hardin's wagon. The studio types may not have been real pleased with Fenn after the Darfur thing, but the last thing they needed was this Hardin guy pissing on their parade. So the studios had leaned on the networks and the networks leaned on Hardin. What Fenn had heard, they had dried up that bastard's pond but good. Fenn figured Hardin was over in some African shithole, begging for scraps. Now here he was in Chicago heading for the luxury boxes. The fucking shrink was right. You had to know what you were angry for, and Fenn was angry that this goddamn Hardin still had him doing the talk-show circuit, pretending he'd let some slimy bastard cornhole him all through junior high, while Hardin was upstairs playing footsie with the high rollers.

Fenn pulled out his cell and called Tony Corsco, mob guy who had consulted on *Cal Sag Channel*, the Chicago gangster pic Fenn had made maybe ten years back. Fenn got on with Corsco, and Corsco liked hanging with the stars. Helped out where he could, somebody needed a new coke connection or whatever. Hardin was the type of problem Corsco could solve.

CHAPTER 5

It was just past 11pm when Hardin checked into the downtown Hyatt on Wacker. Lots of rooms, lots of people coming and going, lots of exits, and it connected to some pedestrian tunnels. He'd stashed his rental in a huge public garage that stretched for several blocks under the fancy new park along Michigan. Short enough walk to the hotel, and he wouldn't have to wait on a valet if he needed to get out quick.

Hardin had no illusions. It had been thirty-six hours since he bounced the couriers outside Kenema. He figured four, maybe five hours after that they were late in Freetown, and maybe another couple hours before their Hezbollah contacts had shit their pants. That meant some pretty bad guys had spent at least a day leaning on anybody who knew anything about the blood diamond trade – and those fuckers knew how to lean. Somebody would remember that Hardin had been nosing around. Hardin wouldn't be the only name on their list, but he'd be on their list by now, so they'd be looking. For $150 million, they'd look hard.

At least he'd seen Stein. Stein set the meet at his luxury box at the Bulls game. Hardin waited until the game was almost over, watching Stein's box for the crowd to clear out. When the Bulls went up big late and it looked like Stein was alone, Hardin made his way up to the suite.

Stein got up and shook Hardin's hand as he came in.

"Long time," Stein said.

"Yeah," said Hardin.

"So, *Hardin* now?"

"My képi blanc name," said Hardin. One of the perks of serving in the Legion – in fact maybe the only perk – was a new identity and French citizenship when you mustered out. Hardin had known Stein from his Marine days, riding shotgun on some weird-smelling Mossad deal in Kuwait (and well up into Iraq, though they weren't supposed to have been there) just after Gulf War I.

"So, a drink? Some ribs?" Stein had quite a spread.

"Let's just get to it." Hardin had eaten breakfast at an IHOP somewhere on the way down from O'Hare earlier and still wasn't hungry. His stomach was on Africa time, and the IHOP breakfast was more calories than your average African family might eat in a week.

"Straight to business with you, eh? OK, so you got some raw rocks, you got no Kimberley certificates on them, and you want to dump them on somebody who can cut them and get them papered up so they go from being useless gravel to being an actual asset. I'm straight on that?"

Hardin got up and started toward the door. "Didn't realize I was wasting your time, Stein. Wouldn't want to saddle you with any useless gravel. Maybe Hezbollah will want to buy them back."

Stein laughed. "C'mon, Hardin. You really want to play footsie with that crowd, after what you pulled yesterday? I'd hate to fire up YouTube in a week or two and watch a video of you getting your head sawed off."

Hardin shrugged. "Kimberley certs or not, you know I can find a buyer. And if these things make their way back to Al Qaeda, your buddies in Mossad aren't going to be pleased with you."

"Sit, sit," Stein said, chuckling. "It's a ballet. I say they're worthless, you say they're Solomon's treasure. I say maybe a little, you say maybe a little more. We eat, we drink, we share the brotherly bonds of commerce–"

"Look, Stein, I was just a working-class kid before I went into the Corps, and I've spent that last couple decades bouncing around the less-civilized parts of the world, mostly with journalists. So what social skills I've got are rusty at best. I just wanna get this done."

Stein held up his hands in surrender. "OK, OK. The customer is always right. So what have you got? A couple of ounces?"

"Eighteen."

Stein's eyes widened. "Eighteen ounces?"

Hardin nodded. "I would have been happier with two, if that makes you feel any better."

Stein blew out a long breath. "How am I supposed to move that kind of weight? Dummying up the Kimberley certs on a smaller amount of carats is one thing, but this?"

"I know, OK? But I also know this is how you and your Mossad buddies keep the green out of Al Qaeda's wallet."

Stein was still for a minute. "You got a number in mind?"

"At $750 a carat retail? That's $180 million and change. What I'd heard was you usually go ten percent."

"I go ten percent when somebody brings me reasonable weight," Stein said. "I'm gonna need a volume discount on this."

"I just want my end. Give me a number."

"Five million," said Stein.

"You want me to get up and start toward the door again?"

"Ten."

"Done," Hardin said.

"You've got a sample, of course?"

Hardin had packed most of the stones into a compartment hidden in his bag. He'd left two stones in the canvas pouch he'd taken off the couriers. He handed it to Stein.

The pouch leaked some dirt onto Stein's pants when he opened it. "Classy presentation," said Stein, trying to brush off the dirt but just rubbing it in. He gave the stones a quick expert examination. "These representative?"

"Yeah."

"And you want cash?"

"I don't want a suitcase of it," Hardin said. "Wire transfer." Hardin pulled a slip of paper from the front pocket of his shirt and held it out toward Stein.

Stein shook him off. "A million or two I do out of pocket. Tel Aviv's good for it. But they're going to have to front the money this time. You can give me the account number when I get the cash."

"How long?"

"Be a couple, three days," said Stein. "How do I get in touch?"

"You don't," Hardin said. "Three days. I'll call you."

Hardin knew the Hyatt was really just an upper mid-level hotel in the States, but after a couple decades bouncing around the bush, it felt like the Alhambra. He'd been going pretty much nonstop for a day and a half since he hit the courier back in Sierra Leone. Flight from Lungi to Casablanca. Air France from Casablanca to New York, connection from Kennedy to O'Hare, then the meeting with Stein. He took a long, hot shower, made sure all the locks were set, put a chair up next to the door, and crashed.

••••

Hardin woke up just after 9am and flicked on the set while he unpacked. Felt a little funny, his whole life crammed into one duffle. He'd grown up in America, understood the life-is-about-accumulating-shit gestalt, and yet everything he owned was stuffed into a four-foot canvas bag. He tried to think what he'd left behind that he'd miss. Nothing came to him. Well, his guns maybe. Had to leave those behind. So far as Hardin could tell, a nice weapon was the only thing that was easier to get in Ghana than it was here.

He took out his wallet, looked at the picture of the girl. Still had that. But he'd brought that to Africa with him, after the trouble with Hernandez. He thought for a minute about looking her up. Might still be in the area. She'd be forty, thereabouts, married probably, kids probably. And she'd invite him over because she owed him, and he'd come because he owed her. And there would be some husband trying to be the nice-guy host, wondering what this shit was about – or maybe knowing, if she'd told him – and her brother's ghost in the room the whole time. Then Hardin would leave, and he'd know that picture was a just a picture now, not a possibility anymore. The picture was the only thing he'd brought from Africa he really cared about, so why fuck that up? If a dream is all you've got, why piss on it?

Hardin shook his head. Almost fifty and the only real relationship he'd had was with a wallet photo. Enough to make a guy think it was time to re-evaluate his life choices.

The TV droned on in the background; just white noise. Hardin dressed, ready to find some food. Just as he reached for the remote to turn off the set, the local station ran its teaser for the noon news show. Some spunky brunette trying to look serious. "This is Kathy

McNally. Stay tuned for more details on the shocking murder of Chicago businessman Abraham Stein at last night's Bulls game. That story, your Cubs spring training update, and the weekend forecast, all at noon."

Hardin flicked off the set. Son of a bitch. Somebody'd offed Stein.

Hardin had no idea how Al Qaeda could be onto him this fast.

But maybe they weren't. Stein had been killed at the stadium, and Hardin had been with him just a minute or two before the game ended. If Al Qaeda was looking for Hardin, why wouldn't they have killed them both?

Either way, he had to figure his name was working its way up the hit parade. Fuck. This left him sitting on eighteen ounces of stones with no buyer and a short clock.

CHAPTER 6

Lynch was on his way into the office when McCord called him on his cell.

"Wasn't expecting to hear from you yet," Lynch said.

"No shit," said McCord, mumbling through whatever he was eating. "Got done with you at what, eleven? I was over at the other scene until after two. But I got something you need to hear. That second stiff, looks like another .22. Haven't chopped anybody up yet, and like I said, I'm not real optimistic on a good ballistics match with anything out of Stein's noggin, so you might have to wait until we get the metallurgy back before we can make the tie for sure. But two guys getting popped with .22s half a mile from each other and maybe thirty minutes apart? Thought you might want to know."

"Has to be the same guy," Lynch said. "Can't picture any of the gangbangers over on the west side using a .22."

"Nah," said McCord. "Anything smaller than a nine, they'd be afraid their pricks would shrivel up."

"What can you tell me about the second victim?"

"You're gonna love this," said McCord. "Guy's name is Membe Saturday. Refugee at some sort of shelter some nuns are running. Guy's pretty much off the boat from Africa. Missing a hand, if that helps. Looks like somebody took it off with an ax a couple years back. Guess he was

41

standing out front, taking the air, when somebody put three through his forehead."

"Three again?"

"Yep."

"Leave any brass?"

"Nope."

"Makes him a calm motherfucker. Picking up the casings in the United Center bathroom, fine. Those had to be right there. But taking the time to find your shells out on a public sidewalk?"

"If it's an automatic. Could be a revolver," McCord said.

"Probably not. We're thinking he had a pretty good suppressor at the UC, and suppressors don't work so hot with revolvers – you get some sound out the back end."

"True, and it looks like the guy still had the suppressor on his piece. This Saturday guy, he was right outside the shelter. You got three shots, and nobody heard anything. Oh, and the three shots? Got a three-inch grouping right in the middle of the forehead. The gate on the fence around the shelter's yard locks and it wasn't open, and this Membe guy dropped straight down right in front of the porch, so the guy was shooting from twenty feet, and shooting damn quick to get all three into the guy's head before he went down. So it's not some spray-and-pray job. Guy can shoot some."

"Swell. Any cameras?" Between red-light cameras, police surveillance cameras in high-crime areas and the private security feeds that have been given access to the city, Chicago was the most photographed city in the world.

"Got a red-light box at the end of the block. Might be close enough to get you something, provided anybody ran the light at the right time."

"You tell Starshak?" Starshak ran Lynch's squad. If they were looking at the same guy that did Stein, then the second shooting was going to get assigned to Lynch.

"Gonna, soon as we hang up."

"So," Lynch said. "We got a shooter, gets himself in Stein's box somehow, gives him the triple tap, then walks up the street and goes all OK Corral on some refugee."

"Looks like."

"Any thoughts?"

"Mostly that it seems fucked up."

"Helpful," Lynch said.

"Sure," said McCord. "Trustworthy, brave, all that other shit, too."

Lynch called Starshak, caught him up. Bernstein would be buried in paper going through Stein's business, so Lynch jumped on Ogden and cut down to Madison toward the shelter. Just like his school days. Off to see the nuns about some trouble.

The shooting had taken place in front of an old three-flat on Madison a few blocks west of the United Center. Place was well maintained – small, neat lawn out front behind a waist-level wrought-iron fence. Madison used to be skid row from the Loop west, but it had been gentrified now, most of the way out to the United Center. West of the stadium, though, it was still a rough neighborhood. Buildings on either side of the shelter were pretty run down. Somebody had put some money into this one, though, and the way upscale was creeping west, the nuns would probably clean up on it somewhere down the line. Of course, you only had to check out the property values on Holy Name and the Cardinal's residence off Rush Street to know that the church understood real estate.

Lynch looked up the street at the red light camera covering the intersection. Two houses up. Probably not the right angle to get anything on the sidewalk, but it might have a shot of the cars parked on the street this far back.

Lynch thought on that for a second. The way the parking worked at the United Center, you could get crammed in pretty good. You had to get out in a hurry, you might be stuck. So, if you're a pro, you probably look for a spot on the street. You make the hit, walk out, find your ride and get gone. Maybe the shooter parked up this way, this Membe guy did something to make him nervous?

Pictures from the red-light camera would be time-stamped, so at least they could see whether a car had left around the right time.

Lynch rang the bell. A short, slim woman answered. Light hair, no makeup that Lynch could see. Strong face, one that had been outdoors a lot. Mid-forties Lynch guessed. Khaki slacks and a plain beige crewneck. She wore a simple wooden cross on a leather thong around her neck.

"You're with the police," she said. Not quite an accusation, but not happy either. Hint of an accent, Scottish from the sound of it.

"I'm Detective John Lynch. I'd like to ask you a few questions about last night." He held out his badge case, showed her his creds.

She looked at them, then closed her eyes for a moment, like she was pushing back something.

"I'm Kate Magnus. I run the shelter for the order."

She stepped aside, walked him into the house. Lynch caught just a glimpse of a huge man off to the right, probably six foot six, hulking, black as coffee. The man glared at him, half hate, half fear. Bad combination. Then the man ducked around a wall, out of view. Lynch followed the woman down a hall and into a small room with a beat-up metal desk, chair behind it, a wall of filing cabinets and a single guest chair. Tiny as she was, neighborhood like this, house full of refugees, Lynch thought the woman would be nervous, but there wasn't a whiff of that. She sat behind the desk; Lynch took the single chair.

"Our residents come from places where any man with a gun is a man to be feared. We had several policemen here last night, for a long time. The residents are still pretty upset. We will talk in here. If you want to speak with any them, I will ask that you make sure that your weapon is out of sight."

"Fair enough, Sister," said Lynch.

She shook her head. "Not Sister. Just Ms Magnus."

"Sorry. With the cross and the order and all, I assumed."

"Dangerous habit in your profession, isn't that, detective? Assuming?" A little dig in her voice.

"Touché," Lynch said.

"I've been with the order since I was twenty. It does good work for good reasons. So far as the cross goes, I have no problem with what it should stand for. Some of the theology behind it, well…" Her voice trailed off and she looked to the side a moment, then looked back. "Vows should mean something. I couldn't take them."

Lynch thought he heard some history behind that, but that wasn't what he was here for and he had a feeling he'd heard as much as he was going to anyway.

"What can you tell me about your residents?" Lynch asked.

"What do you know about Africa?" she said.

"Big place, lots of countries, pretty screwed up. Mostly what I learned looking at maps at the zoo when I was a kid and watching the news. Not sure I should generalize about the whole continent."

"Ignorance of the world is an American luxury. When you have everything you need at home, you don't need to know about anywhere else. Most Americans only learn about a country after we decide to invade it."

"Cynical point of view."

She looked up at Lynch, studied his face a moment. "I've lived in Africa for most of the last fifteen years. People here, they know about Somalia maybe, Rwanda if they've seen the movie. Over there, in most of the places I've lived, for most of the people I knew, that movie never ends."

"Dangerous place for a woman," Lynch said.

She bristled at that. "Dangerous place for anyone."

She had a fire in her; Lynch had seen it before. Some social workers, teachers at some of the inner-city schools, some nurses he knew, even some cops. Some of them, they see enough, and it hits critical mass, it burns all the happy out of them, all the hope, but they keep doing the work, keep throwing more despair inside, hoping someday it will be enough. Probably why she was so small; fire burned so hot nothing stuck, nothing lasted. Just the fire. Lynch could see where she could believe in the cross, believe in the pain, in the sacrifice, just not in the God behind it anymore.

"What can you tell me about Membe Saturday?" Lynch asked.

"Our residents are all refugees from West Africa, primarily Liberia and Sierra Leone. Our order has a very active mission presence there. While the civil wars in these countries have calmed, there is still tremendous tribal violence. For various reasons, all of our guests would have been killed if they remained. We help them secure political asylum and try to help them start new lives here. The man who was killed last night, Membe Saturday, was from Liberia. He had only been with us three weeks."

"I remember Liberia. That Taylor guy, right?"

Her eyebrows went up a fraction, her face loosened a little. Lynch guessed he'd scored some points, not being a complete dumbass.

"Charles Taylor, yes. An amoral thug. He overthrew the government, headed up a group called the RUF. When you meet our guests, you'll notice that many are missing at least one arm. Lopping of limbs is an RUF trademark. Many of our guests were also forced to work in the diamond mines. The famous conflict diamonds – blood diamonds. It's how the Taylors of the region pay for their wars. The men are forced to work in the mines essentially as slaves. If they are caught trying to keep a diamond, they lose a hand, if they aren't killed."

Lynch nodded. "You mentioned tribal violence. These guys here all get along?"

"We don't allow trouble of that sort here."

"You've got all these guys, different tribes, suddenly they get over here and make nice?"

"We don't allow trouble, Detective. And none of our guests have guns."

"Did you see or hear anything unusual last night?"

"No."

"Anything strange about Saturday's behavior?" Lynch asked. "He seem agitated, frightened?"

"All our residents are frightened. They've been abused by armed men in power their entire lives. They've seen family members killed, their wives and daughters raped. They have suffered these horrible mutilations. And most have never been more than a few miles from their homes before. They come here, they're in a completely foreign environment. We work to help them acclimate, but a newcomer like Membe, he's always frightened, always agitated. Anyway, I went through all of this with another detective last night. Do I really need to cover all this ground again?"

"Did you hear about the shooting at the United Center last night?"

"Of course. A rich businessman is murdered and it leads the news. I couldn't find any coverage of Membe's murder at all."

"There is some evidence that indicates that Saturday and the victim at the United Center were killed with the same weapon," Lynch said. "I think the killer may have parked on the street near here – maybe Saturday just saw the wrong guy at the wrong time. Was there anyone parked out front last night?"

"On any night they have an event at the stadium someone is always parked out front."

"Any cars that seemed out of place?"

"Not to me. But I don't know much about cars. Not aside from what I needed to know to keep the thirty year-old Land Cruiser we had in Kenema running."

"Anything special about Saturday?" said Lynch. "Anything that might have followed him over from Africa?"

"I'm not familiar with the details of his life there, Detective, beyond what he has shared with me in the past few weeks. He saw his family murdered, which would be unusual here, but it's commonplace where Saturday was from. He was accused of stealing a diamond, so his hand was cut off. Also commonplace, I'm afraid."

"You must have some records, though. I mean for the political asylum, there has to be an application, paperwork?"

"We don't have those here. There is an attorney downtown who helps us with that. Doug Telling. He'd be able to get you any paperwork from that process."

Lynch buttoned his coat to hide his gun, and then talked with the residents. The huge man Lynch had seen on his way in followed the whole time, always hanging back by the wall, the same frightened, hateful look in his eyes. Only one of the men spoke English, a guy who was sitting on the stairs, the only one that seemed comfortable; had a smart-ass air to him.

"Did you know Membe Saturday?" Lynch asked.

The guy shrugged, smirked. "No more Saturdays for him. Kissi pussy, shoulda stayed home, made baskets."

The huge man came off the wall shouting, lunged toward them; the man on the stairs shouting back, some African dialect. Magnus jumped in front of the big man, her head barely coming up to his chest, put both her hands up, pushed him back, lit in to him in, Lynch assumed, whatever language he had been speaking. The man looked down, ashamed, turned back to the wall.

She turned, snapped at the man on the stairs.

"Go to your room, Isaac."

"You gotta show off for your police boyfriend, eh?" the man said.

She just stared him down. Slowly, he got up, went upstairs.

"Thought you said you didn't have that kind of trouble here," Lynch said.

"That wasn't tribal," she said. "Isaac is an asshole. Besides, I said I don't allow it. I don't."

"You have to jump in like that a lot?"

"It happens."

"Good way to get hurt," Lynch said.

She held his eyes a second, hard. "It happens."

Lynch just nodded. They went through the building, talked to the rest of the residents, Magnus translating. Nothing. One resident with jaundiced eyes and a skeletal face kept following Lynch around with a strange smile, making a gun with his fingers and shooting it at Lynch over and over again.

CHAPTER 7

Bobby Lee watched the blonde walk into the lobby of the Deloitte building at Wacker and Monroe through his hack into the Chicago emergency command center. He'd built a facial recognition match into his software after he'd targeted her at the Route 59 Burlington station a couple days back. She looked like that blonde chick Tiger Woods used to be married to, and that was some hot poontang. He'd heard people saying how they didn't understand how Tiger could step out on that, but Bobby Lee understood. It was the power of strange. World was full of nookie, man. And the nookie you got, that shit don't never take your mind off the rest of it.

Bobby had been part of the team that helped set up the Chicago video surveillance system – one of the most sophisticated in the world. Thousands of cameras – on light poles, on buses, private security cameras networked in. It was on the news now and then, but he figured most Chicagoans just didn't get it, didn't understand that a lot of them were on camera every time they stepped outside. Or inside, for that matter, if they were anyplace public. Bobby understood it – hell, that's why he'd moved out to Naperville. That Big Brother eyes-in-the-sky shit gave him the willies.

But Bobby knew an opportunity when he saw one, and he just might be the best freaking systems guy in

51

the world. The Chicago surveillance gig had been his last
as a wage slave. He'd built a shitload of back doors into
the code, and those gave him run of the system. That's
when he'd gone private. He'd figured there'd be people
who'd pay top dollar for access. He'd figured right. And
then the City had come calling. Bobby's dad had been a
black GI in the waning days of 'Nam. His mom had been
a Saigon mattress girl with enough sense to understand
that the only good thing likely to come out of the war
was a ticket to the States. So Bobby had come squalling
into the world in the VA hospital in Chicago, and he'd
grown up to understand the racial algebra in the City.
Fuck that "Cablinasian" shit Tiger got away with. You
got any black in you, then you're black. And that means
you're a minority. And that means minority contracts. So
when the Chicago PD needed vendors for maintenance
and upgrades for their ever-growing video system, Bobby
tossed his hat in the ring. With his experience in the
system already, he came out with the big prize. Money
was decent, workload was minimal, and it kept him wired
in to the max. It also meant he could cover his tracks.
After a big job, the type that might get people thinking,
he'd close up whatever wormhole he hacked in through,
bury his tracks under a pile of code, and set up a shiny
new way in somewhere else.

Damn, this blonde was hot. He checked his database
– couldn't remember whether he'd hacked anything at
Deloitte yet. Yep. Took a bit, but he found the file for
employee IDs, ran his JPEG of the blonde against the
images they had for their security cards, and up she
popped. Courtney Schilst, senior in the tax practice.
Fifteen minutes after she'd walked in the door he had her
name, salary, cell number, her IP address and where she
lived – an apartment just east of 59, a shade north of Fox

Valley. Ten minutes after that, he was into her Facebook and Twitter feeds, scrolling through, looking for a hook. Courtney didn't know it yet, but inside a week, two at the outside, she'd be another notch on Bobby's belt. Boy had to have a hobby, right?

A warning ping from one of his monitors. Search he was running for Tony Corsco. That Nick Hardin guy, some reporter or something who'd flown in from Africa in the last couple days that Tony wanted run down. A little bit of trouble – the guy had to have at least two sets of ID because none of the hotels or car rental places had popped up a Hardin, but the airlines had. So Lee had his arrival time and the photo from Corsco. That was all he needed. He tracked Hardin from the gate to the Hertz lot, got the license plate on the rental. Some holes in the system between the airport and downtown, but Lee had fed the plate number into his system and set up an auto search. Cameras all over the city had been bouncing all the license plates they picked up off the number, and now he had a hit. The car was in the Grant Park garage, toward the north end, so this Hardin guy, he could be at a few places down that way. Got the Swissotel, got the Fairmont, got the Hyatt maybe. Fuck that shit. He'd give Corsco the car and the location, and if Corsco came back looking for more, then Bobby'd put him back on the clock.

Bobby Lee didn't do charity work.

CHAPTER 8

At least he was in Saigon, thought Munroe. That was the good news. Or Ho Chi Minh City, whatever the locals were calling it these days.

Munroe took a pull on his drink, looked out the window into the wee small hours of the Asian morning. He liked Saigon. The whole Vietnam thing was supposed to be this big black mark, America's lost war, but for a young kid just learning his way around the sharp end of things, there wasn't a better place to be, not back in the late-Sixties. The food, the Eurasian girls, the French panache, road trips to the bush to pick up a few VC scalps, back to the Caravelle by dark for drinks with the journalists and the guys from all the other embassies who were supposed to be aid officers or attachés, but who were all doing the same bad shit Munroe was doing under cover of whatever flag flew over their compounds. Happiest days of his life.

Thrill pretty much wore off by 1975 when he rode the second-to-last chopper off the roof of the embassy, but by then he had enough scalps on his lodge pole, VC and otherwise, to write his own ticket. Which worked out great, because it was right around then that the Church Committee went public with how the Agency had been very naughty and hogtied Langley with a mess of Marquess of Queensberry rules. Hogtied them just about the same time that the Cold War balance of terror started breaking down into a multilateral, asymmetrical clusterfuck where any yahoo with a little scratch in his pocket could stick it up Uncle Sam's ass with anything from a WMD to an airliner full of Koran thumpers.

Just when playing outside the lines got more necessary, it got more complicated. Munroe'd gone one way, a lone wolf Langley could sic on problems that required his brand of discretion.

Sometimes, though, the masters needed a blunt instrument. For that, they had Tech Weaver. He'd taken his group private, set up InterGov.

Munroe and Weaver had both still been on Uncle's payroll, of course, but they were off the grid, untraceable line items bouncing around the federal budget with only one mandate – make sure the bad guys understood that Uncle Sam still had teeth.

Weaver'd been ex-military though. Problem with those guys, they got that chain of command thing in their blood; always need an org chart. When you screwed the pooch, org charts left a place for people to start digging. Weaver'd screwed the pooch big time in Chicago a year or so back. Screwed the pooch so bad, the president ended up putting a bullet through his own head. People started digging.

Now Weaver was dead and InterGov was history – well in that form, anyway. Which meant Munroe was busy.

Another sip at his drink. Better than four decades since his salad days, but Munroe still liked the Caravelle. Conversation at the bar was a little different – it was all thirty-something entrepreneurs talking labor costs and transfer pricing. Little smile at that. Anybody still saying America lost the war? The whole point of the exercise was to keep Vietnam out of the Commie column. You wanted to find a Commie around here anymore, you had to chopper up to the I Drang valley and start digging for bones. Get a couple Vietnamese talking nowadays, and they made your average Iowa Rotary Club member sound like Leon Trotsky. These guys took to capitalism the way their fathers took to black pajamas and AK-47s.

Other than hardly anybody spoke French anymore, Saigon was pretty much the same. Still liked the food, and if you knew how much to slip to which concierge, you could still get hot-and-cold running Eurasian girls sent up to the room with all the fixings.

So Munroe was in Saigon. That was the good news.

The bad news was he'd only sent the girls home about two hours ago, it was three in the morning and his phone was ringing. He looked at the screen. Station chief out of from Lagos. That meant the chatter they'd picked up out of Freetown about a mess of diamonds going missing had checked out. Diamonds with an unsavory pedigree – Al Qaeda by way of Hezbollah. And that meant his Saigon sojourn was over. Munroe hit the talk button.

"This diamond bullshit's not a fire drill?" Munroe asked.

"No. The situation is fluid and some of the information is conflicting, but the best estimate is at least fifteen ounces."

Munroe paused a moment. Fifteen ounces meant at least nine figures retail. That meant the ragheads were up to something big.

"We sure it's not Mossad?"

"They're pissed. Had to talk them down. They thought it was our operation."

Be a lot easier if it was Mossad, thought Munroe.

"I assume you have heard about Stein?" the man on the phone asked.

"Yeah."

"There is something off a video feed from Chicago you should see. I am sending it to your phone."

Munroe's phone dinged and he opened the message. Screen capture of an olive-skinned guy in a topcoat.

"Al Din," Munroe said. "He did Stein?"

"Looks that way."

"But the noise on your end is that the diamonds are still in the air?"

"Yes. And al Din is still in Chicago."

Munroe thought on that a second. Al Din was freelance, so theoretically he could tie to anybody, but for the last few years at least he'd been running almost exclusively out of Tehran.

Islam might be one big happy bowl of ragheads to your average Tea Party dipshit, but Munroe knew better. Iran was Shi'a, and with Iraq castrated, Iran was looking to consolidate its position as the top dog through the whole Shi'a crescent – Iran, Iraq, Azerbaijan, Bahrain, Lebanon, some real pull in Pakistan. Now you had Hezbollah throwing in with Assad in Syria, and it was hard to pick a dog in that fight. Sure, you had the sane people in the Syrian opposition, secular types you could do business with. But you also had a pile of fundamentalists of the Sunni stripe, and it was starting to look like the yahoos had the numbers. Which meant Syria could well go from the dictator column to the Sunni whacko column – that was the side of the balance sheet that Al Qaeda called home. Munroe was more comfortable with a dictator personally, except now Assad owed his ass to Hezbollah, and that meant he owed his ass to Tehran. Whatever piece of it he hadn't already whored out to Putin.

So, the diamonds. Lebanese immigrants in Sierra Leone had pretty much run the West African diamond trade since the first deposits were discovered back in the

Thirties. These were old school Lebanese guys who, on
the Palestinian question, were a lot friendlier with Amal
than Hezbollah. But Hezbollah was pretty much the only
game in Lebanon these days. When you're holding a gun
to some guy's family's heads, muscling in on the diamond
trade gets pretty simple. Which would seem to put the
West African diamond pipeline in the Shi'a column.

Still, even among the true believers, sometimes money
trumps all. When Al Qaeda started looking for ways to
move money around after 9/11, after the West slammed
the door on all their bank accounts, Hezbollah was happy
to play ball. Diamonds became one of Al Qaeda's favorite
financing mechanisms, even if it meant that some Sunnis
and some Shi'as had to make nice.

Whether you were Sunni or Shi'a, though, you could
still hate the Jews, and when you got to the commercial
end of the diamond market, the part in Antwerp and
New York, the Jews still ran the market. So Israel was
wired into it pretty good. Munroe knew Stein had been
working with Mossad to fuck up Al Qaeda's diamond
play, sucking their runners into false buys, whacking
them and taking the stones.

So al Din? Could be he was on Al Qaeda's dime this
time, whacking Stein, trying to clear Mossad out of their
pipeline. Except al Din was still hanging around Chicago.
Not a smart play unless the man had another reason to
stay in town. Munroe had played footsie with al Din
before, couple of times, and he knew one thing for sure.
Al Din had a reason. The guy didn't do stupid.

And that meant the Stein murder was the opening
gambit on a bigger play, one that had something to do
with better than $100 million in stones on the move.
That was a butt-ton of operating capital. Hell, the
ragheads had pulled off 9/11 for box tops and bottle caps

by comparison. Something was up. Something big. And there were too many teams on the field.

"OK," Munroe said to the Lagos station chief. "Three things. First, wake up the Google jockeys at Langley and have them start running scenarios – what kind of mischief could our Islamic friends get up to with nine figures to play with? Could be Al Qaeda boys, could be Tehran. So big-ticket items – loose nukes, whatever. Get ears up in all the weapons markets. Find out who's flush all of a sudden and we'll have a chat with them. Second, whoever has the diamonds has to move them, and these stones aren't papered up. That's gonna take an inside player somewhere, and that means Johannesburg, Antwerp, Mumbai, Tel Aviv, New York, maybe the Russians – there has to be money on the move, and a lot of it. Let's find it. Third, Stein was Chicago, al Din's in Chicago, so I'll be in Chicago soonest. Get me an asset roster. Anybody we got in the Windy City, on or off the books. And anybody we can lean on. I know that Mayor Hurley and his thugs have that place wired up – I want real time access to every camera and microphone in town before I hit the ground. And let's see if we can find out who has the goddamn diamonds, shall we?"

"I'm on it," the man said.

Munroe killed the connection, went to the window, opened it, leaned on the sill and looked out over the city. Three in the fucking morning, but plenty of traffic. New York thinks it doesn't sleep? Nobody's stealing a march on these little yellow bastards. Warm breeze, always that scent of *nước mắm* on the air. An elegiac feeling he had too often these days. Munroe never knew when it was going to be his last time someplace anymore. If this was it for Saigon, he hated to say goodbye.

CHAPTER 9

Liz Johnson sat across the table from Lynch in the booth at McGinty's. Over her shoulder, he could see her on TV above the bar. Not unusual – he saw more of her on TV these days than he did in person.

"You're on the tube," he said. Her and one of the talking heads at CNN. Sound was down, he couldn't tell what they were talking about, but then Hastings Clarke's picture popped up, the former President of the United States who resigned his office by eating a gun after Lynch had dug up his past. He and Johnson had just been starting out then; she'd gotten the story from the inside. Her book on the whole mess was coming out in a couple of weeks. She was A-list talent now. She'd gone from a local reporter at the *Trib* to one of the faces every cable news outlet wanted in their stable. Spent as much time in New York and Washington as she did in Chicago these days.

Johnson turned, took a peek. "PR. Publisher's got me booked solid the next couple weeks. Keep having the same conversation over and over again."

"You've got it down, what I've seen. Things looking good?"

She shrugged. "Going to a third printing, just on the pre-orders. Not Sarah Palin numbers, but good."

Lynch smiled at her and nodded.

"None of that would have happened without you," she said.

"Sure," said Lynch. "Don't forget the little people."

She frowned a little, not sure how to take that. "That a problem?"

He shook his head. "Weird, is all. Got my wake-up from the clock radio the other day, you talking with somebody over at WBBM. I'm half out of it, reach over to the other side of the bed before I realize you're not there."

She gave him a sly smile. "I've got better ways to wake you up, Lynch. You know that."

"That I do," he said. "That I do." She was only in town for the night, back to New York in the morning. But he was glad they were at McGinty's. Not the kind of place where he'd spend dinner watching her sign napkins and pose for pictures.

"This Stein thing going to be another hairball?" Johnson asked. Lynch and Johnson had a deal. Anything they said was strictly off the record unless they both agreed otherwise, and she'd kept her end of the bargain right down the line. Nice to have somebody to talk to, somebody outside the department.

"Don't know what to make of it yet. Second killing just up the street the same night, looks like the same shooter. Some African refugee. Bernstein's pulling Stein's business shit apart. The whole thing's got a funny smell to it already."

Waitress dropped off their burgers, and Johnson took a huge bite, closed her eyes for a moment, smiled. "Jesus, real food."

"They aren't feeding you out east?"

"Oh, sure, all the arugula and overpriced fish I can eat. You go to Komi with Stephanopoulos, you don't get any bacon cheeseburgers."

Lynch laughed. "And how is George?"

"Short. Nice hair, though."

Later, upstairs in Lynch's apartment, she lay on top of him on the bed. They hadn't been together in three weeks, so the first time had been urgent, but now they were rocking gently. Her Blackberry buzzed, vibrating on the table next to the bed. She didn't reach for it, he had to give her that, but he felt her stiffen for a second, and she never seemed to come all the way back to him. He couldn't blame her exactly, but that didn't mean he had to like it. They finished.

"I'm going to wash up a bit," she said, rolling off him. "Have to catch a plane in a couple hours."

"Still back tomorrow though?" Lynch asked.

She nodded, already had the Blackberry up, scrolling through her messages. She took the phone into the bathroom with her.

Lynch lay on the bed, staring at the ceiling. She was the best thing in his life, and she was in the bathroom with her Blackberry. He was in his bed alone.

CHAPTER 10

Nick Hardin was working on plan B.

With Stein dead, he could go to Mossad direct. But he didn't have a personal contact and Mossad tended to play dirty. If he walked into the consulate, he might get his $10 million, or he might get ten cents of lead through the brainpan. More likely, they'd use this as leverage, and ship him back to Africa as their personal indentured asset until his luck ran out. Hardin was looking for an exit strategy, not an unpaid second career as Tel Aviv's sub-Saharan lackey.

No, he wasn't going to Mossad, not without Stein running interference.

What he needed was somebody with the contacts and ethics of a French arms dealer. So he picked up a throwaway cell at a Loop Radio Shack and called one.

Pierre Fouche was living the good life in the south of France, but Hardin had known him when he was Ivan Sidorov, just another Spetsnaz refugee looking to make his way in the Legion after the wheels came off the big Red machine and Moscow stopped paying their shooters. Hardin had saved Sidorov's life, twice.

"Pierre, how's life in Marseilles?"

"Hardin, you bastard. Where have you gone?" said Fouche. "I have been trying to reach you for days. I had a sweet deal cooking in Accra, just needed a body on the ground, and nobody could find you. Then I start hearing stories – a couple of dead Hezbollah couriers, lots of angry camel jockeys looking for you. You're in *beaucoup de merde*, my friend."

"Why do you think I'm calling you? You wanna make a few euros?"

"Dollars, Hardin," Fouche said. "Haven't you been paying attention to the news? We got Greece and Spain circling the drain over here, Italy's being run like a Fellini film, and the Germans are using euros as asswipes trying to clean up the mess. I want to make a few dollars."

"Whatever," Hardin said. "Look, I'm sitting on a shitload of raw stones. I had a deal with Stein. You hear about Stein?"

"Of course, and after I heard about this Hezbollah business, I figured they'd be fishing your body out of the lake up there any day now. Thought for sure it was a two-fer, and they'd just taken you somewhere to ask politely about the diamonds."

"Guess Stein stepped in some other shit," Hardin said. "Anyway, I gotta unload these rocks and get out of Dodge. You got any ideas?"

"Russians like diamonds – mostly they like to keep them locked up and off the market, prop the prices up. I still got some contacts there, could probably find you a middleman. I'll be taking a million off the top, just so you know."

"Wouldn't trust you if you didn't."

"Don't suppose you want to leave me your number?" said Fouche.

"No. I'll be playing musical phones for the duration. How much time you need?"

"It will take two days. Call me then."

Hardin hung up. Two days. So stay put or switch locations? Stay put, and if somebody's got a line on you, then you're toast. Move around and you increase your exposure. Hardin figured if the Arabs had a line on him, they would have made their play last night. So for now, stay put.

Marco "Beans" Garbanzo and Ricky "Snakes" DeGetano sat in a stolen Grand Marquis at the north end of the Grant Park garage, eyeballing Hardin's car. They had Hardin's picture and a cell number. Soon as they see him heading for the car, they make the call and this guy shuts the camera down for a couple minutes, that's what Corsco told them.

Snakes was in charge; Beans was the muscle. Beans was huge, closing in on 350 pounds.

"Been down here half the fucking day," said Beans. "I'm starving."

"Guy rents a car, eventually he'll come down to his car. So just shut up and keep your eyes open," said Snakes.

Snakes heard a low, liquidy rumble. Then the smell hit him.

"Jesus fucking Christ, Beans," said Snake, buzzing down his window.

"Hey, I got a condition."

"What you got is you're hauling like a whole extra person around on account of how you're always shoveling food in your face. You do that again and I'm leaving your body in the trunk."

Garbanzo farted again, on purpose.

CHAPTER 11

Lynch picked up Bernstein at the station and they headed downtown to talk to Telling, the attorney Kate Magnus had pointed him at.

"You say Doug Telling?" Bernstein asked.

"Yeah, know him?"

"If it's the same guy, yeah. He ran in my parents' circles. Used to be a big shot down at MacMillian & Lowe, place Governor Timpson went for his payday after he got done on the public tit."

"Address I got puts him in the Old Colony Building," Lynch said. "That would have been hot shit a century ago, but it's a pretty big step down from the MacMillian digs now."

"So maybe something," Bernstein said.

"Maybe," said Lynch.

Telling's office was on the fourth floor, the hallway lined with tall wooden doors framing long pebbled-glass inserts, the doors all with the old-fashioned transom windows over the top. Old wood, old stone moldings. People would have said faded grandeur maybe twenty-five years ago, but it was still fading. Telling was in 412, "Douglas Telling, Immigration Law" stenciled on the window. The door was ajar; Lynch nudged it open.

Telling was behind a beat-up desk, wearing a dress shirt that was probably expensive when he bought it five or six years ago. Tie on, hanging down, collar open. First impression, the place was a mess, but as Lynch looked at it he realized it was just full of files. Files piled on the desk, files stacked on the metal shelves along the right wall, files lined up on the floor.

Telling looked up. "So you're the cops?"

"Kate Magnus gave us your name," said Lynch.

"About Membe?"

"Yeah," said Lynch.

"And you think this ties in to Stein somehow?" Telling asked.

"It might," Lynch said. "We're checking."

"And that's why you're here, because otherwise Membe's just another dead nigger, and not even a citizen nigger, right?"

The fire again. Lynch turned his palms up. "I do something to piss you off?"

"Didn't have to," Telling said. "I wake up that way."

"Think maybe you can give it a rest for a minute, so we can get through this?"

Telling nodded. "Fine."

"You handled the immigration work on Membe?"

"Yeah."

"Anything in his file you think might have followed him over here?"

Telling snorted. "You've got no fucking clue, do you? If Membe got killed over there, it wouldn't be because he was Membe. It would be the West African version of roadkill – just mean he stepped out in front of the bullet. You guys and your motives and shit. Most of this world, you don't need a reason to get dead. Could be his great-grandfather looked sideways at some asshole's great-grandmother sixty years ago, and the asshole was in the wrong tribe. Could be one of Taylor's former punks was sitting in a bar and couldn't remember whether he had a round in the chamber, so he takes the shot to find out because it's easier than pulling the bolt back and checking. Could be anything at all, but whatever it was would be some dumb-ass trivial bullshit. People don't follow refugees across the Atlantic to kill them over dumb-ass trivial bullshit. They just kill whoever else is handy."

"So why'd he get asylum, then?" Bernstein asked.

"Because his life was in danger."

"You make it sound like everybody's life is in danger over there," Lynch said.

"Everybody's life is. But the sisters can't get their hands on everybody. They get their hands on who they can. And they send me the files. And if I can find a way to make a case, then I make a case."

"I thought asylum had to be based on a specific risk of persecution," Bernstein said.

"You get a look at Membe's right arm?"

Lynch nodded.

"That specific enough for you?"

"What I got from the ME, that was a few years ago," Lynch said.

"You wanna get philosophical, then I'll get philosophical. I don't give a shit. I don't care if it was two weeks, two years, or two decades ago. I work with a number of relief agencies, all over the world. They come to me with somebody who's gonna die where they are and who maybe won't if they come here and I can spin a way to open up the ol' Golden Door, then I'm gonna go for it. Because the rich fuckers that run this country and the racist lemmings that spend their days listening to the bloviating yahoos on talk radio, they want to nail that door shut. Most of this world is a huge fucking cesspool that people shouldn't have to live in. Most of this country isn't."

Little pause after that, not the kind of comment that invited a response.

"Didn't you used to be with MacMillian?" Bernstein asked.

"Yeah. Up until 2004."

"Kind of a change of pace," Bernstein said.

"Always did some immigration stuff to help the firm hit its pro bono targets. I mean the pro bono stuff in a firm like that, mostly it's a joke. Something we use to numb the consciences on the new associates until the work and the money suck out their souls. But I was a proper North Shore liberal. Had a couple million bucks worth of house up in Lake Forest, condo in Aspen, garage full of Beemers. Had a son. Then 9/11 happened, and my son decided to sign up for Bush's jihad, probably mostly to rebel against me and my bullshit. And he got blown up. And my wife turned into one of these America-as-a-fetish Palin worshipers because it was the only way she had for his death to make sense. And I just couldn't go into the office anymore and help another CFO find ways to run circles around the SEC. Because it occurred to me that my son, misguided as he was, stuck his ass out further for something than I ever had. So my wife got the house and condo and the Beemers and the money, and I got this."

"Fair trade?" Lynch asked.

"Screw fair," Telling said.

"This Membe Saturday looks like a dead end," Bernstein said, him and Lynch back in the car.

"Something screwy, though. I mean, why shoot the guy? Because he saw the car? You got people parked all over there every game night. There's no reason for the shooter to think anybody'd be looking at him."

"But if it's not about the shooter, then it's about Stein. So now you're wondering what some refugee has in common with Stein," Bernstein said.

"And I feel kind of stupid wondering that," Lynch said. They drove for a few moments. "Do me a favor, though, OK? We ever get a call out back to Telling's office, let's punt on it. Guy's gonna eat a gun someday. I don't need to see it."

Bernstein's phone went off, some kind of hip-hop crap.

"What the fuck is that?" Lynch asked.

"New ringtone," Bernstein said. "Little Kanye. Upping my street cred."

"Well, answer the damn thing before I put a round through it."

CHAPTER 12

Hardin dumped the room service tray from breakfast outside his door. He'd been staying in the hotel room as much as possible, keeping his head down. He'd taken the underground tunnel from the hotel over to the Macy's on State Street, picked up some clothes. Everything he had he'd bought in Africa, and most of it came from Europe. He couldn't put his finger on it exactly, but over here everybody else's clothes looked just a little different. Different wasn't what he needed just now. Macy's had been a shock. Marshall Field's was gone. He remembered when he was a kid, the Field's out at Fox Valley Mall. Not where he shopped, of course. Sears was splurging in his family. But he remembered hanging around in Field's, the rich people carrying around those dark green bags with the script on them, bags he always figured would smell like money. Field's was the sort of thing that felt permanent when you were a kid, like Pluto being a planet. People liked to switch that shit out on you when you weren't looking, remind you that nothing stuck, that the whole world and everything in it was circling the drain one way or the other.

He fired up his laptop, checked his e-mail. Nothing he needed. Reached for the remote. He'd watched more TV in the last day and a half than he had in the previous twenty years.

And there was that fucker Fenn, some *Oprah* special, tears in his eyes, running through that child abuse crap he started peddling a few years back. And then Oprah had to cue up the tape – the cell phone video from the damn Darfur party that had had a short run on YouTube back in the day.

"That's really when I knew something was wrong with me," said Fenn. "I've been doing the work in therapy, and I've been trying to make it right with people I've gone off on. But I look back at this, and I think of all the damage I did to the good work that Jerry Mooney was trying to do. And I worry about Nick Hardin – he's the guy I'm taking the swing at here. I mean, this cost him his gig with Jerry, and who knows what else a guy like that has."

Hardin noticed they'd cut the tape right after Fenn took his swing and Hardin took his fall. Didn't show Hardin busting Fenn up.

Just great. All Hardin wanted to do was to keep his head down for a few days while Fouche put a deal together. Then he and his $10 million would find some place nice to live out their days. Now his face and his name were on *Oprah*.

Hardin suddenly remembered bivouacking in some pissant village in the ass-end of Benin maybe fifteen years ago, back in his Legion days. This old jou-jou insisted on throwing the bones for them. She threw Hardin's, and her eyes got big, and she grabbed Hardin by the arm. "Beware the black woman with a million eyes. She will be your downfall." It creeped Hardin out a little at the time, but he hadn't thought about it in years. He never figured she meant Oprah.

Too many people had seen him at the Hyatt. If the bad guys didn't have a line on him already, they would soon enough. Time to move. And time to find a fucking gun.

••••

Beans Garbanzo and Snakes DeGetano were two hours into their second morning sitting on Hardin's car when Snakes took a look down at his picture and nudged Beans. "Here he comes. Make the call and pull up behind him."

Garbanzo pulled out his cell.

"Yeah?" the voice answered.

"It's Beans. I'm working that thing for Tony Corsco. Kill the camera."

"OK, you got ten minutes max. Ping me when you're clear .Just remember, I don't need anybody getting curious about convenient camera outages, so grab him and run. Don't leave a mess there, give anybody a reason to start checking for pictures."

CHAPTER 13

Dr Atash Javadi walked along the shore of Lake Michigan on the Northwestern University campus with a slight, olive-skinned man. Javadi had been a youth of twenty in 1979, the year the Shah fell. He had been the intellectual playboy scion of one of Iran's wealthiest families. Now, with degrees from Cambridge, Yale, and Dartmouth, he was one of the West's leading scholars on the Islamic world and the professor of Middle Eastern studies at Northwestern University. An ardent and frequent critic of Islam, he was a regular guest on various news programs and a long-time favorite of the American right.

He was also a devout Shiite and had, for his entire life in America, been an agent for MOIS, the Iranian Ministry of Intelligence and National Security.

"The things that they hoard shall be tied to their necks like a collar on the day of resurrection," said Javadi. "So sayeth the Holy Koran. Cling not to greed, my friend."

"He must pay their wages in full," replied the olive-skinned man, "and give them even more out of his grace. So also sayeth the Holy Koran. And my wages are late. Stein is dead. Heinz is dead. I have your devices. Yet Tehran has my money and I do not."

Javadi smiled an ironic smile. "You quibble over money? Now? On the brink of a triumph that will forever secure in legend the name of Husam al Din?"

Al Din scowled. He had no use for legends and less for names.

He'd only been a few weeks old in 1978 when the Israelis bombed the refugee camp in Lebanon. His parents were killed, and he was just another orphan raised by the PLO. In the camp, they called him Ahmad, but his parents must have called him something. So far as Husam was concerned, Ahmad was just his first cover. A name was just another tool. In New Mexico, he had been Ricardo Orendain. Since arriving in Chicago, he had been Marco Pelligrino and then Dmitri Stavapopolus. With his fine features, light olive skin, and brown eyes, he could pass for everything from a Spaniard to an Indian.

In reality, he was Palestinian. He'd had the religious indoctrination as a boy, the feeble mullahs and their nonsense. There is no God but Allah, and Mohammad is his prophet, the United States is the Great Satan, all the rest of it. But Husam believed that reality was the best teacher.

And reality was this: Any time Israel wanted, the jets came and bombed the camps, and the Palestinians had to hide in the rubble like roaches. If Israel decided to destroy Beirut, they destroyed Beirut. If there was no God but Allah, why then did Yahweh get the F-16s and Abrams battle tanks, leaving Allah's people to fight them with AK-47s and stones? Husam had no more faith in gods than he had in names.

But he had a talent for killing. He had been a very bright student, the brightest boy in any of the classes in the camp. And so the men in the keffiyehs had taught him as well. Pistols, rifles, explosives. How to fight with his hands and with knives. A Kalashnikov – this was a god he could believe in.

When he was fourteen, he had his first exam. He remembered crawling forward in the dark toward the

Israeli roadblock. Watching for a long time to be sure. Two soldiers outside the Bradley Fighting Vehicle, the armored personnel carrier that was another gift to Yahweh from America, Israel's real god. After an hour, the doors to the Bradley opened, and the two soldiers traded places with two others inside. Four soldiers in all.

The instructions for this initiation were simple: Leave the camp, kill at least one Israeli, and return alive. The other boys had all chosen civilians, random killings of unsuspecting targets. And when they had returned to the camp after emptying a clip into some old woman driving back to some kibbutz, he would join in the celebration of their heroic acts. In truth, these cowards disgusted him with their weakness. He was determined to do better.

At any time, he could kill the two outside the Bradley, but the muzzle flash would give away his position. He was not interested in learning how good the soldiers inside the Bradley were with the 20mm cannon and 50mm machine gun. But these Israelis were complacent. It was a quiet sector, routine duty. He watched for an opportunity. It took him more than three hours to move to a slightly elevated position behind the Bradley, giving him a clear line of sight into the vehicle when the doors opened. At the next shift change, all four soldiers were within a narrow field of fire, the door to the vehicle directly in front of him. Ahmad was calm. Many of those he trained with would have cut loose with a long burst of automatic fire, sweeping the weapon back and forth. But Ahmad flicked the selector switch to semi-automatic. Three-round bursts, twenty rounds in the magazine, one spare magazine. Ahmad knew that if he had to switch magazines before the Israelis were down, he was as good as dead. Ahmad sighted on the Israeli standing in the door of the Bradley. If he could drop

him in the doorway, the others might trip over him
trying to get inside.

Ahmad fired, all three rounds hitting the Israeli in the
torso, the soldier falling on the ramp. Ahmad swung the
rifle a couple inches left and hit the second Israeli with
a burst. The target went down, still moving, but down.
The Israelis were well trained. The other two both dove
to the ground, rolling apart so that they were separate
targets. They had seen the muzzle flash. Both brought
their Galils to bear, first one, then the other, raking the
ground in front of Ahmad's position with controlled
bursts. Each moved further out as the other fired – fire
and maneuver, looking to flank. Ahmad slid slowly down
the small embankment and rolled to his left, timing his
movements with the firing by the Israelis to cover the
noise. As one of the Israelis fired at the spot where Ahmad
had been, the other got up to run further right. Ahmad
hit him in the back with a burst. The final Israeli turned
his fire to Ahmad's new position, but Ahmad still had the
advantage of elevation. When he heard the Israeli stop to
change clips, Ahmad sighted carefully, hitting the Israeli
in the face and helmet.

Ahmad had fired four bursts – twelve rounds. He knew
he still had eight rounds in his clip, but he swapped in his
full clip and watched the scene for a moment. The second
Israeli was still moving, trying to crawl toward the APC.
Ahmad put a three-round burst into the soldier's head.
He then put a single round into the heads of each of the
other Israelis, just to be sure. He walked down to the
Bradley and looked inside. He knew he couldn't loiter,
but he wanted his first mission to cement his reputation.
There were two large fuel cans in a rack on the outside of
the APC. He moved them inside the vehicle. He cut both
pant legs from the uniform of one of the dead Israelis,

sliced them in sections, and tied the sections together to make a fuse. He opened the first fuel can, shoved the fabric inside, let it soak a moment, and then pulled most of it out, wadding the end of the fuse in the opening to the fuel can. He set the fuel can in the ammunition storage area inside the APC. He opened the second fuel can, pouring the fuel over the ammunition first, and then splashing it around the inside of the machine. He backed out of the vehicle, trailing the soaked cloth behind him until it ended a meter or two past the end of the ramp. He lit the cloth and ran. Ahmad knew the flame would race up the fuel-soaked cloth and that the fuel can at least would explode and ignite the rest of the fuel within the APC.

He was one hundred meters away when he heard the *whomp* of the fuel can and saw his shadow flash in front of him from the sudden light. Within another hundred meters, he heard the first of the 20mm shells go off, then another, then a staccato cacophony of exploding ordinance; then he was staggered by the force of the blast as the vehicles main fuel storage tanks blew.

Ahmad knew the Israeli combat patrols and helicopters would saturate the area between him and the camps. He ran south, toward Israel.

For two days, Ahmad dodged patrols, slowly making his way back to the camp. By the time he returned, he was a legend. The fourteen year-old boy sent out to kill a single Israeli who had instead wiped out an entire Bradley crew and their machine. And he had a new name, this one of his own choosing: Husam al Din – the sword of faith.

Just because he didn't believe in names did not mean one could not serve his legend.

And his legend grew. As a youth, he became the most feared operative the PLO had. As the power of the PLO faded and Palestinian allegiance shifted to Hezbollah and to Iran, al Din shifted as well. But the movement's increasing penchant for suicide bombings and the attendant promise of heavenly virgins held no attraction for al Din. He had, by then, sampled the earthly variety, and preferred them.

And so al Din struck out on his own. Sometimes, what was needed was a bus full of dead Jews – any bus, any Jews. But sometimes someone – Hezbollah, the Syrians, Iran – wanted one man dead. A well-guarded man. Or they wanted a secure, high-value target destroyed. And when they did, they hired al Din. And they paid al Din. When the New Mexico plan was designed, al Din had been the clear choice.

"Legend?" al Din said. "The Koran also says that he who has in his heart the weight of an atom of pride shall not enter Paradise. In the wisdom of my age, I now reject the legend of my youth and would be only Allah's anonymous servant, who works for his wage alone, not his pride."

Javadi shook his head. "The infidels claim that the devil can quote their Bible for his own purposes. I fear you do the same with our Holy Koran."

"Payment within twenty-four hours to the account designated," said al Din. "Those were the terms. Those always have been the terms. I cannot bring Stein back to life, or Heinz, but I have your devices, and I will not deploy them until I have been paid."

They walked for a while in silence. The brutal cold from a few days before had abated, but the wind was still strong and out of the north, traveling the full length of the lake and driving tall waves into the breakwater along the edge of the path so that a cold spray flew into their faces. It was uncomfortable, but except for one solitary runner who had passed a few minutes earlier, it meant they were alone. And with the wind and spray there could be no audio surveillance.

"Recent events require postponing the final phase of the New Mexico project anyway," said Javadi. "Stein's death was meant to ensure the safe sale of a shipment of diamonds that were to recoup for us what we have spent funding this operation. Once we had the diamonds, we were going to arrange their liquidation in circles monitored by Mossad, circles with established ties to our Al Qaeda friends. The funds from that transaction would replenish the accounts out of which Heinz was paid, accounts we have always maintained through contacts with ties to Al Qaeda. Al Qaeda assets on our payroll then would release the appropriate celebratory videos to Al Jazeera."

"So you wish to give Al Qaeda credit for an Iranian operation?"

Javadi nodded. "The act itself is immaterial. It is the credit for the act that matters. Historically, the Americans are not a patient people. That they have spent more than a decade in Iraq and Afghanistan is a testament to how violently they can react if properly motivated. But now they intend to take their troops and go home. They have already left Iraq, and have a deadline for leaving Afghanistan. Even the American puppet Karzai is calling for them to leave. But leaving will free up both their political and military resources to focus on Iran. This is not attention we desire. Every piece of evidence associated with the New Mexico project will point to Al Qaeda and to Waziristan. After this act, the Americans will not only stay in Afghanistan, but they will double or triple their presence. They will force Pakistan to invade the tribal areas, may even invade them themselves.

That will either topple the American puppet regime in Islamabad or force the Americans to send even more troops to prop it up. India, of course, will take advantage of Pakistan's troubles to press their interests in the region. America will have to spend billions, and will be so busy with Kabul, Islamabad, and Delhi that they will have no time for Tehran. Meanwhile, in two years, perhaps less, we will be ready to strike at Israel. The Americans know we have no weapons that can reach them at home. But if we can keep a few hundred thousand American troops in Afghanistan, the Americans will also know that if they strike back for the Jews, those troops will be consumed in Allah's fire."

Al Din said nothing for a moment, digesting this information. "Such grand designs," he said finally, "and you cannot pay this poor workman his wages?"

Javadi waved his hand as if al Din's comments were without consequence. "This business with the diamonds, it should already have been completed. Your payment, being part of the New Mexico project, was to come from those funds. Alas, it seems that Stein and his Mossad compatriots are not the only ones with a taste for Al Qaeda's diamonds. The fools in Sierra Leone allowed the entire shipment to be stolen. By this man." Javadi pulled a picture and an envelope from his pocket and handed them to al Din.

Al Din looked at the picture of Hardin. "He was with Stein, the night I killed him."

"Trying to sell the diamonds, no doubt," said Javadi. "His name is Nicholas Hardin. His dossier is in the envelope. He needs a new buyer. Find this Hardin, retrieve the diamonds, and kill him."

"Yet another mission, but you still have not paid me for the last two."

"The diamonds are valued at more than 150 million US dollars. Tehran feels a finder's fee of five percent would be appropriate."

"Al Din feels a finder's fee of ten percent would be more appropriate."

"Which is exactly what I told our masters," agreed Javadi.

"In addition, of course, to what I am already owed."

"Of course."

They turned back toward the campus, the wind now at their backs, walking in silence for a time.

It had never been al Din's goal to serve Allah, or, for that matter, Tehran. It was his goal to serve al Din. This new assignment – Tehran expected him to retrieve a huge fortune and return it to them in exchange for a small one. Yet even that small fortune, added to the accounts al Din already had secreted around the world, would mean that he would no longer have to serve the ridiculous whims of his Islamic masters. Instead, he could serve his own appetites.

But he would be serving them in a dangerous world. On 9/11, the Americans were enraged by an attack that, in truth, destroyed more real estate than human life. A mere three thousand dead, and yet one could measure America's rage in a decade of governments overthrown, countries occupied, hundreds of thousands killed. How would America's rage be measured when the streets of Chicago were littered with ten times as many dead?

Tehran intended to pay al Din from the Al Qaeda accounts. That meant that the money trail from the New Mexico project would end with al Din, not with Tehran. Al Din's methods for receiving payment were carefully structured to protect his anonymity, but only a fool considered any method perfect. If there was one thing the Americans understood better than anyone else in the world, it was money.

Al Din decided. He would proceed, but he would maintain control. He would deploy the devices, but only he could decide when or if to set them off. He would secure these diamonds, and then he would decide when and to whom he would sell them. Options and leverage. That is not what he would say to Javadi, of course.

"Agreed," al Din said.

As they neared the campus, Javadi spoke.

"I understand that you killed the good Dr Heinz with a stone?"

"Yes."

"How fitting. Like Goliath, seemingly invincible, yet felled with a simple stone. As soon will be these Americans, who imagine they can impose their will on Allah's people. When all is in place our devices will kill them in their tens of thousands, and with weapons almost as simple as a stone."

Al Din left Javari to wax poetic about his vengeful religious visions. Instead, he took one more look at the picture before pushing it back into the envelope.

Paradise awaited. Not in the next life, but in this. First, however, this Nick Hardin must die.

CHAPTER 14

Hardin had just walked into the garage, popped the trunk to the rental, and dropped his duffle inside when he heard a car stop behind him. He slammed the trunk shut and turned around. A skinny guy in a blue Adidas tracksuit got out of the back seat of a black Grand Marquis holding a 9mm Glock down along his right leg.

"Take your coat off a second, Hardin."

They knew his name. Great. Hardin had no play. He slipped off the jacket.

"Turn around once for me."

Hardin did a slow circle.

"You ain't packing some little sissy gun somewhere, are you?"

"No," said Hardin.

The guy moved away from the door and nodded his head at the back seat. "Get in and slide over. Somebody wants to have a chat."

Hardin got in, scooting over behind the driver. The driver was a hugely fat man wearing some kind of velour pullover. The skinny guy got in on the passenger side and shut the door, staying away from Hardin, holding the gun on him across his lap.

"Let's go, Beans," he said.

The fat man drove the car out the Madison Street entrance, took a left down to Lake Shore Drive, and then headed south. As he cleared the garage, he pulled his cell phone, hit one button. "We're clear, you can turn 'em back on," he said, and put the phone away.

Nobody said anything. They drove past Grant Park to the museum campus, took a curve at Roosevelt then south again past Soldiers Field; McCormick Place sliding by between them and the lake. The driver stayed in the right lane, keeping the car right at fifty, cars flying past on the left. These guys didn't look like Hezbollah. They looked more like something out of a *Sopranos* episode. And this chat the guy talked about, Hardin had a bad feeling he'd already had all the chat he was going to get.

"This about the diamonds?" said Hardin, trying to find an angle.

"Shut the fuck up," said the fat man.

"Just drive the damn car, Beans," said the skinny guy.

Hardin heard a squishy burble from the fat guy, and then the odor hit him.

"Jesus fucking Christ, Beans," said the skinny guy.

They kept heading south, past the Museum of Science and Industry, Lake Shore Drive turning into South Shore drive, heading down toward the abandoned US Steel plant. The fat guy farted again. The skinny guy cracked his window.

"Mind if I open this side?" said Hardin.

"Shut up," said the skinny guy.

"So you aren't after the diamonds," said Hardin.

The skinny guy didn't say anything.

Finally the skinny guy said, "Tell me about these diamonds."

"Better than $150 million in uncut stones. Gotta be about the diamonds," said Hardin.

The fat guy turned his head. "Don't listen to this guy's bullshit, Snakes."

"Shut up, Beans," snapped the skinny guy. "There's a reason I'm riding in the back and you're driving. It's cause your colon works a hell of a lot harder than your brains. Just drive the fucking car."

The skinny guy twitched the gun at Hardin. "Some reason I should believe you ain't full of shit?"

Hardin shrugged. "From the smell of things, there's only one guy in this car who's full of shit."

Skinny guy snorted. The fat guy turned his head. "You ain't gonna be so funny in a few minutes, asshole."

Hardin said, "I'm going to get something out of my coat, so don't get excited, OK?" Hardin had maybe five grand of his cash in an envelope in his inside jacket pocket.

Skinny guy lifted the gun up a little. "Slow and easy."

Hardin nodded. He shifted his hips so he was facing the skinny guy, and then he slipped his hand in his coat, grabbing the envelope and the Air France ballpoint he'd pocketed on the flight over. He dropped the envelope on the seat between him and the skinny guy, top down, so the money spilled out.

The skinny guy's eyes tracked down to the cash, the gun leaning a little away from Hardin.

Hardin did two things. He shot his left hand out and clamped it down on the barrel of the pistol, pushing it away. With his right hand, he backhanded the Air France pen into the skinny guy's trachea. The pen went in deep.

Skinny pulled the trigger, putting a bullet through the back of the passenger seat and into the dashboard, blowing up the radio. Skinny tried to hold on to the gun, but his mind was on getting some oxygen, which wasn't going so well, what with a pen through his windpipe and blood running down into his lungs.

Hardin twisted the gun out of Skinny's hand and slammed it hard against his forehead. Skinny slumped against the passenger door, a little blood bubbling out around the pen in his throat.

The fat guy was squirming, trying to drive the car with one hand and pull a gun off his belt with the other, but his gut was in the way. Hardin put the Glock to the back of the fat man's head.

"OK, Beans. Get the piece out real easy and hand it back here."

The fat man worked the gun loose and handed it back to Hardin.

They were coming up on 86th Street, where it cut across the railroad tracks and onto the old US Steel property.

"Turn in there," said Hardin. "Looks like we're going to have that chat after all."

"OK," said Beans.

"And if you fart again, I'm gonna kill you."

Hardin had the fat man park the car behind a pile of rubble most of the way down toward the lake. The whole US Steel plant was gone, ripped down, nothing but gravel, weeds and empty concrete slabs. Hard to believe. Hardin had an uncle who had worked at US Steel back in the Seventies. He remembered going down to the plant, the sprawling parking lot full of Oldsmobiles and Chevys. Dirty, hulking buildings puking gray-black smoke out over the lake. Clanging noises, thudding noises, the big-ass ore ships in the channels at the south end, and everywhere slope-shouldered men with meaty faces in dirty coveralls. Now it was just a flat expanse, grass poking up through the stone and rubble. It was like the civilization that needed the steel had been gone a thousand years.

Hardin nudged the Glock into the back of the fat man's head. "Gimme the keys," said Hardin.

The fat man tossed the keys onto the back seat. Hardin put them in his pocket.

"Give me the phone, too."

The fat man unclipped the phone off his belt and handed it to Hardin as well.

"Get out of the car, go around the front and get your buddy off the back seat," Hardin said.

The fat man climbed out, went around the hood to the passenger side. When he had most of the car between them, Hardin got out, too, keeping the Glock on the fat man as he opened the rear passenger door, grabbed the skinny guy by his track jacket and dumped him out on the gravel. There was a little gasp out of Skinny when he hit the ground.

"Jesus," said the fat man. "He still alive?"

Hardin came around the back of the car, circling wide, keeping a good five yards between him and the fat man. Hardin looked down at Skinny. Looked dead to him. Probably just some left-over air forced out of his lungs when he hit the ground.

"If he's alive, he'll get over it," Hardin said. "He's got a phone on him somewhere. Get it."

The fat man went through the skinny guy's tracksuit, found the phone, and tossed it to Hardin. Hardin wiggled the gun at the fat man, and then pointed it at the pile of rubble.

"Let's head over there."

As soon as the fat man turned, Hardin took three quick steps and kicked him hard behind the left knee, buckling his leg, and then put the sole of his foot against the fat man's ass, shoving him face down on the ground. Guy seemed docile enough, but at his size, if he got a hold of you, it was all over. Hardin wanted him on the ground. Big as he was, it would take the fat man a week or so to get to his feet – plenty of time to shoot him.

"What the fuck you do that for?" said the fat man, rolling over to sit on the ground.

"Shut up," said Hardin.

Hardin stuck one of the pistols in his belt, stuffed the other one in his jacket pocket. He walked over to the rubble pile and picked up a fist-sized rock.

"So, who you working for?" asked Hardin.

"I can't tell you that," said the fat man.

Hardin took a short wind up and zipped the rock off the fat man's right thigh.

"God!" the fat man shouted.

Hardin grabbed another rock. "So, who you working for?"

"They'll fucking kill me," the fat man whined.

Hardin threw the rock into the fat man's gut. "Been in Africa a long time," said Hardin. "Don't play much ball over there, so it will take a while to get loose Seen this done, though. Get up in northern Nigeria where they're big on Sharia law and they're always stoning someone to death. Usually some skinny-assed chick they think's been sleeping around. Even then, it takes a while. Don't know what your boss has planned for you, but this," Hardin grabbed another rock and hit the fat man in the chest, a little harder this time, "this is one nasty fucking way to go. Big guy like you, I'm gonna get through most of this pile."

The fat man started crying.

Hardin didn't want to do any real damage, at least not yet, but he had to make sure he had the guy's attention. He found a smaller rock and bounced it off the side of the fat man's head, opening up a decent gash. The blood started flowing down the fat man's face and onto his shirt. The fat man put a hand to his head, and then looked at the blood on it.

"Corsco," he blubbered. "Tony Corsco."

"Who's that?" asked Hardin.

Fat man looked up, stopped blubbering. "What do you mean who's that?"

"I'm not from around here, asshole. Who the fuck is this Corsco?" Hardin bounced another rock of the fat man's leg.

"Ouch! Fuck, knock that off! I'm fucking talking, OK? He's the boss – Chicago, Milwaukee, St Louis, the whole Midwest."

"Boss like mob boss?

"Yeah. What the fuck did you think?"

Not that, thought Hardin. "So what's he want with me?"

"He wants you dead. That's all I know. Gave me and Snake the picture, told us your car was in the garage there, told us to take you out."

"What picture?"

The fat man pulled a sheet of paper out of his shirt pocket, unfolded it, held it up. Picture of Hardin at the rental counter at O'Hare. And they'd been waiting when he got to the garage – which meant they'd been looking for him since before the *Oprah* show aired.

"Where'd Corsco get the picture?"

"How the fuck should I know?"

Hardin zinged a rock into the fat man's shoulder, just on principle. "When?"

"Fuck," the fat man said. A huge bubble of snot hung down from his nose, the blood from his head now covering the left side of his face, soaking into his shirt. "Yesterday, right after lunch, OK?"

Hardin knew he should kill the guy. Hell, he'd killed plenty of guys. But something about plugging the fat man while he sat on his ass bawling in the middle of a ruin sat funny with him. Besides, other than Corsco's name, Hardin still didn't know shit. Leave the fat man around, and if he saw him again, maybe he'd know more. The fat man would be hard to miss.

"Give me your wallet," Hardin said.

"Ah, man," said the fat man. He shifted up on his side, fishing the wallet out of his back pocket, and tossed it to Hardin.

Hardin flipped it open. "Garbanzo? Really?"

The fat man shrugged. "Why you think they call me Beans?"

"I was thinking cause you fart all the time."

"Hey," the fat man said, all indignant suddenly. "I got a condition, OK?"

"Sure," said Hardin, sticking the wallet in his hip pocket.

"Can I have the wallet back?" Garbanzo said. "I mean, you can keep the money and stuff. I got a picture of my mom in there. I don't got a lot of pictures of her."

Hardin flipped the wallet back open to a picture in one of those plastic sleeves. Fat woman with an Italian afro of gray hair, speed bags of chicken-skin fat hanging down off her arms. Hardin took the cash and cards out of the wallet and tossed it back to the fat man.

Hardin whipped one last rock at the fat man, right off his kneecap. "I see you again, you're dead," said Hardin. He took the keys from his pocket, got in the Grand Marquis and pulled away, the fat man in the rear view mirror still sitting on his ass in the gravel, not looking like he was in any hurry to get up.

OK, he thought. I needed a gun, now I've got two. Not a bad morning, aside from the whole mob-wanting-me-dead thing.

Beans Garbanzo hurt all over. He'd also shit himself. The gash on his head had stopped gushing and was just seeping now, but the side of his head was swollen up like he was one of them Special Olympics kids. His leg hurt bad, and his chest hurt when he breathed. It was going to be a long walk back to South Shore, and who the hell knew how long once he got there before he could find a phone. Fucking Snakes. He'd told him not to listen to this guy about the diamonds, and now look at this mess. He'd call his sister, he figured. She could drive in from Palos. Then he could get out some feelers, see how much shit he was in.

Up ahead, a gray Malibu pulled in off of South Shore and headed toward him. The car turned right about ten yards in front of him, blocking his path. The driver's window slid down. Olive-skinned guy, hair slicked back neat, dark suit and tie. What the fuck? Did Corsco have somebody out on him already?

The man smiled. "Hello," he said.

"Yeah, hi," said Garbanzo.

"What is your business with Hardin?"

"Who the fuck are you, and what are you talking about?"

The man smiled again." You and your dead companion abducted Nick Hardin from the Grant Park garage and drove him here. Sometime during that trip, he killed your friend and disarmed you. He then knocked you to the ground and threw stones at you until you told him what he wanted to know. Whatever trouble you may be in, and with whomever that trouble may be, you are already in it. I simply want to know what you've already told Hardin. And then I will be on my way."

This actually made sense to Garbanzo. "Yeah, what the fuck. Tony Corsco sent us – Snakes DeGetano and me – to kill that Hardin fuck."

"And who is Tony Corsco?" the smiling man asked.

"Jesus, second guy today hasn't heard of Tony. Who the fuck are you people? Tony Corsco runs the goddamn mob."

"I see. And what was his complaint with Mr Hardin?"

"Look, buddy, he don't explain shit like that to me and Snake. He tells us kill some guy, then we kill him."

"Thank you, you've been most helpful," the smiling man said. Then he raised the .22 from his lap and shot Garbanzo three times through the forehead so quickly that Garbanzo hadn't even twitched before the third round hit him.

Husam al Din drove back north up Lake Shore Drive. So the American mafia, too, had an interest in Hardin. With Stein dead, could Hardin be trying to sell them the diamonds? Had the mafia tried to steal them instead?

Al Din could not know. If not the diamonds, then some other business. But he did know this: guided by intel provided by Javadi from some asset with access to Chicago's surveillance system, al Din had pulled into the garage just in time to see Hardin abducted by two armed professional criminals. They had searched him; Hardin had no weapon. Al Din had followed them south, and, by the time they arrived at the vacant land near the lake, one of the criminals was dead, Hardin was armed, and the other criminal was not. This Hardin was something more than an errand boy for television news people. It was fortuitous that al Din had learned this as a witness and not as an object lesson. He would have to approach this Hardin with care.

CHAPTER 15

When they were done with Telling, Lynch and Bernstein went back to the precinct, started going through red light camera shots from the intersection near the shelter. The problem was the camera only took a shot when someone ran the light, so they had to put all the shots in order, make a timeline, and see if they could pick out any likely cars. Lynch had the tech guy send up shots from the same time of day for a week before the shooting as well. Some of the cars popped up more than once. Had to be locals. They could rule them out.

Starting an hour or so before the game, each shot showed cars cruising the street, hoping to save the $35 it cost to park at the stadium. About forty minutes to tip-off, Bernstein got a clean shot of a Lexus backing into a spot and ran that plate. It was registered to a Harry Weber in Lisle.

"Christ," Lynch said. "You park a car worth forty grand on that street, trying to save a few bucks?"

"No explaining people," said Bernstein.

They flipped through the post-game shots, but the Lexus was gone about half an hour before the shooting at the shelter. Five minutes before game time, a black Escalade that had been parked one spot up from the shelter was gone, replaced by a medium gray sedan with a low roofline. There was an old Suburban in front of it, so they couldn't make out much on the vehicle, just part of the roof and the top corner of the windshield on the driver's side. Again, they flipped to the post-game shots. Somebody ran a light about ten minutes before the shooting and the car was still there. Next violation was twenty minutes later, and the car was gone.

"Looks like a Malibu," said Bernstein. "One of the new ones."

"Yeah," said Lynch. "What's that white spot on the windshield? Some kind of sticker?"

Lynch called the IT guy who had pulled the photos, gave him the ID number on the shot. The IT guy blew it up on his screen. He couldn't get a lot of resolution, but he told Lynch it looked like one of the barcode stickers some of the rental car companies put on the windshields of their stock. Lynch asked him to run through any photos they had around the stadium a half-mile in every direction for the ten minutes before and the ten minutes after the first and last shots of the car, and get him the plate number of every gray Malibu – bonus points if it had the white sticker. Guy said he would, but it was going to take a day or so.

Lynch was about to grab some coffee when the desk sergeant called up from downstairs.

"Got an Ashley Urra here to see you. Says you talked to her out at the UC on the Stein thing?"

"OK," said Lynch. "Send her up."

Urra was less made up, her hair in a ponytail, wearing jeans and a Blackhawks jersey that was too big on her. It hung down off one shoulder, showing the strap to a running bra. Still perky. She sat in the chair next to Lynch's desk. Bernstein rolled his chair around.

"So, Ms Urra. What can I do for you?"

"It's about that man from Abe's box – the one I thought I remembered? I saw him again today."

Lynch sat up in his chair. "Where?"

"On TV. He was on *Oprah*, Well, not on *Oprah*, but on a clip they ran."

"What?"

"You know Shamus Fenn is in town, right, shooting that film? Well, he was on *Oprah*, her Oscar special thing? They were talking about the child abuse stuff with him? You remember, that came out a few years ago? And they showed a clip from that big charity party they had in Africa from back then? When he got in a fight with that guy?"

Lynch had a vague recollection – some stupid drunk celebrity shit. "Yeah, OK, I remember that."

"The guy from the box? He was the one who got in the fight with Seamus Fenn. That's where I'd seen him. I mean I was in high school, but that video was all over the place back then."

Jesus, thought Lynch. I got a dead zillionaire, a dead one-armed refugee, and now some mystery guest at an African charity party who got in a punch up with a movie star – and both him and the movie star are in town?

"The other guy," Lynch asked, "they mention his name?"

"I wrote it down. Nick Hardin. They said his name was Nick Hardin."

CHAPTER 16

Hardin knew he had to move, had to get out of town, get some space. He also needed to get off the grid. Somebody had gotten a line on him somehow, so he had to figure the Nigel Fox ID was shot. Hardin had found Nigel dead in his apartment three months back, the booze finally catching up with him. And Nigel's passport and ID were just sitting there on his table. Date on the passport made Nigel fifty-four – Hardin would have figured he was sixty-five at least, but that's what pickling your liver will do for you. Height and weight were about the same. He knew a guy who could swap the pictures out, and with Hardin's gray hair, he could be a young fifty-four. Always nice to have a spare set of papers, and he didn't figure Nigel would mind.

Nigel had gotten him this far, but from here out, Hardin was on his own.

Hardin drove the Marquis back up to the Loop. Found a metered spot on Columbus, behind the Art Institute. He dumped the Mercury there, walked to the garage, drove his rental back to O'Hare and turned it in, grabbed the L back downtown, then jumped on the Burlington commuter rail out to Aurora. Going home.

Hardin wasn't Hardin when he joined the Legion. He was Mike Griffin. He was home on leave at the end of his second hitch in the Marines, ready to re-up, on the road to being a lifer. It was a few weeks before Christmas. He'd hooked up with his best friend from high school, Esteban Sandoval, and they were heading out to celebrate Esteban's kid sister's twenty-first birthday. Hardin had always been close to Juanita in a big brother kind of way. He knew she chafed a little at the whole macho Mexican culture thing, the limited expectations. She used to talk to him sometimes, and she'd written him pretty steadily while he was in the Corps. The last time he'd seen her was her high school graduation, three years back, it kind of hitting him out of the blue what a looker she was turning into, and her giving him a hug when he left that felt like something other than just goodbye. And she'd opened up a lot in her letters since then. Him too, really, going back and forth about some things he'd never gotten into with anybody else.

And now here she was, walking out with Esteban, and damn. He didn't know what it was exactly, that line where someone's a kid on one side of it and she's a woman on the other. But she'd crossed it.

Griffin had plenty of dough saved from the Corps, there not being much to spend it on over in Sandland, so he was playing big shot. Dinner at Red Lobster out at the mall, and then the old Toyota dealership on New York Street that some guy'd made into a dance club. Juanita was turning some heads. Fuck that, she was turning all of them. And Griffin was falling for her. The first slow dance came on, Esteban clinched up with a girl he'd been working on since they arrived. Griffin stepped back, letting Juanita take the lead, to see if she wanted to stay out for the dance or sit it out. She took his hand, pulled him to her, and he held her as you held a woman. He felt the way she fit against him, and he wanted to say something, felt like he should say something. But she felt graceful and true in his arms and any words he thought to say seemed awkward and false. So he just held her and swayed to the music, his hand moving slowly up and down on her bare back, her backless dress open almost to her waist, hoping that the feeling of his hand on her skin was saying whatever he could not. Then he felt her lips brush against his neck as she stretched up for a minute on her toes, her mouth now right next to his ear, and she said, "I know. Me too."

Halfway through the night, on the way to the men's room, he told Esteban. "I think I'm getting a little thing for your sister, man. Maybe a big thing."

Esteban grinned, slapped him on the shoulder. "Fuck, man, you just figuring that out? You two, you been a thing for a while. Better you than most of the scum in the neighborhood, dude. You gonna be a gentleman, right?"

"Part of the Marine code, hombre."

They danced, they drank – it was the best night Griffin had had in a long time. Best night he'd had, period.

At closing time, Griffin, Esteban, and Juanita were walking out to the car. Halfway across the lot, a stretch Caddy cut them off. Tiny Hernandez and two of his goons got out. Griffin knew Hernandez ran the Latin Kings on the east side of Aurora. He was also the younger brother of Jamie Hernandez, who was a major dealer. Tiny looked like a human cement block – six feet tall, six feet thick, a flat, feral face on a stump neck.

"I been watching you, *mamacita*," he said to Juanita. "You like the finest thing ever been in that dump. I'm gonna take you out, show you where the real players hang."

"I'm not anybody's *mamacita*," Juanita said.

"Thanks for the offer, sport," said Griffin. "But I don't think she wants to go."

"You got shit in your ears? I didn't ask. *Puta* like that, she don't know what she wants. Not till I give it to her." Hernandez's goons got a chuckle out of that.

Griffin caught the look from Esteban – no way was his sister getting in that car. And nothing good was going to come of waiting for the other side to make a move. Esteban yelled for Juanita to get inside, put his shoulder down and drove into the goon on the right – catching him in the gut, driving him back against the Caddy, hard. Griffin feinted toward Tiny, knowing the other goon would rush to help. Then he planted, turned and put the stiffened fingers of his right hand into the guy's throat. Felt something crumple, guy's trachea if he'd done it right. The way the guy went down, Griffin figured he was on his way to dead.

Griffin turned back to see Hernandez with his hand in his coat, a nine coming out. Griffin closed, locking both hands on the pistol, turning it down and in. Hernandez pulled the trigger, blowing a hole through the inside of his own thigh.

Griffin twisted the gun out of Hernandez's hand as he went down. He turned to check on Esteban. The first goon had soaked up the slam against the car, and Esteban must have got in a shot to his face, because the goon's nose was running blood. But the goon had forty pounds on Esteban. The goon got a knee up into Esteban's groin, shoved him back, and pulled a gun.

Griffin shot him through the side of the head.

Hernandez was on the ground, cussing, blood arcing out of his thigh.

"You gonna die, you fuck. You know who I am? You gonna fucking die."

"You first, sport," said Griffin. "That's your femoral artery emptying out there. Unless you're up on your first aid, you got maybe two minutes before you bleed out."

Hernandez looked down at the blood jetting out into the parking lot for a moment. Then he looked back up to Griffin. "Jesus, you gotta help me. I mean, this shit? We let it go, right? Shit happens. But you gotta help me."

"No," Griffin said, turning back toward the club where Juanita was waiting. "I don't."

Griffin had done all the killing, so he took the heat with the cops – said Esteban and Juanita had been inside, he'd gone out to get the car, Hernandez and his goons had said something about taking the girl, Griffin said they weren't, and the shit hit the fan. The DA didn't file any charges. The Aurora cops knew Hernandez, checked on Griffin's military record, and they backed Griffin right down the line. But a week later, some dumb-ass kid, maybe sixteen, made a try for Griffin with a knife while Griffin was in the checkout line at Walgreens. He broke the kid's arm and only had to twist it a little to discover word was out. Jamie Hernandez wanted Griffin's head on a wall, and he'd pay top dollar to whoever delivered it. Even the Marines would be no good – Griffin had seen enough gang signs carved into enough latrines to know better.

Esteban and Juanita drove him to O'Hare the day he left for France.

"I owe you my life," Esteban told him as they shook hands. "Anytime, anywhere, you need me, you call."

Griffin nodded.

Juanita stepped up. "When the time is right, I'm here," she said. She held Griffin's face in her hands, and she kissed him, gently, but for a long time.

Hardin had been dreaming about that kiss for years.

Not always good dreams. Six months into his Legion hitch, Hardin felt clear enough to reach out to some of his Aurora contacts, just to touch base. Found out that Hernandez had killed Esteban a few months before. Which meant Juanita might be on his list, too. Made a call into the Aurora cops, but they told him Juanita had blown town, no sign Hernandez was looking for her. Just somebody at the club had told Hernandez that Esteban had been in the parking lot that night, been part of the scrape.

That put Esteban's death on Hardin's account. He'd skipped town, left him and Juanita behind. He'd thought about skipping out on the Legion, heading back to the US, making sure she was safe. But all that would do is put him back on Hernandez's radar – and point Hernandez at Juanita. No, if she was safe, the best thing he could do was stay away from her.

Forever.

CHAPTER 17

"You're one lucky fucker, Lynch," said Detective Dick Karsten. He was an Area 2 cop Lynch knew going back to his Academy days. "Powers that be got a hard on for you. Every weird-ass case we get, they dumping it on you?"

Starshak had called Lynch and told him to get down and eyeball a crime scene on the old US Steel property on the far south side. Something about more .22s.

"Looks that way," Lynch said. "How it's been going? I hear you dumped that place up in Eagle River." Karsten had flipped a handful of properties in the Northwoods over the years; guy knew his way around a toolbox. He'd helped Lynch out at his place a couple times, Lynch taking some time here and there over the years to pitch in up north.

"Sweet deal," said Karsten. "Some trader started in on his log dream home on Big Arbor Vitae, over toward Minocqua. Know it?"

"Little west of St Germain? Yeah."

"Place is like 3800 square feet. Guy had just got it enclosed when the market tanked. Foreclosure sharks were circling. Swapped my place for his. He still has his Northwoods love pad. I finish this out nice, I make a damn killing. Property's got another little two-bedroom, three-season job on it, too, so I get things fixed up, I can parcel that off."

"Sounds nice. You need some help up there, let me know."

"Gets to where I need the unskilled labor, you're my first call."

Lynch laughed, looked past Karsten to where Bernstein had joined some crime-scene guys who were working around a body – big fat guy on his back. "So what have we got?"

"What you got here is Beans Garbanzo," said Karsten.

Lynch's face went hard. Garbanzo worked for Tony Corsco, head of the outfit in Chicago, the whole Midwest, actually. The gangbangers were bad enough, but Lynch understood them at least. You grow up in public housing, got an entire society shitting on you when they aren't ignoring you, bad shit happens. But the fucking mob, a couple generations of wealth behind most of them, and they just keep going. Drugs, prostitution, protection, robbery, protection rackets, gambling – show them a human weakness and they'll kill for a piece of it. Lynch had been picking up bodies with Corsco's fingerprints on them his whole career, always watching the bastard skate. Watching the media play it like the guy was some kind of charming rogue, just another piece of local color.

Lynch remembered a night his second year out of the academy. Dead girl, fifteen years old. Her older sister waitressed at one of Corsco's clubs, one of them where waitressing meant if Corsco wanted her on her knees giving some slimy bastard head as a favor, then that's what she did. The older sister'd killed herself, but not, evidently before the little sister heard something. She started making some noise. A week later, Lynch is looking at her naked body in a North Side ally, not an inch of her without a bruise on it. Lynch was still in uniform at the time. Nobody ever came close to clearing the case.

What Lynch heard, though, was it was Corsco, personally. Raped her first, then took a bat to her.

"Garbanzo is Corsco muscle," said Lynch.

"Yep. And down yonder where McCord is fucking around, you got Snakes DeGetano."

"And they both got done with .22s?"

"I'll let McCord fill you in on that. Don't want to ruin his fun." Karsten looked at his watch. "I'd stick around and help with the canvass, but canvass what, you know?" The empty US Steel site stretched almost to the horizon. "Damn, almost five. And with the cavalry here, I can make first pitch at Comiskey."

"You mean the Cell, don't you?" said Lynch.

"US Cellular Field my ass," Karsten said. "Fucking deal will run out, somebody else'll buy up the name. Be goddamn Kotex Field or something."

"Be perfect for you pussy Sox fans," Lynch said.

"Yeah, well, this pussy Sox fan is going to be at the game tonight. You're gonna be here eyeballing goombah stiffs. Y'all have fun, now, you hear?"

Karsten took off. Lynch walked over and joined Bernstein.

".22s?" Lynch asked.

"Three of them, nice grouping right in the forehead."

"So what's with all the blood?" Garbanzo had blood all down the front of his shirt, some more on his right leg from the knee down. Three to the head, guy should have been DOA right off. He wouldn't have bled much, especially lying on his back.

"Some kind of trauma to the side of the head. Doesn't look fatal, but he bled a good bit before he got shot."

"You catch the hip holster?"

"The empty one? Yeah."

Lynch turned to one of the techs. "You guys turn up any weapons?"

Guy shook his head.

Lynch looked down toward the second cluster of uniforms. "Guess we better go see what McCord has for us."

It was almost half a mile down to the next body. Bernstein and Lynch stayed way to the right walking down. Little crime scene flags were sticking up out of the dirt every couple yards all the way there, and they didn't want to step in any evidence.

DeGetano was also on his back, some blood on the front of his tracksuit from a wound in his neck. Lynch squatted down and saw a round hole. Shadow fell on him, and he could hear somebody chewing on something. McCord.

"OK, McCord, Karsten didn't want to rain on your parade. So I give, what's up?"

"The fat guy back up toward South Shore, he got it with a .22 for sure," said McCord. "And what made me think maybe your guy again is there's no powder, no stippling, nothing like that. So he got it from at least a little ways off, and the nice grouping looks a lot like your shelter guy. Now, the skinny guy here, this is real interesting. That wasn't a gun at all."

"I was thinking a stab wound of some kind."

"Bingo," said McCord.

"Except I haven't seen a lot of round knives."

McCord held up an evidence bag. "Killer was kind enough to leave the murder weapon in the guy's neck."

Lynch stood up, looked at the bag. "A pen?"

"Yep. Thought you'd like that."

"Can I see that?" Bernstein said.

McCord handed him the bag.

"Air France," Bernstein said. "Interesting."

"Why?" Lynch asked.

"This Hardin guy? From *Oprah*? Before a couple nights ago, all we hear is he's from Africa, right?"

"And?"

"And if you want to fly from Africa – or West Africa anyway – to the US, I'm thinking Air France may be your best bet."

McCord bit another chunk off the Snickers bar he was working on. "Looks like we've got prints on the pen, so we'll run that. If this Hardin's in a database anywhere, you'll have your answer. But if you want interesting, we got interesting. You get a look at the fat guy? The head trauma?"

"Yeah," said Lynch. "Wondered about that."

"OK, we got this one set of tire tracks that stop right here, skinny dead guy right next to them, some scuffing on the ground. The way the blood ran down the front of him, he was either sitting or standing when somebody stuck that pen in his throat, and he was dead or close to it once he hit the ground here. Otherwise we'd have more blood running down the sides of his neck. With the tire tracks and scuffing, I'm figuring he got it in the car, then got dumped here."

McCord walked a few yards toward the lake, toward a pile of rubble. He pointed a few yards south. "We got one set of footprints to here, another that stops maybe five yards from old pen neck over there. Some scuffing on the ground here, some more over there, plus over there it looks like someone was down on the ground and there's some blood – on the ground and on a couple of stones we found. You saw all the flags on your way down from the fat guy, right? Between here and the fat guy, we got a bit of a blood trail. Somebody was dripping. Not bad, not like shot, but dripping all the same."

"Ah, fuck me," said Lynch, seeing where this was headed.

McCord nodded. "Yep. Looks like somebody drove out here with these guys, stuck a pen in Skinny, dumped him, and then bounced a few rocks off the fat man. We'll check the head wound, get some trace evidence, probably match it up to one of the rocks."

"So some guy plays Nolan Ryan with Fatso way down here," Lynch says, "then lets him walk most of the way back to South Shore before he drives up and shoots him?"

"Nope. Our tire tracks here? They loop around and head back out to South Shore. We've got Fat Guy's footprints on top of the tire tracks in a couple of spots. So whoever did Skinny and roughed up Fat Guy, he left before fat guy walked back up there and got shot. About ten feet from Fat Guy's body, you got another set of tracks that pulled up and then pulled away. Different tread, different wheelbase."

"So we got Mr .22 showing up as a second act?" Lynch said.

"Looks that way," said McCord.

Lynch blew out a breath, pursing his cheeks. "I notice Fatso's got an empty holster. Is Skinny strapped?"

"Skinny's got an empty shoulder rig. Haven't done the formal test yet, but Skinny's got some gunshot residue on his right hand. I could smell that."

Lynch looked out at the lake.

"So some guy drives down here with Skinny and the Fat Man. Since they've both got holsters, we gotta figure they're both armed. And I'm thinking our mystery guest isn't, since he stabs Skinny in the neck with a pen instead of just shooting him. Skinny gets a shot off but misses. Then our guy disarms Skinny, disarms Fatso, throws rocks at him, gets back in the car, and leaves. Then Fatso walks back up toward South Shore, and Mr .22 pulls in, shoots Fatso dead, and he drives off."

McCord shrugs. "How it adds up."

Bernstein's phone went off, the Kanye noise again.

"What the fuck is that?" McCord asked.

"Ring tone," said Lynch. "He's working on his street cred."

"You threaten to shoot him yet?"

"Threatened to shoot the phone," Lynch said. "He's next."

Lynch's cell buzzed, he checked the ID. Liz. She was flying back in from her network gig that night, going to be in town for a couple of days. Between her book launch and the network gigs, it was getting hard to see her. Lynch was looking forward to it, though. He took a few steps away from Bernstein and McCord.

"Hey," he said. "You at LaGuardia yet?"

"Yeah," she said.

He could hear it in her voice. "But?" Lynch asked.

"But I'm on my way to LA." A pause, like she wanted him to say something. He had nothing to say.

"I'm sorry, John; it's some film deal thing. My agent just dumped it on me an hour ago. I know this sucks. It's just, with everything going on right now, so much crap is up in the air."

"Yeah," Lynch said. "Look, I can't really talk now. I'm down on the South Shore looking at a couple of stiffs."

"You're angry."

Lynch exhaled. "Not at you. Just, ah hell. Call me tonight if you get a chance." Lynch thinking the "if you get a chance" was a bit of a cheap shot even as he said it. She'd call. He knew she'd call.

"I will. I'll call tonight." In the background, some airport PA noise. "We're boarding," she said, "I gotta go."

Another pause.

"Are we OK?" she asked.

"Yeah," Lynch said, trying to sound like he meant it.
She ended the call.

. Lynch looked out at the lake. What he'd had with
Johnson the last year, it was something he'd given up
on. Figured it just wasn't in the cards, maybe just wasn't
in him. Gotten used to being alone, stopped really trying
not to be. Got to where it didn't matter that much, sort
of the way, if you don't eat long enough, you might be
starving, but you don't really feel hungry anymore. He
was hungry now. He'd gotten used to her being in his
life, in his bed. Now, more and more, she wasn't.

It had been kind of exciting at first, Johnson hitting
the big time. He'd flown out to New York with her once,
been wined and dined with some of the network people,
the publishing people. Lynch getting the star treatment
too, some guy from Harcourt and Johnson's agent tag-
teaming him, trying to talk him into doing a book too.

At the hotel that night, some five-star joint, Johnson
had put her two cents in too, not really understanding
why he didn't want a bite at the apple, Lynch not sure
how to explain it, just that it didn't sit right with him
for some reason, Johnson taking that as a shot at her,
not how he meant it. Been a little tense then, not a fight
exactly, but Lynch looked back at that moment as a kind
of divide. Things had looked up until then. Seemed like
they'd gone downhill since.

Lynch had read it wrong, figured it was a temporary
deal, figured it would calm down. It hadn't. Johnson was
playing in a different league now. It wasn't just the book.
She was smart, beautiful – the Hastings case had put her
on the radar, but she had the chops to stay on it. The *Trib*
was pretty much a part-time gig now. TV was the big

thing. And TV, for a political reporter, meant Washington, meant New York. Chicago was flyover country.

Lynch knew she was working at it, spending more time in town than was good for her, probably. And shit, she'd won the media lottery, it's not like he expected her to give it all up. Nobody's fault, nothing to be done about it. Didn't mean he had to like it.

Lynch had a couple tickets to the Hawks game for tomorrow night – Minnesota in town, and Johnson being a Minneapolis girl, she liked her hockey. It was going to be a surprise. Took his phone back up, dug up Dickey Reagan's number, reporter at the *Sun-Times* Lynch went way back with. Dickey was a hockey guy. Lynch figured he throw Dickey a bone, stay on his good side.

Bernstein worked the phone all the way back to the station, getting background on Hardin while Lynch turned the facts over in his head. The body count was now four: three with .22s, one with a ballpoint. He had a rich trader, an African refugee, and two mob soldiers. On top of that, he had a witness that put Hardin in Stein's box right before the first killing, and now he had a video that tied Hardin to a movie star who happened to be in town. The only other time the two of them had been in the same place at the same time, far as anyone knew, was five years ago in Africa, and the two of them had gone at it then. This Membe guy was from Africa, but better than a thousand miles from Darfur. What's that song from that kid's show? "One of these things is not like the other?" Christ, Lynch would be happy if any of these things had anything to do with anything. This was like a goddamn random clue generator or something.

CHAPTER 18

Lynch and Bernstein sat in Starshak's office, Starshak up futzing with the giant fern that hung in his window.

"What you got on this Hardin, Bernstein?"

"French national," Bernstein said. "For a good stretch, he worked as a sort of logistics and security guy for news crews doing stories in Africa. That's how he got involved with Jerry Mooney. Met him at some point, ended up as his right-hand man, pretty much set up that whole Dollars for Darfur thing for him. That's when he got into that punch-up with Shamus Fenn, not much on him since. Couple of people I talked to said maybe he came out of the Foreign Legion – nobody remembers him saying it, it was just what people heard.

"Anyway, I checked the airlines. This Hardin flew Air France out of Casablanca three days ago – Casablanca to Kennedy, connection on United to Chicago. The flight landed just after 10am the day Stein got shot. I checked the car rental places, working on the hotels, but it doesn't look like he's used the Hardin ID since he got to town. So either he brought a pile of cash with him or he's got another ID."

"Gotta have some kind of ID," said Lynch. "Can't even rent a hotel room without one."

"So maybe something he can flash for a hotel, but that he didn't trust enough to get him through an airport?" said Bernstein.

"Makes sense," said Starshak. "Either way, we've got an Air France pen in the mob guy's neck. You said he was on Air France."

"Yeah," said Lynch. "Listen, we got his arrival time at O'Hare and we got his picture. Get that to the techies, he's got to be on video at the airport, right? Track him out, see does he rent a car, does somebody pick him up, does he take the L, or what."

"That gives us a place to start," said Starshak. "Pretty clear he came here to see Stein. Any thoughts there?"

"He must have had something to sell, all I can think of," said Bernstein. "Stein's got his fingers in a lot of pies. Lots of commodities in Africa, lots of shady deals. If Hardin had the right dope on something, Stein could pony up pretty good for it."

Lynch's cell rang. He checked the screen. McCord. "Yeah?" said Lynch.

"You remember the dirt on Stein's pants; I told you we'd check it out?"

"Yeah," said Lynch.

"OK, first off, this is actual dirt, soil of some kind. When we get something here that looks like dirt, usually it's pollution; road salt, urban grime. So this being actual dirt seemed a little strange. First of all, it's fresh. Not worked into the fabric all that deep and it's not like Stein couldn't afford to get his suits cleaned. Gotta figure he got it on him that night, so that's weird cause there ain't much loose dirt around the United Center. And the weather the last few days, what dirt we got is frozen solid. Second, being actual dirt, it's got geological properties that can tie it to a location. Thing is, this wasn't our usual nice Midwestern sediment. This shit was funky. I had to ship it over to a geology guy at UIC. I'll send you all the fun science – stuff about alluvial deposits and riverine something or another – but bottom line is this: the dirt's from West Africa. And this dirt-specialist guy, he had an interesting question. He wanted to know had anybody brought up diamonds. Said this type of dirt is consistent with the geology around West African diamond deposits."

"Diamonds?" Lynch asked.

"Yep," said McCord.

Lynch hung up the phone, filled in Starshak and Bernstein.

"So diamonds from West Africa, which is where this Hardin just came from," said Starshak.

"Yeah," said Lynch.

"And we have this Membe guy, also from there, who maybe had his hand lopped off for stealing diamonds," said Bernstein.

"Yeah," said Lynch. "Kinda feels like an actual lead."

CHAPTER 19

Munroe stifled a yawn, popped a go pill and looked out his hotel window across Michigan Avenue and Grant Park at Lake Michigan. Needed about ten hours sleep, but the go pill would take care of that. Jet lag was for pussies who hadn't been shot much.

Munroe hated Chicago. His first time had been during the convention in 1968 a few years after he'd officially crossed over to the dark side. Got lent out to track down a Soviet agent provocateur who had been whispering unpleasant ideas into the Yippies' ears, been teaching them to blow shit up. The Chicago cops found that guy bobbing in the lake, bouncing off the breakwater by the Planetarium, bump on his head. They wrote him off as some stoned fuck who didn't know that getting high and going for a swim didn't mix.

Next day, Munroe was out of his hippie mufti, back in his Brooks Brothers, trying to flag a cab out of town, when some long-hair pelted him with an open baggie full of human shit. Shouldn't blame the city, he supposed, but the whole exercise left a bad taste in his mouth. And, of course, there was Hurley the First: classless troglodyte every bit as venal and ham-fisted as any third world thug Munroe had ever had to make nice with. Kind of guy that made you wonder if you were really on the right side.

But the new Hurley? At least this guy loved his cameras.

Munroe was scrolling through a slide show of al Din shots the tech boys had pulled together for him. Pretty clear that al Din knew about the cameras, too, and understood there was no way he could stay off them, so he did the next best thing. He stuck his mug in front of every camera he could find. North side, south side, west side – if there was a camera, al Din was on it. Suburbs weren't wired up, not like the city, but al Din was doing his level best to pop up out there, too. Mall security, ATMs. If Munroe was going to piece together al Din's play based on video footage, al Din was not going to make it easy.

The slippery little bastard still had his ways of dropping off the radar every now and again – an hour here, a couple hours there. Never could track him to a hotel, a base. But that's how you got to the top of the game. If radical Islam had an MVP badass right now, al Din was it.

Munroe's phone peeped. He looked at the screen. Guy at the NSA that was riding herd on the electronic intel for him.

"Yeah?"

"The Chicago PD just ran some prints against the DoD database. An ex-Marine, Michael Xavier Griffin. Two tours, made Scout/Sniper. He mustered out in 1994. This will not be in anything the Chicago police see, but during Gulf War I, he was detailed to Mossad to help on anti-SCUD efforts."

"So he might have a Mossad tie? Might know Stein?"

"Yes. And he is from the Chicago area. He left the Marine Corps after being involved in an altercation with a local drug dealer and two of his enforcers. He killed all three of them. One of them was Jamie Hernandez's younger brother."

"Hernandez as in Mexican cartel Hernandez?"

"Yes. Hernandez put out a contract on him and Griffin left to join the Foreign Legion. He did a hitch there, and has been working as logistics and security support for TV news crews in Africa ever since, using the French ID he received coming out of the Legion, Nicholas Hardin. According to a source with FRANCE 24, he tried to pitch them a story on the evolution of the blood diamond trade a few months ago, but they were not interested."

Munroe closed his eyes a minute, rubbed the bridge of his nose. "You telling me this Hardin has the stones? This whole thing is just a straight-up robbery? Only reason al Din's still in town to run him down?"

"Best theory based on the evidence."

A pause, then Munroe again. "Wait, you said prints. Why was Chicago PD running this guy's prints?"

"Found them on a murder weapon. Two Chicago mafia soldiers were killed at an abandoned industrial site. It appears that Hardin killed one of them."

"One of them?"

"Al Din killed the other."

"What the fuck? Could they be working together?"

"Evidence shows al Din arrived after Hardin left."

Munroe stopped for a minute, trying to decide what to ask next. "OK, so what's the mob's interest in this? Stein got popped and Hardin had to shop for a new buyer, tried them, maybe they got greedy?"

"Don't know."

"Who's playing godfather around here these days?"

"Anthony Corsco. He controls most of the Midwest."

"OK, get me Corsco's info. Me and him need to chat. See if we can get a line on this Hardin guy, too. Play the Legion angle; see who he's in touch with." Munroe paused for a minute, something eating at him. "One more thing. Hardin get hit during this cluster fuck? Did al Din grab him up maybe?"

"No evidence to suggest that. Why do you ask?"

"Trying to figure out why he'd leave a piece behind with his prints on it."

"Wasn't a piece."

"You said murder weapon. What did they find his prints on?"

"An Air France ballpoint pen."

A long pause, Munroe shaking his head. "Sure," Munroe said finally. "Why not?"

CHAPTER 20

Hardin headed east from the Aurora train station, walking through the neighborhood just past the tracks. The area had been pretty Hispanic when he left town and was more so now. That meant there would be enough illegals around that folks here wouldn't be that big on paper checking.

Three blocks in, Hardin found what he was looking for. Ten year-old Honda Civic, pretty beat up, sitting at the curb with a For Sale sign on the dash. Half an hour later, Hardin drove off. The guy had been a little suspicious about an Anglo at his door, but Hardin spoke Spanish (hell, Spanish, French, bits of half a dozen African dialects, enough Italian to get by), so that helped. And paying the ridiculous asking price in cash helped more. The info he gave the guy would never fly with the Secretary of State's office whenever they got around to processing the title transfer, but that was weeks out. If Hardin was still driving the Honda around Chicago by then, he would have way bigger problems.

Hardin cruised through his old neighborhood, taking Spring Street east, cutting down Union to Galena. A decent-sized shopping area had sprung up at Union and New York – bakery, music shop, clothing store, grocery. Hardin remembered when he was a kid, the whites who could afford to all moving out, the Mexicans moving in, all the bad talk about spics and drugs and gangs. It was the same shit his great-grandparents had heard about the Irish back in the day. But the houses were looking better, the shops were going up. It was the way it always had gone. A new wave of immigrants moves in, figures out the game, and joins in on it just like everybody else. On the Honda's radio, some blowhard was going on about immigration and sealing the borders and all the jobs these people were stealing from hard-working Americans. Hardin spun the dial, found a Cubs spring training game on WGN.

Hardin checked into the Motel 6 at 59 and 88. Told the teenager at the counter he didn't have a credit card, so the kid told him he had to leave a $100 deposit against expenses. The kid didn't even look at the expired license he flashed as ID. Anonymous as he could get. He got a room on the ground floor near the back, put his clothes away, and called Fouche.

"Hope you got something for me, *mon ami*," Hardin said.

"I do. The Russians want to play, and they've got a middleman in your area who'll make the buy. Guy named Bahram Lafitpour in some town called Oak Brook. That work for you?"

"Oak Brook's close enough, that's good. Lafitpour, though, that's Iranian. Makes me a little nervous."

"Not that kind of Iranian. Guy went to the US just after the Shah went down. Used to be SAVAK. He's not a Koran thumper, that's for sure."

"OK. How do I get in touch?"

Fouche gave Hardin a number.

CHAPTER 21

Bobby Lee and Courtney Schilst were waiting for a table at BD's Mongolian Grill in Naperville, across Washington from the Barnes & Noble. Twenty minutes on her Facebook, he had all he needed to make his play – the chick was big into poetry, modern guys, liked this Bukowski or whatever his name was. He followed her Twitter for a bit, found out she'd just got dumped, that her birthday was today, and that she was going to spend it "at B&N, with CB, the only man worth loving." So Bobby had done some quick research, found out Bukowski was the poet laureate of American low life and so forth. He got to the Barnes & Noble early, grabbed one of the two Bukowski books they had in stock, slouched into the chair closest to that shelf, and waited.

He was careful not to look when she walked in. Watched out of the corner of his eye while she checked out the shelf. Saw a little frown – she must have wanted the book he had. She grabbed the other one. Bobby had piled his shit on the chair across from him. People liked to sit in the easy chairs along the windows, but one thing he'd learned in Naperville was none of the white folk were going to ask a black guy to move his stuff, not so long as he was wearing his intense Malcolm X face. He'd pulled his backpack and coat off the chair when he saw Courtney grab her book.

She looked at the line of chairs, saw that the one across from him was available, and sat down.

It was like fishing. You couldn't force it. You had to wait for it. Finally, he could feel it, could feel her seeing the book, looking at him. Still he gave it a second. Finally, he lowered the book a little, looked over the top.

She held up her book, the other Bukowski. "I've never seen anyone else reading him in here before," she said.

He shrugged, gave a little half smile, just being polite. Made her make another move.

"I guess, around here, I mean the life he led, that's just not their experience." She was hooked now. She wanted to talk. And he had his play. The Bukowski, the hint of contempt when she said "their experience." She wanted to slum.

"Yeah, well, I ain't from around here," Bobby said. "Where I grew up, I mean I *get* this shit, you know?"

"Do you really?" she said, leaning forward a little now. She was wearing a scoop neck, and it drooped down, giving him a nice shot. "I mean sure, maybe the poverty, but there's something in his take on things, his own genius. I keep thinking I've connected, and then I realize I haven't, I just…How do you get inside that, you know?"

"Don't try," Lee said. Bukowski's epithet, had it on his tombstone. Lee'd read about that. It was perfect.

So an hour of bullshit at the bookstore, then across the street for dinner. Lee had figured her for a project, was ready to invest a week. The way it was going, he'd be boxing her compass tonight.

Lee felt his cell vibrate on his hip, checked his screen. It was a guy he knew in the Chicago PD who'd feed him tips here and there for a little extra scratch. He excused himself and stepped outside to take the call.

"It's Lee. What you got?"

"Hey, Bobby. Remember way back you said if I ever see this Griffin guy pop up to give you a shout?"

Lee had to think for just a second. Hernandez, the drug lord. He'd been referred to Lee maybe a year or so back, some gang shit, somebody messing with his distribution network, wanted some faces run down. Lee had turned the job around in maybe an hour. Then Hernandez tells him about this Griffin. Michael X. Griffin. Just that it was personal, it went back a long way. This Griffin had gone overseas or something, disappeared all the way down the rabbit hole. But if he ever popped up on Lee's radar and Lee got some solid intel to Hernandez, Lee would be looking at a big fucking payday.

"Yeah, OK, Griffin. I remember."

"We just ran his prints. They turned up at the crime scene on some homicide down in Area 2."

Bingo. Lee and his guy settled on a number, the guy saying he'd e-mail Lee a copy of the data as soon as he got off work and could get on a clean keyboard.

Lee headed back into the restaurant. Nice meal, couple hours of blonde stranger for dessert, then see what he could squeeze out of Hernandez. Not like that guy had a budget. Ought to be a lot of zeros coming out of this.

CHAPTER 22

Dave Fansher was pissed. You don't leave a fine animal like this in its saddle, and the way this one was rubbed raw, it had been in the saddle for a few days at least. He'd found it drinking from the ditch along the east road, dirty, matted, sores all along the cinch and the edge of the skirt after he got the saddle off. That pretend rancher, what's his name, Heinz? Guy who'd paid way over market for the hundred acres or so of land the Feds sold off a few years back? Horse had to be his.

Pretend cowboys – the West was getting overrun with them. Make their money doing whatever pencil-neck geek work it was they did, and all of a sudden they think they're John Fucking Wayne. Gotta have their toy ranches, build their big-ass log houses, mistreat their $10,000 animals, have their goddamn family over come summer, tear-assing around on their stinking ATVs, scaring the shit out of his cattle.

Fansher spit on the barn floor, put out some oats for the horse, and gave it a good scratch behind the ears. Wasn't the animal's fault. He would have called that Heinz fuck – let him know he had the horse – if the guy had ever left a number, anything like that, but he never had. Fansher had gone over once to say hello, right after they guy had bought the place. He wasn't crazy about having some rich fuck move in the next spread over, but how he was raised, if you were neighbors you were neighbors. Guy had pretty much blown him off. Said hi on the porch, didn't even invite him in.

Fuck it. Getting late. Animal was OK. He'd cleaned it up, treated the sores, fed it, watered it, got it into a clean stall for the night. He'd run over and check in with Heinz in the morning, let him know where the horse was in case the guy ever wanted to get around to picking it up.

CHAPTER 23

Munroe should have been sleeping, but his mind was humming now, the jet lag all the way gone.

So this Hardin had whacked Jamie Hernandez's brother almost two decades ago. Hernandez had come a long way since then. Cartels in Mexico weren't as big back in 1994, not like today. Mostly they were middlemen, buying off the Columbians, offloading to whatever US networks they could cobble together. Munroe did some quick checking. Hernandez ran powder into Chicago, but had the bright idea of basing his operation out of Aurora, on account of it had a pretty big Mexican population, lots of family contacts he could exploit, and being almost fifty miles west of the Loop, it tended to stay off the DEA radar. That's why he'd had his kid brother up there riding herd on the local gangbangers.

Didn't work out so well for the brother, but Hernandez had come a long way. Ran the most powerful cartel in Mexico. And the most violent. That was his modus operandi – overwhelming, unmitigated violence in response to any challenge, any threat, any insult. Which, Munroe figures, meant he was on his way to town. A guy like that, he hears his brother's killer is in Chicago, he's not going to farm it out.

Which was giving Munroe ideas. Hernandez and al Din in the same place at the same time. Throw in better

126

than $100 million in hot diamonds and two criminal organizations with complimentary problems, and Munroe could whip up a tasty little dish.

See, Al Qaeda had diamonds they needed to turn into cash. And Hernandez had a shit load of cash he needed to turn into almost anything else. Which suited Munroe just fine, because what he needed was a way to turn the foreign affairs spotlight off the Mideast a little bit and get people to pay attention to the southern border.

The Mexican drug situation was getting way out of hand. To your average voter, it was just a crime story and a foreign one at that, but Munroe knew better. Christ, look at Juarez. A few years ago, that city had maybe two hundred homicides a year. Per capita, that was more or less like any major US city. Last year? Something like three thousand. And you could throw a stone into Juarez from El Paso. The violence was ramping up and leaking over the border. That was already raising issues – the possibility that some other bad actor would piggyback on the drug trade to import some serious trouble into the US. And, after the PRI rode the last election back into power, they'd stopped playing nice with the DEA, which wasn't making keeping an eye on things any easier. But the bigger picture was even worse.

The cartels were already states within a state down there, more powerful in parts of the country than the real government. Hernandez was first among equals in that dogfight right now, and the trend was toward consolidation. And once one of the cartels came out on top, the US could end up with a full-fledged narco-state on its southern border. We wouldn't be neighbors with a nation anymore, we'd be neighbors with the world's largest criminal enterprise. Well, the largest if you didn't count Russia. But Putin wasn't in the same hemisphere.

National security, that was Munroe's gig. All enemies, foreign and domestic. Radical Islam? A problem, yeah, but a fragmented problem with too many internal rivalries to coalesce into the threat most people saw it to be. A decade since 9/11 and your average American still didn't seem to understand that it was just a tragedy, not a threat to national security. The ragheads were driven by ideology. That made them predictable. They had no permanent political base. That made them vulnerable. They had to move money through criminal channels to operate. That made them relatively easy to track.

Iran? A bigger threat, seeing as the matter of it building its own nukes was really more a question of when than if. More of an issue for Israel, really, but as long as the US still needed a petrochemical tit in its mouth, then the Mideast was always going to be in play and Iran was always going to be a thorn in the side.

But having Mexico as a narco-state neighbor? And one funded by our own dumb-ass appetites? The cartels were driven by money, not ideology. No telling what they'd do to protect and expand their markets, and they'd have virtually unlimited cash to do it with. Anybody with a wallet and a hard on for the US might be able to lease a base of operations a few feet from our soil. And that would turn our second-longest border into a revolving door for a world of trouble.

That wasn't a problem Munroe could fight, not right now. The War on Drugs? What a crock. Anybody who wasn't looking at the drug problem through a political lens knew the answer. Legalize every goddamn thing the cartels wanted to sell. Drug prices would plummet, the cartels' revenue would dry up. Sure, they could try to go legit, but they wouldn't be having gun fights with each other anymore, they'd be having marketing fights with the cigarette people, the booze people, the Coca-Cola people for all Munroe knew. And there'd be a whole new stream of sin tax revenue to put a dent in the deficit. But the tobacco-sucking, booze-swilling American electorate was convinced that Jesus didn't like drugs, besides cigarettes and booze.

So the War on Drugs was what Munroe had. Problem being, you don't fight a war with policemen and warrants and jail terms. You fight a war with planes and tanks and Marines. You don't send the enemy to jail, you send him to hell. But you couldn't invade a sovereign nation that was supposedly fighting the same enemy you were just because they sucked at doing the job. Not yet anyway.

Not unless you could invent a reason.

With al Din in play and with Stein dead, Munroe could already make a case that Iran had killed a US citizen on US soil. With this Hardin in the middle of it and with what Munroe knew about how Hernandez held a grudge, Munroe could suck Hernandez into the game as well. Then he could paint the lot of them with the same stink; put the cartels in bed with the terrorists. With the money-laundering angle, Munroe could make the case they were solving each other's problems. That would be the new narrative.

Then the cartels wouldn't be drug dealers anymore, they'd be enemy combatants. Then we could lean on Mexico maybe, get them to invite us over the border to help clean house. It wouldn't take that long. These cartel guys, they aren't dug in underground like Al Qaeda – Al Qaeda had been born in hiding, it was in their DNA. You had to root them out one at a time like fucking cockroaches. But the cartel bigwigs? They liked their villas. They liked the high life. They weren't running around free because the Federales didn't know where to find them. They were running around free because they had the cops, the army, the legislature and the judiciary on their payroll, or enough of them anyway.

Give Munroe a long weekend, a green light, a few dozen drones, and some Navy SEALs and he could decapitate every cartel from the Rio Grande to the Panama Canal. Sure, something would grow back in its place, but Munroe would make damn sure it was our something this time. If you weren't going to legalize the drug trade, then the best way to protect the nation was to run it.

Munroe was getting ahead of himself, he knew that. Early in the game, still too many loose ends, too many unknowns, and he'd need some buy-in from way above his pay grade. But it was time to start whispering in a few ears.

CHAPTER 24

The next morning, Lynch and Bernstein were watching the show the surveillance guys had pieced together on Hardin on Lynch's computer. Hardin gets off the plane. Hardin takes the bus to the car rental center. Hardin rents a white Ford Fusion.

They got the plate on that, called the Hertz people. Hardin had used an ID that said he was Nigel Fox. Ran that. Nigel Fox had been at the Hyatt down on Wacker until yesterday. Turned out he was a British newsie Hardin ran with back in Africa. Guy had kicked the bucket a few months back. Ran the plate numbers on the Fusion through the system. Hardin had it parked at the Grant Park garage from maybe forty minutes after Stein got hit until yesterday morning. Then he dropped the car back at the airport, took the L back into town, then jumped a BNSF commuter train to the western burbs. That's where they lost him. No cameras on the trains, and the train he caught was a local: twenty-five stops between Chicago and Aurora.

"He had to drive back from our South Shore crime scene to the garage, right?" said Lynch. "Just before he took his rental back to the airport? But according to the tape, that rental hasn't moved since he parked it. So let's rewind on that, see if we can find the other car."

They got back on the phone with IT. The entrances to the Grant Park garage were all near Hurley's Millennium

Park, the mayor's zillion-dollar-over-budget vanity fiasco. It was like some garish *nouveau riche* attempt to one-up Central Park in ten percent of the space. There was the bandstand that was supposed to be another of Chicago's architectural marvels but looked pretty much like a beer can that had been blown open with a firecracker. There was the Great Lawn, the one the security guys were always chasing the actual Chicagoans off of because they had to keep the grass nice for when the paying customers from the North Shore came down for the concerts. There was the Bean, a giant, stainless steel kidney bean parked right in the middle. It was supposed to be called Cloud Gate. Lynch remembered the artist getting his knickers in a knot when even the media started calling it the Bean. Lynch wondered what it was about Chicago sometimes – some sense of civic inferiority or something – that made the city break out the checkbook for any artist looking for a payday. You had the Picasso, God knows what that was supposed to be, a winged baboon or something. Across from that, next to the county building, there was what looked like a cement amputee with a fork in her head. You had the red spider down by the Federal Building. Had some white carbuncle in front of the State of Illinois building, looked like a giant wadded-up tissue. What was that thing called again? Monument with Standing Beast? Thing always smelled like urine because it had all these crannies homeless guys and drunks could get into when they had to take a leak. Even had a giant metal baseball bat in the West Loop.

One thing about Millennium Park though, it being Hurley's baby. It was wired for cameras, wall to wall.

It only took a few minutes. The IT guy pulled up a shot of Hardin ducking into one of the stairwells off Randolph, tracked him back through the park, got him parking a black Grand Marquis on Columbus, behind the Art Institute. They ran that for a while, saw the tickets stacking up and then one of the blue city wreckers hauling it off.

"Looks like the right ride," said Lynch. He and Bernstein were at the auto pound on lower Randolph, gloves on, taking a first look at the car. The Marquis had some blood on the inside of the right rear door, some on the seat next to it. Also, there was a bullet hole through the front passenger seat. Looked like the round hit the radio.

"Got a shell casing stuck in the seat cushion there," Bernstein said, pointing.

"So if the gun ever turns up, we can match it. Match the blood to Skinny from down on South Shore, and we got this Hardin guy roped in to that solid." Lynch popped open the glove compartment, took out a sheet of paper and unfolded it. It was a picture of Hardin at the car rental place at O'Hare – the same picture the tech guys had dug up for Lynch and Bernstein when they'd started running him down. On the bottom, in block printing, was:

WHITE FUSION GL4 655 GRANT PARK GARAGE
NORTH END

Lynch held the paper out to Bernstein.

"This shit with Hardin and the mob, that went down yesterday early, right?" Lynch said.

Bernstein nodded.

"So who was pulling up surveillance shots before we even knew who we were looking for?"

"Good question," Bernstein said.

"And what were a couple of goombahs doing with Hardin's license number and location before we even had it?"

"Could see where that might kinda eat at you," said Bernstein.

The pound attendant came back down from the office. Lynch had sent him in to run the VIN.

"Got reported stolen up at Old Orchard three days back," the attendant told them. "Retired couple up in Glenview. Plates are off a junker, scrapped better than a year ago."

Lynch pulled out his cell and called McCord. "Hey," Lynch said. "We found your car from South Shore, or at least one of them. You're gonna have to get some techs over to the pound and process it."

"Got something for you too," said McCord. "That pen? Got a hit on the prints. Michael Xavier Griffin. He's in the DoD database. Marines, 1986 through 1994. Nothing in CID, so he's been a good boy, far as we know."

"Sure, except he used to be Michael Griffin and now he's Nick Hardin. You know a lot of good boys who change their names?"

"Don't know too many good boys who know how to kill somebody with a pen either," said McCord.

CHAPTER 25

Hernandez watched out the window of the Gulfstream as it made its descent into DuPage Airport, coming in from the southwest, over the east side of Aurora. From the air, he picked out the parking lot where his brother had died. Where his brother had been killed. The brother he had never avenged.

Sandoval, he was dead. Hernandez had been with the crew that grabbed him, had watched while they used the blowtorch on him, had used the torch himself. He'd cut Sandoval's throat himself, holding Sandoval's head up, starring into the one eye he hadn't burnt out, making sure the *cabron*'s last vision in this world was Hernandez's face. He'd learned all there was to learn from Sandoval.

All these years. His brother in the ground all these years, and Griffin alive and breathing somewhere. Hernandez had never stopped looking. Or so he told himself. But was it true?

You forget, just a little, he had to admit that to himself. His power grew. His wealth grew. The complexities of running the business grew. Whole states in Mexico where he was the power as much as the government, more than the government. Distribution networks – into Mexico, into the US. The gangs in the major cities all over America, managing those relationships, trying to keep over-armed teenagers focused on moving his product instead of on their silly imaginary wars with the gang up the street that looked sideways at their girls.

Had he done all he could? Who could know? He had contacts looking all over the world. Every night, before he slept, his last thought was of his brother. And it was in that moment, the night before, that this Lee had called. Griffin's fingerprints. In Chicago. He'd read through the email package from Lee. The Hardin identity, the murder scene, Corsco's people involved. Hernandez would talk to Corsco.

The wheels hit the tarmac. Lee would be waiting. Hernandez's Chicago contacts would be waiting. Soon, very soon, he would be Griffin's last vision of this world. And by that time, Griffin would be glad to see this world go.

CHAPTER 26

"Is Hernandez on the ground?" Agent Jeanette Wilson asked from the back of the room at the emergency DEA briefing at the Chicago field office.

"Don't know yet," said Brad Jablonski, head of Chicago's DEA field office. "Still sorting through what's coming in from the CIs. We do know this – he's got his whole organization on a war footing, and it's all about finding this Griffin. You guys want to fill us in there?"

Lynch and Bernstein were seated up front. Lynch took the podium.

"We got a hit on a set of fingerprints at a murder down in Area 2 – the South Shore thing down at the old US Steel site, the business with the Corsco soldiers. You've all heard about that. Anyway, the fingerprints match those of a Michael Xavier Griffin in the DoD database." Lynch hit the button to advance the slide show on the screen, a split-screen shot with Griffin's official Marine photo on one side and screen grab from one of the city cam shots on Columbus on the other. "Griffin was in the Marines from '86 to '94, his last six years as a scout/sniper in Force Recon. So he does qualify as a genuine bad ass. You guys already know the story on Hernandez's kid brother. This Griffin was home on leave, out for dinner with some other guy…" Lynch turned to Bernstein.

"Esteban Sandoval," said Bernstein.

"Sandoval, right," Lynch said. "Anyway, Griffin gets in a beef with Tiny Hernandez, that's Jamie Hernandez's kid brother. Thing ended up with Tiny and two of his goons DOA – and it was Griffin who killed all three of them." He hit the advance button again: Sandoval's driver's license picture from '93, and then a crime scene shot from the basement of the crack house on the west side where they'd found his body in March of '95."Cops say Sandoval had nothing to do with it, other than he happened to be out with Griffin the night it happened, but I guess that was enough for Hernandez. This is what Hernandez did to Sandoval." In the back of the room, Jeanette Wilson turned away for just a beat. Surprised Lynch a little. He knew Wilson's rep. She wasn't anybody's idea of a shrinking violet.

"Here's what else we know," Lynch continued. "Griffin has been living for almost ten years as Nick Hardin. French national. Been in West Africa pretty much that whole time, some kind of glorified gofer for TV news guys. Between '94 and the TV gig, we got nothing. Rumor is maybe the Foreign Legion. Which would explain his having a clean French ID. Evidence indicates he was here to see Abraham Stein – got a witness that puts him in Stein's box the night of his murder. Hardin may have been trying to sell some diamonds, but we don't have everything on that yet."

"You like Hardin for the Stein hit?" One of the DEA suits about halfway back.

Lynch shook his head. "Possible, but we don't think so. Our witness saw Stein alive after Hardin left. Could've snuck back in, but it doesn't feel like it. So we don't think it was Hardin, Griffin, whoever–"

Jablonski butted in. "Let's just say Hardin, keep the confusion down."

Lynch nodded. "So, Hardin. With Stein, it could be diamonds. Don't know what's behind the business with Corsco. But whoever shot Stein also killed Beans Garbanzo down at the South Shore site after Hardin had left the scene – left in a different car than the shooter was driving. So again, could it be Hardin, some kind of three-rail shot with multiple vehicles? Could be, but I'd give that about a five percent chance right now. We do know this. Our shooter, Mr .22, whoever he is, he took out an African refugee named Membe Saturday a couple blocks west of the Stadium the same night he shot Stein. So it looks like we got a second party involved here, a shooter with an agenda around Hardin. That's all we know so far. You guys have any tie in on the narcotics side that might clear any of this up?"

Jablonski blew out a breath. "Hernandez and Corsco, they gotta play ball to some degree. Could be Corsco made a run at this Hardin for Hernandez and blew it. Don't know what to tell you about the other guy. Anybody got ideas?"

Some general mummers, but nobody ready to put a hand up.

"OK," said Jablonski. "Work your networks. We got no warrants on Hernandez, but we know how this guy works. If this is about his brother, then he's gonna be hands- on. So it's a real chance to take him down hard. I'll be coordinating with Chicago PD on this, so I want what you got when you got it. We're putting a BOLO out for Hardin. We get him in the bag, get him to play ball, we got a real leg up. Let's hit it."

CHAPTER 27

Hardin called the number Fouche had given, asked for Lafitpour, listened to some hold music for a few minutes, then a voice came on the phone, started giving him instructions – no introduction, nothing.

"There is a self-serve Italian restaurant called Pompeii in Oak Brook Terrace. It is on Route 56 near Highland, in front of the Home Depot." Deep voice, smooth voice, some hard-to-place rich guy accent. A voice Hardin bet people usually listened to. "Be there at 2pm. Sit near the windows. Have a sample with you."

"How am I going to know you?" said Hardin.

"I'll know you, Mr Hardin. You're famous. That's part of your problem, as I understand it."

So Hardin was sitting near the windows, trying to decide whether the pizza was any good, but he'd lost his frame of reference. He hadn't had good pizza in fifteen years.

Hardin was also getting his mind right, same ritual he'd gone through dating back to his days in the Corps, clearing his mental baffles, getting all his thinking done before the shit hit the fan so he wouldn't have to do any thinking when it did. Eliminate the uncertainties, because that's when fear crept in. Fear, when you got down to it, was an idea, a thought, a shadow cast by the memory of pain and the promise of mortality. Nobody wasn't afraid, but you had to be clear on what you were afraid of and why. Then you did the math. Was the risk worth the reward? Had you done what you could on your end to control the downside? Was the current course of action your best bet? If you could answer yes, then your mind wouldn't wander off at a bad time, you could keep your head in the game.

The stakes were pretty clear – $10 million or better against his life. Couldn't think of anything he'd overlooked on the risk control side, and like it or not, the course of action had been set the second he jumped the couriers back in Liberia. Things had gone south some, but there was no way to turn back the clock and, truthfully, he wouldn't if he could. He'd put his life on the line dozens of times – for a Marine paycheck, for a Legion paycheck, for a network paycheck. At least this time he was hanging his ass out for a decent number.

A large man walked in, looked around the room and then stepped aside. A medium-sized man walked directly to Hardin's table. Tan suit, natural shoulder, very Brooks Brothers but a couple dozen notches up the couture food chain. Starched white shirt, maroon tie. His graying hair was combed straight back and gelled in place. He sat.

"You have your sample?" the man asked.

"Nice to meet you, too," said Hardin.

The man smiled briefly, but not like he meant it. "The sample," he repeated.

Hardin pulled the small canvas bag from his pants pocket, the same one he'd given Stein. Lafitpour held it out a little to his side and shook it, still some dirt on it, then held it up at shoulder level. The larger man came, took the bag, and left the restaurant.

Hardin had another bite of the pizza. The man sat across from him, hands folded on the table, looking him directly in the eyes. He didn't seem to blink much.

"I can't decide," Hardin said. "The pizza any good here? Been a while since I had any."

The man smiled again, said nothing. His phone rang. The man held it to his head, listened for a moment, ended the call, put the phone away. He pulled a business card from his pocket, and slid it across the table to Hardin.

"Your sample checks out. Be at this address the day after tomorrow at 8pm. Have your account information and the rest of the material with you. You can bring the pistol you are wearing on your left side under the jacket if it makes you feel any better."

"Thanks," said Hardin. "It does. I will. Do I get my sample back?"

The man smiled again, got up, and left.

"I guess not," Hardin said to the empty chair.

CHAPTER 28

Hardin drove back to the Motel 6, walked into his room, and saw a woman sitting in the desk chair, the chair turned toward the door. Late thirties maybe, medium height, lean, dark hair cut short, gray slacks, white blouse, blue blazer, black S&W.40. Not pointed at him, not exactly. It took a second.

"Hello, Juanita," Hardin said.

She smiled. "Hello, Mike. Or should I say Nick? I like Nick, actually. Suits you. Mike always seemed a little pedestrian for you. And I'm Jeanette, by the way." She picked a leather badge case from her blazer pocket and tossed it to him. Hardin flipped it open.

"Agent Wilson. Nice to meet you."

"We'll see, Nick. We'll see."

Hardin stood, Wilson sat, some kind of charge building between them.

"I guess the time was never right," she said. He didn't have to think about what that meant. "I'll be here when the time is right" – those were her last words to him, all those years ago.

Hardin didn't know what to say. "After Esteban, I just, I don't know. I didn't feel like I had the right."

She nodded. "I wish… I guess I wish a lot of things."

They looked at each other for a long time. She was leaner than she had been, harder. The long black hair he'd loved was cut back to a few practical inches. Hardin tried to see what he used to in her eyes, but there was nothing to read.

"I was thinking about looking you up," Hardin said finally.

"If you had looked for Juanita Sandoval, I would have been a little hard to find."

Hardin closed the badge case and flipped it back to her. "I guess," he said. "DEA, huh? Is Hernandez in this already?"

She nodded. "Your prints turned up at a crime scene and word got around. That and you were on *Oprah*. You stick a pen in some guy's neck yesterday?"

"That depends."

"On what?"

"On who's asking. If it's Agent Wilson, then I guess I need a lawyer."

She set the badge and the gun down on the desk next to the chair. "It's just me."

"OK, yeah. The guy was fixing to shoot me at the time, though."

"Well, you got a lot of people looking for you."

"I was hoping I might be kind of hard to find, too."

Wilson gave a little snort. "Took me about six hours. Of course, I had an idea of where to start looking. But how long before someone else is showing the kid down at the desk your picture? And you'd better hope that someone is just a cop, not one of Hernandez's people. And not one of Corsco's people."

"Guess I'll just have to keep moving," Hardin said.

"How long do you need?"

"A day, maybe two."

Her face went still for a moment, her mouth half-open like she had something to say but had to weigh the words first.

"So my place. No one will be looking for you there."

The statement hung between them a long moment. Hardin shook his head.

"There's no way I'm putting you in the middle of this. I can make it through tomorrow. If you want to do me a favor, then just walk away. If you can't do that, then take me in. I'll go. There's no way I'm hurting you. Not again."

A hard smile from Wilson, her hand moving from the armrest of the chair to the desk next to the S&W. "Hurting me? You're assuming you could."

She sat, he stood, each of them looking at the other, neither of them knowing what to say next.

"I used to think what it would be like," he said, "seeing you again. This isn't what I expected."

"You were thinking a husband, a couple of kids?"

"Something like that."

"Tried the husband thing," she said. "Didn't work out."

"Why not?"

She locked her eyes on his, held his gaze. "Because I kissed this guy goodbye at an airport a long time ago. The goodbye part didn't take." She stopped for a moment, their eyes still locked. "I've thought about seeing you again, too," she continued. "I've thought about that a lot. I've thought about how every good moment in my life falls on the other side of the day you got on that plane. And I lived with that because there was no way not to." She stopped again, then said, "This isn't just your decision."

Hardin felt something turning in his gut, wondered if it could really be like this. She'd been a kid, he'd barely been more than that, and all of it was most of a lifetime ago. Her picture in his wallet all these years, that had been a talisman, a fantasy. And now here she was, and she was no one that he remembered. He thought of some of the things he'd done, what doing those things had made him. And yet for a moment the years were gone. She got up from her chair, took a step toward him, he took one toward her. He went to put his arms around her, but she reached up, put her right hand flat against his chest, her eyes finally leaving his, looking down.

"I'm not who I was," her voice cracking just a little.

He pulled her hand from his chest and held it to his mouth, kissed her palm. He felt her shiver. He lifted her chin until their eyes locked again.

"Who is?" he said.

CHAPTER 29

Lynch was at the UC with Reagan, watched the last couple players skate off the ice before the anthem. Lynch'd always been a baseball guy, a Wrigley guy. Besides, the Wirtz family had acted like such dicks for so long, who wanted to put any coin in their pockets?

Lynch hadn't been to a Hawks game in years. Back when they sucked, you could get in at the old stadium cheap. But old man Wirtz finally died, the Hawks got their organizational heads out of their asses and won the Stanley Cup. Now they were a tough ticket.

Seats were halfway up the mezzanine. Reagan had some fancy-ass camera, some kind of digital SLR rig with a big zoom on it. He was pretty good with it. With newspapers cutting back everywhere, being good with a camera was one more way to keep yourself employed.

Lynch noticed a bit of a commotion up in one of the luxury boxes on the other side of the stadium. Thought somebody looked familiar.

"Hey, can I borrow the camera a second?" he asked.

Reagan handed it to him. He looked up at the booth, cranked the zoom.

Shamus Fenn. Couple other people Lynch knew, too. Davis, one of the old-line aldermen, guy that was always on the edge of every new corruption probe and somehow always ended up not being in the indictment. Couple of union big shots. Some young looker was chatting up Fenn, running her hand up his arm. Another guy was standing next to her, looking pissed – guy she'd come with, probably. Then somebody grabbed Fenn by the arm, pulled him aside. Lynch couldn't see who it was – the looker and her date were in the way, having words. Whoever had grabbed Fenn had his back to Lynch. Shorter guy, in a suit. Whatever this was about, Fenn didn't look happy. Finally, the suit guy turned to leave and Lynch caught his profile.

Lynch clicked the shutter, hoping it worked. Damn camera had more buttons and knobs on it than the space shuttle.

"How can I tell if I got anything?" Lynch asked.

Reagan took the camera, brought the shot up on the screen. Fenn and the suit, clear enough.

"Shamus Fenn and Gerry Ringwald," Reagan said. He lifted the camera, squeezed off some more shots. "Jesus, Davis, some of Corsco's union buddies. It's like an asshole convention up there."

"Yeah," Lynch said.

"You get an asshole convention, somebody ends up with shit on them."

Lynch didn't say anything, but he was thinking about Fenn turning up in that video with this Hardin fuck, about him turning up here now with some mob lawyer, about the dead mob guys down at South Shore.

"You got an interest here?" Reagan asked.

Lynch didn't have any kind of off-the-record deal with Reagan. "Watch the damn game," he said.

"I bet if I looked like Johnson, you'd have an interest."

Lynch just smiled.

CHAPTER 30

Bahram Lafitpour twirled the wine in the glass, took a deep sniff, and then shook his head at the sommelier.

"I'm afraid we'll need another bottle," he said. "This is a little corky."

The sommelier kept a straight face, which impressed Munroe. He wasn't sure which bottle Lafitpour had ordered exactly, some kind of Bordeaux, but in the quick look he'd had at the wine list, he hadn't seen anything much under $300 a bottle, and had seen more than a few that went for four figures. Lafitpour was a four-figure kind of guy.

"It is an earthy vintage, sir. Perhaps you'd care to taste it first?"

Lafitpour looked up at the man with a thin smile that shriveled Munroe's sack just a little. Lafitpour was still a scary bastard.

"The scent was proof enough. I don't need to taint my palate. But if you doubt my judgment, you are free to taste it."

The sommelier raised the glass, sniffed, took a small sip, set the glass back on the table and made a disapproving face. "You are correct, sir. Of course. A new bottle, immediately."

Lafitpour nodded at the glass. "And a new glass."

The sommelier took the glass and scurried off.

"Never actually seen that done before," said Munroe. "Anybody sending the wine back."

"The wine wasn't spoiled, but it wasn't the 1982 I ordered, either. Eighty-two was a banner year, which is why they can charge that ridiculous price for it. They saved a label from one of the few bottles of the '82 they've actually sold and swapped it out for a bottle from an inferior year. Your average tech geek looking to impress some girl he could never hope to bed without his money will order it to show off for the lass and never know the difference. He'll like the poorer year better anyway. Not as aggressive, a little less tannic, more suited to his pedestrian tastes. I suppose I could have just accused them of fraud, but that would have caused a scene and we would likely have been asked to leave. He now knows I know, I've saved him the embarrassment of calling him on his little charade, and he will bring the proper bottle."

Munroe shook his head a little. "You haven't changed much, Bahram."

Lafitpour shrugged. "A little older, a little wiser."

"And considerably richer."

The thin smile again. "Oh, considerably."

Munroe had first seen Lafitpour in Tehran in 1978. Lafitpour was a rising star in SAVAK, the Shah's notorious secret police, and Munroe was an unofficial liaison trying to help the Shah stuff the Islamic revolution toothpaste back in the tube. The demonstrations and strikes had already hit critical mass, though. It was clear the Peacock Throne was circling the drain.

But Lafitpour had built an impressive string of assets throughout the country, so Munroe greased the skids on getting him out. The mullahs would end up running the joint, but Uncle Sam would still want some ears on the ground. Lafitpour had settled in Chicago and made a

huge fortune in the hedge fund business, huge even by
hedge fund standards. There'd been some noise about his
methods, but Lafitpour was careful, and he had friends
in the right places. Munroe was one of them. Given
the Iranian involvement in Munroe's current situation,
Lafitpour had been one of his first calls when he hit
town. Munroe asked him to keep his ears up. Not that
Lafitpour had called back.

The sommelier returned with the new bottle. Lafitpour
went through the necessary ritual, nodded his approval,
the sommelier poured the wine and left. Munroe took
a sip. He could see Lafitpour's point on the aggressive
business. Munroe was sure it was great wine, but he
expected that he and the tech geek would both have
been happier with a cheap Merlot.

"Your friend with the diamonds," Lafitpour said, "this
Hardin? The Russians have been in touch. He's looking to
sell and they'd like me to front the deal. They are offering
$20 million, of which I will keep five. So fifteen on your
friend's end."

"Probably better than Stein offered," Munroe said.

"Probably."

"When?"

"I met Hardin this afternoon to check his sample and
offer terms. I assumed you would still need some time to
make your arrangements, so I scheduled the exchange
for the day after tomorrow at my office."

Munroe nodded. "So we can grab Hardin then. Want
to add a little wrinkle, though. Suppose you actually
made the deal, this Russian money, where's it going to
look like it came from?"

Lafitpour smiled his thin smile again. "The money
will have bounced through several wire transfers at
dependable banks in various countries where secrecy

is still taken seriously, despite the Justice Department's recent best efforts. It will appear to have come from thin air."

"What if I want it to look like it came from somewhere else?'

"Such as?"

"What if I wanted to make it look like it came from Jamie Hernandez?"

"The cartels?"

Munroe nodded.

Lafitpour shrugged. "They are cursed with cash. Of the curses one can have, that's among the best, of course, but it does complicate their lives. They run so much currency through so many laundries that those of us in the financial game have a pretty good idea of who has been washing what, and where. Yes, I can make the money appear to have come from Hernandez."

Munroe thought it through. They had the video on al Din; they'd have the diamonds; they'd have Hardin, who could either recite the right lines or his corpse could offer the mute testimony of Munroe's choosing. It was moving faster than he would have liked. It would be nice to have al Din in the pot too, but Munroe had long since learned about birds in the hand. You have one, you give it a good squeeze, crush the son of a bitch. Hold a live bird in your hand too long, the thing will shit in your palm and fly away. This was probably as good as it was going to get.

"OK," Munroe said. "I'll start clipping loose ends. This will have to get official quick though. I need a public face, a behind-the-podium guy. Somebody who can wrap this whole thing up tight in a flag and make the press salute it. This is your town. Suggestions?"

"Alex Hickman. New US attorney in town."

"He our kind of boy?"

"I have regular dealings with Mr Hickman and have contributed substantially to the political coffers he won't admit to having as of yet. He's proven most useful running interference when the SEC gets a little nosy. He is our kind of boy."

"Can you set up a meet?"

"Lunch at my home tomorrow, shall we say one?"

"You don't have to check with him?"

Lafitpour smiled. "Once a dog is sufficiently well trained, you no longer have to check when you say come." Lafitpour took another sip of the wine. "One question. If this is all going to be pitched as some drugs-funding-terrorism deal, could you arrange the snatch at a location other than my office? It would reflect poorly on my business."

Munroe's turn to smile. "But why, my friend? You have been working undercover in association with elements of US intelligence for months helping to set up this breakthrough in the War on Terror and the War on Drugs. You will provide the inside knowledge concerning how Al Qaeda, Iran and the cartels are cooperating in their money movement and money laundering. You are an American hero, an Iranian immigrant showing your gratitude to this great nation that is the font of your fortune. Just the sort of guy, when the shit hits the fan and we destabilize the Khamenei regime, state might look at to head over to Tehran and run the place, after the free and fair elections, of course."

"Of course," Lafitpour said. "I'd forgotten. But I still take my five million."

"Fine," said Munroe. "But you pay for dinner, I can't afford the wine."

In the cab back to the hotel, Munroe's phone pinged – dossier on Tony Corsco. Thought on that a minute. If everything went according to plan, they should have Hardin in the bag within forty-eight hours. But sometimes things didn't go according to plan. Besides, this business with Hardin and Corsco, it had to be about the diamonds, and Munroe needed to know what kind of word was floating around out there, make sure there were no stray narratives in the mix on game day. Anyway, there was no such thing as too much information or too many assets. So he'd set up a meet with this Corsco fuck. Dossier had a lawyer's name – Ringwald. Work it through him, make it easier. Munroe figured if he gave the lawyer a sniff of his bona fides, it would grease the skids. And he'd had to lean on the mob before– that Carmelo dick out in New York – so he could play that card if he needed it.

CHAPTER 31

Wilson and Hardin barely made it in the door of her condo. She turned to Hardin, clasped her hands behind his neck, her mouth covering his like it was the only way she could breathe. And then she was opening his shirt, and he was reaching for her belt. When he undid it, the weight of the S&W in the hip holster pulled her pants to the floor, the gun hitting the tile with a *thunk*, and Hardin said, "Jesus, I hope the safety is on."

Wilson pulled back for a moment – her eyes on his, sad all of a sudden and a little afraid – and he could see that this was no time for jokes, that she couldn't take it, not if this didn't mean to him what it meant to her.

Then his own pants were dropping, and they were both just flesh. She was unfolding herself like a Cubist sculpture, all of her surfaces – thighs, crotch, stomach, chest, mouth – pressing against him desperately, like she wanted somehow for every square inch of her flesh to press against every square inch of his. He felt the naked admission of her hunger, and he remembered all the other women – a girl in high school, the Marine groupies outside Camp Lejeune, a couple of African girls, the Peace Corps volunteer in Lagos, the economics student from the Sorbonne who he imagined for a time he might have loved – and realized that he had been nude with women before but that he had never been naked. He

155

had never surrendered his distance. He had made love from behind his mental battlements, like a sniper, and this time it would be hand-to-hand, mouth-to-mouth. This time it would cost him a piece of himself.

Then they fell onto her bed, and she wrapped her legs around his waist, her feet pressing down onto his buttocks like hands, and she was already wet and hot and open and he was stripped of every pretense, any idea beyond this moment. He felt himself being drawn into her as if he could somehow spill not just his seed but his entire person into her, and he knew this was the beginning of a private religion. It was the moment in which they became each other's gods.

When they were finished, they both lay on their backs, separate, no longer touching. And then she rolled over, and she took his face in her hands, and she kissed him gently, but for a long time.

"Last time you kissed me like that you were saying goodbye," said Hardin.

"I'm not going anywhere this time," she said, rolling off the bed and standing up. "Just to the john."

Hardin watched her cross the room, the dim light leaking through the Venetian blinds, falling in stripes across her back like the contour lines on a map. Hardin held it in his mind, knowing what a perfect ass would look like if you ever mapped one. He felt the sheen of sweat drying on his skin. All of it turning in his mind, the perfect satisfaction of this moment, the lost years, her brother's ghost.

Then she came back to him, lying on the bed, no effort to cover her nakedness, her head on his shoulder like a part of him that had been missing his entire life.

He'd told her all of it – Fenn, the blackballing, the diamonds, and everything else from all the lost years.

And she told him. Hernandez never came for her. She was just another *puta*. Her parents had both died within a year, after Esteban. They never came back from that. She couldn't stand to look at the town anymore. She got in her car one day, started west on 88, turned south on 35 at Des Moines. The car broke down in Wichita. She got a job waitressing, started taking classes at Wichita State, married a guy with a heating and air conditioning business. People couldn't live without their AC in Wichita. She graduated with a Criminal Justice degree at WSU, hired on with the Wichita PD. Her husband felt emasculated having a cop for a wife, and the marriage came apart pretty quick, mostly because she really didn't care. She was Jeanette Wilson by then, though. Five years later, she joined the DEA in Texas, three years there, lots of violence, too much violence, had been shipped up to Chicago two years ago.

"You were probably supposed to tell them, huh?" said Hardin. "About Hernandez?"

"Yeah."

"Any reason you didn't?"

A pause. "Options, I guess. I always figured there might come a day where things could go one way or the other. And if they went a certain way, maybe it would be better for me if a review board wasn't pawing through my baggage."

"Pretty sure you're supposed to tell them about me, too."

"Pretty sure."

He ran his hand across her face, brushing her hair aside. She kissed his palm.

"So where do we go from here?" she asked.

"South Pacific, Tahiti, in around there. Lots of places down there where my French papers will fit in good. Especially when I've got $15 million to go with them."

She ran her hand over his chest, it resting right over his heart, her fingers curling an uncurling through the hairs on his chest. "Beach bums, huh? Not going to get boring? After the Legion and everything?"

"I'm willing to give it a try," he said. "We can always look up the local DGSE guys; go sink a Greenpeace boat or something. If we get bored."

She didn't say anything for a moment.

"But after we kill Hernandez," she said.

"Right," said Hardin. "After that."

CHAPTER 32

In Starshak's office the next morning, Lynch filled them in on Fenn, Ringwald, the scene at the hockey game.

"Puts Fenn back on the front burner," said Starshak.

"Yeah," said Lynch. "There's more. Remember that gangster thing they filmed down on the south side maybe seven, eight years back? *Cal Sag Channel*?"

Bernstein nodded. "One of Fenn's first big pictures."

"Guess who's listed as a script consultant," Lynch said.

Starshak snorted. "You're gonna tell me Corsco, right?"

Lynch nodded. "Word is Fenn and Corsco, they got pretty tight. With all the chicks hanging around Fenn, he'd get Corsco pussy, and Corsco would keep Fenn in coke."

"Nice symbiotic relationship," said Bernstein

"So maybe this Corsco thing with Hardin? Payback from Fenn out of that Africa bullshit?"

Starshak shook his head. "Big shot celebrity like Fenn taking out a mob hit over some bad PR? Guy's got to have serious snakes in his head to take that kind of risk."

Lynch shrugged. "Weird-ass shit for sure. You got something else that ties Corsco to Hardin, I'm all ears. But Hardin and Fenn, so far as we can tell, they've intersected exactly once and some famous crap happened. Now we got them in the same town at the same time again, and we've got crap happening again."

"Occam's razor," Bernstein said.

Starshak gave him a blank look.

"Occam was a medieval philosopher. He posited that the simplest explanation for any given set of facts is usually the best explanation, even if it seems unlikely. Hardin and Fenn have a history. Fenn's got a reputation as a hot head. Fenn knows Corsco. Corsco made a play for Hardin."

"Just seems so fucking stupid," Starshak said.

"Imagine that," Lynch said. "Hollywood types acting stupid."

Starshak grunted. "So check it out. Something else to rattle Corsco's cage with anyway. Speaking of which, you talk to him on this South Shore business yet?"

Lynch shook his head. "He's ducking us. Lawyer says he's out of town."

"OK, you brace Fenn," said Starshak. "I'll call Ringwald, put a boot up his ass, tell him he doesn't get Corsco to show up soon, we'll go for a subpoena."

"Another thing we haven't thought enough about," said Bernstein. "This second guy, Mr .22."

Starshak nodded again. "Ideas?"

"Refugee makes it Africa," said Lynch, "and that makes it Hardin. Except this guy is shooting everybody but Hardin."

"Which, if Hardin really has some diamonds, maybe makes it about the diamonds," said Bernstein.

"What do we know about those?" Starshak asked.

"Checked on it a little," said Bernstein. "The conflict diamond issue was way bigger ten, fifteen years back when the civil war in Liberia was still going good – how a lot of those guys got money for their weapons. Your mainstream diamond guys – De Beers, the Russians and whatnot – they put this certification system in place.

Kimberley Certificates, to cut down on the black-market business. So if Hardin has uncertified diamonds, he'd have to work through an insider to get them into the system."

"Was Stein an insider?" Starshak asked.

"His family started out in diamonds, back in New York. A lot of Jews in that business," Bernstein said. "He'd know people."

"But how did Hardin know Stein?" asked Lynch.

Bernstein shrugged. "Don't know. Stein, he was real tight with Israel, traveled there a lot. Hardin, we know he was in the Middle East with the Marines. But we don't know what he was up to for quite a while after that."

"So one way or another, Hardin got some rocks off of somebody," said Starshak. "And this .22 guy, maybe he's trying to get them back?"

"Something's still off," said Lynch. "Hardin had just left Stein when Mr.22 showed up and popped him. And Hardin had just been down at South Shore when Mr .22 shows up there, pops another guy. He's after Hardin, how come he's following him around, shooting everybody else?"

"Don't know," said Bernstein. "One other thing? On the diamonds? You've had Lebanese merchants all over Northern Africa for centuries, and they've always been active in the diamond business. Hezbollah, guys like that – a lot of them are out of Lebanon."

Starshak rubbed his face with both hands for a minute, blew out a long breath. "So we got Stein, who's tight with Israel. We got maybe some terrorist types, who don't like Israel. And got this Hardin guy with a big hole in his history."

"Yep," said Bernstein.

A little pause.

"That philosophy razor of yours, you got anyway to shave this down?"

Bernstein shook his head.

CHAPTER 33

It was Corsco's lawyer's office, but Tony Corsco sat behind the desk, leaving Ringwald, and this Munroe guy to take the guest chairs. Ringwald had called him at 7am, sounding a little panicked, insisting he take a meeting with this Munroe fuck. OK, so he was here. But Ringwald was a pussy. Good lawyer, but a pussy. No way was Corsco showing his ass for this Munroe, whoever he was.

"I'll be blunt," Corsco started, wanting to get the first word in, wanting this guy back on his heels. "I'm not used to being summoned to meetings, not on this short notice, and certainly not with your disrespectful attitude, but my lawyer strongly advised that we speak, so I'm here. However, I am a busy man. Whatever your business is, get to it directly."

Munroe turned to talk to Ringwald. "I gave you a number to call. Did you check me out?"

"Yes," Ringwald said.

"Then fill this asshole in. I don't much care for his attitude, either. And I'm not the one with his dick in the wringer."

Corsco's face reddened and he started to rise from his chair, but Ringwald held up a hand.

"Tony, he's from the government, well sort of the government."

"The Feds?" said Corsco. "Is there a warrant?"

Ringwald shook his head. "Not the Feds. The intelligence side of things."

Corsco looked puzzled. "What? CIA? NSA? What?"

"His role appears to be, eh, unofficial. But you need to listen to him. Please."

Munroe finally turned to face Corsco, who was still half standing, his hands on the desk. "I solve problems. I'm not FBI, I'm not NSA, I'm not Agency. I'm not anybody. But I can have anybody I want – Justice, IRS, name it – so far up your ass so fast that you'll think you're back in the prison showers. Or I can make one phone call and you'll be gone by morning. Not just dead. Gone. Jimmy Hoffa gone. I don't send dumb-ass goombahs like you sent after Hardin, I send Navy SEALs. Now sit the fuck down and listen to me, because this is not a negotiation."

Corsco sat.

"What's your business with Nick Hardin?"

Corsco forced a smile. "I'm sure I don't know what you're talking about."

Munroe just nodded and took out his cell phone, hit send, put the phone on speaker and set it on the desk. A voice answered.

"It's for you," Munroe said to Corsco.

A voice on the phone, sounding a little panicked. "Tony? Do what he wants. Whatever he wants. Do that, you're OK. Don't, then we're all against you, all the families. I shit you not, Tony. You want no part of this guy. We've dealt with him before."

"Carmelo?" Corsco said, puzzled.

"Just do what he wants."

Munroe reached out and killed the connection and put the phone back in his pocket.

"What's your business with Nick Hardin?" Munroe repeated.

Corsco looked at Ringwald. "I'm supposed to stick my head in a noose for this guy, Gerry? That's what you're telling me?"

"I have, eh, assurances that Mr Munroe's involvement is of an, eh, entirely extrajudicial nature. There are no legal ramifications attached to this conversation."

"Extrajudicial," Munroe said. "I like that. So, Hardin?"

Corsco opened and closed his mouth a couple of times. "A favor for a friend," he said, finally.

In one smooth motion, Munroe reached inside his coat, pulled out his small, flat Walther, the suppressor already attached, leveled it across the desk and fired, the pistol making a soft bark, the round smacking into the leather of the high-backed chair just to the right of Corsco's neck, so close that it left a crease in the padded shoulder of his suit.

"Jesus!" Corsco gasped.

"I got no time for twenty questions," Munroe said. "So I'll ask one. Guess how many times I can shoot you from here without hitting anything vital?"

Corsco's eyes went wide. "Fenn! Shamus Fenn! Fenn wanted Hardin whacked over that Africa business!"

Munroe's turn to be surprised. "The actor?"

"Yeah."

"What's Fenn got to do with the diamonds?"

"What diamonds?"

"You said the Africa business."

"That Darfur thing. Hardin punched Fenn out, it got on all the news shows, comedians ragging on him, nearly crashed his career."

Corsco and Munroe looked at each other across the desk for a moment. Munroe remembered the Darfur thing. Just never imagined it had anything to do with this.

"What diamonds?" Corsco asked.

"Diamonds?" said Munroe. "Who said anything about diamonds?" Munroe slipped the pistol back inside his jacket. "OK, here's the deal. You guys work for me now – and by guys, I mean your whole organization. First thing, get Fenn under control. There are major issues at play here, gentlemen. Great men in important places are thinking big thoughts. In the end, there will be one story. I'll get you your lines if you're cast for a part. But I don't need some punch-drunk actor pissing on my narrative. Fenn's your problem, you solve him. But if Fenn fucks up my play, I'm charging it to your account."

Munroe took a cell phone out of his pocket, put it on Corsco's desk.

"That rings," Munroe said, "it's me. And you answer it. I don't care if you're throwing a hump into the missus, you climb off and say hello. And there's one number on speed dial – mine. I want a line on this Hardin. This is not optional. There is no Plan B. You found him once, find him again. I don't get some kind of useful intel out of you, then maybe you're dead, or maybe I just send a tape of you confessing to putting a hit on Hardin to the DA."

Munroe got up, headed for the door.

"Tape?" Ringwald said. "DA? You said this was off the record."

Munroe pulled a small digital recorder from his pocket and wiggled it at the two men. "I lied," he said. "I do that sometimes."

CHAPTER 34

The crew for Fenn's picture had staked out the vacant lot on Wells between Randolph and Washington – a mess of trailers parked there with semis loading and off-loading all day, fucking up traffic, a chain-link fence up around the lot to keep the rubberneckers out. Lynch badged the guy at the gate, him and Bernstein getting shunted to some gofer. Kid made half a dozen calls on his handheld, finally took them over to a trailer to see Fenn.

"Shamus Fenn," said Fenn, getting up off the couch along the far wall, his hand out, wearing a pair of chinos and a dago-T, guy obviously spending some time on the weights. Half smile, just a regular guy. "What can I do for you fellas?"

Lynch caught the look from Bernstein. Fenn was playing it all wrong, playing it cool. Cops come to see you and you don't know what it's about, you should be nervous.

"I'm Detective Lynch. This is Detective Bernstein. We're working a homicide. A few of them, actually." Leave it there for a second, see where Fenn went.

Fenn turned his palms up. "I'm not following you here, guys. Somebody I know?"

Bernstein took a picture of Hardin from his pocket, screen grab off the *Oprah* video, handed it to Fenn. "Know this guy?"

Fenn took the picture in both hands, flopped down on the couch, head falling forward, elbows on his knees, picture dangling from his hand.

"Yeah. Yeah, I know him. Nick Hardin. He's dead?"

"We don't know. He's missing."

Fenn blew out a breath. "Look, you guys obviously know what went down with him and me or you wouldn't be here. But I really don't know what to tell you. I haven't seen Hardin since, well -" Fenn held up the picture "- since this."

"Yeah," Lynch said, "we saw the clip on *Oprah*, you and Hardin. And now both of you are in town. Curious, you know?"

Fenn nodded for a long time, not like he's agreeing with Lynch but like he's agreeing with some conversation in his head.

"I can see you guys coming to talk to me," Fenn said. "But I really got nothing for you. Honest to God, last time I saw Fenn, he was busting my nose. And I had it coming." A sigh, a pause. "Look, you guys, you got real jobs, so I don't expect you're keeping up with *People* magazine, don't know what you've heard about me lately. I've been a dick most of my life. I'm trying to get in front of that now. The shit I pulled on Hardin, back in Darfur? What can I say? I took the spotlight off the benefit there. God knows what that cost the poor SOBs in support. And this Hardin guy? He lost his gig over my shit. Seemed like a stand-up guy. If he ended up in something desperate, I mean on account of me, then I gotta carry that too, you know?"

Fenn looked up, eyes filling.

Lynch nodded. "How about Tony Corsco? You talk to him?"

"What makes you think I'd be talking to him?"

"Because he sent his lawyer to brace you at the Hawks game last night. Gerry Ringwald. I saw you two chatting. You didn't look real happy."

Another nod from Fenn, a weak smile. "Your town, right? Gotta figure you'd have it wired. And I gotta learn that my shit is all gonna come back on me. Gotta stop trying to step out of the way."

Fenn got up, went to a fridge at the back of the trailer, pulled out a bottled water. "You guys want anything? All I got is water and juice, trying to stay away from the booze for a bit."

Lynch shook his head.

"OK," Fenn said. "Tony Corsco. I made another picture here a while back, *Cal Sag Channel*? You guys see that?"

Lynch shook his head again.

"Anyway, it was a mob pic, and we had Tony in as, I dunno, kind of a consultant, I guess. What I heard, also he maybe had some money in the picture. Anyway, me and Tony, we hit it off pretty good. This was back in my asshole days, OK? Seemed like a safe source of coke, knew places in town where you could… well, let's just say misbehave. He likes the ladies. I'm ashamed to say, a couple of the girls working the picture – not the A-list talent, you know, but the kids with two lines, trying to break in, the ones who got hired on their looks, think they're gonna grow up to be Meryl Streep? They see me hanging with Tony, and Tony's making his play on them, and I'm going along with it – not exactly saying it's gonna help them out, you know? But not saying it isn't, either. Anyway, I know he did at least a few of them. And he came out to LA a couple of times, looked me up, we'd party, girls would see us…" Fenn looked up. "I really need to go on?"

"You need to tell me why Corsco's got his mouthpiece bracing you at the Hawk's game, yeah," Lynch said.

Fenn nodded. "We set up here for this shoot, and I start getting the calls from Tony. And I'm not returning them. I mean, I'm trying not to be who I was; I don't need Tony Corsco in my life. Guess I should have at least called him back, though. This guy last night, what did you say his name was? He didn't introduce himself."

"Ringwald," Lynch said.

"OK," said Fenn. "He's at that box – local guys with money in the picture – he pulls me aside, asks me who the fuck do I think I am not returning Tony Corsco's calls. I should have manned up, talked to the guy, I guess. Anyway, this Ringwald, I told him, I was out of that shit. I told him to tell Tony."

Fenn looking up now, the tears again, holding Lynch's eyes. Lynch thinking that you could put this guy on a box and he'd flatline the sucker. That right at this moment, Fenn probably actually believed this shit.

"See, what I was thinking?" Lynch said. "This Darfur thing? You took quite a beating over that. Got to thinking maybe you blame Hardin. Maybe you see Hardin here in town. Maybe you think a guy like Corsco, he could even up the score for you."

Fenn sighed. "One thing I've learned through all this, I can't help what people think. And some of the shit I've done? People are going to think some bad stuff. I'm a changed man, Detective. You believe, you don't, nothing I can do about that."

"You don't really know much about Hardin, do you?" said Bernstein.

"Just that he was Jerry Mooney's fixer over in Darfur," said Fenn.

"Before that, he was in the Marines for two tours, including Gulf War I, scout sniper. Know about scout snipers?" Bernstein asked.

"What we hear, the French Foreign Legion after that," added Lynch. "Those are some bad-ass boys, too. And we know this. Guy named Stein got shot at Chicago Stadium the other night. Hardin's the last guy we know who saw Stein alive. We also know two of Corsco's soldiers picked up Hardin. They were armed, he wasn't. He killed one of them with a ballpoint pen. He disarmed the other guy and bounced rocks off him for a while before that guy got shot. Gotta figure he knew who they were working for before he was done. So this Hardin? He gets the same ideas about you that I got, it may not matter much if he's right."

Fenn's head down again. "You reap what you sow. Still learning that, Detective." He looked up again. "Is there anything else?"

"Not for now," Lynch said. "Just hope if I come back here it isn't to look at your corpse."

After the cops left the trailer, Fenn got up, walked to the fridge, and pulled out another water bottle, the one he kept full of Ketel One. Hands shaking a little as he sat back down on his couch, he took off the top. Jesus. That fucker Hardin.

CHAPTER 35

Alex Hickman dabbed at the corner of his mouth with a napkin that felt like it had twice the thread count of his shirts – and he spent a lot on his shirts. He always felt a little like a hick with Lafitpour. Couldn't figure why, except that Lafitpour had more money than God.

"Wonderful meal, Bahram. Unusual. Never had anything like that before," said Hickman. Some kind of chicken thing, cherries in it, some kind of spice that Hickman couldn't place. Good, but a little odd. Hickman was more a T-bone and martini guy.

"Albaloo polow," said Lafitpour. "My granddaughter is learning some of the recipes of my youth. A touch heavy on the saffron, but she is learning."

The other guy, Munroe, tossed his napkin on the table, leaned back in his chair. "Well, she's getting it down, Bahram. Pretty sure the Shah served this once at a little shindig I was at in '78, and it was just as good this time."

"She did well," said Hickman. "How is Hilary?" He'd heard rumors, maybe a suicide attempt, some kind of health crisis. She had been in and out of the dining room of Lafitpour's condo, serving the meal, clearing the plates. Hickman found that a little odd, given the size of the staff Lafitpour had. She used to be a fixture on the Chicago party scene, little Paris Hilton streak in her. Then this incident, whatever it was, maybe a year back. And now here she was, serving dinner.

"Thank you for asking, Alex," answered Lafitpour without answering. Hickman knew better than to press. You could talk to Lafitpour all day, leave not knowing what month it was.

Lafitpour raised his voice slightly, said something in Persian. Hilary brought in a new bottle of wine, poured a sample for her grandfather, waited for his nod, then poured a glass for Hickman and Lafitpour before retreating to the kitchen.

"Shiraz," said Lafitpour. "I am partial to this vintner."

"It's very good," said Hickman.

"Shiraz is named for the Persian city, did you know?"

"No."

"We have been making wine in Persia for more than seven thousand years," said Lafitpour.

"Probably not so much anymore," said Hickman. "I mean with the Ayatollahs and all."

Lafitpour's eyes flashed a little, just a hint. "One of the benefits of a culture seventy centuries old is the ability to take the long view. You Americans, always so impatient. These Arabs and their religion, probably visions Mohammad had in a fever after catching a disease from sleeping with his camels. Look at them. More than a century of oil wealth now for these ridiculous herdsman, and they have done nothing. Their countries make no products, develop no technologies, contribute no knowledge. They can't even run their own oil fields. They have to pay foreigners to do it for them. All they have done is build palaces to hold their egos and use their religion to make slaves of their women. Take their oil away, they will be back living in tents and fighting over their patches of sand in a decade."

Hickman let that ride, took in the view of the lakefront, sweeping south toward the Loop. Lafitpour had the top

two floors in one of the best addresses on Lake Shore
Drive. Hickman knew he was here for a reason, and that
Lafitpour would get to it when he got to it.

Hickman had done Yale Law, a couple years with Justice
in DC, State's Attorney in New York, a few years in the
FBI. Now he was the new US Attorney for the Northern
District of Illinois. Hickman understood the game. It was
all about name recognition. High-profile cases, that was
his ticket, and he intended to ride that ticket all the way
to Pennsylvania Avenue. All he needed was something
national; international even better. So when Lafitpour
called, he was all ears.

Munroe turned toward Hickman. "When you got your
invite, I assume you checked me out?"

Hickman had checked with his sources in Justice, at the
Bureau, even some of the guys from the Joint Terrorism
Task Force in New York. This Munroe, everybody knew
him but nobody was quite sure whose org chart he was
on. A player, though, and at the big boy table. Outside
the lines maybe, but everybody said his word was good.
Hickman nodded. "Bio's a little fuzzy around the edges
maybe, but word is you're a player."

"Good," said Munroe. "Saves me some song and
dance time. Here's the thing. Bahram got approached on
something that's turned out to have some real interesting
connections. You heard about the Stein murder, right?"

"Sure," said Hickman. "You got an in for me on that,
I'm all ears."

"Alex," said Lafitpour. "Have you heard the name
Nicholas Hardin?"

Hickman shook his head.

Munroe filled Hickman in on Hardin, the noise that
had filtered in around the Stein killing, the mob killings,
and now this Hernandez business.

"Sounds like this Hardin is having a bad week," said Hickman.

"That's what the police know, and the DEA," said Munroe. "Here's something they don't know. This other man, the second shooter? His name is Husam al Din."

"And?"

"That translates to the Sword of Faith," said Lafitpour. "He is very skilled. Hamas, Hezbollah, Al Qaeda, they've all used him. But he is run out of MOIS in Tehran now."

"Khamenei's got a pet shooter running around the US?"

Lafitpour took a sip of his wine. Paused a moment. "It is more complicated than that. Al Qaeda has money, billions from Bin Laden alone. But it is impossible for them to move it in traditional fashions."

"Sure," said Hickman. "After 9/11, we froze any account anywhere that even had their scent on it."

"Diamonds are one of their options," Munroe said. "They're small, they're valuable, and they're easy to move." Munroe filled Hickman in on the diamond trade, the Lebanese connection, the ties to Al Qaeda and to Iran.

"And Hardin stole some of their diamonds?" Hickman asked.

"Not just some," said Munroe. "Look, Mossad has been watching the Al Qaeda diamond play for a while. Stein was working with Mossad. Used his network to suck the Al Qaeda couriers into bogus brokers, and then the couriers would get whacked and Mossad would take their stones. So Al Qaeda stopped taking delivery for several months until it was sure it had arranged a safe exchange. This shipment that Hardin hijacked? It was worth north of $100 million."

Hickman let out a low whistle. "No wonder he's attracted so much attention."

"Yes," said Lafitpour. "The gravity of mammon."

"But still," Hickman said, "if we can catch this al Din, then we can tie him to Tehran, right? We've got an Iranian operative killing US citizens on US soil."

"We've got more than that," said Munroe. "This Hardin, he's got a history with the Hernandez Cartel. They know he's on the ground here, and they're looking for him, too."

"I'm not following here. What's that got to do with the diamonds or this al Din?"

Munroe took a slow pull at his wine, sat back, smiled a little. "That's the big question, isn't it? From a certain perspective, what we have here is a major Al Qaeda financing operation, the Hernandez Cartel sniffing around it and Tehran's top trigger man riding shotgun on the deal."

Munroe paused, took a sip of wine, settled further back in his chair. "You've got some idea of what I do, right? Wanna know the three things that keep me up nights? First, has some fundamentalist Islamic yahoo finally gotten enough scratch together to do something really bad, and I don't mean knock down a couple buildings with airplanes. I mean make a mushroom cloud someplace. Second, what's Tehran going to do once they have the bomb, because they're going to, sooner or later? And, third, how do we keep Mexico from turning into a narco state? There are a couple hundred other things I worry about, if you want the full list, but those are the top three. Now, if we control the narrative on this cluster fuck, then what we have is the cartel, Al Qaeda, and Tehran all in bed together engaged in a terrorist conspiracy that includes killing US citizens on US soil. We have an Iran problem, we have an Al Qaeda problem, and we have a Mexico problem. We play this right, we get out in front of all three of them."

Hickman sat back, digesting that for a minute. "Are we maybe missing the bigger issue here? We've got Al Qaeda looking to put better than $100 million in operating capital in play all at once. Shouldn't we be asking why? We've got a major potential terrorist operation, maybe in Chicago, given that al Din keeps hanging around, and you want to muddy the water with some ginned-up cartel connection?" said Hickman. "I'm all for playing hardball, but not if it means we're giving this al Din guy a chance to make the Loop glow in the dark. Don't we need to focus on him?"

Munroe shook his head. "Al Din wouldn't be hanging around if he had an op ready to run. He'd pull the trigger and blow town. That means he needs the diamonds to make it go. Hardin bounced their shipment before it got a hundred miles, and every time al Din turns up, he's sniffing around after Hardin. Al Din isn't here to pull the trigger on 9/11 the sequel. He's here to pull the trigger on Hardin and get the rocks back. We stop that, we stop whatever plot they were going to use the stones to finance."

Hickman thought. Made sense, and this cartel/Al Qaeda/Iran thing, it could work, seen in the right light. "This Mexico to Tehran by way of West Africa thing, there anything to it?"

Munroe shrugged. "Is there? Dunno. I doubt it. Could there be? Sure. Hey, you wanna make the world safe for democracy, you gotta break a few eggs. I'm in the egg-breaking business, and I'm inviting you into the kitchen. I just gotta know if you can stand the heat."

It was Hickman's turn to take a drink. The man was asking if he wanted to plunk his chips down at the big-boy table. If he did, he'd either come out flush or busted. Hickman thought about Munroe's scenario for a moment, and Munroe's track record. From what he'd heard, Munroe had been pulling this type of shit for something like forty years without ever once popping up on anybody's radar. If you're going to go all in, those are the type of odds you want on your side. Thing worked out, he'd be looking at lots of the right kind of face time in all of the right kind of places. And Illinois had a Senate seat opening up.

"What's my role?" Hickman asked.

"Stage manager," said Munroe. "Hardin's meeting with Lafitpour tomorrow night. Once we've got him in the bag and we feed him his lines, then we go public. We need somebody on the scene who knows the local players and can herd the cats. What I hear, that's you. You need to picture the end game here, the press conference. Somebody's gonna be the face behind the podium when we break the biggest War on Terror story since 9/11. Except this time, instead of shaking our fists in the rubble, we're taking a victory lap and waving around some big-name scalps. You want in, then the face behind the podium is yours."

Hickman pushed his chips into the pot.

"OK, I'm in," Hickman said. "But I'm not just your pretty face. You want me to manage things, fine. But we have to do this right. You need to get an official skin on this ASAP. The snatch tomorrow? That's got to be on the record. Get your intel boys to dummy up whatever you need, but I need it tonight. I'll need a warrant, then I've got to brief the FBI and DEA, get them both on board to make the grab. For those guys, credit comes down to who makes the bust, so we want everybody covered in glory, make sure we don't have any inter-agency sniping later if somebody gets jealous. If you freeze them out on grabbing Hardin, then he's not their bust and they have no reason to play ball if anything unravels. Put their faces on the arrest, then they've got a dog in the fight and they'll back your play."

Risky, Munroe thought. Too many people inside the tent too early. But Hickman was right. Give the Feds credit for Hardin's scalp, then they'll help Munroe make it fit on any head he wants.

"Done," Munroe said. "I'm going to put you in touch with Langley, they'll get somebody official out to sit in on your briefings tomorrow, somebody who knows the game plan. Bahram, do you have your story together on the money?"

"Broad strokes, but they will hold up. All I have to do is point the FBI forensic accounting people in the appropriate direction. Once you tell them Hernandez and Al Qaeda are cooperating on finance, they'll find plenty of overlap between their organizations. With the volume of cash Hernandez has to move on a daily basis, and assuming he prefers to do so through banking channels that are not focused on collecting personal data and transmitting it to taxing authorities, then he and Al Qaeda will inevitably be moving money through the same institutions. Switzerland perhaps, the Caymans, the Channel Islands, some of the new players in the South Pacific, Vanuatu and the like. The FBI will find the overlap."

Munroe smiled. "And that will make it their discovery, not something we fed them. Those ambitious fucks, give them a couple of days and they'll be swearing up and down this was all their idea."

Munroe sat back in his chair, warm feeling in his gut. This thing had more moving parts than a Swiss watch, but it ticked like one, too. This was going to work.

CHAPTER 36

Al Din watched the exodus of office workers. Impressive, like watching a nature documentary on the migration of great beasts, a relentless stream of capitalists and their minions, pouring from the doors of the office towers, heading to the elevated trains, to the commuter trains, to the tens of thousands of cars that were jammed in the Loop parking garages. Herds of pedestrians as far as he could see.

Each one of them a perfect delivery vehicle.

Al Din watched from a chair in the window of a Starbucks on Madison near Michigan, a messenger bag at his feet, three of the devices inside, the adhesive attached, ready to be placed. He had placed two yesterday. He checked his watch, took a final sip of his coffee, and then stepped out the door into the flow of commuters to flag down a cab. The cab would drop him right at the door to the target location, and the cameras at the target would go down in seven minutes. He'd make sure the cab ride lasted until then. He could have walked, but it would be best not to turn up on any cameras between here and there in the meantime.

After today, he would have five devices in position. The sixth device was still locked in its case in his hotel room. Should activating the devices prove his best course, then the five would be more than sufficient. Tens of thousands dead at a minimum, even if the Americans responded effectively. Hundreds of thousands dead potentially if the devices worked as Heinz had planned.

So Al Din would keep the sixth device in reserve. What was the name of the American children's game? Show and tell? He might need the last device for that. Once he decided which side he was on.

CHAPTER 37

Lynch put his book on the nightstand, *Devil in the White City.* He was just reaching to turn out the light, when his phone buzzed. He picked it up and checked the screen. Liz. Clock on the phone said 12.42am.

Lynch answered. "How's LA?"

"Jesus, these people, Lynch," she said.

"That's what you said about Washington."

"Yeah, well, I'm not in Kansas anymore. Can't even see it from here. They want to make the book into a thriller. I told them it was a news story."

Lynch let out a little snort. "Was kinda thrilling, the way I remember. I got shot a couple of times."

"Yeah, well, this movie shit ain't happening, not if they can't play this a little straighter." Pause. Something harder coming up. "Got a call from Dickey Reagan."

"Saw him the other night," Lynch said.

"Took him to the Wild game."

"We call it the Hawks game down here."

"Got those tickets for me, didn't you?"

Lynch went to say no, figured BS it, defuse things. Then he figured they didn't face this it would just eat them up anyway.

"Yeah," he said.

He heard her exhale into the phone. "Jesus, John, why didn't you say something? I could have pushed this back a day maybe, moved some shit around."

Could have done that anyway is what Lynch thought, but there was a difference between not lying and being an asshole.

"Not that big a deal," he said. "Just a whim, figured I'd surprise you."

"I do appreciate the thought, John."

"I know."

Another long pause. More of those than there used to be.

"Look, I'm flying out of here tomorrow. I could stop over. Be late probably, but maybe grab dinner, spend the night anyway?

Felt like scraps to Lynch, felt wrong, didn't want to say that either.

"If it works out," was what he said. "I'm drowning in this Stein thing anyway, so I can't promise anything."

Pause again.

"Yeah, might work better when we can plan it out. Things should settle down in a few days. Guess I should get home anyway."

She had a place in New York now.

"Yeah," Lynch said. "You got enough shit on your plate. Look, it's late. I'm not on LA time. I'm dragging here."

"I know," she said. "Sorry about the time. Soon though, right?"

"Sure," Lynch said. "Soon."

He put the phone on the nightstand.

CHAPTER 38

Shamus Fenn sat in his room at the Peninsula, plowing through a bottle. He'd blown takes all afternoon. They'd been shooting a scene along the lakefront – his lover leaving him over all the blood on his hands, tricky emotional stuff that needed his focus. Instead, all he could think about was all the places that fucker Hardin could shoot him from. Jesus, a sniper? Really?

So what were his choices here? Call this Lynch back and roll over on Corsco? Right. Then what? Witness protection? Get a job as a fry cook in Omaha? Where the hell was Shamus Fenn supposed to hide?

Corsco's mouthpiece had told him Tony was pissed. Fenn doing the *Oprah* thing, pretty much putting his hand up and saying he had a beef with Hardin the same day Corsco's guys were trying to kill the guy on his dime. OK, that had been a dumb move. Fenn could see that. But there was nothing to be done about it now. Good news was this drug lord was after Hardin, too. Got Corsco off the hook, the lawyer said. Got Fenn off the hook. All they had to do was sit back and wait. But Fenn'd had no idea that Hardin was some kind of killing machine.

Fenn had called Corsco earlier, Tony pretty much laughing at him. Telling him he was a big pussy. Telling him this Hardin had a full-time job not being dead, didn't have any time to think about Fenn. Telling him Hardin

184

probably thought Tony's guys had been working for Hernandez anyway.

But Fenn wasn't sold. If this cop could put it together, then Hardin could put it together.

A knock on the door. Fenn almost shit himself. He ignored it. Another knock. A woman's voice calling out.

"Mr Fenn?" Little giggle.

Fenn padded to the door, looked through the peephole. He was in a suite at the end of the hall, the door looking all the way down to the elevators, so he had a clear shot. Nobody out there but a couple of hot-looking chicks, a blonde and an Asian. Fenn had a thing for Asians.

"Yeah?" he said through the door.

"Tony said maybe we should stop by? Thought maybe you might be a little tense? No hard feelings, he says."

Fenn thought a minute. He'd had to keep his pants zipped, at least by his standards, during this whole abuse thing.

"And he sent a present." The girl was holding up a little baggie of powder.

And he sure as hell couldn't chance hitting any of his usual connections for some blow. What he needed, probably. Put some mayo in a little girl sandwich, do a few snorts. Tony was right. This fucker Hardin had his hands full anyway.

Fenn opened the door.

Lynch looked at the clock when he heard the phone. *Jesus, 4.17am.*

"Yeah?"

"Get your ass up, Lynch," said McCord. "I'm down at the Peninsula. Your buddy Fenn just OD'd."

CHAPTER 39

"You ever hear of a Dr Mark Heinz?" One of the Google jockeys at Langley on the phone for Munroe.

"Nope. Should I have?"

"Probably not. One of the germ herders down at Fort Dix back in the Eighties. Been out of the game for a bit. Did his twenty, then left for some big pharma gig. But he's on the list of people to watch. Bottom of the list, but he's on it."

"And?"

"And he just turned up dead."

That got Munroe's attention. "Where and when?"

"Week or so back, far as we can tell. Guy had a ranch down near Santa Fe. Looks like he fell off a horse, hit his head on a rock. That's the local ME's take, anyway."

"Got a reason we don't like it?"

"Got an accidental death featuring a guy on the bad bugs list the same week you're looking for some kind of Muslim mischief, so there's that. Also, this ranch of his, it's not like Ted Turner's place or anything, but this thing had to set him back some. And the house he built, at first glance, that wasn't cheap. Maybe he made a killing in the pharma game, I don't know, we haven't taken his books apart yet. But this guy, he came into some serious dough somewhere, and it wasn't his pension from Fort Dix. Just feels like he's worth a sniff."

That was the free radical in this thing – what did the ragheads plan to do with the money once they got it? But, if what they had planned had anything to do with this Heinz character, and if he was already dead, then things might be further along than Munroe thought. Because if Heinz didn't fall off a horse, somebody'd just given him the loose-end treatment.

"Get somebody down to New Mexico," Munroe said. "See what they got. The autopsy especially. I need to know if this guy really fell off a horse. And talk to the AG; get whatever kind of Patriot Act mojo you need to turn this Heinz fucker inside out. I want a line on every cent this guy's ever made or spent. And look up his Fort Dix buddies; see what his deal was down there."

Time to make a decision here. Shut down this Hardin play and put the full court press on al Din in case something bigger was already in motion, or stick with the plan?

But al Din wasn't acting like he was running a terror op. The Stein shooting, the business down on the South Shore? Everything pointed at him chasing the diamonds. If he had what he needed to complete his op, he wouldn't be putting his head up like that, wouldn't be chasing Hardin around.

Besides, al Din had been in town for a week. If he had come to Chicago to start an epidemic, then Munroe wouldn't even be here now. The boys in the biohazard suits would be here filling body bags. Munroe would be somewhere else filling up more with whoever was responsible.

So, for now, he'd stick with the Hardin play. Worst case, and he was wrong? Then he'd run with the same story, but this time, instead of tying Iran, the cartels and Al Qaeda to a financing deal and a couple of murders, he'd tie them to a city full of dead people. Screw a long weekend with drones and the SEALs. Sure, he'd decapitate the cartels, but he'd also get Washington to pull the trigger on invading Iran and carpet-bombing Waziristan.

So, either way, several thousand potential civilian corpses aside, it was a win-win.

CHAPTER 40

"He gonna be able to talk to us any time soon?" Lynch was checking with the doctor at Northwestern. In the background, Fenn was laid out on an ER gurney, tubes running in and out of him, ventilator pumping away.

"You'll be lucky if he ever talks to anybody," the doctor replied. "Him just staying alive is touch-and-go right now. Then we have to see how much brain function he has left. Going to be a few days, anyway."

"Looked like he'd been snorting," Lynch said. He'd seen the rim of powder on Fenn's nostril. "Don't see ODs off that usually."

"With the stuff they brought in with him, you would," said the doc. "Absolutely pure. If he's used to tooting street junk, I'm not surprised this shorted him out."

"OK," Lynch said. Something to think about. "Gonna leave a uniform. Not sure this was accidental. Also, once the word gets out, you're gonna have press up the wazoo."

The doc shrugged. "Not my problem. They'll have him admitted or down in the morgue by then."

Lynch called McCord, who was processing Fenn's room. "Got anything?"

"Been drinking, it looks like," McCord said. "Got through half a bottle of Knob Creek, so that would help him along."

189

"Was he alone up there?"

"Fucking hotel room," McCord answered. "We'll dust it, but we'll get a million prints. He was nude when they found him. If he croaks we can check and see if he got his rocks off anytime recently. Bernstein's talking with the security guys, but no cameras in the hallways up here, so the best we'll get is maybe some lobby traffic."

"Tell Bernstein to have IT run all the faces against anything with Corsco's name on it," said Lynch.

"Will do."

Before Lynch could even put the phone back, it buzzed again. Starshak.

"Yeah?" Lynch answered.

"You guys done there?" Starshak said.

"Close," said Lynch. "Not much to go on. You got somebody from public affairs teed up? Gonna be a shit storm."

"Yeah. Got a mouthpiece on the way down. Fill him in. Then you and Bernstein get your asses down to the Federal Building. We have a meeting. Very mysterious."

CHAPTER 41

Seephus Jones leaned against the window of the commuter train, half awake. Up past three laying pipe with one of his baby mamas, this commuter crime shit killing him. Meant he was moving up in the world, though.

Seephus wasn't wearing his usual. Had a pair of Dockers on, polo shirt tucked in, pants all the way up like some white fucker or goddamn Obama or something. No bling. Stupid computer backpack thing. Course the bag had a kilo brick of blow in it, delivery for the dudes out in Aurora. That and his nine.

Delivery thing was Hernandez's idea, that's what his crew boss told him. Stick some brother in a tricked-out sled, baggy ass jeans, have him drive out to white Irish land with his lid on sideways, tags hanging off it, he was just asking to have some Bubba cop from Naperville popping his trunk just for styling on his roadway. Also, Seephus had to admit, most of the brothers weren't exactly Rules of the Road types, fucking stoplights and shit. Get too many busts coming out of traffic stops.

So Hernandez says get some of the more dependable dudes, guys got a future, dress 'em up all Cosby-like, stick 'em on the train – mix 'em right in with the commuters. Contact in Aurora picks 'em up at the station, they hook up with the LK dudes – guys that handle distribution for the western burbs – and pack the cash in the bag, hop back on the train downtown. Hernandez wanted them on the train early, reverse commuter runs, that way they got the most traffic to mix in with.

Like having a fucking job, though. Up at goddamn seven in the fucking morning.

But Seephus was cool with it. Meant the crew boss thought he was a player. Meant he got to meet the out-of-town crews, build out his network. Might even mean Hernandez knew his name.

Seephus knew one way to get on Hernandez's screen for sure – find this Hardin fuck.

Crew boss, he'd passed the picture around, let everybody know this was a major fucking deal. Didn't say what it was about, just that Hernandez wanted this fucker bad, and that any brother played a part in that, he gonna be one happy nigger. So Seephus had studied the picture good. He was good with faces. Little game he played on the train, watching the people get on and off, trying to remember who goes where. Like the guy up two seat on his right? Guy with that buzz cut white guys like when they start going bald, always got the iPod buds in his ears, always got the laptop open? Got on every morning in LaGrange. Got off at Route 59. Always had a Starbucks cup.

Little tired for it today, though, just leaning on the window, watching the word slide by. Wished he could sleep on the train like he seen so many people do, but he figured he nods off, somebody pinches his bag, he'd end up sleeping on a slab down at the ME's for good.

And then he saw Hardin.

Hardin was going stir crazy. Spent all the previous day in the damn condo. Him and Wilson eating all their meals take out, couldn't even get out, take a run, nothing. Made sense, all the people looking for him, but it was sawing on his nerves. Switched on the TV, switched it off again. Did another hundred pushups. Had to get out tonight, make his deal with Lafitpour. That should be scaring the shit out of him; instead, he was looking forward to it.

She had a lot of books, at least. He flipped the coffee maker on, checked out the shelves; saw *The Mosquito Coast* by Paul Theroux. He'd read a couple of his travel books and liked them, figured he might as well see what the guy could do with a novel. Coffee maker dinged. He poured a cup, walked out on Wilson's small balcony, sat at the little café table she had out there, watched the train pull in to the station.

CHAPTER 42

Seephus looked up again from the *Sun-Times* he'd picked up off an empty train seat when he jumped off. Proud of that move. Gave him something to do 'stead of just standing on the platform. Had the disguise on, he knew, but he still felt like the only brother at a Klan rally. Nobody seemed to be paying him no mind, though.

Been like half an hour now. He'd called in. Boss man told him just sit tight, he'd get a call. Couple of trains had come and gone, one going each way, him still on the bench on the platform. Fucker was still up there, though – second floor, second balcony in from the corner.

Seephus' cell went off: Tupac tone he'd downloaded. Seephus slapping at the phone, trying to shut that shit off, kinda thing get the whiteys looking at you.

"Yo?" He answered.

"Mr Jones, this is Jamie Hernandez…"

Seephus trying to listen through the cha-ching sounds in his head.

CHAPTER 43

Lynch, Bernstein, and Starshak walked into the room full of suits in the Federal Building on Adams. At the front of the room, the new US Attorney, Alex Hickman, was backslapping a handful of brass. Hickman was political as hell, always looking for a camera.

Hickman did the introductions.

Brad Jablonski from the DEA was there, gave Lynch a nod. Hickman's replacement at the Bureau, little guy named Tate, one of Hickman's coattail riders. Handful of other suits, just introduced as "out of DC." Could mean anything. Some gangs-and-drugs guys in from a couple of the larger suburban PDs; Perez, guy from Aurora that Lynch knew; guys from Joliet, Elgin. Wilson, the DEA agent from the last meeting, was in the back.

Hickman hit a switch, dimming the lights, and brought up a PowerPoint show on the screen. It was the same split screen shot Lynch had used, Hardin in his Marine Blues and the cop cam grab.

"Gentlemen, meet Nick Hardin..."

Hickman made his spiel, his DC suits chiming in to back him on a couple points. The diamonds, Hezbollah, the Al Qaeda connection. They threw some kisses out to Starshak and Lynch, blew a little smoke up their asses – kudos for spotting Hardin, running all this shit down in just a few days.

A new shot popped up on the screen. A grainy blow-up picture of some guy taken from a long ways off. Olive-skin, dark hair, on the slight side, a little Omar Sharif vibe to him. He was in a sport coat, open shirt, at an outdoor café somewhere, chatting up a looker in a sundress. Lynch noticed one of the suits, one Bernstein had been eyeballing, tightening up just a touch.

"Husam al Din," said Hickman. "Translates to the Sword of Faith. Intel we've got says he's freelance, pretty much the go-to shooter for fundamentalist Islam." Hickman looked at the Chicago PD contingent. "Lynch, we're pretty sure this is your .22 guy."

"When did you get this?" Starshak said, little edge in his voice.

"Relax, Captain," said Hickman. "This is brand new. We have a dossier for you guys. We're sharing everything we've got."

"Where'd you get it?" asked Lynch.

"Except that," said one of the suits. "We aren't sharing that.

Hickman made his case on Hernandez, claiming he was after Hardin not for personal payback but because Hernandez was playing ball with the Al Qaeda and Hardin had queered their deal.

"We've got two huge criminal organizations, one with substantial amounts of cash that it needs to launder, one with significant non-cash assets it wants to get liquid." said Hickman. "Fred, you want to give them a quick brief from the Treasury perspective?"

A short, heavyset woman got up, took over the laptop, bounced through a few spreadsheets, banks where they'd found overlap, transaction dates that tied together.

Starshak looked at the woman, then turned to Lynch. "Fred?"

"Probably lying about their names, too," Lynch said.

Lynch heard a soft snort out of Bernstein. "Smell a rat?" Lynch asked.

"It's BS. That much money moving around the system, the story would be if it hadn't crossed trails at one institution or another. Of course there's overlap. This isn't proof, it's spin."

When Hickman was done, Jablonski piped up. "Feels kind of out there, Hickman. We've been working Hernandez forever. Never caught a whiff of anything like this."

Tate, Hickman's new Bureau boy, cut him off. "There are other elements of this we can't share. But if we can put Hernandez and this al Din together, then we can throw the War on Terror net over the whole lot of them."

Jablonski shrugged. "Good by me. I've lost enough people to this asshole. You guys want to take him off and waterboard him for a few days, I'm not crying over it."

"Anybody else have questions?" Hickman asked in a tone that suggested no would be the appropriate answer.

"Yeah," Starshak said. "You got a reason I'm not supposed to be worried about some terrorist running around town? Shutting down this money laundry of yours is fine, but I'm kinda wondering about, oh, I dunno, shit blowing up."

"Our intel is that al Din is here strictly as security, protecting the diamonds on the way in and the cash on the way out." Hickman didn't look pleased.

"This the intel we get to know about or more of these other elements you can't share?" Starshak asked.

"The latter." Tate again, the head Feeb.

"We're gonna get something nice and official on that, right?" Starshak pushing it. "Something big enough to cover my ass with if something in town goes boom?"

Hickman smiled. "You're concerns are duly noted, Captain. And unwarranted." Little pause for effect. "Hardin is the key, gentlemen," said Hickman. "The good news is we should have him in the bag tonight."

Meeting wrapped up, a little milling around, Starshak, Lynch, and Bernstein edging out. Near the door, they were next to the Washington suits. Bernstein said something to one of them in Hebrew. The man turned, opened his mouth like he was going to answer, then just smiled and shook his finger at Bernstein.

"What was that all about?" asked Starshak.

"I used to do the Israel thing with the family every summer. Spent enough time over there to pick up that IDF feel on somebody. I told him to say hi to Pardo for me."

"Who's Pardo?" asked Lynch.

"Head of Mossad."

CHAPTER 44

Seephus Jones' stomach was twisting on him. After a while, it seemed like he shouldn't just sit at the station anymore, so he walked across to a coffee shop. He still had an angle on the condo. The yuppies ahead of him were ordering this shit in French or whatever, something-chinos, half this, dusting of that. Fucking coffee. Seephus needed a bump, he got a Red Bull maybe. Got to the front of the line, ponytailed white chick in the apron looking at him.

"That sounded good," Jones said, trying to blend, figuring he'd never get this cap-a-presso-chino shit the guy in front of him had just ordered straight. "Have me one of those." The chick putting this and that in a cup, running it through a blender, spraying shit on top. Stuck some kind of plastic dome thing on top of a big-ass cup, set it, down in front of him.

"That will be $6.50," she said.

Seephus knew places on the West Side he could get his hose drained for $6.50.But he just handed over the coin, got a seat outside, took a sip. Fucking coffee milkshake or something. Weird shit these fuckers do out here.

Hardin guy still on the deck, reading his damn book.

Another hour until Hernandez was supposed to show. Supposed to watch for a black Escalade. Hernandez said he would come down Warren, turn off on Main, park out of sight of the condo. Meet up with them there. Meanwhile, Seephus was just supposed to keep an eye out.

After a bit, he was done with his drink, already read what he could out of the paper, reading not being a big thing with him. He was starting to get looks from the ponytail chick, it coming up on lunch, people waiting for tables. So he went across to this pizza place, got a slice. Couldn't see the condo from there, so he took it back over by the station, found another bench, ate it there.

Then that Hardin fuck went back inside the condo. The door on the side of the building, on Main, Seephus could see that. But a big-ass building like that, there must be a lot of doors. Couldn't watch them all. So he started walking around, watching the front, watching the side. The cha-ching sounds in his head were gone now, replaced with thoughts about what Hernandez was gonna do to his ass, he shows up and this Hardin had booked on him. The pizza and the damn coffee shake were rolling around in his gut now, on top of the malt he'd throated last night.

Wilson raced back to her condo after the meeting, unlocked the door and walked in; saw Hardin standing by the sliding door to the patio, looking out across the tracks.

"How well do you know this Lafitpour guy?" she asked.

"I don't," said Hardin.

"Somebody sold you out. We're going to grab you tonight, at your meet."

"We?"

"Interagency deal, us and the Feebs. Some kind of War on Terror bullshit, the cartels and Al Qaeda cozying up to launder money or some shit."

Hardin nodded, still looking out the sliding door. Black guy in the red shirt was still out there, wandering around, kept looking at the condo, getting real twitchy. "We might have a more immediate problem," he said.

Hardin told her what he'd seen, the black kid hanging around, watching the condo. Wilson opened her closet, reached up on the top shelf. She came out with a couple spare clips for her S&W and dropped them in her pocket.

"Let's go," she said.

"You're not in this yet," said Hardin. "Not to where you can't back out."

She froze. Then she turned and looked at him, her face set hard. "You son of a bitch. After eighteen years, you come back, I bring you home, I spread my legs for you and you say that to me?"

"I just don't want to assume–"

"Fuck assume. We're together or we aren't," she said. "I thought you understood that."

They stared at each other for a long moment, neither moving.

"We're together," he said.

She nodded, reached up and touched his cheek, then turned for the door.

He grabbed his duffle and they left through the garage. Didn't see the guy in the red shirt.

CHAPTER 45

Hernandez sat in the passenger seat of the Escalade. Julio was driving, Miko, Gomez, and Roberto in the back. They were dressed to mix, but Hernandez worried a little about them all being in long sleeves, it being pretty warm. But the ink the rest of them had up and down their arms, anybody knew how to decode that, they'd have Five-O up their asses in a heartbeat.

He had a picture of Jones from the guy who ran his West Side crew. Julio was cruising down Warren, a little under the limit, starting to back traffic up behind them. Hernandez saw Jones, off to the right. Told Julio to turn down Main. Saw Jones get up, start to follow. Julio cut into a little alley on the left. Hernandez and the three in the back got out, and Julio got ready to drive on, start circling, wait for Hernandez's call. Jones turned the corner, jogged up.

"I'm Jamie," Hernandez said, putting out his hand. Seephus reached out and Hernandez took his hand, grabbing Seephus' forearm with his other hand. "I owe you, brother. You ready to do this?"

Seephus nodded. "Got my nine in the bag here. Thought maybe I should toss the bag in the car, though. Got that brick in it still and all."

Hernandez nodded. Seephus shucked off the backpack, dropped it on the passenger seat, unzipped the top,

pulled out his Browning Hi-Power, and shut the door.
Julio took off.

"What I want," Hernandez told them, "is to spend
some time with this guy. So we go up to his place, show
him he got no chance. Then we call Julio, he pulls up,
and we walk the fucker out."

Seephus nodded. "What if he don't play, though?"

Hernandez shrugged. "Time with him is what I want.
What I need is the fucker dead. He don't play, we put his
ass down."

CHAPTER 46

Bobby Lee's brain was racing, trying to think of something he could give this guy that might keep him alive.

Bobby'd been taking a little break. He'd made a good chunk running a quick background check. It was a nice day out, and he'd run up to that Italian joint on Washington, one that made the good sammies. Got himself a beef-and-pepper combo he'd brought back to his place. Figured he'd sit out on the patio in back, watch the whiteys golf for a bit.

Which was when the skinny guy in the linen sport coat walked around the corner of his place, a .22 along his leg with a silencer on it, asking if they could step inside and have a word.

Now he was in his boxers, duct-taped to his office chair, blood pooling on the floor, and his left foot hurting like hell where the guy had cut off his little toe with a pair of pruning shears.

"Man, makes no difference if I tell you anything, you still gonna fucking kill me," said Lee.

"You know that's not true," said Husam al Din.

"You already cut off my fucking toe. Whaddya mean I know that's not true?"

Husam sighed. Americans. No experience with this sort of thing, he supposed. "Precisely because I cut off your toe. The psychological impact of a finger is far greater – and the nerves in the fingers are more sensitive. But you need your fingers to do your work. And my employer values your work. So I will leave you alive and relatively intact if you give me that option."

Husam was actually a little surprised. He didn't have faith in MOIS to do much besides identify his targets and wire his fee. But he knew the Mafia people who had tried to kill Hardin must have gotten intel from the same source he had. They, too, had found Hardin's car. So he had called MOIS and asked them to find the source. They'd gone back through their middle man; someone had hacked through some complex security and tracked down the IP address. And here he was.

"Employers?" Lee blurted. "Who you working for, man? Let's get 'em on the phone, sort this out."

Husam shook his head. "You don't deal with them directly."

"OK, OK," Lee said, thinking maybe he'd get out of this just down a toe. "Just tell me what you need."

"I need to know everything you have given out on Nick Hardin, and everyone you have given it to."

Lee quivered. "Jesus, buddy, you gotta know I can't be ratting out people like that, or they'll be by, start cutting parts off, too. I mean, whoever your guy is, you think he wants me telling anybody who shows up what he got?"

Husam al Din reached down and slid the blade of the shears around the fourth toe on Lee's left foot.

"Fuck you doing, man?" Lee shouted. "You don't gotta… JESUSFUCKINGCHRIST!"

Husam cut off the toe. These were fine shears. He'd bought them at the Home Depot store on Route 59 and they cut through the bone with almost no resistance at all. He would have to pack them when he left. He liked these shears.

"I'm not negotiating," said Husam. "You can give me answers or body parts. And I have done this sort of thing before, many times. I know the people who will tell me what I need and those who won't. You already know you are going to tell me. You are just wasting toes."

Lee spilled – about Corsco, about Hernandez, all of it.

"But you don't know where Hardin is now?" Husam said, leaning forward a little, opening the shcars.

"NO! Man. Fuck no. I mean, I told you. My main gig is Chicago, right? Got eyeballs on everybody down there. Out here? I mean, I can hack systems and shit, been running checks on his Hardin ID, on that Fox ID he used. But I got nothing."

"All right," said Husam, fitting the shears around the next toe.

"FUCKFUCKFUCK! Hey, wait! One more thing. I mean probably nothing, right? But I got a call from Hernandez's guy like an hour back, wanted me to run a check on an address. Turned out to be some chick who works for the DEA. I mean, I didn't tell you cause I figure that's just day-to-day stuff for him, nothing to do with Hardin that I can see, but I mean that's something, right? I'm not holding back on you here."

Husam pulled the shears away from Lee's foot, sliced the tape off Lee's wrists, and turned the chair toward the computer terminal on the desk.

"Print out that address."

Lee clacked away at the keys for a moment. A printer to the left started spitting out a sheet.

Husam al Din shot Lee three times through the back of the head, close enough that one of the slugs punched through, coming out Lee's eye socket, blowing some gore onto the monitor. Amazing what these Americans would believe. He pulled another of the disposable cell phones from his pocket and called a number in Tokyo.

"What do you need?" Al Din asked.

"Are you at the terminal?" answered the voice on the other end.

"Yes."

"Good. Sit down. This will take a few minutes…"

Al Din followed the instructions from the hacker – not the MOIS middleman, but his own contact, one he had used before. After several minutes of entering commands, his contact told him he had what he needed – he could access the Chicago system remotely now. Al Din alone would have access to the surveillance system – not the Mexicans, not the Italians, and not his friends in Tehran. If knowledge was power, sometimes you became more powerful not by learning something yourself but instead by insuring the ignorance of your enemies.

"This system," al Din asked, "you can use it to find specific people?"

"Maybe," said the voice on the phone. "If you've got a good photo and you can narrow down the locations I have to search."

"I'm texting you a picture," said al Din. "He would be in a local hotel."

"OK," said the voice. "If he's in a hotel covered by the cameras, I'll know in a few hours."

Al Din ended the call, pulled up the picture he needed on his phone and sent it to his contact. The Stein murder, the stolen diamond shipment, these things would not escape the notice of Western intelligence agencies. And the size of the shipment would raise alarm. Mossad, they would know about the shipment, and they would want al Din's head for Stein. They weren't beyond operating in the US on their own, but most likely they would work through channels. Their relationship with Washington was too important to them. But how would the US react? Officially? Or had they sent Munroe?

If this was being pursued through normal channels – the theft of the shipment noted, the intel routed to Langley for threat assessment, notices forwarded to CIA residents in the usual places, and then to the FBI for domestic processing, perhaps some coordination with local authorities regarding Stein – then it was just business as usual. The CIA was very good at what it did, but it was bureaucratic, which meant it moved slowly and, to anyone who had dodged them before, somewhat predictably.

But if they had sent Munroe, that was another thing entirely. In al Din's twenty years playing this game, Munroe was the only man who had ever gotten close to him – and he'd done it twice. Al Din's Japanese friend would run the picture, then al Din would know.

Al Din grabbed the sheet from Lee's printer. The address was in Downers Grove, the next town east and on his way back to the hotel. Worth a stop.

CHAPTER 47

Seephus Jones would get his payday. If you want to keep the troops motivated, they have to know that you will hold up your end. But Hernandez hadn't been to war with Jones. He didn't want any second-string talent fucking this up. Julio, Roberto, Miko, Gomez, they'd all shed blood for Hernandez before, theirs and others.

"Jones, you take the corner here," Hernandez said as they got to the side of the condo building. "Watch the garage, watch the side door. You see that fuck coming out, you put him down and call me. You got it?"

Jones nodded, a little relief on his face, the kid not ready for combat. Hernandez knew he'd made the right call.

The condo was on the second floor. Guns out now, Hernandez and Miko took the elevator; Gomez and Roberto took the stairs, just in case. Middle of the day, the building was quiet.

Husam al Din was sitting in the easy chair in the living room of the woman's condo. He had been there for almost twenty minutes. When he arrived, he had knocked on the door, double-checked the paper he had taken from Lee.2B. He had the right door. The hallway was empty, so he stood and listened for a few minutes. He knew what an empty room sounded like. The woman was a member

of the American drug police, so she would be concerned
with security. It took a few minutes with the picks. He
took the .22 from under his jacket and eased the door
open, waiting another moment for any reaction. None.
He stepped in and looked at the back of the door. There
was a thumb lock she could throw when she was inside,
one no one could access from the hall. That's when he
knew for sure no one was home. She would lock that if
she were here. He shut the door. He searched the rooms
briefly to see if there was anything to learn. Then he sat
to wait for the woman to return. Perhaps more to learn
that way. He had the shears and the duct tape in the
messenger bag on the floor next to him.

Roberto and Gomez went up the stairs quickly, Gomez
moving into the hall first, then motioning for Roberto.
The stairs came out one door away from 2B.The elevator
was at the far end of the hall. They would have to wait a
moment.

Hardin and Wilson watched from a table in the window of
the coffee shop, saw Hernandez's group come up Warren.
Hernandez left the scrawny kid in the red polo shirt at the
corner – the same kid Hardin had seen hanging around
the last few hours, eyeballing the condo.

"Looks like you were right," said Wilson.

"Paranoia pays," said Hardin. "You see the Escalade
anywhere?" He'd watched the black SUV turn off of
Main, the kid following it down to the alley.

Wilson shook her head.

"So there could be another guy or two we can't see,"
Hardin said.

"Yeah," said Wilson

"Sorry," he said.

"For what?" she asked.

"I shouldn't have been on the balcony. Dumb move."

"Fuck that," she said. "Water under the bridge."

Hernandez's cell buzzed again, then the ping that told him he had a text. It had buzzed a couple times as he walked up the street, but he wasn't taking calls right now. Only a few people would text him, though. It would be a second before the elevator got there. He checked his screen.

OWNER OF 2B IS A DEA AGENT

Shit. A trap? They bring this Hardin in to set him up? He hit the speed dial for Gomez. No answer. He was about to call Roberto when he heard the gunfire upstairs. He called Julio instead, yanked Miko out of the elevator, and headed for the door.

Husam al Din had waited long enough. There were very few papers in the apartment, nothing that told him anything. A few pictures, the same attractive woman in several of them, must be the drug agent. The woman would probably not be home until the end of the workday, and the building would be more crowded then. Probably not the time to have the kind of discussion he would need. He would come back later, pick up her trail, and find an opportunity. He opened the door to leave.

Roberto was looking down the hall toward the elevator when he heard the door to 2B open behind him. He and Gomez both brought up their 9mms. But it wasn't Hardin, and it wasn't the woman. It was a slight man, a bag slung across his back. They paused.

The man did not. He dove to the floor in almost a somersault, right between Roberto and Gomez.

Gomez snapped off a shot, missing the rolling man, hitting Roberto in the foot.

The man had a gun out now from inside his coat.

Roberto couldn't stand on the damaged foot, but he knew if he went down he died. He leaned back against the wall, weight on his good foot, and fired at the rolling man. But the man never stopped to aim his weapon. He just bounced off the far wall and rolled again, back across the hall.

Roberto's shot punched into the drywall while the man snapped a couple of rounds into Gomez's abdomen. Gomez stopped, looking down at himself like he was surprised he wasn't dead. Then he started to swing his gun back toward the rolling man.

The man kicked into Roberto's bad foot, the pain fogging Roberto's vision as he fired again. The round punched through the carpet, hit the concrete, and whined down the hallway, Roberto tottering away from the wall, between the man and Gomez. The man fired again, one, two, three shots, firing from the floor almost vertically up into Roberto – one of the rounds tearing into his groin, two into his stomach, burning upward.

Roberto went down, and the man shot Gomez twice in the forehead.

Down the hall, an old lady opened her door, stuck her head out. Al Din's gun flashed up…

Hardin and Wilson looked up simultaneously. Gunfire.

"Your place?" Hardin asked.

"Has to be," she said.

Across the street, Red Shirt was looking up at the building, then looking down the street, then pulling out a cell.

"Not gonna be any good way for you to explain this," Hardin said.

"I know," said Wilson. "I think I just became a person of interest."

"Guess we should go," he said.

Hardin had left the black Honda he bought in Aurora a couple blocks north of the tracks. They headed for that.

As they turned up the sidewalk, tires squealed behind them. The black Escalade spun off Warren and up Main, the driver looking over and seeing Hardin, veering toward them. Hardin shoved Wilson up the street, behind a parked car, and pulled one of the 9mms he'd taken from the Italians. He braced his feet, sighted carefully down the barrel, and put six shots in a cluster just above the steering wheel. The engine stopped racing as the driver's foot left the gas, and the car straightened out a little, slowing, crunching into the corner of the parked car next to Wilson.

Red Shirt was sprinting across the street, pistol out, ducking down. As the kid cleared a parked car onto the walk he brought his gun up, snapping off shots. Hardin heard Wilson fire from just behind him and to his left, saw some spray fly off the kid's hip. The kid went down, his gun rattling on the walk. Hardin turned to see Wilson coming out of her crouch, her S&W in hand.

All up and down the street, people where scrambling into stores, ducking behind cars, lots of cell phones coming out.

"Let's take the SUV," Hardin said. "Get a little distance, walk back for the car later."

Wilson nodded. Hardin opened the driver's side door, the Hispanic behind the wheel slumping out. Two in his head, at least two in his chest. He was gone. Hardin dumped him in the street.

He looked up. Wilson was standing over the kid on the walk. The kid was squirming on his back, holding his hands out in front of him. The kid's 9mm was just off to his right.

"I got nothing 'gainst you, lady. I was after that other guy."

"He's my guy," she said.

The kid's hand moved toward his gun. Wilson gave him a double-tap to the head, put the S&W back on her hip, turned and climbed into the SUV.

"Don't ever shove me like that again," she hissed. "You have to trust me to cover your six, not go all Sir Galahad on me."

"Sorry."

Her head swiveled, checking Main as they pulled out. "You see Hernandez?"

"No."

She slammed a fist on top of the dash. "Fuck. FUCK FUCK FUCK FUCK FUCK!"

Hernandez and Miko heard the shots from the far side of the building and jogged toward the corner. They got a view just in time to see the SUV blow north up Main, Julio down in the street, the kid down on the walk. They instantly turned and started walking west.

"Walk up a bit, call the LK crew out in Aurora, have somebody pick our asses up," Hernandez said.

Miko nodded.

"No uniforms, nobody in raid jackets closing the ring. This wasn't any DEA sting."

Miko nodded again.

"Gonna have to think on this."

Miko nodded again. Nothing to say.

CHAPTER 48

Hardin punched it, shooting up a block, turning in, winding through a neighborhood, creating some distance before the cops got to the scene. Wilson had gone quiet.

"That was a little cold," he said. "The kid."

A pause. "Yeah," she said. Strange look on her face, lip quivering a bit.

He waited.

"I got called out on a domestic my third week on the force down in Wichita, some beat-to-shit rental house." Wilson was talking, looking straight out the windshield, perfectly still, nothing moving but her mouth. "We get inside, in the kitchen, this guy's got his wife in a half nelson, got a butcher's knife to her neck. The kids are screaming, the wife's eyes are rolling around, and the guy's yelling about how nobody leaves him. My training officer stays in front of him, holding his attention, and I work around to the side. At one point the guy starts gesturing with the knife, waving it at my partner, trying to make some point, and my partner gives me this look telling me to take the shot. I mean, it's like three feet – no way can I miss. And instead I start talking to the guy, trying to calm him down. I get him to drop the knife, to let the woman go, he lets us cuff him, and everybody tells me what hot fucking shit I am.

"So by the time the whole thing goes through the wash with the DA, the thing's been pled down from attempted

216216 GREED216216 GREED

GREED

murder to some domestic violence deal. The guy does two-and-a-half years on a five-year jolt. Two-and-a-half years and two days later, I get 911'd back to the same address. The woman is duct-taped to a kitchen chair, both the kids lying on the floor with their throats cut all the way to the spine. The woman's gutted like a fish.ME tells me he did the kids first, made her watch. The guy called it in himself. He's sitting in the recliner in the living room when I get there, six empty Bud cans on the floor. And he tells me, 'I told you nobody leaves me.'"

Wilson stared straight ahead, her face frozen. Hardin silent for a moment, looking for the right words.

"That's on him," Hardin said finally. "That's not on you."

She shook her head. "The first time? When I was a rookie? I knew. I looked into his eyes, and I knew. I knew, and I didn't take the shot. I didn't take the shot because I wanted to sleep nights. I guess I thought I could get through without ever having to kill anybody. I didn't take the shot for me. So yeah, the woman and those two kids? They're on me. They're on me for not having the balls to step all the way up."

They drove for a while. Out of the corner of his eye, Hardin could see her jaw clench and unclench, could see her lip quivering.

"All I know is this," she said. "People get a choice to be on the right side or not. You come up on somebody who's made the wrong choice, then you have to step up, every time. You step all the way up."

She still had that look on her face, like she wasn't done. Hardin didn't know what to say.

"That black kid?" she said. "His mother should have told him not to play with guns. And whoever told him he could, they should have told him not to play with me."

Her voice was thin and brittle, and he knew she was locking that kid away somewhere inside. She was tying another knot into a cord, a knot for the black kid on the same cord where she had tied a knot for the woman and her kids and for her brother. A cord she would whip herself with every time she failed to perfect an imperfectible world.

He thought of Africa, of the Legion, of maybe a dozen times they'd been called out for some piss-ant action because some thug somewhere had tweaked some tribal bullshit for his own venial ends. It usually ended with a mess of kids, most of them younger than the one Jeanette had shot today, stinking in the heat with their guts blown out, some of them blown out by Hardin. He'd always told himself that even a postcolonial anachronism like the Legion was on the side of the angels when it came to dealing with the Idi Amins of the world. Except it was never the Amins that ended up showing their guts to the sun.

He took her hand, and she squeezed it like she could force some kind of hope out of his pores.

And then it was over. She pulled her hand away, her face solid and unmoving now, like quick-drying cement. Her foot nudged the backpack on the floor of the passenger side. She picked it up, unzipped it.

"You want to know the bright side?" she said.

"Could use one," answered Hardin.

She pulled the shrink-wrapped brick out of the backpack. "Now we've got the diamonds and at least a couple million worth of coke."

CHAPTER 49

Gonna end up in Iowa, way the day's going, thought Lynch. He was stuck in traffic on 88 coming up on the Route 59 exit, trying to get out to meet Perez and the Aurora PD at a scene out there.

The Downers Grove thing broke loose right after lunch. Jablonski had called Lynch and Bernstein out pretty much as soon as he got a look at it. Three Hispanics down. Based on the tattoos, looked like all three of them were mainline members of the Hernandez crew out of Juárez. And Jablonski knew the guy they found in the street – Julio Ruiz, trigger man, wheel man, guy that usually traveled with Hernandez himself. They also had a black kid who turned out to be a low-level member of one of the West Side gangs that the DEA was pretty sure was tied into the Hernandez network.

Thing was a cluster fuck. Two cartel gunmen and a civilian dead in a second-floor hallway, two outside on the street. The inside stiffs all looked like.22s. The outside guys were larger caliber – 9mms it looked like, at least until they heard different. Witness statements were all over the place as usual. Best they could piece together, the shooting was in the building first, then outside. Couple of people said it looked like a black SUV (got everything from a Navigator to an Escalade to a Suburban on the model) tried to run down a couple on the sidewalk. The man shot the driver. The black kid ran across the street, shooting at the couple, and the woman shot him. Ruiz was driving the SUV, and whoever shot him knew what he was doing, because Ruiz took three in the face and two in the chest, which ain't bad through a windshield when you've got three or four tons of Detroit's finest bearing down on you. Then, while the guy was dumping Ruiz out of the SUV, the woman walked over, capped the kid in the head. Then her and the man hopped in the SUV and took off. They found the SUV dumped about a mile north.

So a couple of interesting things. The shootings inside? It looked like Mr .22 was in play again, although this wasn't his usual triple tap to the head. Stand up fight. The two guys were armed, both got shots off, and he took them both out.

But the real interesting thing was this. The guy who shot Ruiz? Based on descriptions, it sounded a lot like Hardin. And the women he was with? Well, the dead guys were right outside a condo with the door still open. Jeanette Wilson's condo. And things were calming down just a touch by the time this woman strolled down the walk and parked one in the black kid's braincase. Jablonski had shown Wilson's picture around. Consensus was, the woman was Wilson.

That's when Perez had called. They had another stiff, a black guy in the basement of a town house in the DuPage County part of the Aurora, just west of 59.Guy had a deal with one of those Merry Maids crews where they had the keys to get in if he wasn't around. When they let themselves into his place, they found a bigger mess than they had contracted for. Looked like a .22 again. So Lynch left Bernstein to finish up in Downers Grove and headed west.

••••

Aurora was a city of almost 200,000 straddling the Fox River about forty miles west of Chicago. Lynch didn't work with suburban cops too much, but Aurora had its own gang problems, and most of their gangs were tied in to the Chicago gangs. So guys from Aurora would turn up dead in the city, guys from Chicago would turn up dead in Aurora, and guys like Lynch and Perez, they'd sort it out.

Every time Lynch had been out to Aurora before, though, it had been on the east side, usually right in by the river. This was some high-end subdivision just across 59 from Naperville. Goofy-looking McMansions were shoe-horned into tiny lots as he followed the winding street in past the White Eagle sign. He was beginning to think Perez was fucking with him until he saw the black and whites and the crime scene tape in front of an upscale townhouse. Behind the house, a couple of yuppies in ill-advised pants pretended to take practice swings, standing in the fairway while they watched the cops moving around the house. Somebody on the tee must have said something – one of the guys looked back flipped the bird, then topped his ball another thirty yards toward the green. Gapers' block on the fairways.

Lynch parked, badged the uniform at the end of the drive. Guy told him Perez was in the basement.

Lynch could smell the blood before he got to the bottom of the stairs. When he got down, he saw Perez over near an L-shaped office setup. Lots of computer equipment, three different monitors, a rack of boxes and wires – routers and servers, Lynch figured. And a black guy in his boxers, his legs duct-taped to one of those fancy office chairs with that hi-tech mesh for a seat. Some duct tape also hung from the arm of the chair. The guy's head was down on the desk – or most of his head. Looked like some of it was splattered on the monitor in front of him.

Perez saw Lynch, walked over.

Lynch nodded toward the body. "So what have you got here?"

"Stiff's name is Robert E. Lee," Perez said.

"Ironic," said Lynch.

Perez shrugged. "My people are just Mexicans who got stuck on the wrong side of the Rio Grande when you guys stole Texas. I got no dog in that fight."

"You said .22s?" Lynch asked

"Three to the back of the head," said Perez.

"Awful lot of blood on the floor," said Lynch.

"Pedicure," said Pérez. "Your .22 buddy took off a couple of his toes with something before he plugged him."

"Could see where that might be persuasive," Lynch said "Any idea what he was after?"

"Last thing Lee printed out was this." Perez handed Lynch a sheet. Jeanette Wilson's name and address. Mr .22 had been a busy boy today.

Lynch nodded, looked up at Perez, who had a little grin on his face.

"What?" said Lynch.

"Jenks!" Perez called. A metrosexual-looking guy in civilian clothes walked over – flat-front pants, shirt in a you-can't-buy-me-at-Penny's shade of blue, some of those hipster, steel-framed glasses. "Show Lynch here what ol' toeless had been up to."

"Guy's got a great set up," said Jenks. He and Lynch were sitting at a wet bar across the basement from Lee's office area, Jenks on a laptop at the end of a cable that ran over to the dead guy's computer equipment. The crime scene techs were still busy with the body over there. "Highest speed wireless pipe I've ever seen. Would've been tough to crack it, except he had a pad in his desk with all his passwords in it. Stupid, but we all do it, right?"

"I just plug into my cable box," said Lynch.

Jenks shrugged. "OK, so anyway, I start poking around, just looking at recent files, IP addresses, shit like that, and one of the things I get is this." Jenks popped up a series of pictures of Hardin in Chicago: the traffic cam shot Lynch had seen on Columbus, Hardin in front of the Hyatt on Wacker, Hardin's rental in the Grant Park Garage.

"Can you tell when he pulled those?" said Lynch.

"First one, the shot of the car? That was the morning after the Stein shooting."

Couple days before we started looking for it, thought Lynch.

"You know how he got them?"

"Watch this," said Jenks. He hammered at some keys. Kid had fast hands. A video feed popped open. Columbus Street – same angle as one of the Hardin shots they'd been using. It had to be the same camera, except on this screen the cars were moving, people were walking.

"Tell me that's not live," said Lynch.

"Oh," said Jenks. "It's live."

CHAPTER 50

Husam al Din clicked off the television in his hotel room. The shootings in Downers Grove were quite the sensation on the local news stations, which identified the dead men as functionaries of the Hernandez drug cartel.

Strangely, neither Wilson nor Hardin were mentioned on any of the newscasts. The story was being pitched as some mysterious fall out among the Mexican cartels with considerable nervous handwringing about the violence that had been escalating in Mexico for the past several years spilling over onto America's streets. Yet, surely by now the local police knew who Wilson was, knew where she lived, and knew that two cartel members had been killed immediately outside of her door. Surely witnesses had seen Wilson on the street, shooting a young man dead and leaving with Hardin. And surely they had also seen Hardin killing the driver of the large black vehicle. While neither those witnesses or, possibly, even the local authorities might know who Hardin is, they would have seen Wilson leaving with him.

Yet the news coverage included none of that. Which meant that the authorities were suppressing that information. Interesting.

Clearly, the DEA agent, Wilson, was allied with Hardin in some fashion. Al Din could think of no reason why. He had no immediate intelligence he could use to track either of them, but having two people to hunt instead of one doubled the odds of them being spotted. Al Din summarized the data he had on Wilson and e-mailed it to his Tokyo contact, along with her picture. He also instructed the man in Tokyo to research them both in order to uncover the nature of their relationship.

Meanwhile, al Din had another issue.

He had been close to Hardin twice. First, he had been interrupted by criminals working for the American mafia boss Corsco. Today, he had nearly been killed by criminals working for the Mexican drug lord Hernandez. Since both were also looking for Hardin, that made them his competitors.

While al Din had cut off one source of their intelligence, both organizations would be far more familiar with the area. Both would have many other sources of local information. Both had considerable manpower at their disposal.

From Lee, al Din knew that Hernandez wanted Hardin for vengeance. But he had no idea what Corsco's interest was. It was always best to know one's enemies. Corsco himself would be too difficult to approach, would have too much security. Al Din started Googling, looking for a weak link.

In many of the pictures attached to news stories about Corsco, he was accompanied by a short, overweight man identified as his attorney. The lawyer would be more approachable.

Al Din's phone peeped. A daily alarm he had programmed in. He hit a number on his speed dial, waited for the tone that told him the call had connected, and then hung up. Then he started to research Gerry Ringwald.

CHAPTER 51

Hardin and Wilson had been driving the Honda north for better than six hours. Hardin figured a little space was what they needed right now. They'd also been listening to the radio. The Downers Grove shootout was getting some play, but their names were out of it so far, the whole thing going down as a drug turf battle.

It was almost 8pm and they were cruising a neighborhood in Sturgeon Bay, Wisconsin. Lots of bed and breakfasts up here. They figured, with the economy the way it was, nobody was going to get real picky about IDs with someone paying cash.

"That looks nice," said Wilson, pointing at a big, dark green Victorian on the next corner.

"Always wanted to see Door County," said Hardin.

"Secretary at work went her for her honeymoon, always going on about it," Wilson said.

"Might be all the honeymoon we get."

Wilson went quiet, Hardin catching a little swallow out of the corner of his eye.

"It is, isn't it?" she said finally, sounding a little choked. "Our honeymoon?"

Hardin thought about it. No priest, no wedding, no I dos, but he couldn't think of anything that could tie them closer than they already were.

"Yeah. I guess it is."

He turned and smiled at her and she smiled back. First smile he'd seen from her that didn't have a ghost behind it.

CHAPTER 52

"This Wilson throws a wrench in things," said Hickman. "We don't know what the deal with her and Hardin is yet, but Jablonski tells me she knew we were going to bag him."

Bahram Lafitpour stirred his coffee. He, Hickman and Munroe were back at Lafitpour's condo. They'd waited at Lafitpour's office until 10pm, raid assets in place, just in case Hardin showed. He didn't.

"So we have to assume that Hardin knows I betrayed him," said Lafitpour.

Munroe nodded. "You worried he's going to make a run at you?"

Lafitpour shook his head. "People have been making runs at me for thirty years. My security is excellent. Besides, Hardin isn't an ideologue. He's just trying to sell the diamonds. There is no margin in making a move on me. The question becomes whether we still have a play with him."

"So we took a shot," Munroe said. "He's a big boy. He knows all about Plan Bs. And he still needs a buyer. Get word back to his contact that we'll still play ball. Probably gonna cost us though."

"We can't make a deal with Hardin," said Hickman. "We don't just need the diamonds, we need him. We've promised his scalp to the Feds and the DEA, and I've already got the press rubbing the bottle on this. We don't get a genie to pop out of it soon, they're going to get pissed and start asking the wrong kind of questions."

"Yeah," said Munroe. "And with the Feds inside the tent, we started the clock on this thing. We got a couple of days at the outside." Looking at Hickman now. "This Wilson, she was with Hardin?"

"Yeah," Hickman said.

"And she was at your briefing?"

"Yeah," Hickman said.

"So she knows about al Din," said Munroe.

"Yeah."

"What do we know about her?" asked Lafitpour.

"Jablonski's pulling apart her file. Should have word soon."

Silence around the table for a moment, tension tightening.

"So," said Lafitpour, "we need still need Hardin and the diamonds."

"Don't need him alive," said Munroe.

Hickman and Lafitpour looked at him. Munroe wasn't worried about Lafitpour, but this thing was getting sloppy and taking too long. Dead or alive, he needed it done, and dead was always faster and usually easier. Quiet around the table for a minute, Munroe watching Hickman's face. They weren't just talking about a little legal three-card Monte anymore, playing fast and loose with the facts to frame some bad guys. Now, killing people was on the table.

Finally, Hickman shrugged. "OK. But we still need to throw the Feds a bone. If they don't get to make a bust on Hardin, they're going to want something else."

Munroe nodded, keeping his eyes on Hickman. It looked like he had the stomach for the job. "Let's find

Hardin and Wilson, make it sloppy, make it look like Hernandez. Give my guys five minutes with the crime scene and we can hang it on him solid. We let the Feds make the bust on Hernandez. Bigger name anyway. Everybody wins."

"OK," Hickman said again.

"That's Plan B then. Bahram, get back to this Fouche, tell him we're ready to go. Plan C is this – keep the money together and ready to move. Turns out we have to make a deal with Hardin, then we do."

"Plan C?" Hickman asked. "How many plans are we going to need?"

"Someday when I know you better, ask me about Plan Q," Munroe said.

Lafitpour chuckled like he was reliving a happy memory. "That poor bastard."

Munroe had one more asset to line up. He called the phone he'd left with Tony Corsco.

"Jesus," Corsco answered. "You know what time it is?"

"Time for you to answer the phone," said Munroe. "You got anything on Hardin yet?"

"We're working on it. I get anything, you'll now first thing."

"Let me update your orders a little. Intel's still fine. I hear what you hear as soon as you hear it. But if Hardin happens to end up dead, let's just say that's fine, too."

"You putting a contract on him?" Corsco asked.

"Contract is when somebody pays you," Munroe said. "I'm just saying intel's fine, but if that intel happens to be where to find his body, so much the better."

CHAPTER 53

Brad Jablonski tossed a manila folder on Starshak's desk. He'd already sent what he had over to Hickman. Now, he'd stopped by to update Chicago PD.

"Jeanette Wilson used to be Juanita Sandoval," Jablonski said. "Right there in our HR files from when she signed up down in Texas. Maiden name and everything."

"Sandoval as in the guy with Hardin back when he took out Hernandez's kid brother?" Lynch asked.

"Yeah," said Marks. "His sister."

"This never bothered anybody?" Starshak asked.

Marks shrugged. "Should somebody have made the connection? Yeah, I guess. Thing is? It was all legit when she signed on. Changed her name when she married, then got a divorce. She came out of the Wichita PD, they vetted her then. Degree was out of Wichita State. We get a Hispanic female recruit, looks Mexican, talks Mexican, maybe we didn't look at her teeth quite as hard as we could have. I mean, she should have said something. She'd be in deep shit for that if she wasn't pretty much buried in shit already."

"So she's been after Hernandez all along?" Bernstein asked.

"Looks like," said Marks. "She signed up in Texas, which is as close to him as she could get, and she was one hard-ass operator down there. No secret we run a lot of ops across the border, working with the Mexicans. She signed up for that first chance she got, and they loved her. I mean a female across the Rio Grande that could pass for native? That whole macho thing? Bad guys never even looked at her. Thing is, down there? Nowadays, pretty much every bust ends up in a fire fight, which is always a little exciting for the good guys because you never know when one of the people you went through the door with is going to switch teams and shoot you in the back. She had half a dozen kills in Mexico before she got so hot that the Federales said no mas and the brass decided we needed to move her away from the border."

"Sounds like this Jones kid drew down on the wrong senorita," Lynch said.

"Yeah," said Jablonski.

"But she and Hardin go back," said Lynch.

Jablonski nodded.

"I'm getting old," said Starshak. "So lemme just recap here, make sure I'm keeping this straight. We got Hardin, who ain't really Hardin, who ripped off some diamonds from Al Qaeda or maybe Hezbollah, and he wants to sell them. We got Mr .22, sword of whatever, who's after Hardin and racking up a body count like he's Chuck Norris. We got Wilson, who ain't really Wilson, who's after Hernandez. Hernandez has a hard on for Hardin. Hardin is with Wilson and maybe after Hernandez too, for all we know. Corsco's got some kind of angle we can't make out, except it involves Joe Hollywood, who is currently impersonating a houseplant up at Northwestern. We got some suits in from DC nobody knows, and Bernstein here thinks at least one of them is really from Tel Aviv. I missing anything here?"

"Well," said Bernstein, "there's that Lee guy, out in Aurora, who it turns out was watching our TV."

"Right," said Starshak. "There's that. Thoughts?"

"Fucked up," said Lynch.

Starshak got up, picked up the spray bottle off his credenza, and started spritzing the fern in his window.

"So you're the one coordinating with Hickman on this," he said to Jablonski. "Couple days ago you were gonna put out a BOLO on Hardin, now we're sitting on our hands. Why aren't you putting the full-court press on him and Wilson? Looks like they had to leave town in a hurry. She can't use her ID, access her accounts, nothing. Hardin's blown the Fox ID he was using, can't go back to Hardin, can't go back to Griffin. They've gotta be hiding somewhere. We get them on the wire, get their faces up on the tube, we probably get a line on them pretty quick."

"That's how I'd play it," Jablonski said. "But Hickman doesn't want to spook them. He says Hardin takes his diamonds and runs, we might never find them. Say he's worried Al Qaeda will get their hands on them again, which would give the bad guys better than a hundred mil in operating capital. We leave Hardin and Wilson some room, maybe they make a play on Hernandez, maybe we find this al Din, maybe they try to make another sale we can track. If you push him on it, he starts making national security noises, playing the need to know card."

"So now he's worried about what the terrorists might be up to?" Starshak said. "Yesterday he couldn't shut me up on that fast enough."

"Hickman's got some kind of angle he's not telling us," said Lynch. "Cause he's not stupid and that doesn't make sense."

"What I figured," said Jablonski.

••••

After Jablonski left, Starshak, Lynch and Bernstein talked things over.

"Can't just sit on our fucking hands," Lynch said. "What about Corsco? He's tied in here somewhere, and he's still ducking us. I say it's time to sit his ass down."

Starshak nodded, reached for the phone, called Ringwald, told him to have Corsco in for an interview today or Starshak would get a subpoena and serve it on the mother fucker in his box at the opera. He hung up.

"What else?" he asked.

"With these need-to-know fed types in this, they're gonna freeze us out," said Lynch. "This crap from Hickman on the BOLOs, that's just the start."

"Agreed," said Bernstein.

A pause in the conversation. "So what's our move?" Starshak asked.

"So we focus on Saturday," said Lynch.

"Why the African?" asked Starshak.

"This al Din fuck, he's the one leaving bodies behind. And Saturday, that's the one move he couldn't have planned in advance. If he fucked up, he fucked up there. I'm going to go talk to Magnus again, see if I can shake something loose."

CHAPTER 54

Kate Magnus was out front, working in the flower garden along the fence with a few of the residents when Lynch got to the shelter. As he pulled up, he saw a young black kid on the other side of the street wave back between a couple of the three-flats up that way and then turn and jog away from the street, cutting back between the buildings. Lookout, probably. Running a street market.

Magnus was wearing jeans today, what looked like a long-sleeve T-shirt of some kind under a cheap nylon windbreaker. Lynch didn't think she spent much on clothes. Lynch didn't think she gave a shit about that either. She stood up when she saw him, took off her work gloves, said something to one of the men working near her and walked over to meet Lynch at the gate.

"Detective," she said. Neutral at least this time.

"Sister," said Lynch, then, "Sorry, force of habit. Ms Magnus. You've got no idea what twelve years of Catholic school can do to you."

He wasn't sure, but that might have got him a little smile. "Sure I do," she said. "Perhaps it will make things easier for everyone if you just call me Kate. What can I do for you?"

"Something's come up with Membe's case. I've got a picture of a man that might be connected. If he is, it would be from overseas. I'd like you to look at it, maybe show it to your residents."

Magnus was quiet for a moment, looking at Lynch. "I thought Membe was just an innocent bystander. You said he was likely shot because he might have seen the man who killed Stein."

Lynch nodded. "That's what I thought. Might still be what I think. But diamonds tie into this somehow, West African diamonds. And the man in the picture might work for the people who control those."

"You mean Hezbollah."

Lynch's eyebrows went up, she saw that.

"It's not a secret, Detective, not if you've lived over there."

"Yeah," Lynch said. "Hezbollah or maybe friends of theirs."

"So Stein's murder was political."

"I don't know," said Lynch.

She was quiet again, the gate in the fence between them still closed.

"If this is something from Africa, are my other residents safe here?" she asked.

"I think so," Lynch said. "It bothered me a little when I thought about it, Membe getting shot like that. Even if he saw the guy, so what? Just another guy getting into a car. But if he knew him, recognized him for some reason, then it makes sense. So I still think it was just bad luck, bad timing. No reason for the guy to come back after anyone else. Just bad luck, but bad luck that goes back to Africa."

"That's the worst kind of luck," Magnus said. She opened the gate, let Lynch in, said something in a language Lynch didn't know, called the men over.

"What do you want to know?" she asked Lynch.

He took the picture from his jacket pocket, unfolded it and handed it to her. "Just if they know this man, and, if so, from where."

She looked at the picture a moment, then turned it so the men could see, translating, probably a couple of times, Lynch figured, because it seemed like she stopped, then started again in what sounded like another language. None of the men said anything, but one of them, the big man Magnus had to stand down last time Lynch was here, knew. Lynch could tell. He saw the man's eyes widen for just a blink, and then the man looked away, looking at anything but Lynch. The men all muttered, some shaking their heads.

Magnus said something else to them and they returned to the garden, the big man moving as far from Lynch as he could get.

"They all say no," she said.

"But the big one knows him," Lynch said.

"Probably."

"Is he from the same area as Membe?"

"Yes."

"OK," Lynch said. "I'm not going to push him on it now. For now, it confirms what I figured. The shooter recognized Membe. But talk to the big guy. See what he knows. If you can get something from him, let me know. I don't want to jam him up. But I need what he knows."

"Momolu," Magnus said, some edge behind that. "The big guy has a name. His name is Momolu."

Lynch paused, took that in. "Look, I know you think nobody gives a shit, and you probably got good reason. You can believe this or not, but Membe and Stein, they're the same in my book. You kill somebody in my town, if I can make you answer for it, then I do."

Both of them quiet for a minute, Lynch looking up the street. The kid who'd run between the buildings when

Lynch pulled up was back, sitting on a stoop now. Waiting for Lynch to leave so he could give his crew the all clear.

"Alright," Magnus said. "I didn't mean to be rude. But yes. I have reason."

Lynch nodded. "How long you had the drug market going on up the street?"

"A few months. Used to be over on Monroe, but they've moved it a block north."

"Last thing you need," Lynch said. "Weather's getting nice, your guys are going to want to get outside some, aren't going to know the neighborhood, know the code. Somebody flashes a sign at them and they wave back wrong, things could get bad. Don't need some drive-by bullshit or anything."

"Are you going to clean up the drug trade detective, so we can do our gardening?"

"Can't clean it up," Lynch said. "But I bet I can move it a couple of blocks."

"And the people on the block you move it to, do they deserve it any more than we do?"

Lynch let out a long exhale. "Look, I do what I can where I can, OK?"

"I'm sorry," she said. "And thank you."

Lynch nodded. She went to hand the photo back to him.

"Keep it," he said. "Might help when you talk to Mobulo."

"Momolu," Magnus said, but at least she was smiling a little this time.

"Momolu," said Lynch. "Hey, I'm trying."

"Yes detective, I do believe you are."

Lynch turned to open the gate.

"Notre Dame d'Afrique," Magnus said.

Lynch turned back. "What?"

"The church in the background in your picture. It's in Algiers."

"Thanks," Lynch said, wondering to himself why he had to hear that from her.

Back in the car Lynch called a contact in gang crimes, guy that knew the West Wide.

"It's Lynch. Listen, you got somebody running a street market on Madison just north of Oakley. Find out who and tell them that block's off limits. Tell 'em to move their act a couple blocks west or I'm going to make them a hobby."

Wouldn't stop anything, Lynch knew that. But they'd move.

CHAPTER 55

Hardin woke to the smell of gun solvent. Wilson sat cross-legged on the floor in just her panties and a camisole. She had newspaper spread on the rug; one of the Berettas Hardin had taken off Corsco's guys broken down, the slide off, the recoil spring out. She was running a bore brush through the barrel. She looked up.

"It's after nine, you slug. This what time you tough Legion punks roll out of the rack?"

"Late night," he said. "Someone was draining my vital essence."

She held up the rag from her cleaning kit. It was covered with dark splotches. "You gotta start stealing guns off a better class of thugs," she said. "These are a mess."

"Good in the sack and the little woman is cleaning my guns," said Hardin. "I think I'll keep her."

"Careful sport. My .40 is already cleaned, locked, and loaded."

Hardin picked up the remote, flicked on the TV, switched to WGN for the Chicago news. He caught a follow up on the Downers Grove shootings, but still nothing on them.

"You look through that paper before you started?"

She nodded. "Nothing. Also called a guy back at the Chicago office – don't worry, I used a throwaway and I called him at home on his cell. He was making some strange noises about how I wasn't in this too deep yet, and I should call Jablonski and all this could still get worked out."

"Weird."

"Yeah," said Wilson. "We should be all over the news by now. It's like they don't want to catch us."

"Sounds like someone still wants to deal. Guess I better call Fouche."

"You sure you can trust this guy?" asked Wilson.

Hardin shrugged. "If I can't, we're fucked. Unless you know somebody who can move a pound and a half of illegal diamonds."

Wilson set the barrel back in the slide, pressed the spring in place, slid the assembly back on the frame, worked the trigger to check the action, then snapped the magazine into the well. She got up, stretched, the camisole riding up and revealing an abdomen as flat and hard as a piece of slate.

"We gotta think this through," she said. "This Fouche, he's the guy you called before?"

"Yeah."

"Somebody ratted you out, and it's not a very long chain."

"We're running out of options here. We don't cash out, we'll be running on fumes pretty quick."

"Something's fucked here. I've been on the other side of hunts like this. We should be all over the news. Hell, we should be caught by now. Somebody needs to keep this on the QT, which means we've got some kind of leverage we haven't figured out yet."

Hardin thought a minute. "Give me a place to stand," he said, "and I will move the world."

"What the hell are you talking about?

"Archimedes, Greek guy. He was big on leverage."

Wilson snagged a pair of boxers out of the open suitcase on the floor next to her and threw them at the bed.

"Leave the Greeks out of this, smartass, it's complicated enough. Now get your ass dressed and buy me breakfast. Then we'll go lever shopping."

CHAPTER 56

"Shut the fuck up," said Starshak. Lynch and Bernstein were in his office with Corsco and Ringwald. Ringwald had been whining about Lynch insisting they come in to the station, not being willing to talk at Ringwald's office. "Corsco's a crook; you're the mouthpiece that chose to make a living sucking up to him. This ain't a courtroom; you're not on tape, so save it. We been trying to talk to this piece of shit for five days, you guys giving us the song and dance, now you're whining cause we don't show our ass for you?"

Corsco reached over, patted the top of Ringwald's thigh. "It's alright, Gerry. We know to expect a certain amount of abuse from these gentlemen." Corsco was a trim, tall man, dark hair graying on the sides. Expensive suit, expensive shirt, expensive tie.

Corsco raised his eyebrows, looked around the room. "I assume you have some questions for me?"

"Shamus Fenn," said Lynch.

"A fine actor," said Corsco.

"Know him?" Lynch asked.

"We've met. I advised him and his company when they were filming in town a few years ago."

"Which film was that?" Lynch asked.

"*Cal Sag Channel*," said Corsco.

"Advised on what?"

242

Corsco smiled, paused. "Verisimilitude."

"Strange," said Bernstein. "All these years you tell us you're not a mobster, yet when Hollywood needs someone to vet their gangster movie, you're the guy they call."

Corsco shrugged. "I am a simple businessman. If entertainers want to pay for my opinions, well as the saying goes, this is a free country, right?" He turned to Ringwald, eyebrows raised.

"A free country so long as we are vigilant against abuses by the authorities," Ringwald said.

"But you do know Fenn?" said Lynch.

Corsco nodded.

"Talk to him much? I mean since your Hollywood days?"

"From time to time," said Corsco.

"In the last few weeks?" Lynch asked.

"I knew he was in town. I called to say hello. I was saddened to hear of his, well, his health crisis."

"Ever hear of Nick Hardin?" asked Starshak.

Corsco smiled again. "As chagrined as I am to admit it, I did catch the little episode on *Oprah*."

"So you know he had a beef with Fenn?"

Corsco nodded.

"And then a couple of your shooters make a run at him."

Ringwald put his hand up. "First of all, characterizing these gentlemen as 'shooters' and as 'his' assumes facts not in evidence."

Corsco patted Ringwald's leg again.

"Did I know these gentlemen? Yes. They have assisted me with security matters from time to time. But are they employees of mine? No. They are… I suppose independent contractors would be the word. Now,

GREED

because I do have interests in certain industries in which the criminal element sometimes dabbles, I do hear things. And as a gesture of good faith, I will tell you this. It is my understanding that this Hardin has a personal dispute with one of the major Mexican drug lords. In fact, I believe there was an event in the suburbs a few days ago that demonstrates that. I can only suppose that Mr DeGetano and Mr Garbanzo, being security contractors, were pursuing Hardin for Hernandez."

"Convenient for you, isn't it?" said Lynch.

"I'm sorry?"

"This Hernandez turning up."

"Not very convenient for Mr Garbanzo or Mr DeGetano."

Lynch nodded. "Ever hear of Bobby Lee?"

Corsco shrugged.

Lynch pulled Lee's photo from a file, slid it across the desk.

"How long has he been hacking the city's surveillance network for you?" asked Lynch.

Corsco and Ringwald stood simultaneously. "This meeting is over," said Ringwald.

"We're into Lee's system," said Lynch. "Just thought you should know."

"I said this meeting is over, Detective," Ringwald repeated. Corsco and Ringwald left the office.

"Sure you should have given them that, about Lee?" Starshak asked.

"Not like they can get into Lee's system now, change anything," Lynch said. "Maybe they panic, make a move to cover their asses on something we don't know about yet. The more shook up they are, the better."

In the back seat of Corsco's caddy, Corsco turned to Ringwald.

"Two questions, Gerry. First, what might Lee have that could point to us? Second, why isn't Fenn dead yet?"

Ringwald didn't answer, just nodded. The questions weren't rhetorical exactly, he just didn't have answers. The caddy pulled into Corsco's building, dropped Ringwald at his car. He headed home.

CHAPTER 57

The Wilson cunt was Sandoval's sister. Hernandez knew that as soon as he saw her. And he could have killed her easily, years ago. Why hadn't he? Just another *puta*, that's why. Just another warm, wet hole that caught his brother's eye.

The kid hanging from the engine hoist was moaning again. Miko knew. He'd seen Hernandez like this before, and he knew. Until the boss blew off his rage, he wouldn't be able to focus. So he'd talked to the head of the LK crew, got a name. Just a street dealer, dropout who ran a couple corners in Aurora near one of the high schools. But he'd gotten a little greedy. They all skimmed something – almost couldn't trust them if they didn't. But they had to know where the line was. This kid had crossed it. Maybe only put a toe over it really, kind of thing usually you just throw a scare into him. But the boss needed a punching bag, so the kid's wrists were cuffed together, the cuffs over the hook for the engine hoist, the hoist holding him a couple feet off the floor. The LK crew was lined up in the back, bearing witness.

Hernandez picked up the bat again. He'd started with the kid's legs, but those were pretty well pulped now. And Hernandez's head was clearing, most of the poison sweated out. The kid was conscious again, looking at him, face streaked with dirt and sweat and tears. Hernandez felt something like shame, just for a moment – he knew the kid wasn't that far out of line, knew what Miko was doing – and then just pity.

"*Jefe*," the kid blubbered. "Please, *Jefe*–"

Enough, thought Hernandez. *End this here.* Hernandez drew the bat straight back over his head, all the way back until he felt the fat end tap his back, and then snapped it down hard onto the crown of the kid's skull. Heard that crunching, slushy sound he knew too well. The kid hung limp from the chain, blood coming from his ears, his eyes, his nose. Hernandez dropped the bat to the floor, turned and walked from the garage, out into the parking lot, waited while Miko came around and opened his door, sat in the back of the new Mercedes the local crew had provided. Miko got in the front and started to drive.

"Thank you, Miko," Hernandez said.

"*De nada, Jefe.*"

"Let's get to work on Sandoval. We find the bitch, we find them both."

"Wilson, *Jefe*," said Miko.

"Whoever gets to bury her can decide what name to put on the stone. Just find me that bitch."

CHAPTER 58

"Downers Grove, Illinois, my friends. Downers Grove, Illinois." Hardin and Wilson were driving back south through Wisconsin, north of Milwaukee, Hardin poking around the radio dial, looking for something to listen to. The town name caught his attention. One of those right-wing radio hosts, the guy who liked to dress like a Nazi on his book covers.

"That's not Juárez, people. That's not Tijuana. That's not even El Paso or Nogales or some other border town. That's a real nice place. I've been there. Folks like you, real Americans, church-going people, just trying to raise their families, hoping they can still make their house payments and pay their kids' tuition after Washington's through picking their pockets. Folks who are living by the rules. This isn't some slum, these aren't bottom feeders, these aren't the miscreant offspring of some welfare queen who's cranking out kids with every brother on the block to pad her government check. These are honest, hardworking, patriotic Americans. And now they've got the drug gangs turning their quiet little burg into a free-fire zone. If you don't get it yet, let me spell it out for you. I don't care where you are right now. I don't care what you paid for your home, trying to move away from this kind of stuff. If this can happen in Downers Grove, Illinois, then it can happen anywhere.

"And I wish it was just about the drugs, people, I really do. I'm hearing things. I have sources. You know I have sources. There are people inside the wire on this, honest folks like you and me who still know what the flag means, people still in the belly of the beast – that bloated, voracious Leviathan we call a government – and they get word out to me when they can. And you want to know what I'm hearing people? Are you sitting down? Are you ready for this? It wasn't just the drugs. This was a Mexican drug king having a dispute with Al Qaeda over money. That's right. The two greatest threats to our Republic are teaming up. So the next time you hear some bleeding heart talking about immigration reform, you better ask yourself just who they want to let over our borders. You think dope is the only thing they might carry across our joke of a border? How about a chemical weapon? How about a dirty bomb? How about a real live nuke?

"It's time to get real, people. You are at war, and the enemy is bringing the battle to you. And every one of those people who violated our trust, who wiped their feet on the Statue of Liberty by sneaking in the back door when all they had to do was ring the bell like our ancestors did, well every last one of them has always been nothing but just another criminal, just another lazy punk who won't do the work to follow the rules. Sure, they always could have been the slime bag outside your kids' school, the one trying to get your children to throw away their lives for a nose full of crap. But now they may just be something more. Every last one of them could be Al Qaeda's trigger finger. Every last one of them could be the bastard with his finger on the switch that's going to turn one of our gleaming alabaster cities into a radioactive crater. That's right, people, that poncho might just as well be a burqa. And if this doesn't have your attention, if this doesn't have you ready to take your country back from the liberals and the apologists and the diversity freaks and the live-and-let-live, let's legalize-every-damn-thing hippies, then I don't know what will. Back after this word."

Hardin flicked off the radio. "Seems a little worked up," he said.

"Yeah," she answered.

"That make any sense to you?"

"The immigration stuff? That's just right-wing radio noise. But the other stuff, tying Al Qaeda and the cartels together? Even that fat-ass whack job wouldn't make that up. That came out of somebody on Hickman's team. Somebody fed him that story."

They drove for a minute, radio off, tires humming on the pavement. "Something doesn't add up," Wilson said. "We know they want to keep this thing quiet, that's why they haven't gone public on us. But somebody's got America's favorite dickhead bloviating about it on the radio. If they want to sweep it under the rug, why raise the profile on the whole mess?"

Quiet for a minute, passing by a pasture full of Holsteins.

"We queered their play," Hardin said. "They were supposed to have me in the bag last night. Me and the diamonds. Would have given them all the window dressing they needed on the Al Qaeda front. Probably leaked this BS ahead of time. A little public positioning to back their play on the cartels. Question is who's doing the leaking? That Hickman guy, you think?"

Wilson shook her head. "He might be the mouthpiece, but this feels a little above his pay grade. That last meeting we had, there were some mysterious DC suits in the room, and all of a sudden we got the DEA and the FBI playing kissy face, coordinated raid to grab you, lots of background on money movement everywhere from Switzerland to Vanuatu. That wasn't our intel, and I don't think it was the Feebs' either. That smelled like Agency."

"Makes sense," Hardin said. "If somebody was going to pick up some chatter out of West Africa after I knocked over that load, those would be the guys, them or Mossad."

"And they'd know who the diamonds belonged to," said Wilson. "And they know who you are. And they know about Hernandez. So this is their chance to tie all that shit up in one nice, neat package."

"But without the diamonds, they've got no story."

"And without you, they've got no diamonds."

"And," Hardin said, "with this BS story already out there, they're running out of time. I think we just found our lever," Hardin said.

"Something else to think about, though."

"What?"

"Who else was shooting back at the condo?" Wilson asked.

"What do you mean?"

"That shit inside?" Wilson said. "Radio said what, two druggies and an old lady dead in the hallway? Who did that?"

Hardin thought for a moment. "Agency maybe? SOG guys?"

"I don't think so," Wilson said. "Hickman and whoever is pulling his strings, they were looking to get everything official, had a joint raid task force ready to bust you at Lafitpour's office. If they'd known you were at my place, they would have had me in a box and they would have had enough shooters in raid jackets running around Downer Grove to invade Iwo Jima. You never would have made it out of the building."

"Already had the mob after me once," said Hardin. "Maybe Corsco took another shot, ran into the cartel guys, things went bad?"

"Possible, but Hernandez and Corsco? They have to coordinate shit to run their drug territories, so they've got channels, they talk. Seems like they would have talked about this."

"That leaves Al Qaeda. I did steal their diamonds."

Wilson's face went still. "Ah shit. The guy from the briefing."

"What guy?"

"Quick slide they threw up on the screen, some Al Qaeda hotshot. Husam something. I kinda lost focus there for a second, after they announced they were set to bag you."

"Al Din?"

"Yeah, Husam al Din."

Long exhale out of Hardin. "Fuck."

"You've heard of him?"

Hardin nodded. "In the Legion. If the DGSE needed muscle in Africa, my unit was usually it. So I played ball with them a bit. Some after I was out, too. This al Din guy, he's the best the Al Qaeda types have. If that was him up in your hallway, I'm glad we weren't there."

Wilson sighed, sank down in her seat a little, a long look out the window. She talked without turning her head. "So we're dodging a drug cartel, the mob, the cops, the Feds, and some hot-shot terrorist guy." Wilson said.

"Don't forget the mysterious suits," Hardin answered. "Somebody's playing the man behind the curtain. Whoever the Great and Terrible Oz is, he may well be our biggest problem. But he's also probably the guy who might want to buy our lever." Hardin flicked back on the radio, scanned looking for some music. "We should be back in Chicago in a couple hours."

"There's no place like home," said Wilson. "There's no place like home."

"Screwing you, my friend?" Fouche shouting into a phone somewhere across the Atlantic.

Hardin and Wilson were heading west on 90 toward Elgin, big enough town, not one either of them had ties to, close enough to Chicago to operate, far enough out to keep some of the eyes off of them. Hardin put a call in to Fouche to see if he could reopen channels with the other side.

"Screwing you?" Fouche's voice still raised, but calming down a little. "A day ago, I'm expecting my cut on this deal. Now I've got the Russians I roped in making angry Russian noises. And these are the wrong sorts of Russians, those *Eastern Promises* types, gonna show up in the sauna, cut my schlong off for me. And you wanna know am I screwing you?"

"Sorry, man," said Hardin. Reaction he needed. He knew Fouche. If Fouche had played it cool, Hardin would know something was up. "But I had to ask, you know? And I'm getting a little short-tempered over here myself. Second time in a couple of days I've had somebody trying to kill me."

"Somebody's trying to screw you, it's that fucker Lafitpour," said Fouche. "Maybe you should pay him a visit."

"I already know about Lafitpour," Hardin said. "But he's fronting for somebody. I need to know who. I want you to get back to him, tell him I know he tried to fuck me over. Tell him I know he's playing ball with somebody at Langley or thereabouts. Tell him that's a nice story they're selling, this drugs and terrorists bullshit. Tell him I got no problem with that, I love a good story. Tell him I get my money and get out, they can tell whatever story they want. But if I don't, and quick, then I'm gonna start telling my own story."

Pause on the line, some transatlantic hum filling the void.

"Drugs and terrorists?" Fouche said. "You want to fill me in here?"

Hardin gave him the quick version.

"So you have some leverage," said Faust.

"Yep," said Hardin.

"You don't mind, then, if I look to move that ten million figure a little, bump up both our ends."

"Don't mind at all. Oh, and Pierre?"

"Yeah?"

"Since this is supposed to be some cartel-and-terrorist circus now, if they need some coke, you know, to lend a little verisimilitude to the enterprise, let them know I've got a kilo of Hernandez's blow."

CHAPTER 59

Munroe admired the view across Adams Street from Lafitpour's office in the Rookery Building. "Burnham designed this place," Munroe said. "Pretty revolutionary in its time. Metal framing, elevators. One of the first high-rises, the start of the great architectural Renaissance after the Chicago fire."

"Who's Burnham?" asked Hickman.

"The man who was quoted as saying 'Make no small plans, they have no magic to stir men's blood,'" answered Lafitpour. "Large or small, however, we need plans. Hardin's Frenchman has been back in contact."

"Then I guess we're in the right place," Munroe said. "What did Fouche want?"

"Recent events have emboldened our fugitives. Between the rather colorful news coverage and the desultory effort being made to pursue them, they have discerned our plans, at least in broad outline. Hardin knows we need him and his diamonds to make it work. Fouche says that Hardin is happy to play along, but he is having some trust issues."

"I'd be having some myself," said Munroe. "We can always buy a little trust. Everything has its price."

"Price was mentioned. They want $25 million now. It seems they also have a kilogram of Hernandez's cocaine, and they are willing to throw that in."

"The blow will help," Munroe said. "Window dressing on the Hernandez side of things. Push back on the number a little. We cave too easy, it'll smell funny. But settle for whatever you gotta settle for. Just get us a meet. "

"I thought you were tapped out at fifteen," said Hickman.

"I am," Lafitpour said.

"Doesn't matter," said Munroe. "Comes down to an actual deal, we show up with the $15 million, they'll take it, trust me. Right now, I just need them somewhere I can get a scope on them."

"I will get back to Fouche," said Lafitpour.

Munroe looked at Hickman. Hickman was looking thoughtful.

"What?" Munroe asked.

"It's Wilson," said Hickman, "She may have queered us snatching up Hardin, but putting her in the mix really tightens up our story, especially now that we got her toting some blow around."

"How?" asked Munroe.

"We got their back story now, her and Hardin. Old lovers. That will all check out, anybody digs into it. Now we got him coming out of Africa with the diamonds, not too hard to make the case for an Al Qaeda connection there. And we have her coming out of the DEA with a kilo of coke, so we can make her dirty, tie her to the cartel. Them running around together, that bakes them right into the deal. They end up dead? Hey, bad guys meet up, and it goes to guns. Shit happens."

Munroe smiled at Hickman. "So we still pin it on Hernandez, but we paint Hardin and Wilson with the dirty brush, take the sympathy card away. I like it. People think they're with the bad guys, they'll dig at it less." Munroe smiled at Lafitpour. "You were right about this guy, Bahram. He's our kind of people."

CHAPTER 60

A small line of blood ran down the boy's forehead, veering left at the bridge of his nose, dripping from the jaw line onto his T-shirt. Al Din tried to place the character on the shirt. Iron Man, that was it. The movie had been heavily promoted. Al Din waited for the woman to stop struggling against the duct tape that held her to the chair, to stop trying to scream through the gag. The girl's eyes were still open, but she was not moving. Shock, probably. He saw all the resistance go out of the man's face. Always start with the boy, al Din had learned. Men had this strange willingness to sacrifice their sons. So he always preserved the illusion that they could save their daughters.

Ringwald lived in a large, modern house on a two-acre lot in Highland Park. The house had very good locks and one of the better electronic home protection systems, but the large lot meant that no one could see al Din from the street, and, with time, locks and electronic systems were meaningless. The large lot also meant the neighbors would not hear what happened in the house. Once al Din had defeated the system and the locks, he gathered the family and duct taped them to the four chairs from the kitchen table, arranging them in a semi-circle, Ringwald on his left, then the daughter, then the wife, Ringwald's son facing him directly from the right.

Of course Ringwald would not answer the questions at first. Al Din did not expect him to. In fact, did not want him to. Al Din wanted an initial token of resistance that he could meet with complete brutality. That would break the man's will. Then al Din would know that the man spoke the truth. So, once the family was in place, al Din asked a pointless question, allowed Ringwald to say no.

And then al Din shot the young boy through the forehead.

"Completely unnecessary," he then said, turning to Ringwald. "Now you have killed your son. Are you ready to answer my questions? If not, do I shoot your wife or your daughter next? Really, no one else has to die. Will you answer my questions now?"

Ringwald nodded.

"You are Mr Corsco's attorney?"

"Yes," Ringwald said.

"What is his business with Nick Hardin?"

"Hardin used to work in Africa. They had that big charity thing there for Darfur a few years back?"

"I remember," said al Din.

"He was the guy that punched Shamus Fenn in the face. Fenn knows Corsco pretty well. When he saw Hardin in Chicago, he snapped. He came to Tony to put a hit out on Hardin."

"Shamus Fenn, the movie actor?" al Din asked.

"Yes," said Ringwald.

"And he wanted Hardin killed because Hardin hit him in the nose?"

"It screwed up his career," said Ringwald.

"It has nothing to do with the diamonds?"

"What diamonds? Why does everyone keep asking about diamonds?" Ringwald asked.

There was no pause when al Din asked about the diamonds, no sign of recognition. The man would not lie now.

"What about Hernandez? What is Corsco's involvement with him?"

"Hardin killed his brother. Years ago. It's why Hardin left the country. I don't know why he came back, but Hernandez heard about it. He wanted Tony to help track Hardin down. Which was fine with us. It doesn't matter how Hardin dies. Fenn would have had to pay off on the contract either way."

"You said would have had to pay. Because this Fenn overdosed on drugs, he can no longer pay you?"

"Fenn fucked up, went on TV, drew some attention to himself, this whole thing with him and Hardin. The police were talking to him, he was getting nervous. Tony took care of that, cutting his losses."

"Corsco and Hernandez, they are colleagues?"

Ringwald didn't answer. He was looking at the boy, his eyes vacant. Al Din tapped him on the head with the barrel of the pistol.

"Focus. While your wife and daughter are still alive. Are Corsco and Hernandez colleagues?"

"No, they pretty much hate each other. Drugs are a minor revenue stream for Corsco, but there are overlaps between his operations and the local cartel distributors. So they have to cooperate to a degree."

Al Din had what he needed. There was nothing more to learn here. What was the phrase Ringwald had used? Cutting his losses. Al Din liked that phrase. He would have to remember it. It was time to cut his losses.

He shot the woman first. She was an innocent; there was no reason she should have to watch her daughter die. The girl gave no sign she even noticed. Al Din shot her next.

Ringwald was straining against his bonds now, gasping, starting to scream. But not for long.

Al Din shook his head. Corsco wasn't interested in the diamonds at all, didn't even know about them. He was hired to kill Hardin because a movie star got punched in the nose. Al Din turned and left without even looking at the corpses taped to the chairs around him. The strange reasons why people had to die no longer surprised him.

CHAPTER 61

Back at the Hilton, Munroe set down a heavy document, took off his glasses and rubbed his nose for a minute. This Heinz guy, the bug herder who'd turned up dead out west, Langley got the goods on him.

A MULTI-VECTOR APPROACH TO BIOLOGICAL WARFARE: DEGRADING PUBLIC HEALTH RESPONSE THROUGH SIMULTANEOUS DISPERSION OF MULTIPLE INFECTIOUS AGENTS
by DR MARK HEINZ.

The paper was a couple hundred pages long, full of charts and graphs and some really horrible pictures, but the main point was clear enough.

By dispersing several virulent bugs simultaneously, you could first delay consensus on what agent a target community was dealing with because of the overlap in symptomology among the various diseases and their varying incubation periods. Hospitals would initially report conflicting test results. The community's ability to respond would be degraded by the sheer number of cases, their diversity, the compounding effects of continuing infections, and the fact that most of their health care workers would likely be infected with one agent or another by the time they figured out what they were dealing with. Even then, they would be able to treat only a fraction of the infected persons because of the varied list of drugs required, most of which were in limited supply because none of the diseases were common. The paper had several simulations outlining casualty scenarios based on varying delivery vehicles, population densities, and response strategies. Even the most optimistic would lap the body count from 9/11 several times over.

This paper had been Heinz's big claim to fame down at Fort Dix, and he'd been pretty passionate about it. A little too passionate for some of his peers. He had a rep as a cold fish who was a little too fond of his bugs. Langley had put Heinz through the ringer, run down his old cronies, checked him out. Munroe flipped through the transcripts of the conversations, found a quote that set off some alarm bells in his head:

You have to understand that, for most of us, this job is a non-stop horror show. Every day we're working on ideas to contain some truly nasty stuff. And we do it so that someday we aren't in biohazard suits walking through some American town watching people die and knowing there isn't much we can do about it. But Heinz? You never got that vibe from him. You always got this feeling that, if the shit ever really hit the fan, he'd be trying to wrangle a seat on the first chopper in just so he could watch.

On the other hand, Heinz's record was spotless. Honorable discharge once he hit his twenty years, solid career with one of the big pharma companies after, and everybody there thought the guy was just swell. Of course, he had been the brainchild behind one of those boner pills that made the joint a few hundred zillion dollars, so everybody they talked to probably owed Heinz for half the bounce in their stock options.

But Heinz had always been a lab guy, not a C-suite player. Good money, but not Bill Gates money. They'd pulled his finances apart, and if you plugged everything into a spreadsheet, then this Heinz wasn't living beyond his means, not so that you could prove it. But he was living on the edge. The very edge. And the last couple years, when the economy had tanked and everybody else in the world had pulled their belt in a couple notches, Heinz had gone right on spending.

Nothing you could take to court, but it sure felt like he'd picked up an extra income somewhere. So that had Munroe suspicious. That and Heinz showing up dead. Dead guys always made Munroe's nose twitch.

CHAPTER 62

The next morning, Lynch and Bernstein were out in Aurora.

"Nice place," Lynch said. He and Bernstein were shaking hands with Perez in the lobby of the new Aurora PD headquarters. Bright, airy, lots of windows, more like some corporate HQ than a cop shop.

"Yeah," said Perez. "Just moved in a couple months back. You don't get the nice digs in the city?"

"Asbestos, lead paint, Seventies linoleum," said Bernstein. "All the modern conveniences."

Perez wound them through the building back to Jenks' station. The IT guy. Black slacks today, expensive-looking white shirt, some kind of linen thing but without the wrinkles. Jenks walked them through what he had.

"First, you gotta understand we're going to be pulling this apart for months," said Jenks. "He didn't keep much on his local drives – looks like just whatever he had cooking at the time – but he was a bitch for backups. Had a floor safe, pretty high-end piece we had to cut. Backups going back three years. Just scratched the surface on those." Jenks pulled out a file from a drawer, set it on the desk. "Start of an inventory in there. He had the backups sorted by the name of the subject he was tracking."

"OK," said Lynch. "What about these shots of Hardin?"

"He had three Hardin files," said Jenks, "and pretty much the same stuff in all of them. So he had three customers interested in the guy, and he was just reselling the intel."

"Can you tell who the customers were?" Lynch asked.

"I can tell where he sent the stuff," said Jenks. He clicked at his terminal for a minute. "OK, here's customer number one. Gmail account in the name of John Smith, so that's bullshit, right? But I looked at the IP addresses where this account pulled down the data Lee sent. You get a few outliers, but mostly you get the Starbucks downtown at Wells and Madison and you get another Starbucks up in Highland Park. So whoever it is, they're making an effort to say off the grid, keeping it public so you can't tie it to them."

"Not trying hard enough," said Bernstein. "Gerry Ringwald's office is across the street from one of these Starbucks, and he lives in Highland Park."

"Who's Ringwald?" asked Jenks.

"Corsco's lawyer," said Lynch. "Any way we can tie it to him more directly?"

Jenks shrugged. "He's working remote – could be a laptop, could be a cell phone, could be an iPad or something. If he still has the device he did the download with, then I might be able to tie the data to the box. Might even find the files on there."

"OK," said Lynch. "Who else you got?"

"Customer number two, the first few hits were in Juárez, so you have to figure that's Hernandez. Then those start bouncing around. Picked up mail here in Aurora a couple of times, a couple spots in Chicago, all around the area. They're moving around, sticking to public access Wi-Fi, so I can't track this back to any base of operations."

"Same deal?" asked Lynch. "We catch them with the right laptop, we can tie them in?"

"Yeah," said Jenks. "Now, customer number three. This guy's picking up his mail all over the 19th arrondissement."

"The what?" asked Lynch.

"Paris," said Bernstein. "The Arab quarter, actually. Where they had the riots back in 2005."

"So that's al Din," Lynch said.

"Or his handler," said Bernstein.

"Or his handler's cutout," said Jenks.

"Any of these guys do business with Lee before?" asked Bernstein.

Jenks nodded. "He's sent stuff to the IP address in Juarez before, the Highland Park address, the Paris, so my guess is yeah." Jenks spun his desk toward his chair, started clicking away on his keyboard. "Something else I wanted to show you," he said. A slide show of pictures started on the monitor. Stein. Leaving his house, leaving his office, parking at the Stadium. "Part of a file that went to your Paris guy two weeks ago."

Little snort from Lynch. He opened the file on Jenks' desk, ran his finger down the list of names that identified the files Jenks had inventoried. Wide out for the Bears that just got his ass handed to him in a divorce, real estate developer everybody thought had the Block 35 deal tied up before he got low-balled by an out-of-town player, and Mike Lewis.

"Can you pull up what you got on Lewis?" Lynch asked.

"Sure," said Jenks. "Sounds familiar."

"County board race last year," said Lynch. "Remember, that Kroger guy, inherited the seat when his old man keeled over after the primary? Got a little carried away on the patronage, even by Cook County standards? Lewis was the good government candidate that looked like he was going to win the primary, right up until he dropped out a week before the election."

"Now I remember," said Jenks, scrolling down his screen, clicking on this and that. "Real mysterious. Family issues or something."

"That's the guy," said Lynch.

"OK, here we go," said Jenks. Lee ran the file. Lewis leaving his townhouse in Printer's Row, hailing a cab. Couple shots of the cab, tracking it through town, Lewis getting out of the cab at Belmont and Broadway, Lewis walking north and west. Lewis ducking into the Steam Room. Maybe an hour later, Lewis coming back out, another guy with him, the two of them walking a bit west before picking up another cab, the cab dropping them off at the Marriott on Michigan.

"What's that about?" asked Jenks.

"Steam Room's a gay bath house," said Lynch. "Lewis is Mr Family Man, some kind of deacon at one of the black churches. Looks like he was playing on the down low. Hurley, Kroger, or probably one of their guys, they put the eyes on him, knocked him out of the race."

Silence for a second, that sinking in.

"How many files does he have?" asked Bernstein.

"Haven't cataloged everything yet," said Jenks. "So far, better than three hundred."

Lynch's cell rang. Starshak.

"Looks like it's your day for the burbs," Starshak said. "When you're done in Aurora, head for Highland Park."

"Highland Park?" Lynch asked.

"Somebody offed Ringwald. And his family."

CHAPTER 63

"Scenery was nicer in Wisconsin," said Wilson. She was in Elgin with Hardin, in her underwear, pulling back the edge of the curtain in the window of their cheap hotel and looking out across the parking lot at the Jiffy Lube across the street.

"Where I've been the last couple decades, this place gets four stars," said Hardin.

"So we just sit tight and wait on Fouche?"

"I was never big on sitting tight. I just don't know what else to do."

Wilson pulled on a pair of slacks she'd bought at a Wal-Mart in Kenosha on the way back down from Door County. She hadn't had time to pack when they left Downer's Grove.

"This has to be over soon, one way or the other," she said, looking over her shoulder at the mirror. "These things make my ass look like it's wrapped in plastic."

"Think of it as handicapping," said Hardin. "Gives the other girls a chance."

"Fuck the other girls."

Hardin shrugged. "If you insist."

Wilson smiled at him, laughed, strange look on her face.

"What?" Hardin asked.

She shrugged. "This, you and me. Seems like anybody in the world who'd got a gun is lining up to take a shot at us and I can't stop smiling."

Hardin smiled back. "I know."

"I was going to say how much I missed being with you, but we never even had that, not the first time."

"I know."

"Now, odds are, in a couple of days, we're dead. I know that. And you know what? If you told me right now I could turn back the clock a week, I'd pass."

"Me too." Hardin's smile faded and he held her eyes.

"Odds aren't good, are they?" Wilson said.

"No."

"I wait the better part of my life for you to come back, and I get a week if I'm lucky."

"We," Hardin said. "We get a week." Hardin paused a moment. "Want to know the selfish thing? I hope they get me first. I've been in my share of shit, seen people shot, seen them bleed out. That's OK. I can do that. But I don't think I can watch you die."

Her face serious now, too. "So how about we don't?"

Hardin swallowed, nodded. They both finished dressing as he thought about their options, or lack of them.

CHAPTER 64

Lynch and Bernstein stood in Ringwald's kitchen. The wooden chairs were arranged in a semi-circle, Ringwald on the end to Lynch's left, Ringwald's son on the end to the right. The boy, probably four years old, was next to the mother. The girl was between the mother and Ringwald. Lynch was guessing she was seven. Had been seven.

".22s again?" Lynch asked.

"Yeah," said McCord. Some Highland Park cops were milling around, but they didn't get crimes like this on the North Shore. With the .22s and with Ringwald in the mix, it tied into Chicago, so they'd made the call. They were happy for the help.

The blood on the floor was tacky, drying, and the corpses didn't look fresh.

"How long?" Lynch asked.

"Last night, late," said McCord. "I'll know better when I get them in the shop."

"Everybody's gagged except Ringwald," Lynch said.

"Yeah," said McCord.

"So you figure al Din was talking to him."

"Yeah," said McCord.

They both stood for a moment, saying nothing, looking at the bodies. The boy was wearing an Iron Man T-shirt. The girl was wearing a Miley Cyrus T-shirt and a pair of gym shorts. Lynch tried to picture the scene for a moment – everybody getting herded into the room, getting taped to the chairs, getting...

"This guy is starting to piss me off," said Lynch.

"Yeah," said McCord.

"I assume we're going to talk to Corsco?" Bernstein asked.

Lynch just nodded.

"His right to counsel might be a problem, he decides to play it that way."

"Fuck his rights," Lynch said.

CHAPTER 65

Al Din's phone pinged. He opened the text from Tokyo. A photo of a large, older man entering the Hilton hotel on Michigan Avenue.

The Americans had sent Munroe.

If Munroe was in town, then al Din had to assume he was getting close. Time to switch IDs. He checked out of his hotel, drove to O'Hare, returned his rental car, took a shuttle to the terminal, took another to a different rental car vendor, rented a new car under a new name and then headed west, away from the city. Munroe would check the city first. Then he would look near the Interstate highways.

North Avenue was a busy arterial street between Interstate 90 to the north and Interstate 88 to the south. Lots of traffic, lots of stoplights, not an easy place to get away from quickly. That made it a bad choice, which, with Munroe looking for him, made it a good choice.

Al Din found what he wanted – an inexpensive motel with an odd name, not one of the national chains. He checked in. It was late, he was tired, but he was also hungry. He walked across the parking lot to an anonymous tavern.

As soon as he walked in the door, he could feel the emotional buzz of a group sharing some significant experience. Then there was a loud roar from the back of the room. Al Din turned. A basketball game, probably part of this college tournament he'd been hearing talked about all week, this March madness. The team from the University of Illinois had progressed to one of the final rounds and the game was on.

Al Din flashed back to his last trip to the US. He had walked into another bar at almost exactly this time of night, that time in Cleveland, Ohio. The dozen or so people in the bar were not scattered at their separate tables, but were all standing in front of the large television at the back of the room. The American president was on, announcing that Osama bin Laden was dead. The Americans had tracked him to a compound in Pakistan and killed him.

As al Din listened to the tone of the coverage and felt the cathartic reaction of the people in the bar, he realized he had completely misread something in the American character. He'd seen the previous American president standing in the rubble in New York swearing those responsible would be brought to justice. He had heard the same hollow boasts from others over the years, the new president, senators, and congressmen. But he had assumed that it was merely rhetoric. That what really mattered was the pretense the attacks provided, the opportunity it had given the Americans to pursue their aims in Iraq and in Afghanistan. In fact, al Din had long assumed that the Americans had no real interest in catching Bin Laden. They had severed him from his network, so he personally was not a threat. And he served a useful purpose as the monster that inflamed their electorate, a name those in power could always use to manipulate opinion. Al Din prided himself on mastering idiom and recalled the word he was looking for. Boogeyman. Osama bin Laden had been America's Boogeyman.

But Al Din had been wrong. They had never stopped looking. His opinion of the United States hadn't been shaped by the sort of people in this bar; it had been shaped by men like Munroe. But for the average American, for the electorate whose favor those seeking power must court, Bin Laden made things simple. One man who, with his robes and turban and beard and hooked nose, could be made the face of Islam, could be the enemy. With him as a fetish, a totem, the American people didn't even have to try to digest the real picture – the rage of the unemployed young masses in most of the Muslim world. The inbred sense of some historical injustice as they considered the previous grandeur of the Caliphate ground beneath the Crusaders' heels. The Jewish state forced into their midst by the West, even after the West had spent centuries persecuting the Jews. The differences between Sunni and Shi'a, the distinction between secular and religious motivations. Bin Laden was the distillation for all of it, a way to make the complex simple. He reduced an equation involving centuries of history, dozens of cultures, differing religions and competing worldviews into one of their cowboy movies. Good guys and bad guys in the street with guns.

And so America, the most powerful nation on Earth, had spared no effort, no expense, no technical wizardry or human sacrifice in their obsession to find Bin Laden. Even with his fortune, his international network, the open support of the Taliban, the tacit support of Pakistan, the ambivalent support of the Saudis, even with all of those advantages, he could not hide forever.

Al Din stood now in a different bar feeling a crowd of Americans reacting to a basketball victory in much the same way the crowd in Cleveland had reacted to news of Bin Laden's death and realized that, if Bin Laden could not hid forever, then neither could he.

With Bin Laden dead, if al Din completed the New Mexico project, the Americans would need a new face of evil. As Tehran's puppet, its cut-out, as the face at the end of the money trail, al Din would be it. He would be the new Boogeyman, In fact, MOIS would make sure of it, was already making sure of it. That explained the delay in paying him. Tehran would tie the money from the diamonds directly to al Din and al Din directly to Al Qaeda.

Al Din had never considered America to be his enemy, just his target. And he had never considered MOIS or Al Qaeda or Hezbollah to be his friends, just his clients. He had no mission but his own wealth and his own survival. Now it seemed that the best way to preserve both would be to switch sides.

He would make a deal with Munroe. And he would retire in the West, a rich man instead of a hunted one, secure from any threat his betrayal might bring from his current masters, because the Americans, the most powerful nation on Earth, would now be working to ensure his safety instead of his death.

That was his plan, anyway. But it would be a ticklish business. Munroe would value his cooperation. It was clear from the political rhetoric al Din was hearing in the American media that Munroe was using his knowledge of the diamonds and some other angle that al Din did not understand to create a new axis of evil, this one running from the Mexican drug cartels to Bin Laden's corpse. Al Din could give Munroe a way to add Tehran to that axis. The only question was whether Munroe would prefer that al Din cooperate as an ally or as a corpse.

Corpses were much easier to manage.

In the meantime, he would continue to look for Hardin. He would recover the diamonds, not for Tehran, but for himself.

CHAPTER 66

Corsco slammed the door, his face red.

His home. That cop, that fuck Lynch, had the balls to turn up at his home. Show up with his little Jew in tow; brace him in front of his family. Of course Lynch couldn't have exactly called Ringwald and set something up, Corsco knew that now.

Corsco didn't give them shit, of course. Couldn't, even if he wanted to. Corsco had no clue what was going on. Ringwald? Why? Over what? Sounded like a pro – .22s, close range. Lynch told him that much, probably trying to shake him up, which he had.

One of the other families? But why Ringwald? Why give Corsco that kind of heads up if they were coming after him? Hernandez maybe, over this Hardin shit? But again, why the lawyer? And .22s weren't Hernandez's style. He'd have gone in with a chainsaw. This Hardin puke? Did he hear something; figure he could get information out of Ringwald?

Too many fucking questions.

But whatever the hell was going on, he had the cops up his ass like a big-fisted proctologist, which means they'd be digging hard at anything they could get their mitts on. And one of those things was Fenn. Fucking actor, should've known he'd have some kind of cocaine immunity.

Type of thing he'd usually have Ringwald set up, but until he got a new shyster on the payroll, he'd have to use what he had. Took out his cell, called Franco. Franco was solid.

"I need you on a plane to Kansas City," Corsco said. "I want the Eagle on Fenn."

Franco didn't say anything for a second, which Corsco understood. The Eagle made people nervous.

"What kind of number can I give?" Franco finally asked. This was no time to be cheap. First of all, there weren't a lot of hits, not in real life. Hit men were a movie thing. In the mob, mostly they were favors. Sure, you had some guys with the stomach for it, so maybe you used them more than others; maybe they got a little rep. But you didn't have these shoot-the-balls-off-a-gnat, karate-master ninjas who charged six figures a pop that you saw in the movies.

You just had the Eagle. And the Eagle wasn't cheap.

"Whatever it takes," said Corsco. "But this has to be fast, a day, maybe two. Or no deal."

CHAPTER 67

Munroe slid his keycard into the door to his suite at the Hilton. Had to make some calls, check some e-mails.

As he stepped past the short wall that blocked off the bathroom and the closet from the rest of the suite, he saw Husam al Din sitting in the easy chair by the window, a silenced automatic steady in his lap. When a second passed and al Din hadn't shot him yet, Munroe exhaled. Must be here to talk. Or at least to talk first.

"If you would please remove your weapon, release the clip and then pull back the slide," said al Din.

Munroe took out his 9mm, dropped the clip and then jacked the round out of the chamber.

"Drop it in the trash can please," al Din said. Munroe did.

"And the backup," al Din said. "Inside of your left ankle, if my memory serves."

Munroe bent over, pulled out the .32, went through the same routine.

Al Din nodded toward the desk. Munroe saw the extra Beretta that he kept in the nightstand broken down on the blotter.

"My intentions are not hostile," said al Din, "but I thought our conversation might go more smoothly if you weren't focused on getting to one of your backup weapons during our conversation."

"Swell," said Munroe. "You mind if I take a piss first?"

"Be my guest. But I have also removed the weapon you had taped under the sink."

Munroe shrugged. "It was worth a shot. Still gotta piss though. At my age, my bladder doesn't handle having guns pointed at me as well as it used to."

Al Din gestured toward the bathroom with the pistol. Munroe went to the john, came back, spun the desk chair around to face al Din and took a seat.

"Enjoying Chicago?" Munroe asked. "Tried the pizza? Lots of good Italian joints out near the United Center."

Al Din smiled. "I wanted to talk about the boogeyman. Isn't that what Bin Laden used to be? The Boogeyman?"

"Boogeyman?"

"Did I use the term incorrectly?"

Munroe shook his head. "Just caught me by surprise. No, you used it perfectly. Guy's been dead a while now, though. Why the sudden interest?"

"I'm afraid someone else might be planning on making me your new one," said al Din.

Munroe snorted. "You're good, buddy, but you're getting kind of a big head, aren't you? You're not exactly a household name. A boogeyman has to be someone we can shake at the voters when we need to give them a good scare, has to be a known entity. You're under the radar. And I thought you liked it that way."

"That may be about to change."

Munroe paused, considered that information. "So you guys were moving the diamonds for a reason. And you're still in town, so that reason is local."

Al Din nodded.

"Anything you care to talk about?"

Al Din shrugged. "I thought first we could discuss the elasticity of loyalties."

"One of my favorite subjects," said Munroe. "Getting a little disenchanted with Sandland? Looking for an upgrade?"

"To paraphrase your American saying about baseball, terrorism has been very, very good to me. But I'm not sure that retirement in Waziristan is to my tastes. One of the dangers of operating in the West, I suppose, the seduction of comforts. The women, the food, the liquor."

"How you gonna keep 'em down on the farm once they've seen Par-ee? It's our secret weapon. We pretty much brought down the Soviet Union with blue jeans. So, you're looking to deal?"

"Let's call this an exploratory meeting. I'm wondering if a deal is possible. I've already killed several Americans on your soil this week, and we both know they aren't my first."

"Blood under the bridge, old sport. You got a few things in your favor. First, there are maybe ten other people in the country who've seen your whole resume, and they're all pretty pragmatic guys. The shit this week? Maybe your name's been bandied about some, but it's nothing we could take to court."

"I'm not worried about court," al Din said. "I'm worried about SEAL Team Six."

"That's my dog. It doesn't bite unless I tell it to."

"And Mossad? Do you hold their leash, too?"

Munroe smiled. "The Israelis can be a little intransigent, can't they? But what they don't know won't hurt them."

"There's not much they don't know."

"Yeah, but they're willing to pretend they don't know a lot of shit, as long as we keep sending them a few billion dollars of aid every year. I wouldn't plan on vacationing in Jerusalem, but as long as you don't go rubbing their nose in anything, we can reach an accommodation."

"I've already been to Jerusalem," said al Din.

"I know. Off the ol' bucket list, eh? So, you ready to talk turkey?"

"Talk turkey? This phrase I do not know."

"Cut to the chase, get down to business. If you're looking to switch teams, then I'm gonna need some details."

"Let's say I'm ready to explore free agency. As I understand your American sports, switching teams comes down to money."

"Yeah," said Munroe. "And we're the Yankees. We got more money than the rest of the league put together. Plus, if you've been studying free agency, you've heard of collusion. You start trying to get a bidding war going, we're going to whisper in a few ears and dry up your market. You deal with us or you don't deal with anybody. So unless someone from the farm team over in Tehran has put a big number on the table, you're not in a great negotiating position."

"The diamonds are worth $150 million. Hardin was looking to deal with Stein, so I suspect he's now looking to deal with you. Ten percent on Hardin's end, I imagine. Fifteen million dollars. I'll take that."

Munroe shrugged. "Hardin's already offered us the diamonds. And he actually has them. We pay him, we get to turn those around anyway we want and we come out way ahead on the deal. You don't have any diamonds."

"Not yet."

"Maybe not ever."

"True. But I have something more valuable. I have what the diamonds were paying for. Your media tells me America has spent nearly $4 trillion to avenge the three thousand killed on 9/11. How much will it have to spend to avenge ten times that many? Or twenty? Or more?

And how much cheaper would it be to spend a fraction of that amount now to prevent those deaths? And to be able to bring to justice those who planned them?"

Munroe just watched for a moment, tried to read al Din's face, but he got nothing.

"We'd spend a pretty penny," he said. "But we'd need some proof."

Al Din smiled, nodded, sat quietly for a minute, then stood up. "I imagined so. Now that I know an accommodation is possible, I will provide some."

Al Din pulled a cell phone from his pocket. "I will call you on this when I am ready. Now, if you will turn the chair to the desk please, I'm afraid I need to take a minor precaution before I leave."

Munroe turned the chair around, heard al Din close in behind him, thought for a second about making some kind of move, then thought again. Even when he was a kid, he hadn't been in al Din's league, not at the rough stuff.

"This is going to hurt, isn't it?" Munroe asked.

"Not now," al Din said. "But later, yes. I will offer some information for you to consider before our next conversation. A name. You may consider that name to be my bona fides. Bona fides, am I using the term correctly?"

"Depends on the name."

"Dr Mark Heinz."

Oh shit, Munroe thought, just before al Din hit him behind the ear with the butt of his pistol and the lights went out.

CHAPTER 68

Lynch was headed out of the squad room, headed home, when he heard the phone ring back at his desk.

"Slo-mo, wanna grab that? Let me know if I need to turn my ass around?"

Bernstein picked up the phone, listened for a moment, hung up.

"Woman down at the desk looking for you, Magnus?"

"From the shelter," Lynch said. "I'll talk to her on my way out."

Kate Magnus was standing by the desk when Lynch came down, same windbreaker on over a heavy cable-knit sweater. Colder tonight.

"Ms Magnus," Lynch said.

"I thought we'd settled on Kate to ease your confusion. At least you didn't call me Sister this time."

"I try not to make the same mistake three times," Lynch said. "What can I do for you?"

"I talked to Momolu. A couple of times, actually, before he'd say anything. I lost your card, with the number, but I remembered the address. I live a few streets over. I was on my way home. So, it appears, are you."

"Not a problem. I keep funny hours. Do you want to come upstairs and talk, or can I get buy you a cup of coffee somewhere?"

"Coffee detective? I'm Scottish. And I really am not a nun. If you want to buy me a real drink."

"A real drink sounds good," said Lynch.

"You're a little famous, you know." Magnus, with a double Laphroaig, neat.

"My girlfriend's famous," Lynch said.

"More famous maybe. But I remember all of that from last year. Right after I got here from Liberia. You were on the news several times. Your arm has healed?"

"Yeah," Lynch said. "It's fine."

"You're not happy with the famous part? Isn't that the American ambition?"

"I'm a lousy American," said Lynch. "I like ObamaCare. I think taxes are too low, even mine."

Magnus made what passed for a smile, took a sip of her drink. "I'm not used to it here yet. Not sure I'm going to be."

"Take some getting used to, I imagine, after Africa. Where was home originally? Scotland?"

"Aberdeen. Jesus seemed less complicated when I was a child. And the sisters were the only ones I knew that weren't pregnant and married off to some drunk by 19. Thought I'd be one of them. Mostly am, I guess."

Lynch took a pull on his bourbon, quiet for a minute. "I am sorry," he said, "about Membe."

She nodded.

"Momolu knew this al Din?" Lynch asked.

She nodded. "A gunman, an enforcer I suppose is the term. Some diamonds had been stolen. Not one or two by the miners, but a shipment of them. Al Din came and killed several people, Lebanese mostly. Men that Momolu thinks were responsible for moving the diamonds. Not just the men, their families too."

"Killed a family here, too. Last night."

"My God," Magnus said. "Why?"

"Don't know. Lawyer named Ringwald, his wife, their son and daughter. Ringwald was the mouthpiece for Tony Corsco. He's the mob boss around here."

"And he killed Membe? And that Stein man?"

"And a few others. It's about diamonds somehow. Maybe something more. Some funny types from DC have horned in on things, using us as gofers, so there's more going on. And whatever that is, they're welcome to it. But al Din's a killer, and he's killing people here. Not gonna have that."

"Is Momolu safe?"

"Can't think al Din's got any reason to go after him, probably doesn't even know he's there. I wouldn't take Momolu on any field trips until this is over."

Magnus finished her drink, set the glass down, stared down into it for a minute.

"I knew a girl in Scotland, a friend. My best friend, I guess. She was 16. She took up with this guy, older guy, worked the oil rigs. He had money, most guys didn't. He'd come in off his shift, they'd be out on the rigs for a couple of weeks, and everything would be great. Trips into Glasgow, all that. But he'd drink, and then he'd beat her. And then he killed her. And I thought it was the times or the drink. And then Africa, and everyone was killing everyone, and I thought it was just Africa."

She looked up at him. He was expecting tears, but there weren't any.

"It's everywhere, isn't it?" she asked.

"Yeah," he said.

"And there's never a reason, is there?"

"Never a good one."

CHAPTER 69

Late that night, the Eagle sat with Franco in the back of a six-passenger Citation on the way to Chicago. The plane added five figures to Corsco's bill, but that was Corsco's problem. A private plane meant no security, no screwing around trying to get weapons on the other end. It meant getting in when you wanted, getting out when you wanted. Usually the Eagle drove, unless the job was overseas, but Corsco sent this goombah out, wanted a secured target hit on two days' notice because he cocked up some dumb-ass DIY job. Hookers and a bag of coke? Jesus. Amateurs.

Plans for Northwestern Hospital scrolled across the laptop. The Eagle had bought everything – floor plans, wiring, HVAC. That was another couple Gs on Corsco's tab. Worked hospitals before. Hospitals were good, especially big ones like this – mess of buildings, lots of floors. Lots of people coming and going, lots of elevators, lots of stairs, lots of exits. The target was under police guard, though, that would complicate things. But the target had been in for four days, comatose supposedly, no real threat to anyone right now. Security's guard would be down. Probably one cop watching the room. Still, the hospital would have its own security, and some of them would be off-duty cops.

At least Corsco didn't want cute. No air bubble in the IV line, no smothering with a pillow. That made things simpler. Quick hit and run. Probably the .32 with the heavy suppressor. Made the pistol bulky, but it would be bagged up in the special rig, catch the brass and everything. No problem there. Get in the room, shut the door, five rounds center mass. You'd have to be right outside the door to hear it, and you'd have had to have heard a light pistol with a heavy suppressor before to know what it was. Target was medically fragile already; one round close to anything vital should be enough. Pride in the work, though. All five rounds would be right on target. Two rounds for the cop if that was necessary, enough to make sure he went down for the duration. Didn't need him dead. Better if he wasn't. That left five rounds in the clip just in case.

Northwestern was wired up, all the camera locations on the blueprints. So what? Cameras everywhere these days. Still, you study the placements then you know which side of the hall to walk on to give them a bad angle. Put the high lifts in a pair of loafers, those would add a few inches. The gray wig probably. People weren't suspicious of old people. Those silicon cheek inserts with bite wings, add weight to the face, mess with the telemetry if anyone was running any facial recognition stuff, wear the fat vest under the shirt, look forty pounds heavier. A hat. Pick up a Cubs hat somewhere, seemed like the right look for plugging a loser like Fenn.

Get a sweater, something easy to slip on over the rest of the get up, something easy to take off, a cardigan, something like that. Something bright, a solid color, say yellow. It was spring, yellow was a spring color. Give anybody that catches the action something easy to remember. The way it worked with witnesses, you give them one, big flashy detail, they seize on that. So if anybody pulls their shit together quick enough to call

security, they'd tell them look to look for the yellow
sweater. Security'd ask the usual stuff – height, weight and
such, and the witness would be all "I dunno, it happened
so fast. But a yellow sweater. I remember that." Dump
the cardigan in the stairwell, and boom, you're invisible.

From the blueprints, three possible exit strategies.
Closest stairs were to the right, but that meant walking
right past the nurses' station. Guy's in a coma in ICU,
so they'd have him wired up to monitors. Things would
start beeping as soon as the target got plugged, nurses
would be moving. Take the other stairs to the left, at
the end of the hall. Pass the elevator on the way. If the
door happens to open just then, cool. Hop on, ride it
up or down, didn't matter. Long shot on the elevator
though, so the real plan was the left stairs. Target was
on the seventh floor, no cameras in the stairwells. Dump
the cardigan and the wig in the stairwell. Pop out of the
stairs on five, got a bathroom two doors down. Grab a
stall, shed the shirt, the fat vest, the pants, yank the lifts
out of the shoes, spit out the bite wings. Wear scrubs
under everything. Less than a minute, then step out of
the bathroom and bingo, you're just another employee
heading home on shift change. Pictures on the website
showed the housekeeping staff in dark blue scrubs, so
get some of those. Google up the uniform store closest to
Northwestern, they'd have everything in stock.

Shift change was at 8am, so do it then. Not tomorrow,
next day. That was still inside Corsco's forty-eight hour
window. Already working way too much off third-party
intel. Needed to at least do a walk through, eyeball the
set up, get a clear mental image. So recon tomorrow
morning, do the job the next day.

Plane would be at Chicago Executive, up in Wheeling.
Traffic was going to suck, that was the downside to the

shift-change timing, but the upside was worth it. Pilot was getting paid well to be on call. Buzz him fifteen minutes out, have the engines turning over. Worse case, be wheels up two hours after pulling the trigger.

Ran through the plan one more time, tightening it up. Really liked the fat vest considering there was going to be at least one cop involved. Had a Kevlar lining in the fat vest. Too bad about the cop, though. Shoot a cop, that draws heat, even if you didn't have to kill him. But heat was why people called the Eagle. Heat was why they paid the money. Wouldn't be the Eagle's first cop.

CHAPTER 70

The next morning, Lynch and Bernstein walked into Starshak's office, closed the door.

"We gotta talk," said Lynch. "Been thinking. Been so busy chasing our tails on this thing we haven't done enough of that."

"What?" asked Starshak.

"It's al Din," Lynch said. "The Feds bring him up during their little dog and pony show, tell us he's Mr .22. Then they give us the one crappy picture, say that's all they've got. All I gotta do is flash it at the shelter where Saturday got killed and I get more than that, find out it's in Algiers anyway on account of the woman there knows the church. So you gonna tell me that Langley doesn't know where that is? They can't even give us that?"

"You saying they don't want us to find him?"

"I'm saying they're playing us. They're playing everybody. Fine. We've been around that block before. Whatever above-our-pay-grade national security voodoo they're up to, we aren't going to get looped in. But this fuck al Din, he's in our town killing people. Killed a couple of kids now. That shit we don't have to eat."

"So what do we do about it?" Starshak asked.

"I took it down to our tech guy, asked him to start running it against whatever they have from the various crime scenes we can tie al Din to. Guy laughs at me,

290

tells me with that kind of resolution, the bad angle, the lighting, he'd be pulling up false matches by the boatload. Says I got to narrow it down. So I ask him to at least run it against the Stein hit. The stadium has plenty of cameras and we have timing on that down to a tight window. Tech guy pulls up this."

Lynch handed Starshak an 8x10, nice clear shot of a slim, well-dressed, olive-skinned man in the Stadium foyer.

Starshak looked at the picture from the Feds, then at the new one. "So that's al Din," he said.

"Gotta be," said Lynch.

"OK, so have them run that against the other scenes."

"Which is what Lynch said." Bernstein chiming in. "They're already on it. But that might be a problem."

"Problem how?"

"The picture," Lynch said. "The tech guy, before he could even run what the Feds gave us against the Stein shooting, he had to clean up the image quite a bit. Enough, he says, that, if we tried to take it to court, it might get tossed. Get a defense with a good budget, they could bring some digital image expert in and claim we doctored the original enough to get a match."

"And," Starshak said, "if the original gets tossed, then anything we found using it gets tossed. Fruit of the poisoned tree."

"Right," Bernstein said.

"What else?" Starshak asked. "You said questions."

Lynch set the grainy surveillance shot that Hickman had passed out down next to the clean shot they'd pulled from the stadium camera.

"We already know that Corsco, Hernandez, and al Din have access to our surveillance system," Lynch said. "So we know the system isn't secure. You seriously think that Hickman and those suits from DC don't have a way in?"

Starshak sat back, the look on his face telling Lynch he could see where this was going.

"Meaning they could have pulled all the clean shots of al Din that they wanted right off of our own system, probably already knew for certain he did Stein, yet they hand us this crap picture to work with, junk that might queer a case if we ever manage to bring one."

"Yeah," Lynch said. "That."

Starshak sat back, mouth tight, then sat forward again.

"Your witness from the stadium, the waitress chick, she hasn't seen these pictures yet, right? Either of them?"

"No," Lynch said.

"OK, we got a physical description of al Din, right? And we got the piece of junk picture from Hickman. So go back to the techies, give them that, have them run a new search, no doctoring, give 'em a time spread maybe five minutes each side of the good picture, and hope that this pic pops up in the pile. Then we show the whole pile to your waitress chick and hope she picks out al Din. Then we're legit."

"It's still dodgy," Bernstein said. "It would be a problem if anybody hears how we got the clean picture the first time."

Starshak took the good picture; put it in his desk drawer. "What picture?"

"Ah," said Bernstein.

"So let's hope your waitress is good with faces, Lynch. Then we put a BOLO out on al Din. Hickman said not to chase Hardin and Wilson. Fine. He didn't say anything about this fuck."

"You didn't ask," said Lynch.

"Not gonna, either. Anything else?"

"Fenn," Bernstein said. "Got a call from Northwestern. He's starting to show some brain activity.Doc thinks he may come out of it in the next day or two."

"How many cylinders is he going to be running on if he does?" asked Starshak.

"No way to know," said Bernstein.

"They still keeping it quiet?" Lynch asked.

Bernstein nodded. "Yeah. Still handing out the daily update to the celebrity press. No change, no reason to expect any change. But you gotta figure it will leak eventually – nurse, orderly, somebody."

"OK," said Starshak. "I'll make sure our security at the hospital's still good. For now, we keep it under wraps."

"And if it leaks, we watch and see what Corsco does," said Lynch.

CHAPTER 71

"At least that sad little bear is gone," Wilson said.

She and Hardin were at the Phillips Park Zoo on the east side of Aurora, small municipal zoo, but a decent sized park, and had an eighteen-hole golf course. A park Hardin knew pretty well from his childhood, knew the topography at least, had an idea on the sightlines, egress points. Type of place a sharp operator might want to set up a meeting if he had to have a meeting with guys who just maybe wanted to kill him.

"God," Hardin said. "I forgot about the bear."

When he was a kid he used to walk down to the park a lot. One of the few places on the East Side where you'd see a lot of West Siders, kids wearing new clothes, not hand-me-downs, place where you could imagine some other kind of life.

They used to have a bear at the zoo, not a very big bear. Brown bear, Hardin guessed. He was no expert on bears. Fake stone grotto with metal bars in the front and a cement floor that was always puddled with urine and bear shit. Floor of the cage was maybe as big as a decent-sized living room and that bear had been locked inside since the day it arrived. Thing never seemed to move, just lay on the cement, dead eyes staring straight ahead, while kids tossed rocks and sticks at it through the bars trying to get it to do something. Bear had been there the first time Hardin could remember coming to the park, he figured he was four or five. It had still been there two decades later when he left for Africa.

"I hated coming here," Wilson said. "That bear, it broke my heart."

Some things had changed. The golf course had a makeover, new clubhouse. Nice little visitors' center at the zoo, educational stuff for the kids. Big new water park on the south end, on Montgomery Road, place that used to be a big, empty field, place where Hardin and Esteban and some of the other guys from the neighborhood could get up a sandlot game while the little leaguers from the good neighborhoods played real ball on the real diamonds a little to the east. Mastodon Lake was still there, place where some WPA guys had found mastodon bones back in the Thirties when they fixed up the park on the Feds' dime.

And cameras. Of course cameras. Security cam on the visitors' center, another at the parking lot, more probably.

Hardin stood next to a white Camry in the parking lot, turned to face the camera, took off the broad-brimmed hat he'd been wearing everywhere and wiped his brow, did a slow turn, checked all the roads in and out.

He hoped that was enough.

"You sure this is the best idea?" Wilson said. "Our hometown? Seems like the kind of place they'll be watching."

"Fouche gets us a deal, we'll have to make the handoff someplace. Maybe I want a home field advantage."

"And maybe not." Wilson said, smiling.

"Maybe not," said Hardin.

They walked out of the park and down Ashland to the parking lot in front of the taco stand where they'd left the Honda. No cameras there. Not the kind of place that could afford them. But the food was good.

CHAPTER 72

Munroe sat up in bed, reached for his phone. He lifted his head from the desk, felt the knot behind his right ear. That little bastard al Din. Munroe's head was going to be sore for a while. The cell buzzed again. He picked it up, looked at the screen. The surveillance guys.

"Yeah," he said.

"We picked up a hit on Hardin," said the voice on the other end.

"Where?"

"In Aurora. Got it quick because we have a priority feed running on any cams out there. Him and Wilson. They were poking around a big park on the east side, Phillips Park."

"Get it in time to angle anybody in?"

"No. Even with those cams at the top of the pile, there's still like a ninety-minute processing lag."

"What was he doing?"

"Recon's my guess, unless you think he had a sudden urge to go to the zoo."

"Hold on a sec," Munroe said. He opened his laptop, brought the park up on Google Earth. Big place. Got a few ways in and out, more than a few if you're on foot. Trees, some hills it looked like, plenty of stuff to screw with sightlines, but he'd need boots on the ground to get the topography. Public as hell.

And Hardin would know the park. Wilson would know it. The park and everything around it. Might know some people, too.

One more thing caught his eye. A building on the west edge of the park. Munroe switched to street view. Ten stories maybe? Apartments, it looked like.

Munroe knew he'd been brought in on this whole deal because DC wanted subtle. After the cluster fuck in Chicago last year, the last thing they wanted was another firefight. Munroe was still hoping to avoid that, but he was going to need boots on the ground. Boot with guns. This thing went right, then it would come down to one shot. If it went south, though, well...

"OK," Munroe said. "Get an SOG team out there, have them eyeball the place, give me their best guesses on scenarios and solutions. And find out about that apartment building on the west side. Find me a way to get somebody on the roof."

CHAPTER 73

Starshak was happy. The waitress play worked. Took about an hour to get a good spread out of the tech guys, another hour for Lynch to get her in to eyeball it, but she picked out al Din right off, no hesitation. Recognized him, recognized his clothes, said she saw him by the elevators right before she found Stein's body.

Starshak knew eyewitness stuff was crap half the time. But this was solid gold. Cute little All-American girl like that up on the stand? Solid gold.

So now he had a BOLO out on al Din, had the good picture out on the wire, and the tech guys were running it against the rest of this mess. Having a good morning so far.

Then he saw Hickman walking off across the squad toward his office. Fuck. "Lynch, Bernstein," Starshak yelled across the room.

They looked up, followed his eyes, saw Hickman.

"Fuck," Lynch said. He and Bernstein headed for Starshak's office.

Hickman wanted them to pull the BOLO on al Din. "I thought I'd made it clear you were supposed to back off on this," Hickman said.

"You didn't make shit clear to me," Starshak said. "You told Jablonski to lay off Hardin and Wilson, he told me.

You see me running anything on Hardin or Wilson? But we like al Din for..." A pause, Starshak turned to Bernstein, "ah jeeze, what's the count again, Bernstein?"

"Nine," Bernstein said.

"Nine homicides. Being cops and all, we thought maybe we'd take a shot a clearing those."

Hickman nodded. "I understand your frustration, Captain, but there are larger issues in play here. This connection between the cartels and Al Qaeda presents a unique opportunity, and it's something we have to approach with a little tactical discretion."

"Unique opportunity for whom?" said Bernstein.

"Pardon me?" Hickman asked.

"You think we're buying all this shit?" Lynch said. "This whole drug cartel and terrorist pile you keep shoveling at us? We know Hernandez has a beef with Hardin over his brother. And we think maybe Hardin's got some diamonds he stole from some bad guys over in Africa. What we don't see is any evidence that the one thing's got anything to do with the other. But you keep telling us there's this grand conspiracy between Al Qaeda and the cartel. So what Bernstein's asking, I think, is we see an opportunity for you – we're just wondering how it works out for anybody else."

Hickman smiled. "It works out for everybody who's on the team, Detective. I should think you'd be pleased with the idea of taking the gloves off with the drug lords and street gangs for a change."

"Just raises all those line-drawing questions," Bernstein said. "Slippery slopes and all that. But, what the hell. It's just the Constitution, right?"

"Oh my," said Hickman. "Playing the Constitution card already? I suppose I should go home and polish my jackboots. You really worried if we dot every *i* and cross every *t* for a guy like Hernandez?"

"Yeah, and the cameras all over town are nothing to worry about either, not if you're not up to anything," said Lynch. "Except we find out the whole system is out there on pay-per-view and Hernandez is one of the guys with a subscription."

Hickman got up, buttoned his jacket. "Gentlemen, I didn't come here to argue the point with you. I just thought I would do you the courtesy of informing you in person. Given the sensitive national security issues involved, the Stein case, the South Shore murders, the Downers Grove shootings, the Ringwald murders and anything having to do with Hardin, Wilson or Hernandez, all of that is all being taken over by a federal task force under my personal direction. Of course, we still need and value Chicago PD assistance, and your contributions on these matters to date will be both officially recognized and richly rewarded. But henceforward, you are to act in this matter only on my orders."

"Practiced that speech all the way over here, didn't you?" Starshak said.

"This has been cleared all the way up through the commissioner. But feel free to check if you want to rock the boat." Hickman smiled.

"Think I'll skip the boat rocking," Bernstein said. "I feel a little sea sick already."

Hickman left.

"You heard the man," Starshak said. "Pretty much clears your desks for you, so go find something to do with yourselves."

"Cubs are playing this afternoon," Lynch said. "Want us to get up to Addison, direct traffic or something?"

Starshak shook his head. "Hickman said the Stein case, the South Shore thing, Downers Grove, Ringwald, and anything having to do with Hardin, Wilson, or Hernandez.

I was thinking the Membe Saturday case. I didn't hear that mentioned. Did you hear that mentioned?"

"No, come to think of it," Bernstein said, smiling.

"You got anybody you like for that?" Starshak asked.

"Yeah, actually I do," Lynch said.

"So go get him. But quietly. No BOLOs. And wipe the damn smile off your face, Bernstein. You look like a girl."

CHAPTER 74

The tech guy called Lynch. He'd found a clean shot of al Din coming out of a Starbucks on Madison a couple days back. Lynch and Bernstein went down to check it out.

"Guy's good," the tech guy said. "Knows where the cameras are. Watch this series. He's coming out the door, has that hat down, his head angled to the side, no way we get a match. As he clears that frame, he turns, walking sort of backwards, like he's eyeballing the window display there, so the exterior cam gets nothing. But he misses this couple coming up on him, the guy is on his phone, not looking, he and al Din bump pretty hard, al Din's hat comes off and he has to face front. That's where we got the hit."

"He looks pissed," Lynch said.

"Can we trace him from that location?" asks Bernstein.

The tech guy nodded. "Yeah, because now I know that hat." Punches some keys, pulling up street shots, al Din heading north on Michigan, head down, hat low, no angle on his face. "He grabs a cab at Congress."

"Get a number on the cab?" Lynch asked.

Tech guy shook his head. "Bad angle. Plus it's rush hour, so we got a gaggle of pedestrians in the shot waiting for the light to change. Blocks the view."

"How about a time stamp?" Lynch asked.

"Sure," the guy said.

Lynch looked at Bernstein. Might be enough.

CHAPTER 75

Lynch called the cab company, gave them the time and location of the pick-up and they tracked down the driver. Guy named Jackson. Dispatch told him he was on his way in from O'Hare, headed for the Drake. Lynch and Bernstein drove over, met him out front.

Lynch showed Jackson al Din's picture. "You picked this guy up a couple days back. Recognize him?"

Jackson shrugged, scrunched his face up. "Man, you got any idea how many fares I pick up each day?"

"Day before yesterday, 5.17pm, Congress and Michigan. That help?"

Jackson took a look at the picture again. "Yeah, OK, maybe a little. I got stuck on a lot of short hops up and down Michigan for a bit there. I mean daytime, you know? You get the MILFs in from the North Shore, don't wanna walk three blocks, so they flag you down just to take 'em from the 900 shops up to Water Tower. And then they tip you like nothing. Couple of them got in, wanted the Art Institute, some kind of after-hours charity deal, so I drop them and I see this guy in a suit, nice hat, carrying a bag. I'm thinking maybe an airport run. Then the son of a bitch asks me to drop him at Union Station. Dickhead can't walk half a mile? I dropped the guy, ran his card. Got stuck with another local jump from there."

"He paid with a card?" Bernstein said.

"Yeah," Jackson said. "Don't go asking me the name or nothing, though, OK? But that time of day, from the Art Institute to Union, figure maybe five, ten minutes? Call dispatch, they can patch you through to whoever keeps up with that shit. You got my cab number, you got the time, shouldn't be hard to run down a receipt."

"Thanks," Lynch said. "That's major. That's a real help."

"So, you guys you take me out of circulation here, you cost me my spot in the cab queue. Do I get something for my time? Some kind of solid citizen reward?"

Lynch gave him a twenty and his card, wrote his cell on the back. "You get pulled over on some bullshit, you have the uniform call me. I'm not talking a DUI or anything, but you get nailed for ten over on the way out to the airport, hanging in one of the bike lanes or something, I'll get you some rhythm."

Jackson gave him a big smile. "You an OK dude, for a police. That's fucking gold to me, baby."

Jackson got back in his cab. Lynch held up his badge, yelled up to the guy in the monkey suit that was calling the cabs up. "This guy's next." Monkey suit guy waved Jackson up, bumping him ahead of half a dozen waiting taxis. Driver at the head of the line leaned out his window, yelling at monkey suit in an Indian accent. Monkey suit just pointed back at Lynch.

As Lynch and Bernstein climbed into their Crown Vic, the Indian cabbie held his arm out the window, flipping them the bird.

"Another Angry Bird," Bernstein said.

The cab company accounting guy ran down the charge receipt, turned up an American Express card belonging to Ricardo Orendain, guy had been at the Fairmont for a few days, but he'd checked out yesterday afternoon, then used the same card a couple hours later when he dropped a rental back at the Hertz lot at O'Hare.

Lynch and Bernstein drove to the airport. A skinny white kid with bad skin was on the Hertz lot, checking cars in. Manager said he would have been the one on duty when al Din brought the car back. Lynch showed him al Din's picture.

"I don't look at anybody, you know?" the kid said. "I mean I scan the code on the car, take a quick look, make sure there's no dents or anything, check the gas, then I print out their bill, they sign for it, and they grab the shuttle over to the terminal."

"So you don't remember this guy?"

Kid just shook his head. "It says I checked him in, then I checked him in."

Lynch turned to Bernstein. "What's al Din's play here? He's been pretty mobile, so he needs a car. Unless he's blowing town."

"Yeah," said Bernstein. "But he rented this car the day of that Downers Grove thing. And we know he's been in town longer than that. So he's switched rides before. Just being careful. Maybe something spooked him."

Lynch turned to the kid. "How do you get to the other rental places?"

Kid shrugged. "We got the bus that takes you back to the terminal. Avis, all the rest of them, they got their own buses, too. You get back to the terminal, you could hop a bus to any of the rental lots."

"Thanks," Lynch said. He and Bernstein headed for their car.

"If al Din's at the terminal playing musical buses, what do you want to bet we've got all that on video?" Bernstein said.

••••

"Now that I can do," said the tech guy. Lynch had called in, given him the time the car was dropped off and asked him to run their good al Din shot through the system, see if they could pick him up on the shuttles. "Give me maybe thirty minutes."

Lynch and Bernstein drove to the terminal, grabbed a bite. Lynch's cell buzzed.

"Got him," the IT guy said. "Al Din grabs the bus at the Hertz lot at 7.43pm, gets dropped at Terminal 1 at 7.51. He walks over to Terminal 3, hops the Alamo bus at 8.17, gets dropped off at Alamo at 8.26. Drives off the lot in a black Hyundai at 8.41. License SO6 1290. We'll be watching for the plate. It turns up, I'll ping you straight off."

Lynch hung up, told Bernstein.

"Son of a bitch," Bernstein said. "We may actually get this fucker."

CHAPTER 76

"You have the cash pulled together?" Late that night, Hardin on the phone with Lafitpour.

"I do."

"Be ready. Tomorrow morning early."

"And where shall we meet?" Lafitpour asked.

"Think I'm teeing my ass up for you again? Tomorrow," Hardin said. "You get the location then. Just be ready to move. Make sure your Bentley's gassed up."

"Might I have some idea how long this will take so I can plan the rest of my day?" Lafitpour asked.

"I'd clear your calendar, sport," Hardin said. "How long it takes is going to depend on how much you fuck with me."

Hardin hung up. Lafitpour called Munroe.

"Hardin called. He wants to deal tomorrow. He said early."

"Did he say where?" Munroe asked.

"No, but he did tell me to fuel up my car."

"OK," Munroe said. "I'll tell Hickman."

It fit with what Munroe had. After the hit on Hardin at the park in Aurora, Munroe had put the full-court press on him. Hardin had popped up in a handful of other places, all in the western suburbs. Security camera at a driving range and go-cart track joint on Route 47 just west of Aurora, cornfields in all directions. Parking

lot camera at Pottawatomie Park in St Charles, maybe
a dozen miles up the Fox River. Cantigny, some kind of
park and museum complex near Wheaton. Looked like
he was playing al Din's game. He'd figured he was going
to be on camera, so he got on a lot of them. If Hardin was
shopping for a meet site, all the locations would work –
all public, all with some good, defensible spots. Hardin
had to figure they might make another try for him, so he
was spreading them out, giving them so many spots to
cover they couldn't get set up solid at any of them.

But it looked like it was going to be the western burbs.
Hardin and Wilson had both grown up out there, wanted
to play on their home turf. Gonna have to hog some
bandwidth and assets in the morning, have real-time
eyes on all the sites Hardin had scoped out. With a little
luck, Munroe could still get a shooter in place for the
meet. If he couldn't get them there, he should at least be
able to keep eyes on them after, bag them on the road. A
chopper would help. Munroe got on the phone, arranged
for one. He'd meet it at the Aurora airport. Civilian bird,
or it would look like one anyway. But if you slid the
door out of the way, there'd be a swing-out mount for a
minigun. And somebody riding shotgun who knew how
to use it.

Munroe started matching up assets with geography,
deciding who he wanted where.

You plan for what you can. So he gets them at the
meet, takes them on the road and, if he couldn't, then
Munroe would just have to play ball with them until he
could.

World just wasn't that big anymore.

CHAPTER 77

Lynch's cell buzzed. He woke up, checked the clock. Coming up on two. He picked it up, checked the screen. Liz.

"Jesus Liz, you're still in New York, right? Almost three there."

"I know John, I'm sorry. Couldn't sleep."

"You OK?"

"No." Silence for a long while. "It's not going to work, is it?"

"You mean us?"

"Yeah."

Lynch took a breath let it out. "No, probably not. Not much longer anyway."

"I can't give this up," she said. "I know you want someone who can be with you, and I'd love to be with you. But I can't give this up."

"I know. I'm not asking you to."

"And you're never going to leave Chicago."

"No, I guess not."

No one said anything for a long time. Lynch could hear her breathing on the other end.

"You OK?" he asked.

"No," she said.

"Me neither."

More silence.

"I don't want to hang up," she said.
"Me neither."
Lynch heard the line go dead.

CHAPTER 78

Just after 6am, Lynch toweling off after his shower when his cell rang. Bernstein.

"Got a call from Northwestern. Fenn's awake."

"Lucid awake?" Lynch asked.

"Way better than they expected," Bernstein said. "Pretty much a full recovery."

"Meet me there in thirty," said Lynch.

Fenn was sitting up when they walked in, the back of the bed cranked up about sixty degrees.

"Look better than the last time I saw you," Lynch said. "Last time you were down in the ER with all these tubes coming out of you. You remember us?"

Fenn nodded.

"Got anything you want to talk about?"

"Detective, I told you everything I know last time we spoke."

"And then you went back to your hotel and OD'd?"

Fenn shrugged a little. "I don't remember anything about that. I remember getting back to my room. I remember dinner. That's it."

"We got you on possession. You understand that, right?"

Fenn shrugged. "I'll have my lawyer call you."

"And you aren't worried about anything? Doesn't strike you as weird, you talk to me in the afternoon, and that night you end up tooting some virgin powder that just about puts your lights out?"

"As I've said, Detective, I have no memory. And I believe I would like to have an attorney present for any future discussions."

Lynch nodded. "Just so we're clear, I'll be talking to the DA on the drug side of things, so enjoy the hospital food while you can. Stuff in County sucks."

"You really think you'll be able to hold me on some possession charge?"

"We'll see what happens," Lynch said.

CHAPTER 79

Tommy Porcini ran Tony Corsco's juice loan racket for the northwest suburbs. He was having breakfast out in Elgin, fueling up for a long morning of running down deadbeats. Porcini's phone buzzed, he looked at the screen. That puke Pilsen, guy that was supposed to meet up with him this morning and get current.

Porcini opened the phone. "You're late;" he snapped. Flipped open his notebook, ran his finger down to Pilsen's name. Guy was into them for seven and a half Gs.

Porcini could hear the background noise. No other place in the world sounds like the inside of a casino. The dumb fuck was probably down at the Victoria, the riverboat here in Elgin. Juice loan pukes would do that when they knew Porcini was making the rounds, hide out on the boats, cause they knew that was one place Porcini couldn't show his face. Part of that whole keep gambling clean in Illinois sack of shit the politicos sold to the voters, swearing up and down the mob wouldn't get a foothold in gambling in Illinois. Casino security had all of Corsco's guys' pictures. None of them were allowed on the boats. It was all bullshit of course. Didn't mean Tony wasn't getting his rake. Just meant he was getting it through the unions and the politicians now, not skimming it out of the cash rooms.

"I know, Tommy. That's why I'm calling. I'm gonna have it all for you man. Not just the juice, but the whole

shebang. You wouldn't fuckin' believe it, man, but I am
on the prime roll. I gotta be up like fifty right now, easy.
Lady luck, she's giving me a tongue bath. I can't walk on
that. Gotta ride it out."

Porcini thought a second. "You say you're up fifty?"

"Not counting my money at the table, Tommy. Bad
luck. But gotta be fifty. Gotta be."

"Do yourself a favor, Pilsen. Do a little counting. Count
out eight right now and put that in your pocket. You
make sure you leave with eight."

"Eight? Man, I thought I owed like seventy-five
hundred."

"You did. Then you decided to stand me up, which
means you're gonna be late by the time you hang up the
phone, and the juice on late puts you at seventy-seven
fifty."

"That still ain't eight."

"Banks got fees, right? Me too. I got a fee for when I
gotta drive out to fuckin' Elgin, eat some crappy diner
breakfast and get stood up by some hump. So it's eight.
Today. Or else the Victoria may not be the only thing
floating in the river come nightfall."

Big noise on the phone, some kind of whoopee sound
out of Pilsen. "No problem Tommy. Just cleaned up on a
double-down. Eight it is. I'll call you."

Porcini hung up, took a second to admire the ass on the
chick paying her bill up at the register, then took a longer
second to eyeball her and the guy she was with. Son of a
bitch. It was that Hardin dude. Corsco's put the word out
on him what, like a week back? Sent his picture around.

Porcini pulled his out his money clip. Shit. Smallest he
had was a twenty. He wasn't much of a tipper by habit, but
he didn't want to waste time at the register. He threw the
twenty down on top of his $9.73 check and grabbed his coat.

Porcini got in his Buick, adjusted the mirror, watched the chick back out a black Honda, shook his head. What kind of man lets the woman drive? Porcini eased out behind them, hanging two cars back at the light. The Honda hopped on Randall, heading south, staying in the left lane, put its blinker on for the eastbound 90 exit. Tommy got out his phone and hit one on the speed dial.

"Put the boss on," he said to the voice on the other end. Waited a bit, following the Honda down the ramp, tucking in a few cars back and a lane over.

"What do you need, Tommy?" said Tony Corsco.

"I'm out in Elgin. You still looking for that Hardin fuck? I'm on his ass right now."

CHAPTER 80

"You have had time, I assume, to check on Heinz and consider my offer?" 6.30am, al Din on the phone, talking with Munroe.

"Yeah," Munroe answered.

"And?"

"I can go the $15 million, but that only works if you put Tehran in the middle of this. And you're going to have to have some proof to back it up."

"I have been accumulating evidence on my MOIS handler," al Din said. "I have been saving decrypted emails, I even taped my last in person meeting with him. You will be quite pleased. He is local and well placed."

"OK, good. I'm gonna need to eyeball that stuff before we get in bed."

"Of course."

"Plus you're going to get the debrief treatment, you know that, right? Once you come in, it's going to get official. Langley's gonna lock you up in one of their B&Bs for a while. It'll be a nice joint, probably some horse farm in Virginia, but they're gonna wring you out. They'll want your whole history."

"Naturally."

"And I'm going to be adding a tune to your hymnal. Little piece of your history you might have forgotten. You and I need to go over the music."

Al Din smiled to himself, remembering the strange news stories he'd been hearing about a tie between the Mexican drug cartels and Islamic terrorism. "This new song; is it a mariachi number perhaps?" al Din asked. "A little something about drug cartels and terrorists?"

Al Din was sharp, Munroe knew that. Not that he had to be a rocket scientist to piece that together, not with the crap that had already hit the media.

"Yeah, a nice little narcocoriddos tune. I'll have all the lyrics for you."

"I'll brush up on my Spanish," said al Din.

"Then you can look forward to a very comfortable retirement in the West..." Just the slightest pause, just enough to let al Din know that the conversation was about to take an uncomfortable turn. Munroe was about to give him the bad news. "That is if you can help me ensure this diamond mess turns out right."

And now a pause on al Din's end, to let Munroe know he was not happy. "Help you how?"

"Hardin's still running around loose with the stones. And now he's got company. DEA agent named Wilson. Old girlfriend, it turns out. I don't need a couple of free radicals running around waiting to piss on my narrative. And, since you're cast for a major role in this production now, you don't need that either."

"So?"

"So you've been hunting Hardin since you hit town, right?"

"Yes."

"Keep hunting. I'm working Hardin from my end. You keep working him from yours. Until he's off the board, we can't finalize our deal."

Al Din let a little dead air build, let Munroe know he wasn't holding all the cards yet. "I have been hunting

Hardin for Tehran. But I get paid to hunt. The $15 million we've agreed on, that's to tie Tehran to Heinz and to turn in the nasty little surprise they bought from him. If I get Hardin, what am I paid for that?"

"Hardin's still got the diamonds. You get him, then you'll have those. And I need those. So you get Hardin before I do and you double down on your payday."

Al Din smiled, thought of a phrase he had heard many times in America. "What a country," he said.

"Which one?" asked Munroe.

"Who cares?"

Al Din ended the call. The phone had vibrated while he was talking with Munroe – a message coming in from his contact in Tokyo. He had picked up Hardin's black Honda on a tollbooth camera ten minutes earlier. It was eastbound on Interstate 90, heading toward Chicago.

CHAPTER 81

Wilson driving, cussing under her breath, drumming her fingers on the wheel. They were coming up on O'Hare, about to switch from 90 to the Kennedy, but the traffic had slowed to a crawl. Morning rush, and the radio said there was a three-car crash at Lawrence, two lanes closed. IDOT was ripping up 294 again, so cutting down the Tri-State to the Ike wasn't going to save any time. The traffic report on the radio put the travel time from O'Hare to the Loop at over an hour.

"You in that big a hurry?" Hardin said. "We get there, we're either gonna get rich or dead, and I make it 60-40 on dead."

"I'd rather be dead than sit in traffic."

Hardin laughed. "Yeah, me too."

He pulled out his phone, called Lafitpour.

"Get Hickman to your office."

"Why?" Lafitpour asked.

"Because you want to make a deal, and that's one of the conditions. I'll call back in a bit." Hardin closed the line.

"I'll give them the location when we're ten minutes out," Hardin said to Wilson. "If they're going to play nice, then ten minutes is all they'll need. If they're going to fuck with us, the less time we give them the better."

Wilson nodded. Traffic came to a dead stop again. She reached over, took Hardin's hand.

"No matter how this goes, I'm where I want to be," she said.

Hardin squeezed her hand and nodded. "Me too."

319

CHAPTER 82

Corsco thought about the Hardin situation. Hardin was Fenn's contract, but fuck Fenn. The Eagle would take care of Fenn. Not like Corsco was going to see any money out of Fenn anyway, even if he took Hardin down. Never really been about the money anyway. Corsco had to admit that to himself. Been about hanging with Fenn, the Hollywood cool, about the women. Lesson to be learned there.

Still, supply and demand. Hardin was in demand, and Corsco was in the supply business. Question was, who did Corsco feed Hardin to?

That Munroe guy wanted Hardin, but that was just business. As long as Hardin ended up dead, Munroe didn't care how he got there.

Hernandez wanted Hardin, but with Hernandez it was personal. And this past week had caused some serious tension with Hernandez. Corsco didn't need that. Plus, if he gave Hardin to Hernandez, then Hernandez would owe him a favor. That Munroe guy didn't seem like he was the favor granting sort.

Corsco called Hernandez.

"I assume you're still looking for Hardin?"

"Yes. I want to taste that bastard's blood."

Jesus, thought Corsco. These Mexicans. Always with the blood tasting. "I have a man on him," Corsco said.

"Bring him to me," Hernandez growled into the phone.

"Can't do that. But I've got a man on his tail right now, stuck in traffic on the Kennedy. Looks like Hardin's heading downtown. My guy will stay on him as long as he can. If you can round up some troops, my guy will guide them in. What you do with Hardin is your business."

"I will be in touch. If I get Hardin, I will not forget this."

"A favor for a colleague," Corsco said. "You would do as much."

CHAPTER 83

"You have the money ready to move?" Hardin on the cell with Lafitpour. Hardin and Wilson had just cleared the accident at Lawrence, traffic starting to thin out a little.

"Yes, of course."

"What do you need to make the transfer?"

"It only takes a phone call," said Lafitpour. "As long as you have the account numbers and access codes."

"OK. Hickman there?"

"Yes."

"Put us on speaker."

A pause, then Lafitpour, a little distant now, speakerphone voice. "We are on speaker."

"You there, Hickman."

"Yes," Hickman said.

"OK gents," said Hardin, "We're making the deal today. Here's how this works. I will call you with a location, and I will call you soon, so don't step out for coffee or tie up the line. You show up, both of you, but only the both of you. I give you the rocks, you transfer the money. Then we all take a little ride until I'm sure the transaction has cleared and that nobody is trying to bust me again."

Lafitpour chuckled. "And why, exactly, would we agree to be your hostages?"

"Hey, we could have played things nice and civil last time, remember? I wasn't the one who queered that deal. And cut the hostage shit. This whole city is holding me hostage right now. I try to screw you on this deal, there won't be enough room on the planet for me to hide. I'm selling the diamonds, but what I'm buying is your goodwill. Well, not yours. Hickman's and the guys in Washington who are pulling his strings. I fuck you on this, I might as well save myself a few really uncomfortable weeks and just eat my damn gun."

"And if I still don't like your terms?"

"Then I have to find some new friends and some other way to keep safe. Wilson and me? I don't think we can get $15 million for a book deal, but I bet I can get something, don't you? And killing me is going to get a lot trickier after I've been on CNN blowing holes in this drugs and terrorists bullshit."

Hardin heard Lafitpour sigh. "Excitement is rare at my age. I suppose I shall just have to treat this as an opportunity. We will do this your way."

"OK, and don't bother making a call and trying to scramble some assets. You don't have time. I'd see them coming. If I see them coming and I have a clear shot at you, I take it. And then I hit the send button on my phone and reporters from the *New York Times* to *Der Spiegel* get some real interesting e-mail."

"Some days I do despise technology," Lafitpour said.

Tommy Porcini's ass was getting numb, over an hour in this fucking traffic, but it made tailing the Honda pretty damn easy. He was still three cars back, but he could have sat right on their ass ever since O'Hare and they wouldn't have thought a thing about it. Not like anybody could go anywhere.

Corsco'd called back. He was handing Hardin over to Hernandez, given Porcini's number to Hernandez's people. They'd been in touch. Looked like Hernandez had been over on the west side hanging in his crew's territory. Word was he'd loaded up a couple of SUVs, was en route. Porcini was supposed to stay on Hardin's ass until Hernandez got there.

"Al Din is on the move." The surveillance guy talking to Lynch. They'd had eyes on al Din's car full-time since they tracked it down.

"What's he doing?" Lynch asked.

"Just sort of circling around the River North neighborhood right now, like he's waiting for something."

"OK." Lynch waved Bernstein over. "We're rolling."

CHAPTER 84

Hernandez sat in the backseat of a Ford Explorer, one of his best Skull shooters next to him. One of the blacks from the West Side gang driving, a man who knew the streets, another Skull up front. Hernandez had three more shooters in a Lexus that another gangbanger was driving a couple cars ahead in the left lane. They'd cut north up some surface streets, got on the Kennedy at Fullerton headed back south. Hernandez was on the phone with Corsco's man. He should be close – a red Cadillac CTS behind a black Honda in the right lane.

Corsco saw a red Caddy five cars up.

"Tap your brakes twice," Hernandez said into the phone.

The brake lights on the Caddy winked.

"Hardin still in front of you?" Hernandez asked.

"One car up," said Porcini.

"OK, we got him." Hernandez hung up the phone.

Hernandez tapped his driver. "Get in the right lane. Call the other driver; tell him to get over, too."

A few cars ahead, the Lexus cut into the right lane. The red Caddy pulled over into a middle lane. Hernandez's driver cut into the vacated spot. Hernandez could see the Honda now. The Lexus was immediately in front of it. The Honda signaled a turn, getting ready to take the Randolph Street exit. The other driver was paying attention – he led the Honda up the ramp.

Hardin picked up his phone and dialed. He and Wilson were coming up on their exit. Time to get Lafitpour and Hickman moving.

"You two ready?" Hardin asked.

"Yes," said Lafitpour.

"OK. Both of you take off your jackets. Either of you has a gun, put it on your desk and leave it there. Hickman got his phone with him?"

"Yes," said Lafitpour.

"Have him call this number. That will be Wilson. He stays on the phone with her until we meet. You stay on with me. Don't want you calling any friends, trying to arrange any surprises."

Wilson's phone rang, she answered.

"Just keep talking," she said. A pause. "I don't care about what asshole. Recite the fucking alphabet if you have to. Just make sure I keep hearing an open line."

"OK," said Hardin. "The two of you get outside – you're taking a little walk."

"We will lose our cell signals in the elevator," said Lafitpour.

"Then take the stairs. There's a parking garage at Franklin and Washington. Walk there now. Right now. Should take you ten minutes. Take the elevator to the sixth floor. Walk to the east end of the floor and stand by the wall, right in the middle. You aren't there when I pull up, we're done. And keep the phone by your mouth. You aren't that interesting so you don't need to keep talking, but I better hear you breathing."

Hardin could hear street noises through the phone, could hear Lafitpour's breathing picking up a little. Ten minutes meant he and Hickman had to hoof it, but Hardin didn't want them relaxing, didn't want them thinking. He just wanted them moving. Hardin hit the mute button on his phone. Wilson did the same.

"Hickman still there?" Hardin asked.

"Yeah," said Wilson. "He's saying some uncharitable things about you."

"Looks like we might be alive for lunch," Hardin said.

"Be able to afford a nice one if we are," said Wilson.

Wilson cut up the Randolph exit, took Clinton south to Washington, and then turned east.

Hernandez sat at the left turn lane at the light at Wacker and Washington, the Honda in front of him, the Lexus in front of the Honda. The light changed and all three cars headed east down Washington. Just before the end of the block, the Honda turned into a parking garage. The Lexus couldn't make the turn.

"Lost the other car," the driver said to Hernandez as they turned into the garage, the Honda halfway up the ramp ahead of them.

"Tell them to circle the block," Hernandez said. "Have them pull in, block the exit."

The driver made the call.

The shooter next to Hernandez looked over; saw the boss stroking the barrel of the MP5 like he was trying to make it cum. The shooter smiled. He knew exactly how the boss felt.

CHAPTER 85

Al Din was near the Merchandise Mart when the Honda exited the Kennedy, Tokyo on his phone now, on speaker, guiding him in.

"Take a right, cross over the river on Wells. The target is eastbound on Washington. You'll intercept in a couple of blocks."

Al Din caught the light at Wacker, caught the next one at Lake, too. Almost enough to make him wish he believed in Allah so that he could also believe that Allah was smiling on his efforts.

Al Din stopped for a red light at Washington.

"Should have caught them on the traffic cam right at your intersection," Tokyo said. "They turned in somewhere. Hold on." A very long couple of seconds. "OK, I've got them on a security cam. Parking garage directly across from you on the right. Do you see it?"

"Yes," al Din said.

"There's an exit off of Wells. Turn in there."

The light changed. Al Din accelerated through the intersection and signaled his turn into the garage.

Four cars back, Lynch cussed the jackass who double-parked, blocking traffic.

"We're going to miss the light," Bernstein said.

Lynch muscled the Crown Vic left, cutting off a taxi, getting a blast on the horn for that, shot ahead, cutting back to the right lane and into the intersection just as the light turned yellow and al Din's car disappeared into the garage.

Bernstein got on the radio and called for backup.

CHAPTER 86

Wilson looped around the third floor of the garage, still full, caught the ramp up to the next level. On the fourth level, she started to see some open spots. The SUV behind them wasn't pulling in to any of them. Shit. She had really hoped they were just looking to park.

"Got a black Explorer on our six," she said. "Picked it up just before the exit. Still behind us."

"Yeah," Hardin said. "Saw that."

"Looks like four guys in it."

"Yeah, saw that too."

"So I guess we shouldn't make those lunch reservations yet."

Hardin took out both of the 9mms he taken from Corsco's men, held one in each hand.

"Not yet," he said.

"Get up on their ass," Hernandez said.

"Can't lose them in here," the driver said. "We hang back, let them park, hit them as they get out of the car."

Hernandez nodded. That was the smarter play. Had to relax. Too much blood flow to his cock, he guessed. Just like being with a hot woman. The little head turning off the big one.

CHAPTER 87

Munroe had the chopper spun up and was hightailing it for the Loop. He was tracking the GPS on both Lafitpour's and Hickman's phones. Pretty clear they were on foot, walking north across the Loop. And neither one answering – calls going straight to voicemail.

Had to give Hardin credit. The whole west burbs thing was smoke and mirrors. Now he was crashing the deal, pushing Lafitpour into some fast meet where Hardin pulled all the strings.

"How long?" Munroe asked into his mic.

"Be downtown in thirty. Don't know where I'm going to put this down, though."

"Wherever I tell you," said Munroe.

Munroe took a breath, let it out, started thinking. There was what you wanted and there was what you had, and they were almost always two different things. So Munroe started working through what he had.

The deal with Hardin was going to go through. Lafitpour would punch in the numbers and the $15 million would go wherever Hardin had him send it. Munroe was pretty sure that as soon as the money turned up wherever it was going, Hardin would have someone waiting on the other end to spread it out and make it disappear. That was the smart play and Hardin hadn't done anything stupid yet. Munroe wasn't going to be able to yank the chain on the transfer, pull the money back.

And, with $15 million and a twenty-minute head start, Hardin could get seriously gone.

Feds in raid jackets had been the plan for the first Hardin meet, but Munroe was hoping this to keep this one unofficial until after Hardin was dead. Guess that wasn't going to happen. Had to do something to slow Hardin down.

Munroe called the director of the FBI – he didn't have time to explain who he was to the field office guys in Chicago.

"What can I do for you Munroe?"

"I assume you have a rapid response team on call in Chicago?"

"Yeah."

"Got a short clock situation here, Bill. Hickman, US attorney in Chicago; used to be one of your guys?"

"Yeah?"

"He's being held hostage by a Nicholas Hardin and a DEA agent named Wilson."

"This the thing we were supposed to be in on a few days back? Terrorist, drug lords, lots of other bullshit?"

"Gotten a little hairy since then, but yeah. I don't have time to explain now, but I'm going to link you to the GPS on Hickman's phone. Get a tactical team on that signal soonest – and I mean in like ten minutes. I'll be there in twenty. It is imperative that Hardin and Wilson don't get in the wind. And tell your boys these are dangerous folk. Hardin's former scout/sniper, former Foreign Legion. Wilson's got a mess of cartel notches on her belt, and they've both killed people this week."

"You telling me you don't want us reading them their rights?"

"You can read them. It just might be better if they can't hear them when you do."

"Do what I can, but you may get there before we do."

Feebs were on their way, but them being on time was going to be a close thing. But the whole operation had officially gone sideways. Things were going to get loud and messy, which was exactly not what the big boys in DC wanted when they tabbed Munroe for this assignment. Munroe went through his mental ledger, started making calls, calling in chits, firing up the threats-and-favors apparatus. When you know you're gonna ruffle some feathers, it's good to have all your carrots and sticks lined up.

CHAPTER 88

Lafitpour and Hickman stepped out of stairwell and started across the sixth floor of the garage. Half empty up this far. They walked to the wall Hardin had told them to.

"We're here," Lafitpour said into his phone.

"Hang tight," Hardin answered.

Al Din took his ticket from the machine, waited for the gate to go up, and then started up the ramp.

"Do you know what floor they are on?" he said to the phone.

"They just passed the cam on five," Tokyo answered. "Only got six and the roof left."

Al Din accelerated.

On five, Hardin started seeing more empty spots, things really thinning out at the back of the floor, toward the ramp to six. That's why he'd told Lafitpour to meet on six. Hardin had scouted the garage a couple days earlier. This time of day, six was still mostly empty. Hardin didn't want to go up to seven. Seven was the rooftop, no overhead cover. If somebody managed to put a long gun in play, he didn't need to make it easy on them. Wilson cut the wheel, started up the ramp to six.

The SUV followed, half a floor back.

As soon as they made the curve on the ramp, out of sight of the SUV, Hardin nudged her arm. "Floor it. When you hit six, get to the far end as fast as you can. I'm going to roll out behind the pillar there. Pull in to the right, wait until you see them make the turn at my end, then get out. You'll have the car for cover. If they don't see me, we'll have them between us."

Wilson nodded, her face hard and unmoving.

She shot out of the ramp on six and across the floor, slowed as she made the turn at the far end. Hardin opened the door and rolled out onto the cement. Wilson sped away.

Lafitpour and Hickman stood by the wall at the east end of the sixth floor, turning to look as they heard a car accelerating up the ramp. A black Honda shot out and across the floor two rows to the west of them. Lafitpour just caught a glimpse of Hardin as the car passed. The black compact slowed radically as it turned at the far end. Lafitpour had just enough of angle to see Hardin roll out of the passenger door and come up with a pistol in each hand.

He heard another engine straining and saw a black Explorer erupt from the ramp, four men inside, the man in the passenger seat holding a submachine gun at port arms.

"Where's the fucking car?" Hernandez yelled as the Explorer charged onto six.

"There," the driver answered. "To your left." Hernandez saw it, parking head in near the elevator. Bad angle, too much shadow to see in the windows. The driver pushed the truck hard, braked, tires squealing as he made the turn at the far end, circling back toward the Honda. The driver's door opened, the woman got out.

••••

Hardin squatted down on the west side of the pillar making himself as small as he could, a minivan to his left, blocking the view from the direction of the ramp. He heard the truck accelerate across the floor. He didn't look, just straightened to a crouch as the truck passed behind him, screeched around the curve. Hardin held both pistols out in front of him. He'd be more accurate one handed, but he was a good shot with either hand, or with both, and there were times when more lead mattered.

"Where the fuck is Hardin?" Hernandez said as the truck curved around the pillar at the far end of the floor and zeroed in on the Honda. Better angle from here. Wilson was standing on the other side of the car and he couldn't see anyone in the passenger seat.

Wilson dropped down behind the Honda's engine block, her S&W in a two-handed grip, her arms braced on the hood of the car. To his left, Hernandez sensed movement and turned just in time to see Hardin, to see the back driver's-side window shatter, to see the Skull shooter's head explode. Hernandez rolled forward, trying to squeeze down into the footwell, feeling a ripping burn across the back of his shoulders as a round tore a furrow through his flesh. The air was full of the sounds of gunfire, a steady staccato beat from behind and to his left, Hardin firing, and then a slightly higher pitched ripping as Miko cut loose with his MP5 out the front passenger-side window.

Hernandez started to straighten, went to swing his MP5 up at Hardin, but a flurry of rounds slammed into the window pillar of the driver's side, into the back of the driver's seat. The driver slumped forward and the truck slewed left. Hernandez lost his balance, tipping against the front passenger seat. The dead Skull fell across Hernandez's lap, knocking the MP5 from his hands.

Hardin saw the truck make the curve. The driver couldn't shoot, not while he was driving, so Hardin took the guy in the back passenger seat first. Kill shot, the guy's head exploding. Big guy on the far side of the seat dropped down, might have been hit, might not have been. Might have been Hernandez.

Hardin turned, tracking the car, putting out as many rounds as he could at the driver. Must have hit him. The Explorer swerved radically left, then slowed, drifted.

Hardin looked toward the Honda, Wilson behind the engine block; arms locked, rock steady, squeezing off shots. He heard an automatic weapon rip from the SUV. The left drift gave the guy in the passenger seat a straight shot at Wilson. Hardin saw a line of holes stitch across the Honda's front passenger side, creeping up, a furrow opening across the top of the hood, Wilson not even blinking at that, just firing. Then the firing from the truck stopped and it rolled into a green BMW across from the elevators, crunching to a halt.

Hardin holstered the pistol in his left hand, ejected the clip from the one in his right, slammed in a spare, pulled the slide. He advanced on the SUV, the single pistol in a two-handed grip and trained just over the sill of the rear passenger window. He still didn't know about the guy in the right rear, but if he saw even a hint of movement, he was ready to open up. Wilson came out from behind the Honda, reloading her S&W, closing on the truck from the other side.

The guy in the front passenger seat tried to rise up. Wilson put two through his head, changed her angle just a touch, and gave the driver a double tap, too, just to be sure.

Hardin got to the driver's side of the SUV, looked in the back window. Shooter on his side was done, down across the seat, half his head missing. Hernandez was bent over behind the passenger seat, trying to dig a weapon up off the floor.

"Don't fucking move," Hardin said.

Hernandez looked up, froze for a second. "Why not, so you can shoot me?" Then Hernandez made another frantic move for the pinned weapon.

"No," Hardin said. "So she can." Hardin stepped to his left, out of Wilson's line.

From the passenger's side, Wilson's S&W barked five times, tearing off the top of Hernandez's head and shredding his back between his shoulder blades.

Wilson straightened and looked across the top of the SUV at Hardin.

"Thanks for waiting," she said.

"I figured you had dibs," Hardin answered.

CHAPTER 89

"You gotta go faster, man." Paco, one of the Skull shooters Hernandez had up from Mexico. He was riding shotgun in the other SUV, two more Skulls in the back, the black gangbanger driving.

"You want some cop lighting us up? Doing the best I can. And keep that fucking gun down, will you? Some do-gooder sees it and 911s us, we're gonna have company we don't need." The Skull kept holding the submachine gun up across his chest. He lowered it to his lap, below window level.

The driver was pissed. Fucking snakebit damn Honda turning into that garage behind them; hadn't seen that coming. He taken a quick right onto Wells figuring he'd have to circle the block, shot left around a FedEx truck that was blocking the right lane, and that meant he saw the Wells Street entrance too late to make the turn. Next cross street was Madison, but that was one-way east, went through that intersection, cut up Arcade, more of an alley, really, but it would get him back to Wacker. Except there was a truck blocking it, hazards blinking, some kind of delivery. Reversed back out to Franklin, over to Munroe, up to Wacker, more red lights, the whole thing taking forever.

"Buzz your guys," the driver said to the Skull while they sat at the light at Wacker and Madison. "See does he still want us in the entrance or what?"

The Skull made the call, loud Spanish voice, sounded worked up; driver couldn't understand any of that shit, but then gunshots. Lots of gunshots. Didn't need any translation for those. The Skull yelling into the phone, nobody answering.

The driver punched it. Way they timed the lights on Wacker, if he hauled ass, they'd make the green at Washington, be in the garage damn quick.

Al Din was halfway across the fifth floor when he heard gunfire from six. A lot of gunfire. It was time to pause, assess his situation. He parked at the end of the row. He could hear at least three different weapons, one of them automatic. Then the shooting stopped.

"There is shooting on a floor above me in the garage," he said into his phone. "Do you have anything on camera?"

"Uh, I got a black SUV crunched in to what looks like a green Beemer, got some windows shot out. OK, I got a guy walking up to it. It's your guy, Hardin. And here's Wilson."

Al Din heard a tightly spaced group of shots. Five of them.

Tokyo spoke. "Um, I don't know who was in the SUV, but I hope they weren't friends of yours."

"Competitors," al Din answered.

Al Din thought for just a moment. Hardin and the woman had taken out the men in the SUV. It would be just the two of them, alone. They had no reason to suspect he was here. And al Din had been in his share of firefights. When you have won, when you have survived, your system crashes a little, the adrenaline bleeding off. You let your guard down. Right now Hardin and the woman would be sloppy.

He wouldn't drive up the ramp. A car they would hear and there was still plenty of parking on the floor below them. They would know that. They would be sloppy, not stupid. But the door to the stairs was behind him and to his right. He could be on six in seconds, could enter quietly, with any luck could get at least one of them before they even knew he was there. That would leave one. They were both good, but al Din would take his chances one-on-one with anyone in the world.

He got out of the car and ran for the stairs.

To his right, he heard a car roar up the ramp, heard the tires squeal as it turned hard toward him, heard it screech to a halt, still running. He turned his head, still running toward the door. He saw a black sedan stopped almost even with the stair doors, but in the main traffic row, two rows in from the wall. Both front doors flew open, two men out, weapons coming up.

"Al Din! Police!" The taller man shouting. The man on the driver's side.

Without slowing, al Din swung his weapon taking the first available shot, the smaller man on the passenger side, firing two shots, the first slightly, high, but adjusting, the second punching through the window of the open door, hitting the smaller man in the chest.

Lynch had just nosed the Crown Vic onto the ramp up to five when he heard shots from above.

"Sounds like we're late to the party," Bernstein said.

Lynch put the hammer down, rocketing up the ramp and onto five. Halfway across the floor, he saw a man sprint from the line of cars parked to his left headed right and toward them at an angle. It was al Din.

He slammed on the brakes, him and Bernstein both leaping from the car, bringing their guns up.

"Al Din! Police!" Lynch shouted.

••••

Al Din heard the car behind him, did the geometry in his head, got ready, but kept moving. He was in the open, wanted to be closer to the door if it came to shooting. But when he heard the policeman call out his name, he knew he had to change the equation, put their heads down, buy some time.

He made sure the weapon was at chest level as he turned. He didn't want to have to worry about elevation, just had to be ready to squeeze the trigger when he tracked across the target. A smaller man on the passenger side of the vehicle. Al Din fired twice, his bullets punching through the window of the car. Early on the first shot, but he knew the second was on target.

That should freeze them for a moment. He continued his spin, kept running for the door.

Al Din surprised Lynch. Didn't even pause, just spun, firing twice. Lynch heard glass break, heard a grunt, saw Bernstein drop out of the corner of his eye.

Al Din was almost to the door of the stairwell. Lynch sighted there. Al Din would have to slow to get in the door.

Al Din knew he would have to pause at the door. But he had the range now, could picture the larger man behind the driver's door of the car. Just before the door to the stairwell, al Din spun again, the weapon leveled, waiting for the barrel to cross its target. He fired, fired again, shocked that the man wasn't moving, wasn't down. The first shot should have been perfect, but it slammed into top of the car's window frame just in front of the man's chest. The second shot may have been wide. Still, it should have been enough, should have had the man ducking for cover, but the man stood perfectly still, gun steady.

The larger man fired. Al Din felt the round hit him near the right shoulder. Didn't mean it was over – al Din had been shot before. He switched the pistol to his left hand, was raising it for another shot when the next round slammed into the center of his chest.

Al Din fell back against the door, slid to the floor, his brain still racing through his options but his body no longer cooperating. How wide was that window frame? One inch? Two? That was the difference. His shot had been perfect. The other man should be down; al Din should be through the door, gone.

Al Din saw the man come out from behind the car, his weapon still raised, still trained on him. Al Din looked down at the pistol in his left hand, concentrated, could still feel the fingers, tightened them on the grip, focused on his arm, started to raise the weapon.

Just before he got to the door, Lynch saw al Din spin, fire again. Nothing Lynch could do, just hold his ground, aim. First shot hit something metal. Lynch heard the sound. The second tore through the fabric of Lynch's coat sleeve, just below the left shoulder. Either it didn't hit him or he didn't feel it yet. Lynch figured if the little fuck was gonna shoot at him with a .22, then he'd better hit him solid.

Lynch fired, the first round hitting al Din high in the right chest, near the shoulder, al Din not skipping a beat, just switching his weapon to the left hand, starting to bring it up. Lynch fired again, center chest. That drove al Din back into the door, al Din sliding down, leaving a smear of blood behind on the green metal.

Lynch came out from behind the car, gun up, closed on al Din. He saw al Din look down at his weapon, start to raise his left arm, trying to bring the gun up. Lynch emptied the rest of his clip into the bastard's chest, everything hitting on the midline between his collarbone and belt buckle. Al Din's hand opened, the pistol dropped, and he slumped to the side, his eyes fixed and open.

Lynch ran around the front of the car, slid to a stop next to Bernstein, who was on his back gasping. Lynch looked for a wound, saw nothing. Then Lynch saw the hole in the breast pocket of Bernstein's blazer. He lifted the coat open, looking for an entry wound, nothing, a small tear in the shirt, a little blood from a shallow gash.

Something fell from the pocket of Bernstein's blazer. His iPhone, the screen shattered, the silver back of the device dented, split open a little at the apex of the dent.

"I should have let the fucker live," Lynch said. "He killed your damn phone. Fucking thing saved your life."

Bernstein tried to laugh, grunted in pain, drew in a shallow breath. "There's an app for that," he said.

CHAPTER 90

On six, Hickman and Lafitpour emerged from the cars they had been hiding behind.

"What the fuck?" Hickman said.

Lafitpour said nothing, still holding his phone.

"You can hang up now," Hardin said. "Transfer the funds."

"We had nothing to do with this," Lafitpour said.

"I know. It was Hernandez. Transfer the fucking money. We don't have much time."

Lafitpour pulled a sheet of paper from his pocket, started dialing. "Damn," he said, killing the connection, starting again.

Hardin pressed the muzzle of his gun to the center of Lafitpour's forehead. "Concentrate," he said.

Lafitpour dialed the number in one try, made the transfer. "Done," he said.

Hardin looked to Wilson. "Wanna watch them a second?"

She leveled her S&W at the two men.

Hardin holstered his pistol, pulled out his phone, called Fouche.

"Can you confirm the transfer?" Hardin asked.

"I've been watching the screen, *mon ami*; it just hit your account."

"OK. Start spreading it around. If somebody tries to take it back, I don't want them to find anything."

"In five minutes, there will be no trace and no trail."

Hardin hung up, looked at Lafitpour. "Give me your phone." Looked at Hickman. "You too." They handed their phones to Hardin and he threw them over the wall onto Wells Street.

"We're leaving," Hardin said. "You're not. If I see you following us, hell, if I see you ever, it isn't going to end well."

Hardin and Wilson turned and walked toward the stairwell. Cab would be safer than the Honda now.

Just before they reached the door, they heard a shout echo up the ramp from the floor below.

"Al Din! Police!"

Then gunfire.

"That's between us and out," Wilson said.

"Hate to get shot now that I'm rich," Hardin said.

"And things were going so well," she answered.

They ran for the stairs.

CHAPTER 91

Lynch heard another engine coming up the ramp fast, then tires slamming to a stop, doors opening. He stood, looked back over the roof of the Crown Vic, saw a white Lexus parked in the middle of the lane, all four doors open, four shooters getting out, three with submachine guns, one with a pistol.

Lynch grabbed Bernstein under the arms and dragged him away from the Crown Vic into the line of parked cars toward the inside wall. Bernstein grunted, his teeth clenched, clutching his chest, but as Lynch dragged him, he grabbed the pistol he'd dropped when the round hit him. Bernstein pushed with his feet, the two of them scrambling behind the engine block of an old Buick just as the first burst tore into the sheet metal.

The four gunmen were only fifteen yards back, and closing fast. Lynch had already punched out the clip he'd emptied into al Din, slammed in a new one. One more clip left after that. Couldn't waste rounds, but he couldn't let these guys just close on him, either. He reached up over the hood of the Buick, picking the line from his visual memory, squeezed off three quick shots.

Bernstein rolled to his stomach, fired a couple rounds from under the car, aimed at legs, clipped one guy on the calf, a shout in Spanish, the guy hopping into a line of cars toward the inside of the garage, another guy, the driver, bobbing into the same row. The two from the passenger side went right, toward the wall.

"We don't get some backup, we're fucked," Lynch said.

"Called it in when we entered the garage, figure a couple minutes," Bernstein said.

Another burst ripped into the Buick, closer this time, better angle.

"Be about a minute more than we got," Lynch said.

Lynch hit the ground and rolled to the back of the Buick, watching the floor on that side, looking for legs, looking for the two guys who'd moved in toward the wall. Bernstein wedged himself as far under the front end as he could, watching the right for the other two shooters.

Another burst, from the left this time, glass from the windows dropping on Lynch.

Lynch saw a foot, aimed, fired. Someone screaming in Spanish.

Another burst, the bad guys learning their lesson, somebody on Lynch's side had laid his gun flat on the floor and pulled the trigger, rounds zipping along the floor, popping noise and then a long, fading hiss from the rear tire on the other side of the car.

"Son of a bitch," Lynch grunted. One round had skipped up, ripped a bloody line down the outside of his right thigh.

Hardin covered the stairway down to four while Wilson looked through the narrow, wire-meshed window out into the fifth floor of the garage.

"Got a couple cops pinned down by a Crown Vic in the middle lane. A guy named Lynch and another guy."

"You know them?" Hardin asked.

"Know him a little," she said. A pause. "We leave, they die."

Hardin closed his eyes a minute, swallowed, then nodded. They were who they were and they had done what they'd done, but Wilson had been a cop for a decade now, a good one. Hardin knew she couldn't walk away from this and live with it. Truth be told, neither could he.

"OK," he said. "Let's go."

Wilson nodded, looked back out the window. "Crown Vic is the cops. Got a white sedan on the far side, four shooters, looks like three with subs and a handgun."

A single shot from the cops' position, one of the bad guys gave out a yell, hopped into the line of cars across the center aisle, another bad guy following him. The other two moved between the cars on the near side, toward Hardin and Wilson. One of them straightened up, put a burst on the Buick, then a single shot from the cops, more cursing in Spanish, on their side this time. Then a burst from across the aisle.

"We take the two on our side first," Wilson said.

Hardin nodded.

"Ready?"

He nodded again.

Hardin grabbed the door handle. It would open from Wilson's side. She stood back a step, her S&W steady, waiting for a line. Hardin pulled the door back slowly, felt a weight pushing it. Al Din's body fell into the stairwell, shot to hell.

Wilson went through the door, hugging the wall, working for an angle. Hardin came out behind her.

One of the shooters on the far side shouted something in Spanish, turned toward Hardin and Wilson, fired a round that splattered into the concrete wall between them. Hardin knew better than to rush. You got shot, you didn't get shot, not much you could do about that. But if you kept your shit together, aimed, you'd at least hit what you were shooting at. Nothing fancy, center mass. Hardin fired, drilling the guy just below the solar plexus, dropped him in his tracks.

A guy with an MP5 popped up two cars in front of them, firing wild, the first rounds hitting into the back quarter of a minivan, just right of Wilson, the guy trying to adjust, swinging the gun her way, his finger still locked on the trigger, the glass in the minivan busting out as the bullets tracked toward her. Wilson didn't even flinch, just aimed and put her first shot into the middle of his face. Two down.

Lynch and Bernstein heard the new shooting on their left. Bernstein saw the shooter on the far side catch a round in the gut and go down.

"Cavalry's here," he said.

"But who are they?" answered Lynch.

"You care?"

"Nope."

Lynch looked ahead under the car. "Can't pick a target on this side. Let's light up the other fucker over your way, at least keep him out of the game."

Bernstein nodded; they both rose, squatting at the hood, firing right. Lynch's leg tried to buckle on him, so he leaned into the car, keeping the weight on his good side.

The other shooter on Wilson's side popped up, right along the wall, his short burst just missing her, slamming into the windshield of the minivan. Wilson hit the floor, spun, looking for his legs.

Hardin heard the burst, saw Wilson drop, didn't know whether she'd been hit or not. Brought both guns to bear on the guy by the wall just as the guy saw Hardin. Hardin put six shots into the guy's chest just as the guy pulled the trigger on him. The guy dropped, Hardin felt his left arm yank back, lost the pistol in that hand, then felt the burn. Caught at least one round high up, close to the shoulder.

"I'm OK," Wilson called.

Hardin twisted, looked across the aisle. Should be one more shooter over there. He saw the first guy he'd hit, gut shot guy, rolling toward the aisle, reaching for his weapon. Hardin lined him up and put two in his brain pan, saw the last guy coming out. Hardin fired again, three rounds hitting the target high center mass before the slide locked back. Empty.

Hardin went to reach for his spare magazine with his left hand, but his left arm wasn't working. Felt more pain then. Hardin dropped the empty pistol from his right, squatted down, picked up the one he'd lost when he got hit. Didn't know what he had left in that one.

Nobody was shooting, nobody was moving.

Wilson was back up, gun out, swiveling. "That everybody?"

"Yeah."

She saw his arm. "You OK?"

"Will be," he said.

From below, they heard sirens, lots of them. Sounded like half the Chicago PD was pulling into the garage.

Behind them, the two cops stood up from behind the Buick, the short one's left arm hanging, the bigger one hobbling around the front of the car, his right leg bloody.

"You're Hardin and Wilson, right?" the tall guy said.

Hardin nodded.

Both cops raised their weapons. "Not that we don't appreciate the help and all," the tall guy said. "But you're both under arrest."

"And we're really hoping you'll put the guns down," the short cop added. "Cause I think you're better at this shit than we are."

Hardin, shrugged, set the 9mm down on the roof of the car next to him. Wilson laid her S&W down next to it.

"Which one of you got al Din?" Hardin asked.

"Me," said the tall guy.

"Then you're pretty good yourself," Hardin said.

CHAPTER 92

A couple of units reached five, lights going, sirens going, stopping at angles on either side of the Lexus that blocked the aisle. The cops leapt out, going to guns, but Lynch and Bernstein had moved to the center of the aisle, holding their badges out, and everybody calmed down.

"Radio for some buses," Lynch yelled to one of the uniforms. "Here and on six."

"How many?"

"Lots," Lynch said, "Hold on."

He yelled over the sirens to Hardin.

"Anybody wounded upstairs?"

"Not unless I'm slipping," Hardin answered.

"How many?"

"Four."

"So four on six, at least six here," Lynch said to the uniform, raising his voice over the commotion. "Gonna need crime scene, ME, fuck it, we're gonna need everybody."

Five minutes later, the first two ambulances arrived. The EMTs wanted to transport Hardin and Lynch, but Lynch told them to wait. He was on a gurney they'd pulled out, his right leg out straight, the pants leg cut off halfway up his thigh. One of the techs was cleaning the wound, shooting a local into the leg in a few spots. The back of

the gurney was raised so Lynch could sit up. Hardin sat
on the bumper of the second unit while a short woman
cleaned and bandaged his arm. Another EMT was
wrapping Bernstein's ribs. When one of the techs tried to
look at Wilson's head, she told him to fuck off.

Hickman came out the door, holding up his creds,
walked over to Lynch.

"I don't know what happened here detective, but this
whole crime scene is under federal jurisdiction."

"Fuck you," Lynch said.

A plainclothes car stopped, half on the ramp. Starshak
got out. He walked over to the gurney, looked at Lynch.

"Get to a fucking hospital," he said, turned toward
Bernstein. "You too."

"Just as soon as Hickman stops trying to Bogart my
crime scene. He says this is a Fed deal."

Hickman stepped between Lynch and Starshak. "Your
people stumbled into and very nearly ruined a long-
running and extremely sensitive federal investigation
involving matters of national security that I am not at
liberty to disclose at the moment. I might add, Captain, that
you were told to stay away from this case, that it was a task
force matter now." Hickman was trying to be pedantic, but
it wasn't working because he was shivering. He was still in
his shirtsleeves, and the temperature was in the fifties, a
cold wind gusting into the garage from the east on and off.

"Membe Saturday," Starshak said.

"What?" said Hickman.

"Refugee guy by the Stadium," said Lynch. "We liked
al Din for that, too. Nobody said anything about not
clearing that case. Guess it wasn't sexy enough for you
Fed assholes to work it."

Hickman shook his head, waved a hand. "Clearly that
was connected. At any rate, I'm telling you now, this is a

Federal matter. Transport your injured people, back your uniforms off to the street so they can control access to the garage, and get everybody else out of my crime scene."

"Not gonna happen," Starshak said. "Homicide is a state crime, not federal. And right now, all I've got is a multiple homicide. We haven't even ID'd any of the victims yet, No way in hell I turn this over on your say so, especially since I got you on scene. Right now, you ain't the US Attorney, Hickman. You're a material witness. Maybe a suspect."

Starshak turned to a nearby uniform. "Hardin, Wilson and Mr Expensive-tie, I-don't-say-shit over there," Starshak pointed at Lafitpour, who had come out the stairway door with Hickman and was standing by the wall, "link them up and process them." Starshak poked a finger into Hickman's chest. "And if this dick interferes, cuff his ass and run him in, too."

"Cap," Lynch said, "just so you know, Wilson and Hardin saved our asses."

Starshak looked at Hardin, then at Wilson. "Well don't this just get curiouser and curiouser."

From above, Lynch heard the beat of a chopper getting louder, closer, then shutting down. Sounded like it landed on the roof. From below, the sound of more sirens, on the street, then some shouting. Starshak walked over to the wall, looked down at Washington Street.

"Mess of Feebs. Who called them?"

CHAPTER 93

Lynch watched a powerfully built older man walk down the ramp from six. One of the uniforms stopped him, but the guy just smiled handing the uniform a cell phone, the uniform listening for a second and then stepping aside, still holding the phone to his ear. The guy was at least sixty, probably more, looked like he could still throw a punch if the mood struck him. Expensive suit, spring weight camel hair coat. Guy looked like Brian Dennehy maybe ten or fifteen years back. He walked directly to Starshak.

"Captain Starshak, before you fuck things up to the point where I can't unfuck them, perhaps you and I could have a word."

Starshak ignored the guy and looked past him to the uniform who'd let him pass. The uniform looked back sheepishly, still holding the phone like he didn't know what to do with it.

"Too busy playing Angry Birds to do your damn job?" Starshak barked. "Who is this hump and what is he doing in my crime scene?"

The cop opened his mouth and then closed it, didn't know what to say. The Brian Dennehy guy took the phone from the cop's hand.

"Actually, the phone's mine," the man said, handing the phone to Starshak. "And it's for you."

Starshak took it, listened, his face impassive. He listened for a long time. He never said anything. Then he handed the phone back to the big man and turned to address the cops.

"Listen up, people," Starshak yelled. Everybody stopped, turned. Starshak pointed at the big man. "This guy's name is Munroe. Don't ask me who he works for, cause I don't know. But I've heard from the chief, who's heard from the mayor who, for all I know, has heard from the fucking President. Good work on al Din, that's the word. Atta boys all around. Now we dumb-ass local yokels are supposed to step back and let the big boys do their jobs."

"This is totally fucked," said Lynch

"Tell me about it," said Starshak.

"Will somebody get me a damn coat?" Hickman said, sounding whiny.

"Shut up," said Munroe.

Lafitpour said nothing at all, standing to the side, not moving. He wasn't asking anybody for a coat.

Bernstein walked over. The tech was done with him for now, ribs wrapped, left arm in a sling, bound tight to his chest, his ruined blazer and a raid jacket draped over his shoulders.

"What's he doing here?" Bernstein asked, nodding toward Lafitpour.

"Don't know," Lynch said. "Hasn't said a damn thing. No ID on him, don't even have his name. And I get the feeling Joe Washington here likes it that way. But he's awful damn quiet, that's for sure. I guess the cat's got his tongue."

"Persian cat, I bet," Bernstein said. He stepped up to Lafitpour, directly in front of him, got in his personal space, staring him down. "Bahram Lafitpour, Chicago's mysterious wizard of Wall Street. What are you now? Second richest guy in town? Won't do interviews, not even with the financial press, don't like having your picture taken. And here you are, playing cops and robbers in your shirtsleeves."

Lafitpour's eyes flashed with anger, his jaw tightening.

"Careful, Slo-mo," Starshak said. "I don't think he's used to the help talking to him that way."

"Wait until I try it in Hebrew," Bernstein said.

Lafitpour spat in Bernstein's face. Starshak nudged Bernstein aside and drove a fist into Lafitpour's gut, doubling him over for a second, but Lafitpour straightened quickly, glared at Starshak.

"I don't give a shit what your connections in DC say," Starshak said to Munroe. "A suspect spits on a cop, that's assault. We don't do assault."

The Munroe guy chuckled a little shook his head. "You know what? You shut up too, Bernstein. Fucking Jews. Always too smart for your own good. You wonder why everybody's pissed at you all the time."

Bernstein turned toward Munroe. "Do I know you?"

"Nope," said Munroe. "But I know everybody. Oh, and this guy?" He nodded toward Lafitpour. "He's not here anyway."

CHAPTER 94

An hour later, Munroe slid the Do Not Disturb sign aside and stuck the key card into the door at the low-end motel out on North Avenue. Card had been in al Din's wallet. He'd left Hickman to ride herd on the FBI team that was processing the garage in the Loop. Little worried about Hickman. He was getting scared and whiny now that they had a little excrement on the fan blades.

Starshak, Lynch's boss, he didn't roll easy, raised quite a stink, trying to get Chicago guys to process the scene, saying the shootings were homicides, and homicides weren't federal. Munroe had to make some more calls, push the Chicago PD brass to get a better leash on their people. He needed the locals all the way outside the tent on this thing. Fuckers were smarter than he thought, Bernstein putting an ID on Lafitpour; that was a free radical he didn't need.

And Lynch, Munroe knew about Lynch from the whole cluster fuck the year before. That guy was like Joe Frazier, punch him in the head all day long and he was just going to keep coming, next thing you know you've busted your hand on his skull and while he works your body, cracking your ribs one at a time. Had Chicago PD on ice for now, but he knew they be picking at whatever they could pick at. Just needed to box this mess up, get a bow on it, and blow town.

Munroe pulled on a pair of latex gloves. He'd check the room first; decide what he wanted going into the official paperwork. And what he didn't.

Two beds, shitty desk and chair, cheap dresser, Laptop on the desk, laptop bag on the floor by the chair. He'd be taking that, send it east, let the tech weenies out at NSA see what they could wring out of it. Al Din had a phone in his pocket, which was in Munroe's pocket now. Put that in the same pouch. Nothing in the drawers. Underwear, socks, some shirts all neatly folded in the suitcase that lay open on the second bed. Three more phones in there, all the same make and model. Throwaways, probably, picked up at a 7-Eleven somewhere. Munroe powered them up one at a time, checked. No call history, no messages, no texts. Leave those for the Feebs; give them something to play with.

Bathroom. The usual shit, although the bottle of Acqua di Gio next to the sink went for something like seventy bucks. Looked like al Din's tastes had gotten a little too refined for Sandland. Munroe was more of an Aqua Velva guy himself.

Closet. Pants and shirts, all ironed and hung up, couple of sport coats. Munroe checked the labels – Armani, Cardin, all high-end stuff. On the floor, next to a couple of pairs of expensive loafers, an aluminum case.

Munroe put the case on the bed, tried the latches. Locked. Bastard. Munroe pulled a leather case from his pocket, took out a couple narrow metal picks, had to fuck with the case for a minute. Out of practice. Didn't do that much breaking and entering these days, not personally. Better than usual locks on the case, too. But the latches popped. First one, then the other. Munroe lifted the lid.

The case was lined with stiff black foam, six identical slots cut into it. Five of the slots were empty. In the sixth,

Munroe saw a flat black metal tube with a couple of buttons on it. Pretty sure he knew what that was.

The little fucker had deployed the other five, probably some kind of failsafe play. If Munroe made a move on him, al Din could set them off. Or maybe just a safety net, make sure, when he came in, that he had a hole card, something to play if he didn't think Munroe was honoring the deal. Or maybe he was gonna jack them up for more cash.

The why didn't matter. Munroe had five devices in the wild that he needed to find ASAP.

He pulled out his phone dialed a number, gave the guy on the other end the address and room number. "I need a runner here soonest. Then get on the phone to Fort Dix, find out the closest Level 3 biohazard lab we've got around here, one we can use on the QT. I got a device I needed eyeballed yesterday."

"Got it," said the voice. "Anything else?"

Munroe had an uncomfortable thought. Al Din had a phone on him. Gotta figure, if the devices were his failsafe, then he could set them off remotely. That scene in the garage? Did al Din have time to push a button?

"Yeah. Monitor the emergency channels." Munroe thought through parameters. They'd been tracking al Din as best they could ever since Munroe got the call in Saigon. Fucker'd been everywhere. "Following counties: Cook, Lake, DuPage, Kane, Will, Kendall. Tap their public health systems, too. You start hearing anything unusual, anybody calling CDC for advice, anything like that, I need to know."

Munroe ended the call, packed al Din's computer into the laptop bag and closed the metal case. Did a quick scan. Fuck, power cord had come loose from the computer, plugged in under the desk, lying on the floor.

Feebs find that, they're going to start asking about the missing computer. Munroe bent down, yanked the cord, stuffed it in the bag. There was a single knock on the door. Munroe slipped out his Walther, cracked the door. Small guy in motorcycle leathers, Kawasaki Ninja in the spot behind him, next to Munroe's car, black helmet on the seat.

"I'm your runner," he said.

Munroe gave him the packages, called Hickman, told him the Feebs could toss the room now, looked at his watch. Not quite 11am. Long day already, and it just got a hell of a lot longer.

CHAPTER 95

The Eagle was in the stairwell at Northwestern Memorial, coming down from eight to seven. Nudged the door open just a fraction of an inch to make sure it was unlocked. It was. Supposed to be unlocked in hospitals, but needed to make sure there was no exception due to the security around the target.

Been on the floor earlier, sticking to the far end, past the nurse's station. The cop was leaning on the desk, chatting up a blonde who was doing some charts. See where he was tomorrow, then make the call whether to come from the right or the left. Liked the layout, the way the nurse's station was tucked in to an alcove, the seats facing away from the target's room.

Already been down the other stairwell, the exit stairwell. Nice little gap under the stairs at the bottom of each flight, space enough to dump the sweater and wig. Be a while before anyone found those. A little variety on the scrubs, but the dark blue was dominant, so go with that.

Nothing more to see here. Time to do a little shopping.

CHAPTER 96

Starshak followed the ambulance to the ER, Bernstein riding with him. Took a while for the docs to finish up with Lynch, stitches on the outside of his thigh from a few inches below his hip damn near to his knee, his whole thigh wrapped in bandages. Starshak on the phone a lot while the docs worked. The brass, DA, review board, seemed like pretty much anybody from any federal agency anywhere that felt like calling him.

Bernstein got X-rays: did in fact have a cracked rib. Not much to do for that. Nurse wrapped him back up.

When they were done, Starshak drove them to Bernstein's place first, Bernstein grabbing a sweater he could work his arm into. Then they headed to Lynch's condo, Lynch pulled on an old BC sweatsuit, the only thing he could fit over his thigh.

Then the three of them sat at Lynch's kitchen table.

"You guys OK?" Starshak asked. Bernstein nodded, said nothing.

"Just a scratch," Lynch said.

"Big fucking scratch," said Starshak.

"Yeah," said Lynch.

"That wasn't what I was asking."

"I know."

The three of them quiet for a while.

"Never been shot at before," Bernstein said. "Never shot at anybody." He sounded a little hollow.

"You did good," Lynch said.

"Right," said Bernstein. "Took a round in my iPhone, emptied my clip, I think I got one guy in the calf."

Lynch shrugged. "Four guys, three with machine guns, you stood your ground, did your job. You weren't there, I'd be dead."

Bernstein nodded. They were quiet again for a while.

"We got lucky," Bernstein said.

Lynch nodded.

"Hardin and Wilson hadn't stepped in…" The thought trailed off.

"They say why they did that?" Starshak asked. "They could have walked clean."

Lynch shook his head.

"You got any ideas?"

Lynch pursed his lips, looked out his window for a moment. "They're just on the right side, I guess."

"Running up quite a body count for being on the right side," said Bernstein.

"I'm OK with the bodies," said Lynch. "Corsco's goons? Hernandez's goons? And from what I can see, nobody that didn't come after them first. Hardin stole some diamonds maybe, but not in my jurisdiction, and look who he stole them from? And Wilson? Stand up cop, up until this week. You look at their history, what we know about the two of them now, this shit with her brother, Hardin does two tours, then gets chased out of his own country by some punk hood, spends a decade in Africa taking out other people's garbage. I don't know. You've got the law, and that's great. Most of the time, for most people. But the law never did shit for either of them. So I think maybe they just go by right and wrong, now, as best they can. I hope they come out of this OK."

Quiet again. Lynch got up, walked stiff legged to the cabinet, got out a bottle of Bushmills, three rocks glasses, set the glasses on the table, poured them each a couple of inches.

"You were on the phone a lot," Bernstein said, looking at Starshak.

"Yeah. Lots of new friends."

"Any idea what's going on?"

Starshak just shook his head. "You two would know better than I would. Seems you two were participating in an operation vital to national security and helped to derail a significant terrorist plot. That's what I'm told."

"Felt like we were just getting shot at a lot," Lynch said. "There's something else, though."

"What?" asked Starshak.

"Hernandez, al Din, I mean fuck it, right? What are we going to do? A couple of Chicago cops? We're gonna clean up the international drug trade, stop terrorism? But that shit with Ringwald, al Din taking out his whole family, that points at Corsco."

"The South Shore thing, too," said Starshak.

Lynch nodded. "Corsco we can do something about."

"You got an idea?" Starshak asked.

"Maybe," said Lynch. "Hey, Bernstein, what do we hear about Fenn?"

"Expecting a full recovery, give or take. They're keeping him another couple of days."

"Let me think on that," Lynch said. He looked up. "Anybody hungry?"

Bernstein looked surprised. "Yeah, actually."

"We can head downstairs, get something. Big fucking heroes like us; maybe Starshak explains that to McGinty, we get a freebie. Besides, we gotta keep our strength up. You can sweat the moral dilemma all you want, Slo-mo, but you're going to find out the true human tragedy of pulling your piece."

"Which is?"

"Paperwork."

"Actually, that's the good news," Starshak said.

"There's good news?" said Bernstein. "Something from one of your phone calls?"

Starshak nodded. "Yeah. The good news is no paperwork. This was a task force deal, remember? Evidently you were on loan. They'll write up your paperwork, you'll just have to sign it."

"For the best, I guess," Lynch said. "How am I supposed to write it up when I don't know what the hell is going on?"

"We get to perjure ourselves?" Bernstein said. "That's the good news?"

"Maybe," Starshak said. "You gonna be able to prove that anything they feed you isn't the truth?"

"Will my lips still move when I speak?" Lynch asked.

"Of course," said Bernstein. "The dummy's lips always move."

"Thought I felt somebody's hand up my ass," said Lynch.

Starshak's cell rang. He answered, listened for a minute, then hung up. "We're supposed to get down to the Federal building, some kind of pow-wow, learn all our lines."

CHAPTER 97

Munroe was in a windowless conference room in the Kluczynski Federal Building at Adams and Dearborn, and he was in a good mood. Turned out al Din's computer security wasn't that great. Still a lot to work through, but Munroe had Atash Javadi cold. That was huge. Javadi, he was the right wing's go-to guy on Islam, half the politicians in Washington had him on speed dial. Hell, Langley'd had the bastard in to consult more than once. SOG had already snatched Javadi up, nice and quiet. Had him on a Lear out of Mitchell up in Milwaukee, headed for the proverbial secure, undisclosed location. If they could flip him, run him as a double, they'd have their best set of eyes ever into Tehran. Even if they couldn't, the stuff they'd get out of him? Priceless. And they would get it out of him. They always did.

Munroe had the early rundown on the device from al Din's room from some slide-rule types down at Argonne National Laboratory in the southwest 'burbs. It was Heinz's bio-terror cocktail. Really pure, professionally weaponized shit. Remote trigger; ran off a cell phone. But Lynch must have got al Din before he could push the button. Because if al Din had pushed the button, there'd be weird cases popping up in ERs all over hell by now. Techies said give them a week and they'd work out a way to get the receivers to send out a signal. Then they'd fly in some boys from Fort Dix, pick the rest of the devices up on the QT. Said the things should be safe until then.

But you never put all your eggs in one basket. Not in this game. So Munroe kept up the full court press on al Din's timeline. If he could find the devices faster, he would. All around the room, he had guys cataloging, mapping and time-lining every al Din sighting since he hit town. Data out of the Chicago system, various municipal feeds around the suburbs, the toll way cameras, private security. He'd pulled some strings, had some pocket protector types feeding everything into a couple of Crays out at Livermore. Sped the processing way the hell up. They were filling in the gaps pretty quickly.

He had his chat with Hardin and Wilson. They already had their money and Munroe couldn't get it back. He'd tried. OK, win some, lose some. They'd gotten what they wanted out of the deal – they got to kill Hernandez. They pretty much knew the rest of the story and were ready to play ball, just so long as Munroe understood that, if he ever came after them, or if they even thought that he was trying, they'd go all Snowden on his ass. They had the whole story spooled up online somewhere ready to pop up in unfriendly inboxes. We'll see about that, Munroe figured. People get careless after a while. So friends for now. In a year or two, Munroe's story would go from being news to being history. Once it was history, anything Hardin might say wouldn't be a competing story in the media cycle; it would be revisionist nut-job conspiracy babble. Munroe would revisit his feelings toward Hardin and Wilson then.

Munroe's phone pinged. The Chicago PD crew was on its way up. The last bit to lock in place.

••••

Starshak, Lynch and Bernstein got off the elevator, some suit with an ID badge ushering them to the end of the hall and into a big conference room on the right overlooking the Calder statue in the plaza below, Lynch gimping along stiff-legged. The suit stood in the corner like a chaperone, hands clasped in front of him.

Hardin and Wilson sat at the table, backs to the windows, Hardin finishing the last couple bites of a sandwich. Nothing on Wilson's plate but crumbs. Mess of food on the credenza against the wall to the left: big basket of kaiser rolls, cold cuts, pasta salad, fruit, platter of cookies and brownies.

Wilson looked up. She had a bandage on the left side of her face, near the hairline. "You guys here to get your minds right?"

"That seems to be the plan," Lynch said. "Food any good?"

She shrugged. "Better than no food. I've been hungry for lunch all day. It was looking like I wasn't going to get any."

"I know what you mean," Lynch said. "If I'd known breakfast was going to be my last meal, I would have paid more attention."

Hardin swallowed the last bite of his sandwich. His left arm was in a sling

"You OK?" Lynch asked.

"No damage to the joint, just the meat. I'll be fine. You?"

"Just stitches. Thanks again, by the way."

Hardin shrugged. "Hey, thanks for not shooting us on sight. I've got a feeling that was the plan with pretty much everybody else."

"Couldn't have shot you if I wanted to," Lynch said. "My trigger finger was tired by that point."

The door across the hall opened, Munroe stepping out. Lynch just got a glimpse into the room before the door closed – pictures and street maps wallpapered everywhere, mess of guys in shirtsleeves and ties milling around, mess of laptops on the table.

Munroe crossed the hall, stepped into the big conference room.

"You guys get enough to eat?" he said to Hardin and Wilson.

"Sure," Hardin said.

"Yeah," she added. "Stunned by your largesse."

Munroe smiled, turned to the suit in the corner. "Nobody was talking out of school in here, where they?"

"Just small talk," the guy answered.

"OK, take Hardin and Wilson upstairs. I'm gonna have a word with these guys.

The suit paused a second, opened his mouth once, then closed it, then opened it again.

"Sir, Hickman asked that an agent witness all interviews."

Munroe chuckled. "You're taping all the interviews, right?"

"Yes sir."

"Seems kind of redundant then, doesn't it?"

"Yes sir, but I have orders from Hickman."

Munroe's smile went away. He stepped up close to the agent. "You piss off Hickman, what's the worst that can happen to you?"

"I could lose my job sir."

"You piss me off, what's the worst that could happen to you?"

The man didn't answer for a moment.

"I'll take Hardin and Wilson upstairs, sir."

The suit left the room, led Hardin and Wilson down the hall toward the elevators.

"You guys hungry?" Munroe asked, his smile back. "Help yourselves. Want something we don't have, I can get it."

"Beluga caviar, maybe a bottle of Moët Chandon," Bernstein said.

Munroe laughed. "Fucking Jews. Always busting my hump. I hear you were asking about Pardo a little ways back. You want some pastrami, I'll send for it. You want Beluga and champagne; I'll call Chuckles the Suit back and have him shoot you."

Hickman came storming into the room.

"Damn it, Munroe, you agreed I could have an agent at all interviews. We need to do things buy the book now."

"Now?" said Starshak. "Gee, that would imply that maybe some rules got broken earlier. Hard to imagine."

Hickman reddened a little.

"Yeah," Munroe said. "Tell the nice police officer what you mean by 'now'."

"I mean by the book now and always," Hickman said.

Munroe smiled again. "And when we get to the interview, we'll call the agent back. Right now, we're just a few old warhorses shooting the shit over lunch. Anybody with a battle scar is welcome to stay. That leaves you out, counselor."

Hickman's face got even redder.

"Don't feel bad about the scar thing," said Bernstein. "I just got mine this morning."

Munroe closed in on Hickman, his smile disappearing again.

"Hickman, why don't you go take a leak or something, so you don't hear anything you'll have to deny at a confirmation hearing someday." Hickman stood his ground for a second, then walked out of the room. Munroe closed the door.

"Shut it off Morty, all of it," Munroe said.

"OK," came a voice from the ceiling. "You're clean."

Munroe got up, walked to the coffee pot over on the credenza, poured a cup. Walked back to the table, sat down. "I'm going to play it straight with you three, see how that works out. What I tell you, there's no record of it, not anywhere, so you start shooting your mouth off, it's your word against mine, and I don't exist. So basically you'll be talking to yourselves about what the voices in your head told you." Munroe took a sip of the coffee, set the cup down. "Shit got out of hand. But the bottom line is this. We were flipping al Din. Hadn't wrapped the deal yet, but we were close. He gave us the scoop on Iran running a fake Al Qaeda op here in Chicago. Seems, Khamenei and the mullahs over in Tehran were worried that, with us pulling out of Afghanistan, that was going to free up our resources to start paying more attention to them and their nuclear ambitions. So they were planning 9/11 the sequel. Plan was to pin that on Al Qaeda, keep us chasing ghosts around Waziristan for another decade or so. So that's one thing.

"The other was this. The deal the Iranians were planning, al Din would have been the guy pulling the trigger on it. Guess he watched the Bin Laden take down, realized we hold a grudge about this kind of thing. Did the math, figured out, best case, he'd spend the rest of his life hiding in some dump somewhere waiting for Uncle Sam to zero a drone in on him. That's where the Iranians miscalculated. Turns out al Din isn't very ideological, just wants his payday and a nice place to enjoy his sunset years."

"So you were making a deal with him? Guy we've got lined up on at least nine homicides, he was going to spend his time on some beach on the taxpayers' dime?" Starshak said.

Munroe shrugged. "You say homicides, he says targets. I say collateral damage. It sucks, no way to unsuck it. But yeah. The deal was he gets paid off, we get to wring out his brain, and we get what we need to call Tehran on its bullshit."

"Those homicides?" Starshak said. "How is it some guy who doesn't exist gets to make a deal that has to come out of the Cook County DA's office?"

Munroe shook his head. "You never charged him, you never even had him in custody, and now he's dead, so that all pretty much falls into the spilt milk category. Where we still got a problem is we got a parking garage full of bodies to explain, OK? And I'm sorry a couple of you guys got nicked up, but it looks like you're both gonna be fine. But here's the thing, we had al Din on one side of this deal and Hardin on the other. Hardin got stuck in town with a shitload of hot rocks after Stein got whacked, he needed a buyer, and he was talking to us. Then this business with him and Hernandez cropped up and that presented a whole new opportunity. Gave me some terrorist diamonds and Hernandez in the same place at the same time, everything I need to sell a whole new war on terror story and put a real dent in the mess down in Mexico."

"You're admitting to a criminal conspiracy, you know that, right?" Starshak said.

"Grow the fuck up, will you?" Munroe with an edge to his voice now. "Who do you think is winning this goddamn War on Terror? Us? In 2001, we were running a surplus. The economy was humming. Iraq and Iran gave us a nice little balance of power in the Middle East, and the fact that Tehran had to worry about Saddam getting another invade somebody bug up his ass kept them plowing most of their defense budget into conventional weapons. Then

Bin Laden pulls his little surprise party. We gut Iraq for
no good reason other than George Jr thinks maybe they
dissed his daddy back in the day. We spend something
like two trillion chasing ragheads around camel town.
We turn whatever rep we had on the Arab street into
ass wipe by acting exactly like the Crusader fuck ups Bin
Laden knew we would. Pakistan, in case you don't read
the papers, is teetering on the edge of becoming the first
fundamentalist Islamic state with its own nukes, Iran's
working on becoming the undisputed power in the
region – and if their Hezbollah puppets manage to keep
Assad on top in Syria, they might actually pull it off. Our
economy is in the toilet, and Congress and the President
are pissing on each other in the kiddie pool trying to
decide how not to default on our debt. Hardin's a big boy.
He decided to steal a mess of diamonds from a mess of
terrorists. He didn't think that could end badly, then he
should have thought again. And this Wilson or whatever
her name is, she got into bed with Hardin knowing who
he'd been screwing with. That ain't safe sex. Things are
seriously fucked, but Tehran has finally stepped on its
winky with this deal, and I've got a chance to start the
unfucking process by bloodying their nose but good.
And what you gentlemen have to understand is I will do
whatever is necessary to get that done."

"You got a point to get to here?" Lynch asked. "Or did
you just need an audience to practice your neocon spiel?'

"OK boys," Munroe said, "Here the pitch. Turns out
this Hardin's got all kinds of interesting friends, including
some DGSE types from back in his Foreign Legion days.
We spin that into Hardin being an operative with a
friendly Western power, and an ex US Marine at that,
then he's not a thief anymore, then we got him inside
this operation in a role that will pass the smell test with

the media. That's just crooked enough that the Frogs have
signed off on it. They love this kind of shit. All we gotta
do is let them send some guy over from the Consulate
so he can take a bow during the press conference. With
Hernandez putting shooters on the field, God bless his
psychotic little heart, we got everything we need to sell
this drugs-for-diamonds financing thing. Wilson is the
DEA's inside player, another hero. And you boys, you're
Chicago PD's contribution to the proceedings, the tough
guys with the local know-how to make this whole thing
work out. And Lynch, thanks to the tabloids, you're
already everybody's favorite hot cop. Now you'll be the
guy who put out al Din's lights. What the press gets is
this: US and French intelligence penetrated an Iranian
false flag operation. Tehran was financing the deal by
selling blood diamonds to the Cartel to make it look like
an Al Qaeda play – and most of that is true, if that makes
you Boy Scouts feel any better. In cooperation with the
Chicago PD, we bounced the exchange today, terrorists
were killed, brave men were wounded, and Chicago
was saved from a fate worse than 9/11. Hardin and his
girlfriend get their payday, the French back our play, I
get on with the business of making the world safe for
democracy, and you guys get to be heroes. All you gotta
do is smile for the cameras, take your bows, and keep
your goddamn mouths shut."

Long pause. Lynch could see a vein popping on the
side of Starshak's neck.

"This fate worse than 9/11, you wanna fill me on that?"
Starshak said.

Munroe shrugged. "Biological attack. Our guys
projected between thirty and a hundred thousand dead,
depending."

"That's been taken care of?"

Munroe was coming as close to leveling with these guys as he did with anybody. For one thing, he liked them. Damn good cops. Smart, tenacious, big brass ones, and Lynch did take out al Din before the little fuck could pop the cork on his toys. Second, these guys had real good bullshit filters. He knew their type. If they thought he was feeding them a pile of crap, they'd start picking at it, trying to find something that made sense. No, the right play was to give them as much of the truth as he could, hope they saw the reasons for it, show them they were boxed in on all sides, and hope they could live with it. Hell, they were cops; they were used to living with shit. Warrants tossed because of bureaucratic slip ups, psychos walking because some shrink sold a jury a sob story, civil liberty types tying their hands any way they could. At least this time all the bad guys ended up dead. They even got to kill one of them. The worst one of them. No threats, not with these guys. A guy like Lynch? Threaten him and he'd never stop coming after you. Threaten him and you had to put him down. Munroe didn't want that. He liked the guy. Put him down if he had to, of course, he'd put all three of them down if he had to. Just wouldn't threaten them first. That would be a waste of time.

So he fed them all the truth he could, but he sure as hell wasn't telling them there were still five devices hidden around town. They didn't need to know how close this had come to going south.

"Yeah. That's been taken care of," Munroe said.

Everyone sat there, nobody talked.

Starshak's cell rang. He answered, listened for a while, hung up. "The chief," he said to Lynch and Bernstein. "Nobody's got our back on this. And nothing we do is going to change any of it. Our orders are to play ball."

Lynch choked down his anger, trying to keep his mind clear. He'd never been Don Quixote, never imagined the world could be perfect. Do the best you can with what you got, that was his compass. This sucked. But he'd always known shit went on outside the lines. Sometimes it was bad shit done for good reasons. Lynch couldn't stop this, he couldn't change it. All he could do was try to get some good out of it. Serve and protect, that was the deal. Not the entire free world, just his city. Lynch wanted something for Chicago.

"If I play ball, I want something," Lynch said.

"What?" Munroe asked.

"I want Corsco."

Munroe's smile was back, broad and expansive. "Tell me what you need."

"Hardin," Lynch said. "I need to borrow Hardin."

"Done," said Munroe. The big man pulled a small digital recorder out of his pocket and tossed it to Lynch. "And I'll throw this in for free."

Lynch hit the play button. A little tinny without earbuds, but he could make it out. Munroe jacking up Ringwald and Corsco, Corsco confessing to putting a hit out on Hardin.

"Won't do you much good in court," said Munroe, "what with me not existing and all, and I did kinda point a gun at him. Well, shot a gun at him. But if you need it for window dressing, knock yourself out."

CHAPTER 98

Munroe took his cell out of his pocket. It had been vibrating all through his chat with his Chicago PD buddies, but he didn't want to take the call, break the rhythm.

He checked the number. The lab. He hit redial.

"What?" he asked.

"We got a problem. The device, it started ticking."

"What do you mean ticking?"

"It's got a secondary program. A failsafe. It's set up to detonate remotely off a cell signal. Looks like al Din had this thing set up so he had to call the cell's number every day to reset the timer. If he didn't, then the device starts counting down. Al Din didn't call today. This sucker is ticking."

"And you can't shut it off?"

"No so far."

"How long?"

"You got till 1730 hours."

Munroe looked at his watch. Almost 3.00. He had until 5.30. No time, and he didn't have the manpower on the ground to run any kind of search off the books. He had two plays. Option one, call Starshak back, get Chicago PD on this, give them everything they'd worked out about al Din's timeline and hope to hell they found these things before they went off. Option two; just let the

379

clock run out. Have to ice the two guys out at Argonne, wouldn't do to have it get out Uncle Sam had known tens of thousands of Americans were going to die and just sat on his hands. Once he'd heard about the bio angle, Munroe had made some preparations on the QT, had a shit load of Cipro in a National Guard armory up near O'Hare, had a mess of other shit either in town or teed up and ready to wing in on his say so – isolation units, HAZMAT suits, body bags. Had rough outlines for a couple different quarantine scenarios he could ram down the National Guard's throat if it came to that. Of course, the Guard would only be running things until they could get regular Army in here. And he knew what was in the weapons, the medical confusion they were meant to cause. Be able to get word out so everybody knew exactly what they were dealing with. That meant they'd keep the body count down to the very low end of the projections. Problem being the low end was still around ten thousand – three times as many as 9/11.

Upside would be this. The coverage you'd get. Every talking head in the world doing stand-ups in front of the bodies stacking up in temporary morgues, some ghost town shots of the Loop, CDC guys wandering around in spacesuits, hospitals with beds lining the halls. Couple days of that, Munroe could probably get the President to sign off on nuking Tehran. And the Mexican problem? Tea Party ass hats would have to give up on their border fence. That thing would have to come down so we could get the armor over the border.

He walked over to the window, looked down at the plaza where they had the Calder sculpture. Thing looked like a giant red spider. Town sure did like its funny statues. Lots of people walking back and forth, a mom chasing a couple little ones around the legs of the sculpture, one of the kids giving out a happy squeal loud enough he could just hear it through the glass.

Not much of a shot. Have to get lucky as hell. Sensible thing was to let it play out, cover his tracks. But everybody's got a line they won't cross. It's just that Munroe had never hit it. Was starting to think he didn't have one. Turned out he did.

The Chicago guys would still be in the building. He called Hickman, told him to round them up and bring them back.

CHAPTER 99

Fifteen minutes later, two hours and twenty minutes to go. Starshak, Lynch, Bernstein and Munroe were on one side of the conference table in the windowless room across from the conference room they'd been in earlier. Hundreds of photos of al Din on the walls. Hardin and Wilson stood across the table. Munroe figured they'd been playing footsie with al Din all week, they might come up with something.

"Most of this is out of our system," Lynch said.

"Your system and elsewhere," said Munroe.

"So where was all this when you were supposedly cooperating with us?"

Munroe shrugged. "You really want to waste time on that right now? All this will be over one way or another in a few hours. You wanna step outside then, find out if you're as big a badass as you think you are, fine."

Lynch clenched his jaw, nodded, looked down at the pictures.

"Fucker's been everywhere," said Starshak. "Got him at Sears Tower, Aon Center, the Hancock. Hell, he's been in and out of anything over fifty stories at least once. Pretty much every hotel within pissing distance of downtown. Illinois Center, all the pedestrian tunnels in there. It'll take us a week to search that alone."

"You'll want to get into the HVAC centers for the bigger buildings," said Wilson. "Get the building maintenance guys in there with them, they should know if something's out of place. He gets one of those to pop into the duct work..."

"Good thought," Munroe said, looking at her a little sideways.

"My ex was an AC guy," she said. "Always said if you wanted to gas a building, that was the way to go."

Starshak made calls, got units headed to the HVAC centers at the bigger targets.

"You sure we shouldn't be starting an evacuation?" Lynch said.

"No time," Munroe said. "Besides, evacuate to where? We got pictures of him in," he picked up a sheet of paper, "Schaumburg, Aurora, Naperville, Joliet, Elgin – pretty much every population center you've got in fifty miles out in any direction. Malls, hotels, where you going to send 'em? And cranking up the pedestrian traffic while we're looking for these things is just going to make it worse. Everything we got that can help is on its way here – drugs, docs, we got quarantine contingencies in place for every option we can think of. You let me worry about the worst case, you worry about finding the damn devices."

Lynch stared at the pictures. Something was itching at him, and he couldn't think what. Also, Munroe being in the room was hurting his concentration, because every time Munroe opened his mouth, Lynch wanted to stick a gun in it.

"Munroe, your guys took one of these apart," Hardin said. "How do they work?"

"How about we have shop class later?" said Starshak.

"Hey, it's a weapon," said Hardin. "You understand how it works, then you know how it should be deployed."

Starshak just nodded. Munroe held up an 11x17 sheet, exploded view based off the device.

"When the time hits zero, a CO_2 cartridge is going to blow, rupturing the membrane at the end of the container and shooting the bugs out. This stuff is really fine. A particle of talcum powder is ten microns; all of this is smaller than that. Once it's out, it's going to float around very easily. Most of these infections will be through inhalation, but a couple of these agents will work transdermal. So his best bet is a confined space with high pedestrian traffic."

"Which means he doesn't have to get these up high to get people to inhale anything," Bernstein said. "Particles that size, they'll float around on the air. You could dump it on the floor, it would get kicked up like dust."

"Yeah," Munroe said.

"You're al Din, you want to plant these somewhere public because you want traffic," Hardin said. "You either have to break in and plant them when a place is closed, which ramps up your risk. Or you have to plant them while people are around."

"If he was going to risk a break in, then he'd go for the HVAC system," said Bernstein. "Maximum damage. Why risk a break in just to stick them somewhere he could hide them during business hours?"

"OK, that makes sense," Starshak said. "We got people checking HVAC. So how's he gonna do it if he's in public? How do we narrow it down?"

"Shoulder to waist," Munroe said. "Basic tradecraft, like marking a dead drop. He isn't going to climb up on anything, get down on the floor, bend over, anything that draws attention."

"Pointed up, I'd guess," Lynch said. "If airborne is better, then get it airborne. Why wait for people to kick it up?"

Starshak waved his hand. "Best we're gonna do. So, waist to shoulder height, somewhere he can just reach in quick, probably pointed up."

Munroe nodded. "Tell your guys to just walk and look, ask themselves where they'd stick something if they had to."

Starshak relayed the instructions to dispatch.

Bernstein was leaning on the table, looking down at the pictures.

"Something's fucked up about this," he said.

"That's what I thought," said Lynch. "Just can't think what."

Bernstein started picking up pictures at random: al Din in the lobby at the Hyatt, Sox cap on, but a good side angle, green nylon messenger bag on his shoulder. Al Din in the pedestrian tunnel running from City Hall to Macy's, Bears' cap this time, still with the messenger bag. He flipped the pictures over to check the dates and times. He picked up another photo. No cap this time, still with the messenger bag, pretty much looking dead into the camera. He flipped it over. Just a number on the back.

"Where and when?" he asked.

"The numbered ones are shots we've got in from suburban locations," Munroe said. "They aren't on the city grid so we don't get the time stamps on the photos. We've got them cataloged. What's the number?"

"317."

Munroe checked the database. "Woodfield Mall, Schaumburg. That's off an ATM. Two days ago, 8.12pm."

"An ATM? You get any ID off the withdrawal? Might give us something."

"Ah shit," Munroe said. "Hold on." He made a call to the tech guys, gave them the time and the ATM location.

"Can we sort these by time, day, anything like that?"
Bernstein asked.

"Yeah," said Munroe. He pointed at the laptop on the
desk that was plugged into the projector. "They're all
loaded into a database. You can sort that any way you
want."

Bernstein started tapping away at the computer,
plotting locations and times.

"So, until you get out to the 'burbs, he hasn't been
west of the river?" Bernstein said. "Just the Loop, then
up Michigan over in River North?"

Munroe shrugged. "Make sense, density wise. Sticking
with all the good targets."

Bernstein nodded.

"Time?" Starshak asked.

"We got an hour and seventeen minutes," said Munroe.

Munroe's phone rang. It was the tech getting back
about the ATM.

"Fuck." Munroe snapped the phone shut. "Nothing.
Just picked him up passing by."

Bernstein shook his head. "No, no, no, that's not right.
Where's that fucking picture?"

Munroe found it, passed it across the table.

"He's maybe two, three feet from the camera, looking
right at it. He's not passing by. He's making sure he gets
seen. He's out of the city, so he's not sure where the
surveillance is. But he knows damn well that the ATM
will pick him up."

"He's building his haystack," Munroe said, "making us
find his needles in it."

Bernstein nodded, tapped a sort into the database,
pulling up suburban pictures. "We got dozens of these
full-on ATM pics in the burbs. He's advertising. The
suburbs are a red herring. It's downtown."

Munroe nodded. "Part of their mindset, too. You look at all the major attacks, New York, London, Madrid – they want that name recognition. Schaumburg isn't going to have the same cachet as Chicago."

Bernstein held up a hand, cut him off. "There's something here, just shut up a second."

Everyone was quiet. Lynch looked at his watch.

"Yeah, OK. I'll pass it along," Starshak talking to dispatch. "People are getting out of work. Getting real crowded out there."

Bernstein slammed his hand down on the table.

"Nothing west of the river," Bernstein said. "Son of a fucking bitch. The train stations. Union and Ogilvie – pull everybody you've got and get them to the stations. That's why the motherfucker never crossed the river. Both of the major commuter stations are west of it. That's why the things are timed for at 5.30. Stations will be crammed. Check the entrances, concourses, the trains – the devices have to be in there somewhere."

"You sure we want to go all in on that?" Munroe said. "The stations are totally wired, and we haven't got a single shot of him in either of them, not one."

Hardin shook his head. "When those guys snatched me out of the garage, the fat guy did something weird when we pulled out. Called somebody on his cell, said they were clear, that he could turn them back on. I bet you guys don't have them snatching me on film, do you?"

"No," Lynch said. "And we know al Din bought access to the system. If you can buy access, what do you want to bet you can get somebody to turn off a camera for you, too?"

"We're running out of time," Starshak said. "We have to go all in on something."

Munroe nodded. "OK. Let's go."

CHAPTER 100

Ad hoc team – a mess of Feds that were on hand, handful of uniforms that were close enough to be useful. Starshak, Bernstein and Munroe took half to Ogilvie. Lynch, Hardin and Wilson took the rest to Union. They had 32 minutes.

Meanwhile, Munroe had other resources closing in. At 5.25, he'd seal the stations – nobody in or out. If the devices were really all at the stations, then he'd keep the secondary infections down to practically nothing. Get the Cipro in quick enough, maybe he'd keep the body count down. Or maybe not. You get dusted good by that shit, maybe the Cipro wasn't going to help much.

Got lucky early. Only took four minutes to find the first one. Lynch heard Bernstein on the comm channel through his earpiece. "Got one. Tucked in behind a magazine rack at the newsstand, waist high like we figured, facing out into the concourse. So nooks and crannies facing the concourse, figure waist up, places you could stick your hand in quick without drawing much attention."

Lynch was glad about the waist up business. Couldn't bend his leg at all, and it was killing him as it was. Munroe had passed out thick black bags, some kind of rubberized fabric with a heavy zipper. If you found a device, it went in the bag. Munroe said it would contain everything if the devices blew.

Twenty-eight minutes to go. Then nine minutes of nothing.

"I'm sealing the buildings at 5.25." Munroe in Lynch's earpiece. "Get your asses out before then."

"Fuck that," Lynch said.

"Seconded." Wilson.

"I go where she goes." Hardin.

"Stop wasting our time." Starshak.

"OK," Munroe said. "We run it out. The Cipro will be close. Not sure what good it does if you're sitting on top of one of these when it goes off."

Nineteen minutes to go.

"Got number two." Wilson from the far end of the concourse at Union. "Back of a trashcan in the food court."

Sixteen minutes.

"Got another one," one of the uniforms from Ogilvie in Lynch's earpiece.

Twelve minutes.

That made three. Munroe had scotched evacuating the stations, said they could never get everyone out in time, that the panic would make finding the devices impossible. Lynch tried to focus on the search, kept getting distracted by the people going by. Heard a guy on his cellphone, sounded like he was arguing with his wife, nothing horrible, just a little marital friction, wondered if that would be it, the last the woman ever heard from the guy would be some stupid angry words over something that didn't matter. A young couple, early twenties, sitting at a high top in the bar along the south side of the concourse holding hands across the table, the girl telling the guy she'd gotten the job, the guy's face lighting up. A dad hustling a boy, maybe seven, into the men's room, the kid grimacing, holding the front of his pants.

Ten minutes.

"Number four." Munroe. "Inside a planter near the escalators."

"That's three at Ogilvie," Bernstein said. "Have to figure the last one is at Union. He'd want to balance the dose as much as possible."

Quiet over the channel for a minute.

Eight minutes.

Not enough time for anyone to get from Ogilvie to Union and help.

"Good luck over there." Starshak.

"Yeah, well keep looking," Lynch said. "Hate to have one of those things go off in your face while you're patting yourselves on the backs."

Lynch started running his hand along the undersides of the tables along the edge of the bar, then remembered that they stacked those up every night. No way al Din could know where the table would be any given day, whether it would be near the concourse. And with people handling the tables, it was too likely somebody'd find the thing.

Stuck his arm in behind the display case at the popcorn shop, ran it down, guy walking by giving him a look, shaking his head. Felt like he was just flailing at random. Saw a family go by, mom and dad in their mid-thirties, daughter about ten wearing a sweatshirt from the Shedd Aquarium with the Beluga whales on it, a boy, younger than two, sleeping in a stroller, the daughter laughing and yakking a mile a minute, tired smiles from the mom and dad.

An older guy, fifties probably. A raincoat with a couple more years on it than it needed, off-the-rack suit. Looked tired, worn out, not a guy whose dreams had come true, just pushing the stone up the hill one more time, trying to get home to a beer, maybe a couple hours of TV before going to bed, getting up, doing it all again.

All those lives pressing down on him.

"The McDonald's is clear." Wilson from the north end of the concourse.

"Nothing in the coffee shop." Hardin.

Five minutes.

Lynch pictured the stations. The three at Ogilvie had been spread out. One at each end of the concourse, one near the middle. The one at Union had been at the south end of the concourse near the food court.

"North end," Lynch said. "From the popcorn shop to the escalators, everybody work that."

Had to take a shot. Only four minutes left.

Lynch stepped out into the lobby where the escalators came down, took a quick look, didn't see anywhere you could hide anything. The escalators were all still running, but no one was on them. At the top of the vestibule a line of uniforms were blocking the door, commuters starting to stack up in the plaza outside. Nobody was getting in now.

Or getting out.

Lynch turned back into the station, saw Wilson head to the ATM that was up against a pillar in the middle of the concourse just north of the popcorn shop. She muscled in front of a line of people waiting to get cash and started running her hands along the top and sides of the machine. A guy she'd pushed in front of pulled on her shoulder. Young guy, khakis, oxford shirt, windbreaker, laptop bag.

"Hey, there's a line here, bitch."

Lynch limped toward them, but Wilson spun, slapped the guy's hand away, held open her jacket. Lynch couldn't tell whether it was the badge on her belt or the S&W that made a bigger impression, but the guy backed up, hands out.

Lynch got to the machine, Wilson squatting down on the right side. Lower than waist high now, the machine didn't even come up to Lynch's shoulder, but it felt right and he was out of ideas anyway.

Two minutes.

"Anything?" Lynch asked.

"Fucking dark," she said, her arm behind the machine to her shoulder. "I feel something. Can't reach it." Lynch grabbed the top of the ATM and wrenched it away from the pillar as hard as he could, felt some of the stitches in his leg tear loose. It moved a few inches, made a beeping noise.

Wilson got her arm in deeper, grunted, came out with the last tube. Lynch held his bag open, Wilson dropped the device in, and he zipped it shut.

"What the fuck?" said the guy that Wilson had backed off.

"Servicing the machine," Lynch said. The screen now read ATM OUT OF SERVICE.

"Asshole," khaki guy said, scowling at him.

Lynch just smiled. "Got the last one," he said into the comm. "Call off your dogs, Munroe. We're coming out."

He and Wilson headed up the stairs toward Adams Street. He heard a soft thump, felt the bag bounce on his hip.

"Guess we'll find out if those bags work," said Wilson.

CHAPTER 101

A little after 8pm now. Back at the Federal Building. Munroe gave them an update on their lines. They had the device back up from Argonne for show and tell. At least they had the germs out of it. Wave it around, talk about intercepting several of these on US soil. Nothing about the train stations, of course. Nothing about pulling five of these out with seconds to spare. Munroe needed the public pissed, he explained, not scared shitless. Press had asked, seeing as how they'd had dozens of uniforms in both stations in the middle of the afternoon rush. Just precautionary was the response. Given the day's events, just making sure.

Lynch and Bernstein sat on a bench in the hall behind the briefing room where they were going to hold the press conference, both of them too drained, too tired anymore to fight any of it. The brass wanted the Chicago PD contingent on the dais, dress blues, front and center. Starshak had taken their keys, sent a unit to bring their uniforms down. Bernstein had to wear his jacket open because of the sling. Lynch couldn't get the pants from the dress blues over the bandages on his thigh. Department press guy had them open the side seam up, the guy positively giddy with the results, saying that the two of them looked like that Spirit of '76 painting, the bloodied patriots, Lynch telling the guy to get the fuck away from him.

Munroe stopped by, his camel hair coat on.

"Not staying for the show?" Lynch asked.

"TV? I don't exist, remember. Besides, I've got to catch a plane to Nevada."

"Vegas?" Lynch asked. "Haven't gambled enough for one day? Or do you want to pick up a couple of hookers?"

"Hooker sounds good about now," Munroe said. "But no. Other business."

"Not Vegas," Bernstein said. "Henderson. The air base."

Munroe shook a finger at him like he was naughty.

"Henderson?" Lynch asked.

"They fly the drones out of there," Bernstein said. "Pakistan, Afghanistan, Yemen, wherever. Every time you hear about some yahoo getting a Hellfire up his tail pipe, it's some joystick jockey at Henderson pushing the button. While I was waiting for our show to kick off, I caught the crawl on bottom of the screen on CNN, something about the Mexican president jetting up to DC for emergency consultations. That has to be about the cartels. Come morning, I'm betting a few people south of the border are going to wake up dead."

Munroe shook his head, smiled again. "Bernstein, you ever want to move up in the world, get in touch. Of course, I'd probably have to kill you some day. You do get on my nerves."

"Get in touch?" Bernstein said. "How am I supposed to do that?"

Munroe just smiled again, turned and left.

A minute later, Hardin and Wilson walked down the hall. Hardin in some kind of military uniform, Wilson in a pants suit.

"Halloween?" Lynch asked Hardin.

"Foreign Legion duds. The French want to play up their end."

"And they just keep a set at the consulate for emergencies?" Bernstein asked.

"Hell if I know," Hardin said.

"DEA don't have a monkey suit for you?" Lynch asked Wilson.

"I'll stand by their damn podium, but they can't make me say anything, and they can't dress me up like a goddamn Barbie."

Lynch just nodded. Wilson had more balls than the lot of them.

Hardin looked at Lynch. "Munroe said you need a favor."

Lynch nodded, grunted up to his feet. Leg was really barking at him now. He hobbled a few yards down the hall, Hardin following, Lynch talking for a couple of minutes, Hardin nodding.

Hickman stuck his head out the door to the briefing room looking like somebody'd shot his puppy. He'd been bumped to the back row. The Secretary of Homeland Security was taking over MC duties, flew in from Washington to get his face in front of this operation which, evidently, had been his brainchild. That's why the whole show got pushed back another couple of hours.

"OK," Hickman said. "Let's go."

An hour later it was over. The DC crowd was hanging back, schmoozing the press. Lynch and Bernstein slid across the back of the room toward the side door.

Johnson was there, of course. She saw Lynch, excused herself, walked over.

She looked down at his leg, looked up.

"You OK?" she asked.

Lynch gave her a half smile. "You keep asking me that. I will be."

She nodded, gave a weak smile back. "Me too, I guess."

She held his eyes for a moment, then leaned forward, put her hand on his cheek for a moment, then left.

"You two through?" Bernstein asked.

Lynch just nodded.

CHAPTER 102

Shamus Fenn was out of the ICU and in a private room at Northwestern, watching the press conference on TV, talking on the phone.

"You square things with Corsco?" Fenn asked. He was talking with Bernie Alger, his lawyer and agent.

"He hasn't called back yet," Alger said. "But we gotta talk about how to spin this coke deal. You were making progress with the whole abuse thing, so I've chatted up some of the high-profile TV shrink types, got a couple of them ready to give you a pass on the OD, chalk it up to some kind of post-traumatic stress. You'll have to go on their shows, though. But we need to get our story straight on that, make sure we keep it all consistent."

"Get that guy in from LA, what's his ass, the shrink I've been seeing. I'll play it out with him, and then we'll get him to make a statement," Fenn said.

"Yeah, OK. You're clear on the Chicago end. They aren't moving ahead with any charges. So you're good there. Only free radical is this Hardin fuck."

"What I hear, he's got enough problems," said Fenn.

They talked for a bit, working out their PR strategy. Suddenly Fenn stiffened in his bed, bumped the volume up on the TV. They were marching everyone out for the press conference. Saw that Lynch fuck and his partner. And next to them, Hardin.

Fenn listened, dropped the phone to the bed after a minute. From what Corsco had told him, Hardin was dead or was going to be. Now he was a hero.

"Shamus?" Alger said. "Shame? You there?"

Fuck, Fenn thought. Fuck fuck fuck fuck.

Starshak and Lynch stood in the back row. The room the Feds were using for their press conference was hot as hell, seeing as they had an overflow crowd, every damn network and cable outlet trying to cram a crew in, dozens of light rigs baking everybody. They'd rushed the show, getting it out just in time for 10pm news, getting the first draft out in front of everybody before the media had a chance to start developing theories. They were slapping a national security Band-Aid over the whole deal. It was a good way to keep anybody from taking too close a peak at the forensics or details, because God knows some of that was going to smell funny.

Hardin and Wilson were in the front row with the stars, the Secretary of Homeland Security spinning Hardin's history – decorated US Marine, decorated veteran of the Foreign Legion chased out of his own country by the scourge of drugs, a living symbol of the world's united front against the forces of darkness. Way the story went now, Hardin was a DGSE asset working with the CIA and Wilson was deep-cover DEA.

Everybody said their lines, everybody took their bows. Fade to black.

Fenn sat slack-jawed watching the end of the press conference, then he called Alger back.

"You catch that shit?" Alger asked.

"This Hardin, he's like the French James Bond. You think he doesn't know? We gotta do something."

"Do what?" Alger said.

"I dunno," said Fenn. "I dunno."

CHAPTER 103

7.30am. Lynch picked up Hardin and they drove north on Michigan.

"Michigan Avenue still looks the same anyway," said Hardin.

"Lived here all my life," Lynch said. "Everything changes, you don't really notice, until you look up one day and it's a whole different world. Gotta be strange for you, back after all this time."

"Haven't had a chance for much sightseeing," Hardin said. "But it's weird. I mean I stopped into one of these Super Wal-Mart's with Wilson? I saw more consumer goods in fifteen minutes than I've seen in the last fifteen years. Twelve different kinds of electric toothbrushes."

"You counted them?"

Hardin shrugged. "I was curious."

"Mean anything?"

"What do I know?" Hardin said. "It's too much shit, though. I mean all that crap in Wal-Mart, then Corsco's guys, they drag me down to the old US Steel site, and there's nothing there, just busted concrete and weeds. Too much of one thing, not enough of the other. Something's not right."

"You work it out, drop me a postcard," Lynch said.

Lynch pulled into a reserved slot near the ER entrance at Northwestern, turned to Hardin.

"Sure you're OK with this?"

"Little shit tried to get me killed. I'm good to go."

CHAPTER 104

The Eagle was working the phone, working some sources, running the meter on Corsco, another ten Gs promised out this morning chasing info.

Got to Northwestern at 7.00, wanted to do a quick recon, be set up, ready to go at 8.00 on the dot. But they'd moved the target. He wasn't in his room, wasn't in the ICU at all. Did the guy die? That would be handy. Take credit for it anyway, tell Corsco to pay up. Corsco would. They always did. They knew the other option.

"OK, thanks." Closed the phone.

Fenn wasn't dead, he was getting better. They'd moved him to nine, private room.

The Eagle looked up the floor plan on the smart phone. Layout was almost identical, even better maybe. Fenn was a couple doors closer to the good staircase and almost straight across from the elevator. A couple minutes to eight now, employees coming in, others getting ready to leave. Perfect conditions. No time for a walk through.

Take the elevator; be ready with the gun when the door opened. If there was a cop at the door, take him, go straight in, nail Fenn, then hit the stairs. The cop going down would draw some eyeballs, so it might get ugly, but if the guy was down the hall chatting up the nurses again, maybe get in and out without anybody seeing a thing. So roll the dice. That's why you get the big bucks.

CHAPTER 105

The city still had a uniform outside Fenn's door, patrolman Lynch had worked with before. "Hey, Lynch," the guy said. "Figured you'd be sleeping in, maybe lining up an agent for your book deal."

Lynch gave a little snort. "Yeah. Listen, I have to talk with Fenn for a few. You get any breakfast yet?"

"No," the uniform said.

"Why don't you run down and grab something. I'll be here a bit."

The uniform looked at Hardin. "This guy with you?"

Lynch nodded.

"Cool. See you in a few." The uniform got up from his chair, headed for the elevators.

Fenn was on his cell when Lynch and Hardin walked in to the room.

"Tell 'em they can have the exclusive if–" Fenn saw Hardin and his jaw locked open.

Lynch could hear the voice on the other end of the call. "You there Shame? Shame?"

"Tell them you have to go," Lynch said.

"I have to go," said Fenn.

"Tell them you'll call them back," Lynch said.

"I'll call you back," said Fenn.

"These aren't the droids you're looking for," said Hardin.

401

"What?" said Fenn.

"Hang up the fucking phone," said Lynch.

Fenn hung up.

"How've you been, Shamus?" Hardin asked, walking around to the other side of the bed. "Long time."

Lynch stepped to the side, leaned on the wall in the corner by the door. Fenn sat in the bed, unmoving.

"You OK?" Lynch asked. "Need the doctor? Having some kind of flashback here?"

Finally Fenn spoke. "You can't bring him in here. For Christ's sake, you're supposed to be protecting me."

"From what?" Lynch asked. "Hardin? Why would you need protection from Hardin? He's a freakin' hero."

"I just, I mean, you know, Africa. I kind of screwed him up over there."

"Water under the bridge, buddy," Hardin said. "No, it's the contract with Corsco I've got the real problem with."

"I don't know what you're talking about," Fenn said.

"That's fine," said Hardin. "Thing is, I've got this policy. Nobody gets to try to kill me twice. If you've been paying attention the last day or so, then you know I got to a drug lord and an international terrorist. You gotta ask yourself how much trouble I'm gonna have getting to you. Hell, Corsco damn near took you out with a hooker and a bag of coke."

"Are you threatening me? Lynch, you hearing this?"

Lynch wiggled a finger up near his ear. "Been a lot of shooting lately. Hearing's a little iffy. Thing is, I did hear this." Hardin pulled the digital recorder from his pocket, pressed play.

Corsco's voice. *"Fenn! Shamus Fenn! Fenn wanted Hardin whacked over that Africa business!"*

A different voice. *"The actor?"*

Corsco's voice. *"Yeah."*

Lynch clicked off the recorder. "There's more, but that's the gist of it."

Fenn shaking his head. "No, no, no."

"You gotta understand your position here," Lynch said. "With the tape, and Hardin testifying, we got you and Corsco. We don't need to deal with anybody. But I don't want you. You're nothing. You're just another Hollywood piece of shit. I want Corsco. I want him nailed down and bleeding from every extremity. I get you on top of Hardin, then it's a lock. And I've already greased the skids on your deal. You roll, you walk. You don't, then I take my chances with what I got. And maybe you end up in the pen, too. That'll be something to see. *People*'s Sexiest Man Alive on the yard with the big swinging dicks."

"What do you figure, Lynch?" Hardin asked. "Cute guy like Shamus here, all the brothers lining up for a shot at him, I say two weeks before you could rent his asshole out for off-street parking." Hardin turned to Fenn. "But, Shame, the other thing is this. Even if you beat it, pull an OJ and get some jury to suspend disbelief, then you still got me. So basically, you roll or you die."

"I need my lawyer," Fenn said. "I gotta talk to him."

"You want to talk to somebody," Lynch said, "then I got a stenographer and a video guy waiting downstairs. You wanna fuck around with your lawyer, then I'm done."

Hardin picked up the watch off the table next to Fenn's bed. Top-end Rolex. "Nice watch," he said. "Take a look at the date, Fenn. Six months. You take Corsco down or that's what I'm giving you. Some day in the next six months."

Fenn locked his lips shut, his chin quivering. Then he started to cry. "It's not fair," he said.

"Screw fair," said Lynch.

CHAPTER 106

The elevator door opened. The Eagle had a hand in the shoulder bag, wrapped around the .32, ready to nail a cop if there was one there. Practiced shooting through the bag all the time, accurate as hell at ten feet, never fired from further out than that.

Nobody. Fenn's door closed, hallway empty. Don't question luck, just push it.

Walked straight across, pushed the door open, gun ready, picking up the bed, the target, squeezing off one shot before the door was even fully open, catching Fenn low, got the hip maybe. Aim off because there was another guy standing on the other side of the bed. That was a little distracting. Swung the gun up to get him. Fenn wasn't going anywhere.

Fenn was ready to fold when the door flew open, blocking Lynch behind it. Lynch heard a barky, coughing sound, saw some blood spray off Fenn low on the torso, a leather shoulder bag coming past the door with a hand in it, some old lady coming in behind it. Yellow cardigan, five nine maybe, chunky, gray-haired, swinging the bag up at Hardin, Hardin dropping for the floor.

Lynch hit the door hard, knocking the old broad sidewise. Lynch snatched out his gun. The broad had good balance, hadn't lost her feet. She was, spinning, swinging the bag at him now, must have the gun in there, another fucking suppressor. Lynch wanted to drop, but couldn't bend his leg, got half behind the door, just his head and his right arm out with the pistol. Bitch snapped off another round, hit the door close enough to Lynch's face that he could feel it. Fuck it. Lynch lit her up, six rounds, all to the body, punching her back, the broad grunting, but not dropping, started bringing her bag up again.

What the fuck?

The Eagle was ready to pull the trigger on the second guy when she got blindsided by the door, almost lost her footing. Felt the long-forgotten urge toward panic, fought that down. Improvise and adapt. The guy behind the bed went down to the floor, so she spun toward the door, saw a big guy there, the guy going for his belt, sliding behind the door, narrow target now, head and arm out, arm with a gun at the end of it now. Gonna have to be pretty fine with this.

Her first shot was just wide, hit the door maybe two inches right, had the range now. That's when the guy opened up and she took the first round in the fat vest. And the second third fourth fifth sixth. She'd tripled up on the Kevlar in the fat vest – plenty of room, no need to be skimpy. Didn't make getting shot in it any more fun. Still felt like taking a baseball bat to the gut.

The guy behind the door paused a second, probably trying to figure out why she hadn't gone down yet. Gave her the break she needed, she brought the bag up, not rushing it, getting her line. He was doing the same thing, switching his aim point up to her head now, too.

Gotta be a vest, Lynch figured. That or she's some kind of android Terminator. He brought the gun up, got a sight picture on her face and fired, her gun going off so close behind his it was almost a single noise. The edge of the door splintered, blowing bits of wood into Lynch's face, stunned him. But a good chunk of the old bitch's head was wallpapered on the far wall and she was down on the floor, hand out of her bag now, not moving except for a little twitch in her right foot.

Fenn was screaming on the bed, Hardin scrambling up from behind the bed, the old broad was bleeding all over the floor. Maybe not that old. The gray hair was a wig, half off now.

"What the fuck?" Hardin said.

"Don't know," said Lynch. "Tell you this, though. I am really fucking tired of getting shot at."

Lynch put a hand to his face, some blood, splinters. Felt around. Nothing seemed serious. Close thing. Damn close thing.

Fenn stopped screaming, blubbered something.

"What?" Lynch asked. His ears were ringing.

"I'll talk!" Fenn said. "I'll fucking talk!"

CHAPTER 107

An hour later, Lynch was sitting on a gurney down in the ER. Nurse was finally done picking shit out of his face. Hardin was sitting in a chair across the way. Lynch told him he could go, knew he was blowing town, but Hardin said he'd stay, wanted to hear how things worked out.

Starshak and Bernstein walked in.

"How you doing?" Starshak asked.

Lynch just shrugged. "What's up with Fenn?"

"Round skipped off his pelvis, nothing serious. Already trying to talk to us, told him he has to wait until he's out from the anesthetic. DA says his being under could screw the deal. But I think they'll have to sedate his ass to shut him up. We'll get what we need. Doing the interview in an hour. Hickman's getting a warrant ready on Corsco. Trying to get on our good side, I guess."

"Trying to get his face in front of another camera, more likely," said Bernstein.

"What about the old lady?" Lynch asked. "What the fuck was that? Corsco?"

Starshak smiled. "You want to tell him, Bernstein?"

"You bagged the Eagle," Bernstein said.

"The Eagle? That was the fucking Eagle?"

"I know," Bernstein said. "I expected somebody a little more badass."

"From where I was sitting, she looked pretty badass," Hardin said.

"You weren't sitting, tough guy," said Lynch. "You were hiding under the bed."

Hardin laughed, stood up. "So we're good? We got our happy ending?"

"Yeah," Lynch said.

"That shit you told Fenn about me testifying, you know that's not happening, right?"

"Yeah, I know." Lynch said. "We've got what we need. Corsco's toast."

"And that's all you wanted out of this?"

"Fuck what I want. Not like I'm gonna stop the drug trade or solve the Middle East. But this is my town. Corsco's been shitting where I live."

"Glad I could help," said Hardin. "Now, I have a flight to catch."

"Someplace nice?"

"Tahiti," Hardin said.

"That's pricey."

Hardin shrugged. "Say what you want about Munroe, he pays well. You ever want a nice South Seas vacation, let me know. On me."

"Wilson's going with?" Starshak asked.

"Yeah," Hardin said.

"Don't know if I could relax with her around," said Lynch. "She scares me a little."

"Scares me a little, too," Hardin said. "I just figured that was love."

CHAPTER 108

Five hours later, Hardin and Wilson were in a limo on the way to O'Hare for their flight to Papeete. "Wish I'd had time to pack," said Wilson.

"They've got stores there," Hardin said. "Nice stores."

"So we're really rich?"

"Really, really rich."

Hardin heard Corsco's name on the radio, asked the driver to turn it up a minute.

"Tony 'the Blade' Corsco was arrested at his residence today on charges of conspiracy to commit murder. US Attorney Alex Hickman told reporters that further charges are expected. In a stunning development, actor Shamus Fenn, who is recovering from a drug overdose, is reportedly involved in the case and has provided key evidence—"

"You can turn it off," Hardin said.

They rode in silence for a moment, Wilson leaning over and resting her head on Hardin's shoulder.

"Think anybody will come after us?" Wilson said.

Hardin shrugged. "Have to deal with us if they do. By the way, you'll need this." He pulled two French passports from his jacket pocket and handed one to her. She flipped hers open, then took his and looked inside.

"Jean and Fantine Bernard. Really? I didn't know that Fantine had a last name."

"I don't think she did, but you need one for a passport. Bernard is kind of like the French version of Smith. Fouche arranged the papers. He thought the names were romantic."

"Husband and wife, huh? This makes it official?"

Hardin pulled her hand up, kissed it. "All the sacrament I need."

Wilson turned toward the window a moment, her hand went to her face. Hardin thought she might have brushed away a tear. Then she turned back.

"Fantine," she said. "I'm stuck with that?"

"I could call you Fanny, I guess."

"I may have to kill Fouche for this someday."

"That's probably harder to do than it looks," said Hardin.

"Isn't everything?" Wilson said.

ACKNOWLEDGMENTS

Man, doing a second acknowledgements page is tough. I mean what do you do? Thank all the same people again? Um, in some cases, yeah, you do.

So thank you again to my agent Stacia Decker and to my Team Decker stable mates Chuck Wendig, Joelle Charbonneau, John Hornor Jacobs, Steve Weddle and Seth Harwood who have all lent support, and, occasionally, booze.

Hat tip to my siblings, Tom, Maura, Brendan, Marty and Pat, who have put up with me longer than anyone. (Marty gets special mention for making his in-laws and friends buy their own copies of my last book when they asked to borrow his.)

Thanks again to Emlyn Rees and the team at Exhibit A. A special thank you to Paul Simpson, without who's sharp eye I would have embarrassed myself a couple of times. And to Stewart Larking, what can I say? Another stunning cover.

There's this weird little universe of people out there you get to know if you're a crime writer, online reviewers, magazine and e-zine publishers, folks taking a shot at starting up new imprints. They aren't getting famous, they sure as hell aren't getting rich, but they do a hell of a lot to help authors breaking in to this game get a little exposure.

So thanks to Jon and Ruth Jordan, the masterminds behind *Crimespree Magazine*, behind Murder and Mayhem in Muskego, the driving forces behind a couple of Bouchercons and just nice people.

Thanks to the Shotgun Honey crew, past and present – Kent Gowran, Sabrina Ogden, Chad Robacher, Ron Earl Phillips, Jen Conley, Chris Irvin and Eric Arneson.

Thanks to the Snubnose Press guys, Brian Lindenmuth, Sandra Ruttan, Jack Getze and R. Thomas Brown.

And to fellow writers and Noir at the Bar emcees Scott Phillips, Jed Ayers, Eric Beetner and Stephen Blackmoore, thanks for the stage and the mic. I'm told I had fun, but it's all a little fuzzy.

Finally, to Elizabeth A. White, who first reviewed a version of this book way back when it was an online experiment, I hope you like how it turned out. We'll always have *Mammon*.

"A non-stop adrenaline rush, beginning, middle and end... a bona fide blockbuster."
OWEN LAUKKANEN, author of The Professionals

DAN O'SHEA
Introducing Detective John Lynch

PENANCE

One dark secret is about to rip a whole city apart...

In 1976, four boys walked into the jungle. Only three came out alive.

In 1976, four boys walked into a jungle.
Only three came back alive.

DAN
NEWMAN

THE
CLEARING

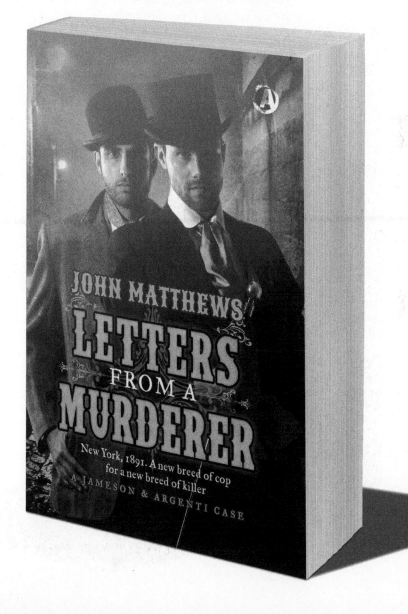

JOHN MATTHEWS
LETTERS
FROM A
MURDERER

New York, 1891. A new breed of cop
for a new breed of killer

A JAMESON & ARGENTI CASE

A taut, timely thriller ripped from today's
headlines. Blisteringly paced, authentically
told, here is a novel that demands to be read
in a single sitting."
James Rollins, New York Times *bestselling
author of* The Eye of God

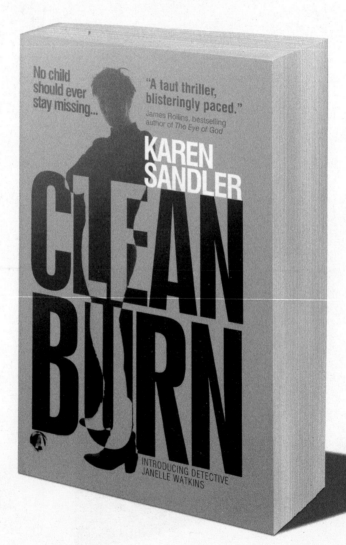

No child
should ever
stay missing...

"A taut thriller,
blisteringly paced."
James Rollins, bestselling
author of *The Eye of God*

KAREN
SANDLER

CLEAN
BURN

INTRODUCING DETECTIVE
JANELLE WATKINS